Miss Hillary
SCHOOLS a
SCOUNDREL

SAMANTHA
GRACE

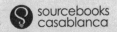
sourcebooks
casablanca

Published by Sourcebooks Casablanca, an imprint of Sourcebooks, Inc.
P.O. Box 4410, Naperville, Illinois 60567-4410
(630) 961-3900
FAX: (630) 961-2168
www.sourcebooks.com

Printed and bound in Canada
WC 10 9 8 7 6 5 4 3 2 1

To Lori for reading everything I've written, for leaving
encouraging—sometimes rambling—voice messages
along the way, and for always being up for lunch.
Thank you to G. & S. for you being you. You fill my life
with joy. You make me laugh. And your sibling squabbles
were inspiration for the relationship between Drew and Gabby.
Kevin, you made it possible for me to follow my dreams. Plus,
you didn't complain when I turned the upstairs room into an
office, even though I insisted it had to be a guest room when we
moved in. I love you for both of these reasons and many more.

One

London, England
May 26, 1816

Two types of men crowded the Eldridge ballroom this evening: the dashing gentlemen whose ardent, but proper, pursuit any debutante would welcome. And *then* there were the ones who pursued Lana Hillary.

While the pretty ladies, like the shy Miss Catherine Mitchell and her intimate circle of acquaintances, captured the hearts of the handsome Lord Gilfords of Town, Lana hid behind a potted fern, hoping the desperate Lord Carrington and those of his ilk didn't spot her without the protection of her brother.

How long did it take Jake to collect two glasses of punch? *Drat!*

Carrington's black gaze locked on Lana. With a satisfied smirk accentuating the viscount's droopy jowls, he came straight toward her, jostling past the elegant guests awaiting the first dance. Lana's less than subtle discouragement last evening had obviously failed.

Where *was* her blasted brother when she needed him? A quick perusal of the crowded ballroom proved futile.

Carrington stalked in her direction, a destitute predator in expensive evening dress. Rumor had it duns circled the viscount's property like merry children around a Maypole, ready to seize the last of the small luxuries left to him. He was desperate. Determined. But then so was she. Lana would never consent to become the third Lady Carrington given marriage to the lout transformed the sweetest of debutantes into empty vessels with no will to live.

He shouldered his way through the crowd, coming closer. Dread washed over her. If word of his interest reached her mother... Lana shuddered. Why, Mama would wrap her in gilded paper with bows and have her delivered to the viscount's doorstep posthaste. Nothing would thrill Mama more than hoisting her off on *any* gent. A title would simply be the icing on the wedding cake.

Dashing into the crush to evade the gentleman, Lana threw a hurried glance over her shoulder. Carrington followed, proving as skilled at tracking as the bloodhound he resembled. She reached the perimeter of the room only to realize she had nowhere to go.

Carrington flashed his rotting teeth in a triumphant leer. He had her where he wished, trapped between a wall of French doors opening to the terrace, a completely unacceptable alternative, and a doorway leading to the inner maze of the house.

Heaven help her. On impulse, Lana darted into the deserted corridor moments before Carrington reached her. She would hide in the retiring room.

The first bars of a country dance floated from the ballroom and faded as she made her escape. Lamps mounted on the damask walls spilled pools of light on the polished wood floor. Staying to the shadows as best she could, she glided down the wide passage past gilt-framed landscapes she had no time to admire. She didn't slow her pace until she rounded the first corner.

Lana released an elated breath. She had done it, thought quickly, and orchestrated her own rescue. She smiled as she continued to the retiring room, a newly acquired bounce to her step. Who needed Jake, or any of her older brothers for that matter? She could handle the odious viscount without their assistance, thank you very much.

"Miss Hillary?" Carrington's voice rang out in the empty corridor.

She wheeled around with a gasp. *Oh, blast it all!* He followed?

"Miss Hillary, did you come this way? I desire an audience." He sounded closer and winded, as if he hurried after her.

Lana would rather die than be discovered alone with him. Abandoning all regard for etiquette, she ran. The whisk of her slippers grew silent as she reached the thick Turkish carpets lining the corridor.

"Miss Hillary." He sounded exasperated and much too close. She would never reach the retiring room in time.

Would the blackguard truly ruin her reputation to acquire what he wanted?

"Miss Hillary, I *demand* you wait."

What had she been thinking to leave the ballroom? If caught in his presence without a chaperone, Carrington could demand anything once her parents forced them to marry. A shiver of revulsion shook her frame. Well, she'd not let that happen.

Lana tried the next door she came to and, finding

it unlocked, slipped inside before closing it again with an almost imperceptible click. Leaning her ear against the solid oak surface, she listened for evidence of the blackguard dashing past. Minutes ticked on a clock from somewhere in the darkened room, but there was only silence from the corridor. No imperious demands, heavy footfalls, or arduous wheezing. Where was the pudding head? He should have passed the room by now.

She pressed her ear closer to the door and strained to hear any little sound. Only the thundering of her heart filled the silence. Had he abandoned his pursuit? Lana wilted against the door with a relieved sigh.

What a narrow escape. She would never do anything so foolish again. And this time she meant it. Lana brushed a hand over her skirts to set herself to rights. She really should return to the ballroom before she stumbled upon more trouble. Lana reached for the handle as a bump shook the door. She scurried backwards, banged her hip on a corner of a sturdy chest, and uttered a soft cry of surprise.

Carrington was still out there.

If any member of the *ton* discovered her and the viscount in a darkened room, her mama would *kill* her first and then force her marriage to the man.

Frantic, Lana searched for an alternate exit. *The window.*

She ran across the room, lifted the lower sash, and poked her head outside. A glow from the lanterns lining the garden pathway provided enough light to assess her situation. The second story definitely presented an obstacle, but not an impossible one. Lana eyed the rose-laden trellis, looking for footholds.

Double drat!

The thorns would rip her to shreds.

Dismissing the trellis, she contemplated a maple tree growing close to the house. If she sat on the ledge and stretched, she could reach one of the sturdier branches. Climbing trees proved easy for Lana, a lesson she'd learned as a girl with four older brothers happy to teach her. Scaling a tree in a ball gown, however, was a feat she'd never undertaken.

She glanced between the door and window. For a long time, nothing but the constant whirring of crickets on the balmy evening air filled the silence and diminished her fears.

Now who's the pudding head?

She studied the long drop to the ground. Had she really considered such a foolhardy plan? Her parents would have her carted to Bedlam if they knew, which sounded surprisingly more appealing than marriage to the bloodhound.

Lana twittered nervously. She really should return to the ball before her brother organized a search.

The door handle squeaked.

Oh, drat, drat, drat!

Lifting her skirts, Lana scrambled to sit on the window ledge before stretching one arm toward a lower branch.

"Miss Hillary, come out, come out, my sweet." Carrington's hushed voice invaded the space. "I know you're in here. I heard your laughter, you naughty temptress. I grow weary of these childish games. Allow me to claim my prize."

Of all the—

Lana whipped her head around to deliver a sharp retort and knocked herself off balance. She pitched forward, barely grabbing the branch with both hands before slipping from the window ledge. One second she swung through the air and the next she came up short.

Oh, heavens above. Something caught her skirt, causing it to bunch up around her waist and expose her drawers for all God's tiny garden creatures to see.

Lana tightened her grip and suppressed a whimper. Why did she leave the ballroom? Giving the miserable lout a cut direct in front of the *ton* at large would have been wiser. Now, certain death might be the reward for her hasty decision. Nevertheless, one thing remained absolute; Lana would risk breaking her neck before she would call out for Carrington's assistance.

❦

Andrew Forest, the Duke of Foxhaven's youngest son, tossed his cheroot to the ground and sprang forward to rescue the young lady dangling from the tree. He had been watching her with curiosity ever since she poked her head through the open window. Only a fool would have bet on her rash action. What were ladies about these days, throwing themselves from windows? She'd barely saved herself from a nasty fall, and she remained in a precarious predicament.

"Miss Hillary?" A perplexed male voice drifted out the window.

Drew froze in place, not wishing to draw the man's attention outside. Any young lady desperate enough to escape the gent's company by means of a second-story window wouldn't wish her effort for naught.

"Are you in here, dearest?" A loud bang, like the barking of a shin against a solid piece of furniture, sounded in the room. "Bloody hell. It's too bloody dark to see a bloody thing in this damned room. Bloody, no-good chit."

Drew raised his eyebrows. Quite inappropriate language if the lady were in the room, but as luck would have it, the no-good chit swung from a tree branch with her skirts up around her middle. Drew glanced between the lady and window, debating on whether he should give away her location to save her foolish neck or trust her to hang on a smidge longer.

The room brightened a brief moment followed by the slamming of a door. The foul-mouthed gentleman gave up his search without ever checking the open window, but who would have imagined any woman so bold as to climb out a window? Drew's interest was piqued.

He hastened to the dangling debutante. "This must be my lucky night," he drawled. "It's raining ladies."

The chit kicked her legs. "Oh, get me down at once, sir. Can't you see I'm in a compromised position?"

The lady's *position* revealed a great deal of shapely ankle and long leg, a poor motivator to rush to assist the damsel under normal circumstances. "It appears your skirts are caught on the trellis. I'll climb up and release it."

"Oh, please hurry. I—" Her voice caught on a sob.

He hurried up the trellis, ignoring the pricks and pokes of thorns through his gloves. Having had his share of narrow escapes through windows, Drew held some sympathy for the young woman, but damned if he'd ever gotten himself into a pickle like this one.

"Almost there. Just a moment longer and you may let go." Drew spoke to her as he would a spooked filly while he worked the hem of her gown loose. He climbed halfway down the trellis then jumped to land with a thud. "Looks like a trip to the retiring room will be in order, but otherwise, you'll go unscathed, Miss Hillary, is it?"

The lady must be related to the Hillary men, a younger sister. What had Langford been moaning about at the club as of late? Something in the way of doubting his admiration for the miss could overcome his aversion to her mother.

Reaching up, Drew grasped her thighs in a hug. "You may let go, Miss Hillary. If you don't mind my asking, what manner of gentleman drives a lady to flee out a window?"

"Only the most despicable curs, I suppose." A violent tremor raced through her limbs despite her bravado.

Miss Hillary released the branch and even though they tottered, Drew held tight, unwilling to let her fall at this juncture. Once he had steadied them, he loosened his hold. She slid down his front, his hands brushing her delectable backside. It was a fleeting reward for his gallant act. He'd certainly received greater rewards from the fairer gender for less heroic acts.

When her feet touched the ground, his arms encircled her slim waist. She felt quite nice in his embrace and smelled like lily of the valley, sparking visions of a wild romp in a field. Perhaps he would keep her.

Her delicate hands rested against his chest. "You may release me, sir."

A flicker from the lanterns behind him illuminated her plump lips. Damn, she had fine kissable lips. Did she feel it too, this heat between them? He urged her closer and sensed the quickening of her breath. "They say if a gentleman snags a debutante, he's allowed to take her home."

Her fingers curled softly against his waistcoat and sent blood rushing to his groin. Inclining his head, he grazed his lips over hers, testing her receptivity.

She gasped and shoved her fists against his chest, twisting her face away. "Oh! Release me at once, you scoundrel."

Her commands brought a lazy smile to his face.

How he'd love to hear her sultry voice issuing orders in the bedchamber. But alas, he wouldn't drag her there without consent.

"As you wish." Drew dropped his hands from her waist, but he didn't step away and neither did she. Her heat and perfume enveloped him, urging him to abandon all semblances of manners and kiss her anyway.

"I have a good mind—"

A twig snapped, causing him and the temptress to startle and knock heads.

"Ouch," she hissed and held a hand to her forehead.

"Drew?" Lady Amelia Audley called out in a hushed voice. "Did you come out here?"

Bloody nuisance. This was the last time he'd play hero to a lady in distress.

He had hoped to avoid a scene when he had spotted the widow in attendance this evening. With a tiny push, he directed the alluring Miss Hillary toward the house.

"Run along before we're discovered," he whispered.

Two

LANA NEEDED NO FURTHER ENCOURAGEMENT TO RUN from the scoundrel, or her utterly humiliating reaction. His touch made her tingle all over. It was shameful.

She flattened herself against the rough exterior of the house and tried to calm her accelerated heart. The rogue had placed his hands on her bottom, for heaven's sake, and he'd kissed her. Lana's body heated as a trill of excitement shot to her belly and swirled around inside.

Stop it. No, no, no. Hadn't she just promised never to do anything foolish again? Thrilling or not, his touch had been scandalous. Men like her rescuer were the reason chaperones warned innocents away from darkened gardens. Lesson learned. She'd practice better judgment in the future, though the man *had* saved her life. Perhaps she should seek him out in the ballroom. He at least deserved proper thanks, whoever he might be. With the torchlight behind him, shadows had obliterated his features.

"With whom were you speaking, Drew?"

Drew? Lana knew no one named Drew.

"I heard a lady." Lana tried to place the voice but was unsuccessful.

"It was no one, angel. Must have been the wind you heard."

Lana rolled her eyes. Only a simpleton would believe such rubbish.

"I know I heard a woman." The angel's voice trembled. "Is she hiding in the bushes?"

"Hell's teeth." Drew's audible sigh expressed his exasperation. "I came outside to escape the crush. Nothing more."

"But there *are* other women, aren't there?"

Lana held her breath. She shouldn't eavesdrop, but perhaps the couple should choose a more secluded spot before engaging in an intimate tête-à-tête. Quietly, she inched away from them.

"I never lied to you," Drew said, his tone as calm as if he discussed the weather. "I made my intentions clear from the beginning. If you seek a commitment, you should search out another gentleman."

Gentleman. Lana clamped her lips together to keep from laughing aloud. He was no *gentleman*. This Drew character, with his wandering hands and callous discarding of ladies, was a rakehell just like her deplorable former fiancé. He and Lord Paddock could go hang.

Gentleman indeed.

Lana stole around the side of the house, berating herself for her earlier inclination to seek the gentleman out in the ballroom. She needed to focus her attentions on finding a respectable husband and banish fanciful ideas about rakes and kisses. And good heavens above! Entertaining thoughts of kissing that particular rake was unacceptable.

Slipping back inside through a servants' door, she paused to determine which way she should go. Two identical wigged footmen gaped at her, but neither said a word.

She smoothed her skirts and lifted her head with as much dignity as she could muster, which, given her disheveled appearance, wasn't a lot. "Is there an alternate route to the retiring room? I've lost my way."

They pointed in unison toward a doorway.

"The back staircase will take you to the hallway, miss," one of the twins said. "'Tis the first door on your left."

"Thank you." She maintained decorum until she was out of sight then dashed up the stairs.

The retiring room attendant's eyes bulged when she took in Lana's rumpled appearance, but she mended the torn hem without a word before securing Lana's hair with pins. With her appearance set back to rights, Lana returned to the ballroom. The palms of her gloves were worse for the experience, but not noticeable enough to warrant leaving the ball.

She took a deep breath before she stepped into the brightly lit great hall, squinting against the glare. Jake would be furious with her for disappearing. Before she could ponder what excuse to offer her brother or even to gather her wits, a gentleman spoke at her ear.

"Miss Hillary, how splendid."

Lana squealed in fright and whipped around to discover Lord Gilford, her friend Charlotte's brother.

His brows pulled together in concern. "Are you all right? You appear peaked."

Her hand rested over her pounding heart, but she forced a giggle. "You really know how to flatter a lady, Gil."

"Where's your brother?" He frowned as he searched the area. "Well, come dance with me so we may speak without stirring up gossip."

Fixing a polite smile on her face, Lana accepted his arm, ignoring the prick of hurt. Of course Gil wouldn't want others to think him enamored of *her*. She had no desire to be linked with him either, but it would be nice if a decent gentleman considered her a desirable candidate for a wife.

The string quartet played a lively quadrille, not a dance conducive to conversation. After the requisite hops and heeltaps, she and Gil linked hands to travel in a circle.

"Did you speak to her?" he asked, but they joined arms with another couple before she could answer.

A few more steps brought them back together and twirling around the polished floor. "You should call on Miss Mitchell soon, my lord. She mentioned Lord Bagley brought her white roses yesterday and took her on a reckless drive down Rotten Row."

Lord Gilford's face fell as they parted for yet another round of hops, but when they came back together, Lana quickly relieved his anxiety. "Miss Mitchell prefers orchids and strolls along the Serpentine. And she finds your nose to be a much better fit for your face."

"Indeed?" Lord Gilford's chest puffed up and a wide smile stretched his lips. The music ended and he escorted Lana from the dance floor.

The soft-spoken debutante had two admirers vying for her attention at that moment, neither gentleman as amiable as Gil. "Miss Mitchell is especially fond of the minuet."

Gil squeezed Lana's hand. "Thank you, Miss Hillary," he whispered. "I would kiss you if it were proper."

Memories of her improper near-kiss in the garden caused her insides to quiver. "Go win her heart, Gil. You are a perfect match."

Her dance partner offered a generous smile before dashing off to woo the lady of his dreams.

A deep chuckle sounded behind her, and she spun around to face her brother Jake.

"Lana Hillary, are you here to play matchmaker or find a husband?"

She huffed and placed her hands on her hips. "*Where* have you been?"

"Retrieving punch. I've circled the ballroom several times. I take it you've been gathering information from Miss Mitchell in the retiring room."

Lana accepted the glass of Negus he offered and sipped it rather than tell him a lie. The spicy drink seemed too heavy for the spring evening, but she enjoyed the tingle on her tongue all the same.

Jake grinned, his eyes crinkling at the corners. "Do you expect Mother will be pleased when she hears of your successful matchmaking endeavors this season? Let's see. There was Lord Busick and Lady Eleanor. Then the Walter brothers' engagements to Misses Oliver and Collier."

Lana didn't expect their mother would be pleased by much anything she did, nor did she expect her understanding.

"Oh, yes," Jake added with a smirk. "We cannot forget Mr. Turner's betrothal to Miss Johnston. You've been busy this season."

Lana tapped her toes in time with the music. "Surely, you don't envy the couples their happiness."

Jake chuckled. "Of course not, and I'm touched by your concern for their states of bliss. Nevertheless, if I didn't know better, I might think your charitable work served as a means of deflecting marriage proposals aimed in your direction."

She rolled her eyes. Their proposals had hardly been aimed in her direction given each gentleman had already set his sights on a different match. Lana wanted a man who desired her and only her, not one who wished to form a union with her dowry, and certainly not a gentleman who pined for another lady. In Lana's way of thinking, if the gentleman was not for her, why shouldn't she offer her assistance?

"Were you not listening to Mama this evening? I must secure a husband this season." The moment their mother had returned from Sussex last week she had pointed out with great conviction the necessity of Lana catching the eye of a respectable gentleman and bringing him up to scratch at once. Her mother's harping amplified Lana's humiliation. She truly was trying to catch the eye of a desirable bachelor, but none of them looked her direction.

Jake lowered his voice, no longer smiling. "I'm sorry for teasing. I dismissed Mother's irritable mood as a symptom of her lingering illness, but I see it bothers you. Mother is disappointed in *life*, dear sister, not you. You cannot take it personally."

Lana blinked back tears. Jake could always read her too easily.

He bumped against her shoulder affectionately. "And Mother is wrong about Nicholas. He'll provide for you if you remain unmarried, and if he won't, I will."

Her heart overflowed with affection for her brothers. It was because of her love for her family that she couldn't bear to fail them. She feigned a happy smile. "Just what I need, lifelong protection from one of you addle-pates. Now do your part and assist me in my search. Do you see any new faces?" Lana hoped her inquiry sounded casual enough. Despite her resolve to forget the scoundrel in the garden, her curiosity demanded satisfaction. One glimpse would do.

"Just the usual dullards are in attendance."

"Well, put your height to use and look again. After all, time is of the essence. As Mama says, no decent man will court me if another season passes without an offer."

Jake's sharp bark of laughter gave her a start. "Wild boar will take to the air the day gentlemen stop pursuing you, my dear."

Or her dowry, more to the point.

She flashed a toothy grin and batted her lashes, grateful to be distracted from grim reality by her older brother. "Oh, look. You're sprouting wings. I see the day has arrived."

He snorted, making her laugh. What would she do without Jake? Five years her senior, and yet he was her dearest friend.

She caught a glimpse of Lord Carrington hovering nearby and stepped closer to Jake. "Isn't it your job as chaperone to make certain the gentlemen *aren't* chasing me?"

"I only make certain they don't catch you without a proper marriage proposal. Nevertheless, if you have need, I'll be happy to discourage any gentleman's suit."

Lana nodded in Carrington's direction. "I have need."

Jake glanced at the foppish gentleman. "At your service, dear sister. Will you hold my glass?"

Her brother drew himself up to full height, glared at Viscount Carrington, and took a threatening step forward.

Lana giggled as Carrington scrambled backwards, tripped on Lady Eloise's skirts, and nearly careened into a marble pillar. Red infused his face from his forehead down to his neck as he darted from the ballroom.

"How great to have an older brother," Lana said with a sigh and held out his glass.

"I'll remember you said so the next time I've angered you." Jake's smile softened. "She's here," he murmured.

Lana searched out the object of his attention, the young widow, Lady Audley. Although the classic beauty was too attractive to be a wallflower, she stood alone by the same potted fern where Lana had sought shelter earlier.

Lana gazed back at her brother. *Good heavens above.* Jake's expression practically shouted of his infatuation with the lady. "Perhaps you should ask for her dance card," she prodded.

"Perhaps I will," he answered, but his sudden stormy countenance confused her.

Returning her attention across the room, she saw a gentleman had entered the ballroom from the terrace. Lana nodded toward him. "There is a new face. Who is that gentleman?"

"A gent I won't allow anywhere near you," Jake said on a growl.

Lana cringed. *Too late.*

Something in the man's swagger, and the fact that he had come from the gardens, told her he was her rescuer. And drat it, he was far too handsome by half.

Three

DREW SIGHTED AMELIA MOMENTS AFTER REENTERING THE ballroom. He didn't know if it was by design or accident that she hadn't ventured far from the terrace doors after she stormed from the gardens in a fit of pique. Experience, however, suggested this was no coincidence. Despite his past efforts to spare her discomfort, he could not make her happy this time. It was better to end their association definitively, and allow the lady to progress on to the next interested gent.

Besides, Drew had neglected Phoebe long enough. If his elder brother learned he had ventured from his sister-in-law's side for even a moment, he was in for a tirade of phenomenal proportions.

He stopped to lean against a pillar and scanned the ballroom for his sister-in-law. There was a risk of Phoebe being cross with him for neglecting her for too long, but at least she wouldn't demand his constant attention all night.

He glanced around the thick pillar, his gaze snagging on a pair of shrewd brown eyes peering at him above the lacy edge of a fan. Like all the other members of the fairer gender, the robust lady engaged in a flurry of whispers with a companion. Both ladies turned to study him with unabashed interest.

A twitch began at his temple. *Mothers*.

Under normal circumstances, his position as third-born son of a duke provided blissful invisibility, especially with two hearty brothers unlikely to meet their maker for years to come. Yet, with his godfather's bequeathal—an estate that raised his fortune almost on par with his eldest sibling's—Drew's bachelor status afforded him notice by those in search of a spouse for their daughters.

The Earl of Overton, the last of his line, had taken a liking to him practically from his birth, but Drew had been surprised by the contents of his godfather's will. And grateful. Drew's newfound wealth afforded him a leisurely existence, but his inheritance placed burdens on him as well: an uninhabitable town house in desperate need of repairs, requests for loans, and undesirable attention from ambitious mamas.

He moved on before either lady entertained ideas about him. In theory, he seemed a prize to be captured. In reality, he wanted nothing to do with the institution of marriage.

"Look! It's Lady Phoebe." The enthusiastic pronouncement rang through the ballroom and shattered his musings. He craned his neck to find his honey-voiced debutante from the garden, the delectable Miss Hillary. Across the room, she attempted to draw her brother in the other direction, but Hillary wouldn't budge. His murderous glower landed on Drew, persuading him to look over his shoulder to see if someone disagreeable stood behind him. There was no one.

Drew's muscles tensed. *Devil take it*. Had Miss Hillary told her brother of their encounter in the garden?

He hoped not. His plans did not include rising before noon on the morrow.

When Hillary didn't surrender to his sister's wishes, she threw her hands in the air and marched away in a huff. For all that he shouldn't pay attention to such things, Drew found Miss Hillary refreshingly amusing to watch.

She hurried across the room and captured his sister-in-law's hand. "Lady Phoebe."

Pheebs squealed with apparent delight. Neither lady paid notice to the rumble of disapproval over their public display of friendship.

Miss Hillary's carefree manner eased his guard to some degree. Surely, she would not behave with such cheerful abandon if her brother planned to issue a challenge to defend her honor. Yet, this evening Miss Hillary *had* proven herself unique amongst her contemporaries. Drew didn't know what to expect from her next, which simply added to his curiosity. How providential that Miss Hillary and Phoebe were on intimate terms. His sister-in-law provided the perfect excuse to further his acquaintance with the lady.

A quick glance at Jake Hillary revealed his frown had not waned, but fate smiled on Drew when the man turned on his heel and stalked off into the crowd. If that wasn't an invitation to approach Miss Hillary, he didn't know what was.

With her brother's blessing and an eager grin, Drew started toward the ladies, but came up short when Lord Hollister stepped into his path.

"Lord Andrew, what a surprise. Tell me, how are the duke's hounds?"

Just what his evening had lacked, a conversation with a canine-obsessed popinjay.

❧

Lana held Phoebe at arm's length. "I had no idea you were back from the continent. Oh, how I have missed you."

Phoebe laughed, her glow originating from someplace inside of her. Lana had never seen her friend look so radiant. Apparently, travel agreed with her. "And I have missed you, Miss Hillary. You haven't changed a bit."

Lana might be the same, but something was different about Phoebe, though she couldn't for the life of her say what the difference was. "When did you arrive in London?"

"Yesterday. I apologize for not calling on you. Our Stephan has been ill, and then Richard came down with a chill this afternoon."

"I hope it is nothing serious."

Phoebe squeezed her hand. "It is a cold, but the doctor assured me they are hearty and will recover. Still, I didn't want to leave either one, but Richard insisted I attend Lady Eldridge's ball. He knows another minute away from your company would have been intolerable."

"Don't tell me *you* are the cause of my misery this evening," an amused voice piped up from behind Lana.

A shiver ran up her spine, her body recognizing the baritone voice before her mind did. She spun around to face the ne'er-do-well from the garden, her breath catching when he bestowed a slow, sinful smile on her.

Double drat. He was so very dashing up close.

Lana pulled herself up to her full height, which was impressive for a lady, and tossed an icy glance in his direction before ignoring him completely. Perhaps his handsome looks made other women swoon, but Lana refused to turn into a ninny at the sight of his perfect white teeth and evenly proportioned lips.

She had been dancing with dashing gentlemen for the

last two seasons, and never once had she swooned. Of course, those gentlemen simply sought her assistance with their courtships of other ladies while her rescuer desired something different, something that caused a fluttering in her chest and made her knees weak. Nevertheless, she *never* swooned and wouldn't start at this juncture, even if her head did feel a little fuzzy.

Phoebe tapped the scoundrel's arm with her fan in a familiar gesture as he sidled up to her. "*There* you are. I had come to believe you had deserted me."

Lana balked. Surely, Lady Phoebe wasn't one of his *other* women. Why, she had a perfectly lovely husband at home.

"Desert you, Pheebs? Never." The rogue flashed his dratted smile again as his gaze settled on Lana. "Have I earned the privilege of an introduction?"

Phoebe placed a hand on his arm. "Please, forgive my lapse in manners, Drew. Miss Hillary, may I present my brother-in-law, Lord Andrew Forest?"

Egads. Drew was Phoebe's relation? Perhaps Lana would faint after all.

She curtsied. "My lord."

Drew—*Lord Andrew*—gathered her hand in his and placed a kiss on her gloved knuckles. Amusement sparked in his blue eyes, the same shade as forget-me-nots. "Pardon me, Miss Hillary, but I believe we *have* met."

Lana swallowed wrong and launched into a coughing jag.

Phoebe stepped forward and patted her back. "Good heavens, Lana. Are you all right?"

Lana drew in a shaky breath. "We... we've met?" Her voice squeaked. "I believe you are mistaken, my lord."

"No, I'm certain we've met. Let me think. Where did we make our first acquaintance?" More dimples. The scoundrel was enjoying himself. He snapped his fingers. "I recall now. Last season your parents hosted a dinner party, one of those rare occasions when I was not otherwise engaged."

Lana almost collapsed with relief. "Of course. Yes, lovely to see you again."

She searched her mind to place Lord Andrew before their run-in tonight. Honestly, how could she ever forget the gentleman? He was quite gorgeous in his black formal dress, although he knew he cut a pleasing figure if his smug smile was any indication.

Lana returned his smile with a weak one. "I apologize, my lord, but what were you saying a moment ago?"

Phoebe gazed toward her brother-in-law with fondness. "Drew has been complaining all evening about escorting me to the ball."

Lord Andrew shrugged shyly, a complete act on his part. There had been nothing shy about his wandering hands in the garden.

"Do you oppose dancing, my lord?" Lana feigned naïveté, suspecting his reluctance had more to do with jilted lovers ambushing him in the gardens.

"If I may be frank, Miss Hillary, I oppose the marriage market. I try to avoid it at all costs."

"But Richard insisted I have an escort to the ball," Phoebe added. "Drew kindly agreed to accompany me, but these affairs are not part of his usual repertoire."

Lord Andrew raised a brow, a twinkle of mischief in his eyes. "Lady Phoebe insinuates I don't enjoy an evening with a beautiful lady." A toffee-colored lock of hair fell forward on his forehead, adding to his annoyingly boyish charm. He brushed it away with his fingertips. "Nothing could be further from the truth, Miss Hillary."

As she well knew.

Jake joined their group, taking up sentry over her as if he protected the crown jewels. "I doubt anyone would accuse you of disliking the company of ladies, Forest," he said.

Lana might have frowned upon his insult of Lord Andrew's character if she didn't know it to be an accurate account.

"Jake Hillary, long time," Lord Andrew greeted with a magnanimous smile. "Was it Oxford? No, it couldn't have been that long ago."

"It was last evening at Rendell's." The unspoken word "jackass" seemed on the tip of her brother's tongue, but he censored his language in polite company.

Lord Andrew laughed. "How could I have forgotten? Seems you lost all but your waistcoat and boots."

Jake's fist tightened as if he would relish thrashing the gentleman.

Phoebe linked arms with Lana and attempted to direct her away from the men. "Let's allow your brother and Drew to catch up, shall we?"

Lana dragged her feet, curious to overhear what they might say to one another, and a bit hopeful her brother might challenge the rake to fisticuffs after his deplorable treatment of Lady Audley. Lord Andrew had been horrible to her, had he not? He'd lied to the lovely woman, at least about Lana's presence in the garden. And he'd obviously taken advantage of Lady Audley's affections. Oh, why must Lana remind herself of Lord Andrew's faults? He was a rascal, no questions about it.

Lord Andrew's voice carried faster than Phoebe could lead her away. "Still in a temper over the barmaid, Hillary? She *was* more my type."

"Did she have a pulse then?" Jake practically growled.

"Hmm, hot-blooded chit."

"Heavens." Phoebe, cheeks blazing with color, put more force behind pulling Lana toward the refreshment table. Once out of earshot, she cleared her throat. "Yes, well. What was I saying?" She clicked open her ivory fan and waved it in front of her face. "Oh, right. We're returning to the country in the next day or two, as soon as my gentlemen can travel."

Love lit Phoebe's countenance when she spoke of her family. It almost made Lana queasy, except it was Phoebe, her guileless and darling friend.

Longing tugged at Lana's heart. She had never hoped for a loving marriage herself. What her friend had with Lord Richard was a miracle, because no one else married for love. If a couple was fortunate, they might be equally suited for parlor games. Perhaps they may even find each other amiable, or tolerable, or at the very least, neither induced nausea in the other.

"Richard must see to the tenants for his father before we travel north for hunting season," Phoebe said. "To be honest, Miss Hillary, I sought you out tonight to extend an invitation to visit Shafer Hall. I thought I might be more successful in persuading you in person. Of course your family is welcome as well."

Lana eyed Phoebe. Something was amiss. "You know I don't condone the stalking of defenseless animals. And *you* have never shied away from riding in the hunt. What's behind this invitation, my lady?"

The pink blooming in Phoebe's cheeks painted a fetching portrait. She almost glowed as she leaned toward Lana. "Riding isn't recommended for women in my condition," she whispered.

Lana matched her volume to Phoebe's whispers. "You're with child?"

"Stephan is to be a big brother," she confirmed, clutching her hands over her heart.

Lana gathered her friend in another enveloping hug. "Congratulations, Phoebe. What a blessing."

"Richard's father believes Shafer Hall is better suited for lying in wait. Less noise and more privacy. I should be grateful for the offer of his property, but I fear I will be bored to tears." She retrieved two glasses of punch and handed one to Lana. "The duchess has planned a grand house party at Irvine Castle to alleviate the tedium. Richard has promised I may enjoy some of the activities, but I would appreciate the company of a dear friend. Please say you'll come north."

"I would be more than honored to come for an extended visit." She glanced toward Lord Andrew, who was engaged in conversation with Lord Hollister a few paces away. "Will *he*—Lord Andrew—be in residence at Irvine Castle?"

Phoebe chuckled. "Drew holds no interest in hunting or travel. You are as likely to see an elephant on the grounds as to cross paths with my husband's brother."

The tension in Lana's shoulders melted away. With a lighter heart, she tossed her hands into the air. "Splendid suggestion, traveling north. But why wait until autumn? My trunks could be packed within the hour, anything to escape the dullness of being marketed like horseflesh."

Lord Andrew ambled up to the women in time to overhear Lana's last comment. "I thought ladies liked shopping. I hear husbands are quite in fashion."

For the love of… Where was Jake now? Lana scanned the room and discovered her brother detained by an earnest young woman and her mother. His brows drew together, and he rubbed his forehead as if in pain. She stifled a giggle. It seemed Jake needed someone to protect *him*.

Pushing her amusement aside, she offered Lord Andrew a dispassionate stare. The man was too cheeky, by far. She had been jesting, at least to some degree. Husband hunting was a dull, albeit necessary, occupation. "I am *not* most women."

"I cannot dispute your claim, Miss Hillary, but perhaps that is your strategy," Lord Andrew said with a self-satisfied grin. "Pretending to run from gentlemen until you snag a husband is a wise tactic. Most men enjoy a good chase."

Oh, he thought himself so clever. She lifted her chin. "You would be the expert, my lord. I imagine chasing skirts is your forte."

Although Phoebe gasped, Lord Andrew broke into warm laughter. His entire being lit from within and the musical sound of his voice wrapped around her, soothing her temper despite her determination to be cross with him.

He bowed, his eyes shining with merriment. "Touché, Miss Hillary."

Four

LANA COULDN'T BANISH LORD ANDREW FROM HER thoughts for several hours following their encounter. She recalled their conversations verbatim as the Berlin carried her and Jake home to Hillary House at the end of the evening. Frustrated with her inability to cease thinking on Lord Andrew, she huffed and shifted her position on the carriage seat again.

Jake crossed his arms and scowled. "For goodness' sake, Lana. What's with all the huffing? Are you laying an egg over there?"

She lifted her nose and refused to dignify Jake's question with a response. He needn't take out his surliness on *her*. She shifted on the bench once again as an idea occurred to her. Maybe she would benefit from some of her brother's knowledge of Lord Andrew's rotten vices, because surely he had many. Perhaps if she knew the entire list of his sins, her foolish musings on what it must feel like to surrender to his kiss would go away.

"Tell me the reason you dislike Lord Andrew," she demanded.

Jake grunted and stared out the window. With the lamp burning inside the carriage, there was nothing beyond the glass but a sea of darkness. "This isn't an appropriate subject to discuss with a lady."

"Away from everyone, I'm not a lady. I'm your sister."

"In the ballroom, you *are* a lady," he argued, "and that blackguard ruins ladies."

Lana gasped. "Like Leo… Lord Paddock ruined Miss Bettis?"

Jake dropped his head back against the seat and groaned. "Must we discuss Forest?"

"You cannot imply Lord Andrew ruins young ladies and then refuse to share the details. It's very unfair."

Her brother grimaced. "Allow me to rephrase. I have no direct knowledge of any action leading to the ruining of innocents. However, his liaisons tend to be brief and varied."

"Oh," Lana said on a breath of air. "Well, that is entirely different, isn't it?" She slumped against the seat, relieved to learn Lord Andrew wasn't in the same class as her former betrothed, and yet disappointed to have her observations of the gentleman confirmed. Lord Andrew was a scoundrel.

"I was surprised to find him in attendance tonight," Jake said. "Forest doesn't typically keep company with polite society, which no doubt explains his lack of decorum this evening."

"Yes, he was rather forthright in his discussion of the barmaid. No beating around the bush with the gentleman. I suppose one might admire that quality."

Jake's expression darkened and his white teeth flashed in the dim interior of the carriage. "You'll steer clear of Forest or there will be the devil to pay."

Lana dropped her head a fraction of an inch and raised her eyebrows in mock amusement. She wasn't one to tolerate threats, much less from her brother, and she wouldn't abide a raised voice. "Don't think to intimidate me, Jake. I shall keep company with whomever I wish."

"Good God." Jake pinched the bridge of his nose and blew out a forceful breath. "This is for your own protection. You *will* abide by my rules."

Her brother's boorishness crossed the boundaries of her tolerance, which he must have deduced when Lana folded her arms over her chest and set her jaw.

"Lana, be sensible." His voice bordered on pleading. "You have your pick of fine gentlemen. Anyone you want. You've no cause to associate with libertines."

She sighed. Of course, she wouldn't seek out the company of such scandalous gentlemen. She sincerely wished for a tidy match with a respectable sort, but her brother wore blinders in the ballroom. She *didn't* have her pick of upstanding gentlemen. She had overbearing, destitute viscounts clamoring for her hand.

"Tell me the true reason you dislike Lord Andrew," she said softly.

He hooked a finger between his cravat and neck to loosen it. "What do you mean by the true reason? I hardly need an additional reason to dislike any scoundrel found sniffing round my sister's skirts."

"He wasn't—He—" Good heavens, if her brother only knew the accuracy of this turn of phrase. "The—the man barely knows I'm alive."

"Oh, he knows, Lana. The gentleman came perilously close to salivating in your presence."

She scoffed as a rush of warmth infused her body. Jake behaved as if she was the Queen of Sheba, but she kept a looking glass in her bedchamber. She knew her unfashionable red hair and the freckles sprinkled across her nose were abominations. Her mother reminded her almost daily. Lana couldn't help it if her ivory skin spotted just thinking about the sun.

"Please, trust my intentions, Lana. I don't want to see you hurt. Not again."

Her mouth dropped open but no sound came out. Her brother referenced Paddock, delivering the equivalent of a gut punch. Humiliation engulfed her, and she couldn't squeeze out any words around the lump forming in her throat.

Lord Paddock had duped her entire family, but Lana had been the biggest cake of all. She had ignored the ample evidence that he'd been with other women, the lip rouge on his cravat, his waistcoat reeking of lavender. Only a simpleton would believe a visit to his elderly aunt accounted for the blood red smears and cloud of cheap perfume clinging to his person.

Lana had made excuses to her family to explain a missed afternoon stroll or his late arrival at the theatre. She'd accepted his flimsy tales with wide-eyed naïveté, convinced she only needed to be a better fiancée to make Leo love her as she had thought she loved him.

Even when rumors of his mistreatment of Miss Bettis circulated, she had confronted him with the secret hope he would vehemently deny the accusations leveled against him. A foolish part of her believed Leo would reassure her everyone was mistaken, that he wasn't responsible for the young lady's injuries. That he'd never even made her acquaintance.

Lana shuddered. She could have been in Miss Bettis's shoes just as easily. Closing her eyes, she breathed deeply to gather her strength.

Her brother had no reason to fear. Lana would never become enamored with a rake again.

"One must offer one's heart up in order to have it broken," she said. "I shan't be hurt again since I'm aware now that love is rubbish."

She opened her eyes to discover Jake's unwavering stare. Sadness flitted across his features as he scooted across the carriage to assume the seat next to her and place his arm around her shoulders.

"Please, don't say that," he implored. "Love isn't rubbish."

"Perhaps not for you," she murmured.

Jake didn't argue. Instead, he squeezed her in a brotherly hug, making tears prick the back of her eyes. She sniffled a few times before inching away and twisting sideways on the bench to face him.

"Will you tell me of your infatuation with Lady Audley?"

Jake's eyes widened for one fleeting moment before his expression went blank. "I don't know your meaning." He directed his gaze forward; his jaw tightened. Clearly, he did know her meaning, but she would honor his reticence for now.

Sadness rolled off him in waves. Jake cared deeply for the young woman, more than Lana had guessed. And he obviously required assistance in his pursuit. Lucky for him, Lana was the perfect one to further his cause. After all, Jake *had* accused her of being an effective matchmaker. Why shouldn't she use her talents to help someone dear to her?

Lana tapped her finger to her chin as an idea formed in her mind. The visitors at Shafer Hall would spend most of their days engaged in activities at Irvine Castle, the Northumberland residence belonging to Phoebe's father-in-law, the Duke of Foxhaven. Perhaps Lana's friend could arrange an invitation to Irvine Castle for the beautiful widow.

"Pay me no mind," she said. "I see you harbor no fondness whatsoever for Lady Audley."

෧෨

Drew's routine had returned to normal after the Eldridge ball, the soiree proving to be nothing more than a tiny bump on the otherwise smooth road to debauchery. In fact, he'd almost succeeded in banishing the entire encounter with the fiery Miss Hillary from his mind. Almost. Nonetheless, her memory plagued him more than usual this evening, and he found himself wondering what event she attended tonight.

He'd been loitering at Brook's for the past three hours, bored with the same scene, the same faces. He considered, and dismissed, the idea of heading to the gaming hells or paying a visit to the lovely new wench under Madame Montgomery's employ. Even those prospects sounded dull.

Drew had always relished his decadent existence: imbibing, gambling, and a different woman to bed every night. It was his calling. His father expected it of him. While his older brother, Rich, was the responsible one, Drew's exploits provided entertainment to his sire. But as of late, his usual pursuits brought him little excitement. When had everything in his life become so mundane?

"Down on your luck, Forest?"

Drew glanced up to find his childhood friend, Anthony Keaton, Earl of Ellis, meandering to where he sat nursing a drink. They had first made each other's acquaintance as young boys barely out of leading strings, having grown up on neighboring estates. Later, they attended Eton followed by Oxford the same years.

The prospect of challenging Ellis to a game of billiards

and recalling old times cheered Drew a smidge. "My luck is improving with your arrival."

Ellis flopped into an adjacent chair with a grimace. "My gambling days are over."

"Since when?"

"Since I lost nine hundred pounds the last time I played faro with you. What are you drinking?"

Drew jiggled his near empty tumbler. "Scotch."

"Let me buy you another." Ellis signaled for a footman. "Another scotch for my friend and I'll have a brandy."

When the man returned with the drinks, Ellis sank back in his chair. "How's your family?"

Drew raised an eyebrow in bemusement. "The same."

"And your mother and father? How are they?"

Egads. If he had hoped for sparkling conversation from Ellis, he was disappointed so far. "Both are in excellent health. Thank you for inquiring."

"I suppose your sisters are fit as well. Gabrielle and… um, the other girls."

"Indeed. I've received no notice of any dire illnesses afflicting any of my siblings."

"What are the other girls' names?" he asked absently.

Drew chuckled. "Damnation, Ellis. Are you drafting my biography?"

His friend laughed as well. "I wouldn't wish to put readers into a sleeping trance."

"Then explain your line of questioning before you place me in a sleeping trance."

"It's nothing. I've simply been thinking how long it has been since I visited the Forest brood. Have they departed for the country?"

"Good God, man. Spit it out. What is it you wish to know?"

Ellis gulped his drink instead of answering. Then he pursed his lips, seeming to ponder his next words. He sat up straight before leaning forward to rest his forearms on his thighs. "I wish to inquire after Gabby."

Every muscle in Drew's body tensed. "You mean my sister, *Lady* Gabrielle?"

Ellis twitched. "Yes, of course, Lady Gabrielle." He chuckled, but it came out strained. "It's difficult for me to think of her as a grown woman. I meant no disrespect."

Drew banged his glass on the table beside him. "She's not a grown woman, so stop thinking about her at all."

"You're right, of course." Ellis sipped his drink, studying Drew over the rim. "But will she be presented next season?"

Did Drew detect a note of hope in his friend's voice?

"What has gotten into you, gent? Do you fancy yourself in love with Gabby?" Drew's eyes narrowed on his friend as the magnitude of what Ellis's objectives might be dawned on him. "Don't tell me your intentions with my sister are dishonorable unless you'd like to schedule a dawn appointment. Since we have a history, I would only wing you, but you may lose use of your arm."

The earl smiled indulgently, not intimidated in the least despite his knowledge of Drew's abilities with a firearm.

"Rest assured that I have no intentions with Lady Gabrielle. I am simply curious. She seemed to be of age at the duke's birthday celebration."

"Well, you are mistaken. It could be two years yet before Gabby is presented." Drew hoped to discourage his friend, because despite his denial, Ellis wore a familiar lovesick expression. His brother, Richard, had adopted a similar smitten appearance once he met Phoebe.

"Two years," Ellis muttered. "In two years it is."

Bloody hell. The earl was making a mental note. What type of illness plagued Ellis and Rich? First Drew's brother leg-shackled himself to Phoebe, a lovely young woman to be sure if one *must* select a spouse, and it appeared Ellis desired to follow his example. *But Gabby?* She was a mere girl. How could Ellis consider her otherwise?

Listening to any more of his friend's drivel would either drive Drew batty or compel him to issue a challenge to defend Gabby's honor. Neither prospect pleased him, so he dragged his weary frame from the chair. "I'm off to Rendell's."

"Yes, well, good luck," Ellis mumbled.

As Drew gathered his hat and cane from the porter, Jake Hillary strolled into the gentlemen's club. His lip curled as his sight landed on Drew. Although Drew wouldn't have claimed friendship with Hillary, he had never considered them enemies. What had gotten into the man that night at the Eldridge ball?

"Hillary." He called out a jovial greeting, willing to overlook the other gentleman's hostile behavior. "Released from your escort duties tonight, or did you leave that peach of a sister to fend for herself?"

"She's none of your concern," Hillary snapped. "And don't bother making the rounds. She is under the safety of our father's roof tonight."

Make the rounds? The ballrooms were the last place Drew wanted to be. He'd finally managed to extricate himself from his association with Lady Audley and preferred to avoid any future contact. Not even the prospect of catching a glimpse of Miss Hillary would compel him to visit the horrid places.

Jake handed his hat and gloves to the porter. "Rest

assured Lana will be under *my* protection when we visit your brother's estate in a few days."

Hell's teeth. What care did Drew have for the Hillarys' affairs? He tipped his hat and tried to pass, but the gentleman blocked his way.

"I suggest *you* stay in London and away from my sister, if you know what's good for you."

Hillary was dicked in the nob. All this fuss over a skinny redhead made no sense. *Skinny redhead.*

Drew pictured Miss Hillary as she had been that evening hanging from the tree with her skirts bunched around her waist. A more accurate description might be to call her a ginger-haired beauty with long legs and an arse out of Botticelli's *Primavera.*

He met Hillary's fierce glare without blinking. Maybe he *should* go to Northumberland, if for no other reason than to defy this prig doling out unsolicited advice. The travel, however, was grueling and the activities mind numbing. Good Lord, what was he thinking? He wouldn't punish *himself* to spite the bugger.

Drew offered a sardonic grin. "I have no intentions of traveling north when everything I could want is here." He stepped around Hillary and left for Rendell's.

Five

THE NEXT MORNING DREW SAT DOWN TO A PLATE OF baked eggs with chives, toast, and a cup of hot tea moments before the butler entered the breakfast room. The Talliah House residents had departed for Irvine Castle two days ago, leaving Drew as the only occupant of his father's town house. As the duke's living quarters were more comfortable than Drew's rented rooms, he was certain his father would not mind.

Wesley held out a calling card. "My lord, you have a visitor."

Drew squinted at the scrolling black letters. What the devil possessed Norwick to call this early? A mere five hours ago, they had spoken at Rendell's. Drew couldn't fathom that his friend had anything of importance to convey that couldn't wait until later.

The earl had been heavily into playing the dice most of the night, but when Drew left at dawn, it seemed Norwick dominated the table. Perhaps his friend's luck had soured.

Drew pressed his lips together and settled against the seatback. "Send him in."

A moment later Norwick bound into the breakfast

room with a wide smile. "Forest, here you are. You missed the annihilation at the table."

Norwick wasn't here to borrow funds after all, much to Drew's delight. "Congratulations. Would you care for something to eat?"

"No, no." Norwick waved his hand as he dropped onto the mahogany carved dining chair. "Well, perhaps just some eggs. And a piece of toast."

Drew nodded at the footman.

The servant set a plate in front of the Earl of Norwick. "Make it two pieces of toast, my good man." Norwick patted his belly and grinned. "I didn't acquire *this* body from turning down food. Hard as a boulder. And almost as large."

Drew chuckled. "Indeed. You possess a remarkable frame, my good friend. So, will you be back at the gaming tables this evening?"

Norwick bit into his toast and pocketed the food in his cheek. "I leave for Northumberland in an hour. It's a dreadfully long journey, but I was pleased to receive the duchess's invitation. Perhaps we can get the dice rolling at Irvine Castle. When do you depart?"

Drew gave a distasteful look. "I'm afraid you must proceed without me."

"You're not going? What fun will that be?"

"It's not, which is the reason I stay in London."

Norwick's shoulders slumped forward. "Bloody hell. I suppose it is too late to back out. I've already accepted the invitation." An instant later, his jovial mood returned. "On the bright side, a country party has its rewards. A few of the ladies attending are quite fond of doling out favors, I'm told."

Drew's eyebrows shot upward. This soiree didn't

sound anything like the typical gathering at his family's northern estate, all hunting and no fun. Had Mother finally wrestled control from Father?

Norwick waved over the footman, requested more eggs, then returned his attention to Drew. "Rumor has it Hillary almost drew your cork at Brook's last night."

"Untrue. The damned bugger was fortunate he didn't receive a facer himself when he blocked my path. I found his dire warnings to stay away from his sister irritating."

Norwick speared another bite of eggs. "Then I suppose what happened to Hillary last night left you in high spirits."

Drew looked expectantly at his friend.

"You didn't hear? Hillary was deep in his cups and took a tumble leaving Brook's, though Lord knows how a man trips over his own two feet. Broke his leg. He'll be laid up for weeks."

Oddly, Drew did feel pleased by the report of Hillary's bad fortune, not that he would have wished it on the gent. But since he hadn't caused Hillary's injury, he could take a bit of satisfaction in the result.

"Which brother will accompany the little sister to Shafer Hall?"

"Do you refer to Miss Hillary? I imagine her mother will chaperone alone."

"Indeed? I'm surprised she would wish to travel so soon after returning from Sussex." He frowned. "Miss Hillary has three other brothers, yet none of them may be relied upon to lend their protection?"

Norwick shrugged. "The elder Hillarys aren't residing in Town at the moment. They're engaged in their own pursuits, I suppose."

"Debauchery, drunkenness, and excessive gambling, no doubt."

"That sums up the Hillary men." Norwick shoveled another bite of eggs past his lips. "A brood of Corinthians, similar to you and me, chap."

Drew bristled at being included in the same category. He might enjoy his vices, but he wouldn't neglect his family to pursue them, at least not intentionally.

"The injured Hillary excluded, of course," Norwick said with a scowl. "He seems rather protective and uncommonly aligned with his sister's wishes. Refused to convince her to dance with me once."

Drew leaned back in his chair and crossed his arms with a wry smile twisting his lips. "You don't attend balls."

"I did last year, one or two. Thought I might select a wife. Miss Hillary seemed an acceptable candidate, but the bloody gent blocked my way."

Drew bit back a grin. Miss Hillary hardly needed her brother's protection against Norwick, not when the chit scaled trees.

❧

Her mother's harping to find a suitable husband in the country vexed Lana. She was well aware of the urgency without her mother's constant reminders. Mama had lectured most of the way from London, and Lana thought if she had to endure much more, she would have Jake's other leg broken when they returned to Town.

Mama seemed quite committed to the task of brokering a marriage on Lana's behalf, which might be appreciated if Mama behaved with any decorum. Lana dreaded the coming days of her mother hounding young men to pay court to Lana. It was mortifying.

"We'll get one up to scratch," Mama said with a

slightly wild gleam in her eyes. "A baron at least. Just you wait and see."

Lana's gut tightened. Despite her father's reassurances all was well with her mother, Lana wasn't certain. If Mama suffered another one of her spells, would she know what to do?

Blast it. Papa should have accompanied them in Jake's place. Lana had never comprehended the underlying animosity between her parents.

Her mother fluffed her skirts before folding her hands in her lap and frowning. "Good heavens, your hair is a mess. I do hope Lady Phoebe's maid is as skilled as she boasts. You'll need all the help you can get if you are to attract suitors."

Lana's moment of wondering why her father had declined to travel with them evaporated. "Are you listening, Alana? If a third season arrives, you're as good as on the shelf. No gentleman desires a lady others have passed over. By the grace of God, we have received one last chance to secure a match this year. How industrious of you to have cultivated a friendship with Lady Phoebe."

Lana sighed and resisted the urge to roll her eyes. "I *like* Lady Phoebe, Mama. I had no design in mind."

"I know, darling. You would never befriend anyone to earn an advantage." She winked. "It's simply *fortunate* the friendship bloomed as it did."

Forget breaking his leg, Lana would strangle Jake when she next saw him. Traveling alone with her mother was torture.

Arriving at Shafer Hall at last, a footman assisted them from the carriage as Phoebe's butler came forward.

"Lady Phoebe regrets she is unable to greet you upon

your arrival, but sends her warm welcome. Please, come inside."

The butler charged a footman with showing them to separate bedchambers and ordered their trunks taken upstairs. Despite being assigned individual quarters, her mother trailed into Lana's chambers. She strolled around the room inspecting every vase and figurine. Holding a crystal glass up to the light, she apparently found no spots and replaced it on the sideboard.

"You're an attractive young lady," her mother said, "and Jake assures me many gentlemen hold you in high esteem. Still, no one calls at home. Young men these days... I fear there is something very wrong with them."

Finally, they had discovered common ground.

A stout maid gathered up the wrinkled dresses and left the room.

"Take Lord Paddock, for example," her mother continued.

Lana flopped on the bed belly first. "Mama, *please*. I wish to forget all things Paddock related."

"And who could blame you?" Her mother stomped her slipper-encased foot. "Poor Miss Bettis. What type of degenerate deflowers a girl barely out of leading strings? Paddock is lucky he escaped castration, in my opinion."

"Mama."

She flicked her hand. "Oh, please, Lana. You've lived in a house with five men. Don't pretend I have offended your sensibilities."

Lana pulled a pillow over her head to cover her ears. If she never heard her former fiancé's name again, she would be forever grateful. Fresh waves of humiliation and anger washed over her.

When Lana had confronted Leo and realized the truth of the allegations against him, she'd broken their betrothal on the spot. While she had been prepared for an argument, his attack on her person caught her off guard. Paddock had not been the Quality she had thought him to be. Nevertheless, Lana managed to deflect his blows with a book long enough for Jake and Daniel to storm the room and subdue him.

Subdue him. Such a mild word to use in connection with Lord Paddock's injuries.

Her mother's weight barely dented the bed as she sat down beside her and hauled the pillow from Lana's head. "My dear, you'll find better than the likes of that scoundrel."

"And what if I don't?" Lana's eyes filled with tears, but she blinked them away.

"Heavens. How can you think such a thing? You are a beautiful young woman."

Lana rolled to her back to confront her mother. "Come, Mama. You've said more than once that I would be prettier if only I would cover my face."

Her mother laughed. "Lana, I've said *no* such thing. You make me sound like a monster. Asking you to wear a hat in the sun does not indicate I find you the least bit lacking in beauty."

"You hate my freckles, Mama. You call them an abomination."

"*Your* freckles are adorable, you foolish girl. Never once have I spoken a bad word against them. If you haven't noticed, we share similar coloring." Her mother's hands fluttered to adjust her hat. "I realize I've complained of my own spots in front of you, but I never meant to give the impression I thought you were anything less than perfect the way you are."

"I know for a fact I am imperfect. Paddock was kind

enough to catalogue my flaws in excruciating details when I cried off."

Red spread up her mother's neck and face like wild-fire. "That no-good devil's spawn. What did he say?"

Lana refused to meet her eyes. Repeating his insults was too mortifying. "It was nothing."

"Well, regardless of whatever misguided thing that blackguard said, he was wrong. A lead ball is too good for him."

Lana covered her face. She hadn't wanted anyone to know of her additional humiliation. Everything else had been bad enough.

Her mother pulled Lana's hands from her face and urged her to sit up. "My sweet daughter." She gathered Lana into her arms and cradled her against her bosom. "Don't listen to the ramblings of a madman."

She felt like a small child again. A lump formed in her chest as she fought back her sadness.

"You must put your sentiments aside and make an advantageous match while you still have time. The good Lord knows I made the mistake of listening to my heart, and you can see what a lonely existence I enjoy."

Six

DREW LEANED FORWARD AND URGED THE BLACK stallion his father had presented for his expert opinion into a gallop. The Thoroughbred was descended from the Godolphin Arabian and bred for swiftness and agility. His father would be pleased the animal possessed a perfect blending of both qualities to render him a superior foxhunter.

The magnificent beast's strong flanks propelled them forward at impressive speeds, and the wind whipped through Drew's hair. He laughed aloud. How easy to forget pleasures afforded by the country when residing year-round in Town.

He spied Shafer Hall in the distance and reined in the horse to allow him a cool-down before reaching the mews.

As he rode up the circular drive, he spotted Phoebe in the gardens with his nephew. His sister-in-law leaned down to examine something the boy cradled in his palm. Drew's heart warmed. Rich had a family and it was a lovely one.

He dismounted, left the horse in the care of the footman, and jogged toward the gardens.

"Phoebe. Stephan," he called.

Both of their heads popped up. Stephan's fist closed to entrap whatever he held. "Uncle Drew, come see what I found."

He grinned, pleased with the way the boy accepted his presence at his home without question as if it were an everyday occurrence.

Drew knelt on one knee beside his nephew. "Let's take a look." Stephan opened his hand to reveal a black beetle. "My, he's a big one. Will you keep him in a jar?"

"Mama says he'll miss his family, so I have to let him go. It's terrible to miss family. Do you not agree, Uncle Drew?" Stephan wandered off with his bug secured in his hand without waiting for a response.

Yes, missing family was a terrible condition, and missing out was even worse. Drew glanced up at Phoebe, her abdomen rounded from the baby growing inside, another tiny nephew or niece. "You look amazing, Pheebs."

Her hand moved to caress her midsection as her arched brows pulled together. "Yes, well, thank you and good heavens. What are you doing here?"

He laughed and got up from his knee. "That's a better welcome than I received from Mother. I believe her words were along the lines of 'you *cannot* be here.' There is no room for me at Irvine Castle. So, here I am."

She tipped her head to the side, her brow furrowed in confusion. "That explains why you are at Shafer Hall, I suppose. But what brings you to Northumberland? You haven't been here in years from what I've gathered."

He shrugged. How could he explain the yearnings he had been experiencing? He'd grown restless in Town, and had been for weeks. It seemed there should be something more, although hang him if he knew what it could be. He thought the ennui would pass after a time, but it hadn't. Not yet, though he didn't want to voice any of this to his sister-in-law.

"All of London is *here*, my lady. I've no one to entertain me."

"Poor Drew," she said with a touch of playful sarcasm. "No one to love him in Town. I suppose we can find room for you."

"How gracious of you, my lady." Before they turned to approach the house, Drew caught sight of a willowy figure in the distance. "Who comes this way?" he murmured.

His heart skipped a beat. *Miss Hillary.*

He couldn't mistake the fiery hair bouncing around her shoulders. Her hat swung carefree in her left hand while she grasped a fat bouquet of colorful flowers in her right. Her steps slowed when she seemed to realize Phoebe had a visitor.

A close-up view revealed cheeks flushed pink from the fresh air and exercise. Why did women make themselves up with powders and perilously balanced hairstyles when their natural state proved so beautiful?

Phoebe stepped forward. "Drew, I'm sure you remember Miss Hillary."

He nodded. "It is a pleasure to see you again."

Miss Hillary's eyes narrowed on Phoebe. "Lord Andrew, how *unexpected* to see you again. Did you by chance arrive on an elephant?"

"I can't say I did, Miss Hillary." He winked at Phoebe, a wide grin stretching across his face. "And I thought people in the country were friendly. I'm beginning to feel unwanted."

A corner of Miss Hillary's mouth lifted.

"Oh, Drew," Phoebe cried. "Of course, you are welcome. Please, come inside and we'll find a room for you."

He didn't miss the roll of Miss Hillary's eyes. "Perhaps if you had sent word, Lord Andrew, we would have formed a parade to greet you."

"I'll keep that in mind for the future, Miss Hillary. Thank you for the suggestion." He gestured to the bouquet in her hand. "Are those for me?"

"Oh," she said, remembering the flowers. "I hope you don't mind if I bring them inside, Phoebe. I'm a fool for wildflowers, and these were too beautiful to resist."

"Hmm." Drew lifted an eyebrow. "I believe I've used that excuse myself a time or two."

His sister-in-law frowned, but a chuckle slipped from Miss Hillary before she forced a chastising look. At least someone had a sense of humor, even if she were loath to admit it.

Stephan raced past as the three of them walked toward the house side by side. Drew glanced sideways at Miss Hillary. She looked quite radiant, even more appealing than the last time he had seen her.

"The fresh air agrees with you, Miss Hillary."

She missed a step and stumbled, but Drew reached out in time to steady her. Her green eyes met his. "Th-thank you, it seems to agree with you as well."

Drew sipped a brandy as his brother paced the length of the study at Shafer Hall. Rich had summoned him minutes after his arrival and seemed intent upon stomping holes into a perfectly good floor.

His brother skidded to a stop and scowled. "I don't know why you chose *this* year to make an appearance."

Drew crossed his ankle over his knee. "Last year you were on the continent."

Rich glared. "Phoebe's friend is *off limits*, Drew. Allow me to lay down the rules for you. You cannot, under *any* circumstances, be anywhere within a hundred feet of Miss Hillary at any time. Do I make myself clear?"

Drew chuckled. "Is the dining room table long enough, or am I to take my meals with the hounds?"

His brother crossed his arms over his chest. "You know my meaning. And don't tempt me."

"Yes, yes," he said on a sigh. "No seducing the delicious redhead. I understand."

"Drew, you have to take this seriously. I forbid you to risk Phoebe's or the baby's health by upsetting her."

Rich could be quite fierce, especially in protecting his family, but his brother didn't intimidate him. Drew was fond of his sister-in-law and loved his older brother. He would never do anything to bring them harm. He could easily submit to their demands, since he had no designs on Miss Hillary. Still, this entire hullabaloo over the forbidden female piqued his interest.

"I have no intention of luring an innocent to my bed, Rich. Too many strings attached."

"And we all know how you like being unattached."

Drew frowned at the censorship in his brother's tone. "As did you once upon a time, as I remember." Once upon a time, before his brother met Phoebe.

Rich seemed happy with being leg-shackled, but marriage was not for Drew. It seemed a man should love a woman if he married her, and love apparently wasn't in his cards. He had sampled some of the finest women in England and many across the continent while on his grand tour. None of them left him with stars in his eyes or inspired him to write poetry, not that anything would inspire him to write a poem, silly dribble that it was.

Nevertheless, Drew had felt nothing beyond a stirring in his loins, and he'd accepted the truth long ago. He wasn't made for love, not from the heart anyway.

He would keep his promise and stay away from that little vixen during her extended visit. But he wouldn't pledge to remain celibate. There were plenty of other attractive, not-so-virtuous guests staying at Irvine Castle to whet his appetite.

He downed his drink and set the glass on the side table with a thump. "Consider your duty dispatched. Reassure your wife I'll be as good as I know how."

"That. Is. Not. Good. Enough." Rich bit out each word.

"Very well." Drew threw his arms wide. "I'll aim for sainthood. Just don't be angry if I miss the mark."

Rich stared in silence for a minute before a knowing smile stretched his lips. "Just watch where you shoot your arrows."

Drew tossed his head back in laughter. His brother wasn't destined for sainthood any more than Drew was, no matter how much Rich pretended.

Lana took a slow, deep breath before leaving her bed-chamber to join the rest of the inhabitants of Shafer Hall. Her stomach tied itself in knots as she fretted over the carriage ride to Irvine Castle where everyone would dine for the evening.

What was Lord Andrew doing in Northumberland?

She reached for the door handle, changed her mind, and hurried to view herself in the oval looking glass. Her cornflower blue dress had no wrinkles, and every strand of hair stayed in place.

Thank goodness.

She hoped her appearance made up for the disheveled mess she had been earlier when Lord Andrew had arrived. Her embarrassment over being found so out of sorts lingered.

Of course, neatness was all she had going for her. She couldn't boast great beauty like Phoebe. Nor was she petite and plump in all the right places. Yet, Lord Andrew *had* complimented her earlier.

Don't be a ninny. Lana scrunched her nose and stuck her tongue out at her image.

She had asked after Lord Andrew following their encounter at the ball and learned more about his peccadilloes than she cared to know. She couldn't allow his empty words to flatter her. Everyone knew for Lord Andrew flirtation came as naturally as breathing. His reputation rivaled Paddock's when it came to charming ladies out of their drawers. Lana's cheeks burned at the thought.

Unlike Paddock, however, Lord Andrew was reportedly direct about what he desired. He didn't pretend to be anything other than what he was—a rogue with no intentions of marriage. In fact, Lord Andrew's forthrightness made him seem safe given Lana knew his game and wasn't foolish enough to play with him.

With a renewed sense of optimism, she left her room with a spring in her step. The Forests and her mother waited for her in the drawing room.

"Everyone is accounted for," Lord Richard announced. "Shall we go, ladies?"

Lana scanned the room. "And Lord Andrew?"

"He left about an hour ago," Phoebe replied.

"To London?" Her voice held a note of alarm, which she immediately regretted.

"No." Phoebe spoke slowly as if Lana had lost her mind. "He departed for Irvine Castle."

"Of course." *Drat!* Maybe she was a fool after all.

Seven

D REW HAD SPED BACK TO HIS PARENTS' RESIDENCE AS soon as Rich informed him of the dinner party planned for that evening. With his mother in charge, there would be a grand procession, which meant taking a gamble as to which lady he'd escort to dinner.

He would rather navigate through a jungle of quicksand than leave the choice of his dining partner up to his mother. Chances were he knew a fair number of female guests a little too well, and if the lady in question hadn't given up hope of rekindling their affair... Well, these situations could be tricky. The last thing he desired was a former lover latching on to him for the entirety of his stay.

Drew breezed into his mother's chambers as if he hadn't a care in the world. "I can't believe my own mother wouldn't find a place for me to sleep," he teased.

She looked up from the sheet of foolscap she held in her hand. A look of concern darkened her gray eyes. "Don't tell me Richard refused to put you up?"

Drew bent down to kiss her cheek, enjoying the way she always smelled like flowers. "Of course he did, Mother, but I cannot allow you to turn me away without needling you a bit."

She smiled ruefully. "Darling, I love you dearly, but why did you show up unannounced? I've been working diligently since this morning to rearrange the seating for dinner, and it is no easy task."

He moved behind her and leaned over her shoulder to view the list she held. "I'm sorry. Allow me to make amends. I shall take on the task of rearranging the guests."

She jerked the paper away as he tried to take it. "I'm perfectly capable, Andrew. And there's no need for atonement."

He sighed, moved to a chair beside her, and dropped down on the thick cushion. "May I at least see the list? Please?"

Her eyebrows shot up as she held it out to him. "Mind you, I'm not making any more changes."

He scanned the names.

Hell's teeth. His promenade partner was Lady Audley. Did his mother despise him? He directed a surreptitious glance at her before shaking off his suspicions. His mother possessed no knowledge of his escapades. He rushed through the list.

No.

No.

Bloody hell! There was barely an appropriate lady on the list.

"What if I sat by Phoebe? I haven't seen her in…" He trailed off when faced with his mother's scowl.

"I said *no* changes, Drew. Besides, you know your brother refuses to part from her for more than a few minutes at one of these events."

He sighed again. "Sick bugger," he mumbled.

"Andrew."

He bolted upright in his seat. "I beg your pardon."

A small smile pulled at the corner of her lips as she inclined her head, accepting his apology.

Drew studied the names again. His mother paired Lord Reinhardt with Miss Hillary.

That old gent? His eyesight must be shot at his age. How was he to appreciate the charms of a beautiful lady?

Drew handed the list back and smiled. "I see you have handled everything beautifully, Mother. I'll see you at dinner."

Drew wrapped the kitchen maid into his arms. The room outside the pantry hummed with activity. With only a sliver of light from where the door stood ajar, he had difficulty seeing her face, but from what he'd glimpsed earlier, she was pretty enough.

"Are you ready, love?" he asked.

"Aye, my lord."

Drew loved the way women breathed their words when he held them, but there wasn't much time to savor the experience. He placed his lips over the maid's for a thorough kiss. A tremor raced through her body.

He broke the embrace then set her away from him. "Don't forget, you must convince the duchess there is a crisis in the kitchen. I only require a few minutes."

"I shan't forget, my lord. And you won't forget your promise either, will you?"

"I've delivered the kiss you requested. Our bargain is almost complete."

"But, Lord Andrew," she purred, "it needn't stop with one kiss. I could visit your chambers tonight."

He placed a peck on her cheek to soften the rejection.

"You deserve better than me, Bridget. Marry that nice boy you told me about earlier."

"Do you think I should?" Her voice held a note of uncertainty.

How would he know? Only a crackbrain would listen to his advice on marriage. "Depends on if you love him, Bridge."

"I think I might, but how am I to know for certain? Have you ever been in love, my lord?"

"Never, but the fools who are seem to enjoy it." He grabbed a jar of something he couldn't identify and shoved it into her hands. "Run along and try to distract the kitchen staff. I'll slip out after you."

About five seconds after the wench left him alone in the dark, a shrill scream pierced the air followed by the sound of shattering glass.

"You clumsy girl," a woman yelled.

"I saw a mouse." Bridget screamed again. "Over there."

More screams erupted. "Catch him, you worthless bumpkins."

During the pandemonium, Drew stuck his head through the crack in the door to discover everyone's backs were to him. He crept from his hiding place and escaped the kitchen undetected.

Upstairs, he lingered on the edge of the drawing room, waiting for the kitchen staff to summon his mother. She had almost completed the task of pairing the guests when the butler appeared by her side and whispered in her ear. She arched her neck to see the kitchen maid standing outside the door. A look of panic crossed his mother's countenance before she bustled from the room.

Lord Reinhardt's ridiculous wig stood out among

the more fashionable guests' coiffures, and Drew darted toward him before his mother returned to discover his scheme.

He slowed his step as he approached before sidling up to the gentleman. "My lord, I believe you are in the wrong spot," he said. "You are to escort Lady Audley."

"Pardon?" Reinhardt bellowed. "Can you repeat that, young man?"

Drew amplified his voice. "I said you are to sit with Lady Audley."

Miss Hillary leaned forward to see around her dining partner.

Lord Reinhardt scratched his head, upsetting his wig. "Are you certain, young man? I thought Her Grace said I was to escort *this* young lady."

Drew shook his head. "No, no. I'm positive you are to be with Lady Audley."

Lord Reinhardt's face was a picture of confusion as he turned toward Miss Hillary.

She regarded him with rounded eyes, offering a look of innocence no one would question. "I believe the gentleman is correct, my lord."

"By the saints…" Lord Reinhardt chuckled. "I suppose I should move on to the appropriate partner. I bid you a good evening, miss."

"Thank you, my lord."

Drew took the spot he vacated and offered his arm to Miss Hillary as his mother hustled into the drawing room without taking much notice of anyone. She assumed her place beside the Duke of Sagehorn, ready to follow his father, who escorted the duke's wife.

A footman drew himself up to full height. "Dinner is served."

"That was devious of you, Lord Andrew," Miss Hillary murmured.

"No need to thank me."

She snaked her free hand over and lightly pinched the arm linked with hers. "Who are you trying to escape? Lady Audley?"

"We both benefit from this arrangement, Miss Hillary. Lord Reinhardt has a tendency to spit when he talks."

She leaned her head closer to his, sending a ripple of desire through him. "And *what*, may I ask, is Lady Audley's foible?" she whispered.

"I'm not at liberty to discuss such matters."

She reached over and pinched him harder.

"Ouch," he muttered. "I'm having second thoughts."

She giggled softly. "As you should."

When they arrived at their appointed seats, Drew sensed someone's eyes boring into him. His brother sat several seats down on the opposite side of the table, staring daggers.

Drew shrugged and mouthed the words, "Talk with Mother."

❧

Lana picked at the roasted goose in front of her. Although the meal was lovely, a generous cut of sumptuous golden brown bird surrounded by sliced green apples, she wasn't hungry any longer. Her stomach performed acrobatics she never knew it capable of doing.

The acute awareness of heat radiating from Lord Andrew's body didn't help her frazzled nerves, and she shifted away from him. When his fingers brushed hers, she almost jumped to the ceiling.

"Is my brother's glaring making you nervous?" Lord

Andrew murmured, his warm breath caressing her neck. "I find it very distracting."

Lord Richard sat beside Phoebe on the opposite side of the table, several chairs away. Whereas the gentleman typically showered his wife with attention, tonight he didn't shift his gaze from their position for one second, even as he sipped his wine.

"Lord Richard looks angry," she whispered back.

"I knew he'd be upset about Walter."

She twisted to face Lord Andrew. "Who is Walter?"

"His pet goose. He cherished that bird, but unfortunately…" He dragged his index finger across his neck then nodded toward her plate. "I believe you have Walter's left wing."

She covered her giggle with her napkin. Lord Andrew might be a rogue, but he was an entertaining one.

"That is the silliest story I've ever heard, my lord."

Lord Andrew raised his goblet in his brother's direction and flashed a smile. "Yes, well, I feel it is my duty to report Rich is quite a silly man."

Lana laughed fully and sank against the seat back. She hadn't realized how rigid her spine had been until this moment.

Lord Andrew nodded toward where her mother sat, a wry smile twisting his lips. "Who's the gentleman courting your mother?"

She stretched her neck to study the flaxen-haired gentleman who had her mother quite animated. "I've never made his acquaintance. Do you not know him? He looks like your type."

"My *type*?"

"Yes, you know, rascally."

His face lit up and dimples pierced his cheeks.

"Perhaps I am of a higher class of rascals, because I've never met the man."

"Or lower class," she added, smiling sweetly.

"Miss Hillary, your honeyed words and charming smiles will not win me over."

Lana heated with pleasure when he beamed.

Her mother chatted excessively with her dining partner, gesturing with her hands and glancing in Lana's direction every few seconds. Lana suppressed a groan. Was her mother husband hunting already? She couldn't meet the gentleman's gaze for fear she would see in his eyes the appalled disbelief he surely felt at being accosted by her mother before dessert had even arrived. After dinner, the women adjourned to the drawing room. Taking Lana's elbow, her mother steered her to a corner. "You'll never believe what happened at dinner."

"Mama, thank you for your good intentions, but I am capable of attracting a husband on my own."

Her mother rushed on as if Lana hadn't spoken. "The gentleman seated next to me at dinner is Lord Philip Bollrud, great-nephew to Lady Dohve, the baroness."

"That is fascinating, Mama." She tried to interject the appropriate level of excitement in her voice, knowing any lack of enthusiasm on her part could precipitate an avalanche of critical words heaped upon her. "I should find Lady Phoebe. It would be rude to abandon our generous hostess."

Her mother gripped Lana's arm. "Silly," she hissed, "that wasn't the interesting part."

Lana's lips stretched into a strained smile. "And I suppose you must share the part you found interesting?"

Her mother puckered her mouth as she always did when displeased. "Lord Bollrud was to accompany his aunt, but she fell ill at the last minute. The baroness insisted her nephew travel without her."

Lana's good humor waned. "And being a doting nephew, he left her to fend for herself. You are right, Mama, that is a fascinating turn of events."

"Honestly, Lana. You try my patience. Perhaps you don't take husband hunting seriously enough, which would explain your lack of success over the last two seasons."

Lana sucked in a deep breath, embarrassed by her mother's blunt manner. She glanced around to see if any of the other ladies overheard, but if they had, they were polite enough to pretend otherwise.

"Here's the part I found interesting," her mother said. "Lady Dohve insisted her nephew attend the party without her, because she knows he seeks a wife."

Perhaps her mother was rushing into an association with the gentleman. They knew nothing about him.

"Mama, where has Lord Bollrud kept himself all this time? I never made his acquaintance in Town. Does that not strike you as odd? One would think he would participate in the season where he'd have more variety with his selection."

Her mother punched her fists to her hips. "Then lucky for you he has been on the continent."

Lana drew back. If her mother had slapped her, it would have been less shocking.

"Lord Bollrud has been on the continent for the past ten years." She leaned closer to Lana and spoke in a hushed tone. "I think this is a sign. You are meant to find your husband here in Northumberland, I'm certain of it."

Lana sighed. Would her mother truly wish her carried off to the continent? She hadn't realized how desperate

Mama had become to be rid of her. She bit down on her bottom lip to still its slight quiver. "Mama, I cannot ignore Lady Phoebe alone any longer. Please excuse me."

She released Lana's arm and allowed her to walk toward her friend.

"I promised your first waltz to Lord Bollrud," her mother called.

Lana faltered in her footsteps and winced. The poor man likely had no choice in the matter. She just hoped Mama hadn't browbeaten him too badly.

Eight

DREW STOOD SENTRY ON THE FRINGES OF THE DANCE floor as the country bumpkin Mrs. Hillary had recruited to waltz with her daughter twirled the beautiful miss around the ballroom.

Perhaps manhandled would be a better description. Drew had never seen a man as pathetic on the dance floor.

Miss Hillary's strained visage belied her longing for the waltz to end, and Drew couldn't agree more. He'd been enjoying a nice conversation with her and Mrs. Hillary before the bumpkin barged in and towed the beguiling redhead away. A moment later, her mother retreated to an alcove, seemingly uninterested in her chaperone duties now that she'd procured a suitor for Miss Hillary.

"Hell's teeth," Drew muttered.

Despite what his brother might think of his intentions, he only wished to watch out for the chit. Obviously, her mother wouldn't provide her with the proper protection she deserved. How could the woman be blind to the fact this man was a fortune hunter? Drew had seen more than his share of down-and-out gentlemen in the hells of London, and Bollrud's ill-fitted breeches and unfashionable coat gave him away in an instant.

A small group of young ladies, close in age to Gabby, meandered to where Drew stood, blocking his view of the dance floor. One of the bolder ones stepped forward.

"Good evening, Lord Andrew."

The others giggled and batted their eyelashes.

He spared them a perfunctory glance and followed with a slight bow. "Ladies."

They didn't move away as he had hoped. Instead, they loitered, fingering their dance cards.

A raven-haired beauty smiled at him but spoke to her friends. "I have one or two open dances, but my card is filling quickly."

"As do I," another added.

They all giggled, some behind fluttering fans.

He sighed. Now he recalled the reason he avoided balls. All that twittering gave him a headache.

As the last strains of the waltz carried on the air, he moved away from the girls to allow for a better view of Miss Hillary. She broke contact and stepped a respectable distance away from her dance partner, waiting for him to lead her from the floor. Yet, the man didn't move. Even from a distance, Drew could see Miss Hillary's cheeks turning red as she seemed to vacillate between walking from the dance floor without her partner and standing there in awkward silence. Eventually, she gestured toward the alcove where her mother chatted with several other matrons of the *ton*, paying no attention to her daughter.

When the beginning bars of the next dance began, the man snatched her hands and dragged her into position for a quadrille. Miss Hillary's mouth dropped open and her eyes widened, but she recovered her composure quickly and attempted to fall into step.

Drew's jaw tightened, and he stalked closer to the dance floor. If the blackguard thought to force Miss Hillary into a *third* dance, he was mistaken. Drew would see this debacle ended on the spot.

As soon as the quartet finished the set, Miss Hillary pushed away and appeared to be begging off. Nevertheless, the man grasped her elbow and guided her toward the punch bowl. Drew followed, closing the distance with purposeful strides.

In the refreshment room, Miss Hillary shrunk away from the bloody bore as soon as he released her arm to retrieve punch.

"I believe Mama said you're Lady Dohve's nephew? Lord Bollrud, is it?" Her voice quivered slightly.

The fop bowed with comical flourish as if he were engaged in a parody of genteel manners. "Philip Bollrud, at your service."

Drew fought the urge to squeeze off the gent's air supply. He abhorred the insincere gestures and prancing like peacocks most suitors did to gain a lady's attention. But something deeply bothered him about this particular gentleman.

Drew reached Miss Hillary's side, smiling when she moved closer to him. "Did you say Mr. Bollrud?" he asked.

"It's Lord Bollrud," the man answered with a lift to his nose and frost in his words. Bollrud held out a glass of punch for Miss Hillary, but Drew took it and sipped the drink.

"Much appreciated," Drew said. "Bollrud? Am I acquainted with your family, sir?"

The man sneered. "Highly unlikely. My father was a Bavarian nobleman, a count, and now I've inherited the title."

Drew wondered if he was expected to be impressed. Much to his pleasure, Miss Hillary appeared unaffected.

"I spent most of my life on the continent," Bollrud said. "Lady Dohve is my great-aunt on my mother's side."

Drew hadn't realized he'd requested a recitation of the man's family tree. He collected another glass of punch and presented it to Miss Hillary. She held Drew's gaze, the slight lifting of her lips and twinkle in her eyes encouraging. Devil take it. Her eyes were blue. He would have bet money this morning they were green. He tore his attention away from her mesmerizing eyes and focused on Bollrud again.

"Pity you've been away from England so long," Drew mused. "I suppose that explains a lot."

Bollrud scowled. "A pity? I don't know your meaning."

"I'm referring to your lack of manners, sir. Perhaps in Bavaria it is acceptable to monopolize a lady's attention, but you're far from home." Drew offered a polite bow to the lady, more than ready to dismiss the gent. "Miss Hillary, do you intend to deny the pleasure of your company to the other gentlemen eagerly waiting to dance with you?"

An impish grin played on her lips as she checked her dance card. "Never think it, Lord Andrew. We have the next dance, do we not?"

Drew started at her reply. Upon his grave, he hadn't intended to request a dance. Yet, he couldn't bow out without offending the lady, and he didn't intend to leave her in Bollrud's company, not a sweet morsel such as her.

"I believe you are correct, Miss Hillary. You did give your word."

He offered his arm and led her to the floor, determined that when the dance ended, Lana Hillary would be as far from Bollrud as possible. As they took position for another waltz, he shot a look in his brother's direction. Less than a day had passed since he had given his word to stay away from Miss Hillary, and here she was in his arms.

His brother's back was to the dance floor, and he engaged in a lively chat with Phoebe and Lord Henley. Drew couldn't count on Rich's preoccupation for long, however, and expected he would receive another dressing down later.

He smiled down at Miss Hillary. "On the ride back to Shafer Hall, please mention to my brother I rescued you from a giant leech."

She arched a delicate brow. "Who said I needed rescuing?"

"It was obvious to all except the leech. Obligation required me to lend my protection. You are my brother's houseguest, after all."

Drew tilted his head and studied her eyes again. He detected flecks of gold, but were they blue or green? It was hard to discern in this lighting.

They glided around the floor in time with the melody, Miss Hillary's movements graceful as if she floated on a cloud. If he was to catch hell from Rich for dancing with her, he might as well do something to deserve the lecture. Trailing his hand slightly lower on her back, Drew pulled her closer. Her hips brushed against his, and an attractive blush brought color to her face. Yet, she hesitated before drawing back.

Drew swallowed the groan rising in his throat. He'd never been one to find pleasure in denying himself, and he regretted giving his promise to stay clear of Miss Hillary. Given her response to his simple touch, keeping his word could prove an impossible task.

He cleared his throat. "Where's your bullish brother when you need him?"

"Jake had more important things to do, such as mend a broken leg," she replied with a touch of surliness.

"How thoughtless of him."

Her deep-throated laugh inflamed his body even more. "Let me ask you, Lord Andrew, how can you be certain playing the distressed damsel is not a tactic I'm using to catch a husband?"

Drew missed a step and she laughed again. The little vixen mocked him. His grip on her hand loosened and he returned her smile. "So you haven't forgiven my teasing at the Eldridge ball."

"Yes, well. I've barely given it a thought. Might I add, sir, you were wrong about ladies and our desires."

"Indeed? How very intriguing." Nothing would please him more than learning of Miss Hillary's desires. He hoped they might align with his own.

The waltz ended, but Drew didn't excuse himself when he escorted her off the dance floor. Instead, he guided her to a corner where they could continue their conversation. "Tell me more of ladies' desires."

Color infused Miss Hillary's cheeks again, but she boldly met his gaze, so unlike the innocents he had encountered in the past.

"You assume all women wish to secure a match, perhaps with a gentleman such as yourself. After all, you are in possession of a modest fortune and noble blood." She wrinkled her nose and frowned. "Well, my lord, I can assure you, not all women find you as pleasing as you believe yourself to be."

Her frank assessment made him smile. "I'm hurt, Miss Hillary, for you failed to mention my charm or handsome face while listing my attributes. I believe those add to my marketability."

She tossed her head, fire sparking in her spectacular eyes, and barreled on as if Drew hadn't spoken. "Some women possess no desire to marry at all, my lord. Mayhap these ladies in question prefer devoting their lives to academics or a pursuit of the arts rather than wifely duties and such."

"I see." Drew nodded, doing his best to hold back his grin.

"Perhaps they wish to invest their funds or take up a profession to support themselves like their brothers."

Miss Hillary became more intriguing each moment. He had never met a woman who didn't care if she secured a husband. He found it difficult to believe one existed.

"Do you have something against marriage?" he asked. "Do you wish to remain unmarried?"

"I wasn't referring to myself—" Her mouth snapped closed and she scowled. "Why is it society finds it acceptable for a man to remain a bachelor, but a woman becomes an anomaly if she wishes to remain unwed; something for young boys to jab with a sharp stick?"

"I see you hail from the rougher section of Mayfair," he said with a chuckle.

Her face darkened as her eyes narrowed. "Does mocking me amuse you, sir?"

"What do you take me for, Miss Hillary? You think me a gentleman who would take pleasure in the act of mocking you? No, it's your fiery temper that provides me with much entertainment, and it requires so little effort to stoke."

She issued a huff of outrage and crossed her arms, pushing her breasts upward.

Determined to ignore her enhanced neckline, he offered his most disarming smile. "Come now, Miss Hillary. Did you not just tease me a moment ago?"

The corners of her perfect pink lips lifted slightly. "I suppose I did."

Drew studied her. How had she grown more beautiful since that night in the garden? "I suppose you're avoiding my original question," he said softly. "Do you truly not wish to marry?"

Her eyebrow arched. "It is every lady's duty to secure a good match, sir. I will thank you to cease your impertinent questions."

Drew spotted Bollrud's towhead moving through the crowd in their direction, and a flicker of irritation ignited in him.

"Come along, Miss Hillary. You're in need of rescue again."

As Drew guided the lady toward her mother and Phoebe, his fingers brushed the soft skin of her upper arm. Hell's teeth, what luxury. It was a shame he would never have the opportunity to discover if she proved as silky all over.

"I thought you were rescuing me," she mumbled as they approached the alcove.

"I am." If he stayed in her presence any longer, he would no longer be responsible for his actions. She was as intoxicating as his father's best bottle of scotch. "Thank you for the lovely dance, Miss Hillary. I trust you will enjoy the remainder of your evening."

He meet Phoebe's gaze then flicked his eyes to Bollrud, hoping she understood his warning. In case his message was lost on his sister-in-law, however, he retreated to his side of the ballroom where he could watch over Miss Hillary for the remainder of the evening and held his post until Miss Hillary left Irvine Castle.

Once he saw her safely removed from Bollrud's clumsy clutches, the tension drained from his body, and he chuckled under his breath. When had Drew become the protector of women rather than the reason they needed protection?

Of course, Miss Hillary's circumstances were unique. Because of her close association with his family, she earned his loyalty by extension; at least that seemed the most logical explanation. Besides, it was apparent she required protection her mother was ill equipped to provide. Why, the noddy woman had allowed Drew to monopolize her daughter's attention in a secluded corner of the ballroom for a good ten minutes. Granted, he and Miss Hillary had remained at a respectable distance, but a man of his reputation shouldn't be allowed anywhere within the vicinity of an innocent unless one wished her name tarnished.

Drew turned to leave the ballroom and spotted Norwick heading his way.

"There you are, chap." His friend lowered his voice as he drew closer. "What in the devil's name are you doing in the ballroom? Don't you know there is a private party?"

Drew raked his hand through his hair, not in the mood to deal with his usual crowd. "You will have to proceed without me."

Norwick laughed, but when Drew didn't join in his merriment, the earl's eyes rounded. "Oh, you are serious. But there will be cards. And brandy. And, and certain *amenable* women."

"It was a grueling trip from London," Drew said. "Perhaps tomorrow."

He scanned the ballroom, meeting eyes with Lady Audley then glancing away before she received unintended encouragement. What had possessed his mother to extend an invitation to Amelia?

Norwick stared openly at Drew's most recent lover. "Ah, I see now, you scoundrel. You've arranged a private party of your own."

"Stop ogling Lady Audley like a sailor after eight months at sea."

"As you wish. I wouldn't think to interfere." Norwick winked. "You laid claim to her first, my friend."

Drew blew out a long breath. "I'm taking my leave, Norwick."

"Indeed, have a nice time."

Damnation. The earl could be a real dullard.

Fatigue washed over Drew. Returning to Shafer Hall seemed a prudent choice at this time rather than cards or bedding a wench, but after a good night's rest, he'd be up for his usual activities. That is, if he could catch any sleep with visions of Miss Hillary plaguing his mind.

Nine

DREW BOUNDED FROM HIS BED AT DAWN THE NEXT morning, filled with renewed enthusiasm for life. He couldn't recall the last time he woke at sunrise, although he had experienced many debauched evenings ending with the sun's appearance. The novelty was a welcome change. Perhaps that was all he needed to cure his ennui, variety in his routine.

Dressed and prepared to return to his parents' home for the festivities an hour later, he trotted down the stairs to see if households served breakfast at this early hour. In the breakfast room, his brother and Phoebe leaned their heads together, speaking in hushed tones. Miss Hillary and her mother were absent, likely still abed like normal folks.

Devil take it. This would be a grand opportunity for his brother to rip into him without the houseguests being any wiser. Drew turned on his heel in an attempt to escape the dressing down he knew forthcoming.

"Stop right there," Rich ordered.

Drew halted with a sigh, then plastered on a jaunty grin before facing his brother and sister-in-law. "Good morning, favorite family members. I take it you both slept well."

"Enough of the pleasantries," Rich replied.

"Richard, remember what we discussed." Phoebe placed her hand on her husband's forearm. "Please stay calm."

His brother's jaw went slack, and he inhaled deeply in response to Phoebe's touch, leaving a more peaceful adversary for Drew to face. He would be wise to stay on his sister-in-law's good side.

Drew held up his hands in surrender. "Listen, I know what you wish to discuss, but in my defense—"

"Have a seat." Rich nodded sharply toward a chair, his stormy eyes merely cloudy after Phoebe's intervention. "You know my thoughts on your association with Miss Hillary. We needn't rehash it this morning."

Drew dropped onto the padded seat and eyed the gold-rimmed plate set in front of him. "Really, Rich, must you be so judgmental? Miss Hillary is a delightful girl if given a chance."

His brother gritted his teeth and snarled. Phoebe had her work cut out today.

"Drew, please don't antagonize him," she pleaded.

"My apologies, dear sister, but antagonizing Rich has become a habit. I'll try to refrain from provoking him further this morning, but only in deference to you." He tilted his head and regarded her, his thoughts shifting from his brother's temper to a more pleasing topic. "Pheebs, what color eyes would you say Miss Hillary has? I thought they were green in the garden, but later they appeared blue in the ballroom."

She blinked. "I… They… I-I think… Hmm, I can't really say, Drew. Now that you mention it, her eyes do appear to change color."

He grunted and shoveled a bite of eggs in his mouth, happy to have his observations validated. When he glanced up from his plate again, he discovered Rich's cheeks matched the strawberry jam on his toast.

"Drew, do you recall you are to stay a hundred feet away from Miss Hillary? That means her eye color, alabaster skin, or… or anything *else* about her person should not be the topic of conversation at breakfast tomorrow."

Drew chewed thoughtfully while creating a mental inventory of Miss Hillary. "Nor freckles, I imagine."

"Excuse me?"

"You failed to mention the sprinkling of freckles on her alabaster skin. I'm assuming I should not discuss those either."

Rich simply growled as Drew had hoped he would.

He would have speculated aloud whether Miss Hillary had spots elsewhere on her body to irritate his brother further if Phoebe hadn't been present. But despite her marital status and the babe in her womb, his sister-in-law remained rather innocent in her thinking. It wouldn't do to embarrass her for the sake of bothering Rich.

Phoebe bit her lip and shot a glance toward the doorway. "Could we speak of something else? Lana and her mother may join us any moment."

Rich caressed her shoulder. "Of course, love."

Raising his eyes to the ceiling, Drew shook his head. Rich found excuses to touch his wife every two minutes, yet everyone labeled *Drew* the depraved one.

He crammed the last bite of toast into his mouth and shoved from the table. "I'm leaving for the castle. Perhaps our paths shall cross later."

"Mother wishes to speak with you," Rich said.

Drew skidded to a stop and looked over his shoulder. "Mother wants to speak with me? And *why* does she want to speak with me?"

His brother grinned, clearly pleased with himself. "I'm sure she didn't appreciate your stunt at dinner."

"I hardly think she noticed on her own, traitor."

"Bottle-head," Rich shot back, a spark of amusement shining in his eyes.

A corner of Drew's mouth slanted up and he squared his shoulders, preparing to engage in a verbal duel. "Miss Molly."

"Toad-eater."

"That is *enough*, boys." His sister-in-law wore a disgruntled look, but he and Rich smiled from ear to ear. Drew had missed his brother this last year while Rich traveled. Nothing ever filled the void left by absent family members, he had come to realize.

"Saved by your wife again," he said then hurried from the breakfast room and sprinted up the stairs. He rounded a corner in the upstairs hallway on the way to his chambers and almost mowed over Miss Hillary.

"Oh." She covered her heart with her hand. "My lord, you frightened me."

A moment alone in the corridor with Miss Hillary? His day had gotten off to a great start.

"You hardly seem to be a shrinking violet, Miss Hillary." Drew leaned closer and breathed deeply, detecting the light scent of lily of the valley. "Though I dare say, you smell like one."

She rolled her eyes. "Violets have no scent, silly man."

"Really? Allow me to try again." This time he leaned even closer, his lips almost grazing her slender neck. God, she smelled scrumptious, like ripe innocence ready to be plucked from a tree branch. "What are you wearing, peach?" he whispered.

"Ahem."

They both jumped away from each other, and Drew spun around to encounter Mrs. Hillary's chiding stare.

"Good day, Mrs. Hillary. I was just commenting on the delightful aroma wafting through the hallway." He stepped toward her, yet kept a respectful distance. Sniffing the air, he allowed a magnanimous smile to spread across his lips. "I believe I have located the source. Is that a new scent you're wearing?"

Miss Hillary released a soft snort behind him.

From her mother's scowl, he clearly hadn't fooled her. "You are too kind, Lord Andrew. Have you consumed breakfast this morning?"

"I have. A delicious spread awaits you."

"Then you will excuse us so *we* may partake as well." Mrs. Hillary motioned to her daughter to accompany her. Drew moved aside to let her pass. Both women floated down the red-carpeted hallway, Miss Hillary's hips swaying ever so enticingly.

Did the little minx know what she was doing? If she kept that up, he'd have to bed her. Consequences be damned.

Drew replayed the scene in the hallway with Miss Hillary on the ride to Irvine Castle. The chit had become irresistible overnight. Had her mother not interrupted when she did, Drew would have backed her against the wall and kissed her thoroughly.

Shaking off the temptation she presented, Drew focused on the horizon. He would do well to recall Miss Hillary remained an innocent and turn his attentions elsewhere. There were many beautiful, accommodating ladies waiting at Irvine Castle. He simply needed to bed one and give up his fantasies of Miss Hillary. Several women had exhibited signs of their willingness to accommodate his needs last night, but damn him, even the thought of a supple body beneath his lacked the allure of watching Miss Hillary from across the room.

Drew recoiled. He would rather *watch* Miss Hillary than tumble a fine wench? He required a doctor. Although he suspected the true cure for his affliction remained out of his reach, thanks to his damned brother.

"Hell's teeth." Drew sat up straight in the saddle. Why hadn't it dawned on him earlier? Miss Hillary was forbidden, and what man didn't desire what was denied him?

He issued a relieved chuckle. A physician's assistance was unnecessary. Drew knew how to remedy his situation. He only need gain full access to Miss Hillary, and once he knew with certainty he could tumble her, he would lose interest as he did with every other woman. Well, his interest usually waned *after* he had bedded the object of his desire, but Drew only needed to possess the knowledge he could win Miss Hillary. He needn't actually claim the prize. He possessed some willpower, after all. His promise to his brother would remain unbroken— perhaps bent a little, but still unbroken—and he would be able to return to a normal existence like the one he enjoyed before meeting Miss Hillary.

Drew frowned and gripped the reins tighter. But how could he navigate her mother without leaving the impression he intended to offer for the chit? Mrs. Hillary's drive to find a husband for her daughter proved treacherous terrain for a man like him. Of course, she hadn't been the most attentive chaperone last night. Distracting her should be easy.

In reality, Miss Hillary's mother was the lesser of his two concerns. The true challenge lay in getting what he wanted without upsetting Phoebe and incurring Rich's wrath. An idea began to form as the battlements of Irvine Castle loomed into sight. He had to seek out his sister.

❧

"Why should I help you?" Gabby flounced across her chambers and dropped onto the chair in front of her dressing table. Crossing her arms, she frowned fiercely.

Drew wagged a finger toward her mirror. "Princess, you might want to take a gander. You have something unattractive on your face."

She gasped and swiveled to catch her reflection in the looking glass. Nothing was there, and she swung around again to pierce him with another dark look.

He shrugged, a huge smile pulling at his lips. "My mistake. That *is* your face."

"Drew." Gabby jumped from the chair and charged, smacking his arm hard.

"Ouch." He laughed when she delivered a few more blows he halfheartedly tried to deflect. She had actually been quite adorable before succumbing to her temper. "I was only teasing, princess."

"Stop calling me that." She stamped her foot, bouncing her ebony curls in the process. "I hate it when you tease me."

"But it's so entertaining," he countered.

"Not for me."

She hit him once more before stomping back to the chair and collapsing on it. Her bottom lip trembled.

"Gabby, look at me."

She turned away in stubborn defiance.

Drew sighed and crossed the room to kneel in front of her, trying to gain eye contact, but she dodged any attempts he made. "I'm sorry. Would it help if I confessed to lying?"

Her furious gray eyes shot to his. "It would be more shocking to admit you ever tell the truth."

He suppressed a laugh and patted her knee. "You've grown into a beautiful young woman. No longer are you the little girl I loved annoying. I would be smart to recognize this fact and treat you like a lady."

Suspicion darkened her eyes. She would be difficult to convince, but Drew had nothing to lose.

"If I didn't recognize your maturity, why would I come to you for help?" He glanced toward the ceiling certain lightning would strike him dead any moment.

"Again, *why* should I help you?"

"Don't you like Miss Hillary? She was here two years ago. Did you not spend time with her then?"

Gabby snatched a book from her dressing table and buried her nose in it. "I like Miss Hillary fine, but I'm not fond of *you* at the moment."

This was going nowhere. He rose from the floor and sank into an armchair, a pink, fuzzy, childish piece of furniture. Running his hand along the armrest, he discovered the soft fabric actually felt nice under his fingertips, much like Miss Hillary's silky skin had last night. Back to the task at hand.

"Don't you long for more freedom?" he asked.

Her head jerked up. "I desire more than a *taste* of freedom, which is what you propose. I wish to come out next season, but Mama refuses to allow it. It's unlikely she would grant permission for me to participate in the festivities."

"If I can convince her, will you assist me?"

Gabby appeared to mull over the decision before lifting the open book to block his view of her face. "I can't."

"Why the devil not?"

Gabby peeked over the edge of the book. "Despite my desire for liberation, I cannot be a party to heartbreak."

"What are you talking about? No one's heart will be broken."

Laying the book on her lap, Gabby stared hard. "Tell me your intentions with Miss Hillary. Why do you want to chaperone me? And why do you ask me to spend as much time with her as I can? You want to get close to Miss Hillary, don't you? But I'm afraid you will only hurt her. She is a nice young woman."

He slumped in the chair and rested his chin against his propped-up hand. "*Everyone* thinks I'm the devil. I don't intend to hurt Miss Hillary. I simply need this."

"*What* is it you need?"

"I can't put it into words," he snapped. "You couldn't possibly understand."

She frowned. "Then you may seek assistance elsewhere. I have to know what I'm doing if I join this venture with you."

They sat in silence, Gabby never wavering in her stare. Looking into her eyes for the first time, Drew detected a hint of compassion.

"If you must know, I'm unable to banish Miss Hillary from my mind," he admitted in a quiet voice. "She has plagued me for weeks, ever since the Eldridge ball."

"Indeed?" A gradual lifting at the corners of Gabby's lips raised his spirits. "Very well, Drew, but you must do something for me in return. Secure Mama's permission for me to be presented next season."

"I beg your pardon? Why, that is coercion, Gabrielle." Clever girl. He winked. "I'm impressed."

An hour after his conversation with his mother and father, he questioned the wisdom of accepting full responsibility for Gabby. His sister pranced down the stairway in her lavender riding habit at the appointed hour, drawing the notice of every gentleman loitering in the foyer. Good God, when had she grown into a beautiful young woman?

When Gabby reached the landing, she bubbled with excitement. "You did it, Drew. I'll never underestimate your cunning again."

"Shh, let's keep it our little secret." He lightly grasped her elbow and whispered in her ear. "Now do not forget your part of the agreement. As soon as Miss Hillary arrives, I want you on her like a tick on a dog."

Gabby's face screwed up as she pulled away. "Ew. I hope that isn't an example of the sweet nothings you typically whisper in a woman's ear."

He chuckled. "Sorry, princess, but that's exactly the types of things men whisper in young women's ears, so don't allow them the opportunity to get too close."

"Oh." Her innocent eyes rounded, making his heart swell with tenderness.

He cleared his throat to dislodge the lump forming. "So does Lizzie hate you forever?"

"That was her declaration when she heard the news. Of course, that is her declaration every fifteen seconds lately." Gabby lifted her nose and sniffed with disapproval. "Fifteen-year-olds are extremely childish."

"Just remember, she's the only sister you have. You cannot do away with her."

"Drew, aren't you forgetting about Katie?"

"Oh, right!" He winked. "Well, since you have a spare…"

She giggled. "You have a macabre sense of humor, dear brother."

"True, but you laughed." A flash of auburn hair at the entrance to the castle caught his attention. "There. Miss Hillary is just arriving. You know what to do." He gave Gabby a tiny shove in the lady's direction.

"Yes, yes. A tick on a dog," she mumbled.

Ten

LANA HELD NO INTEREST IN THE HUNT, BUT SHE WOULDN'T pass up an opportunity for a group ride on a gorgeous day. Granted, her mother's fear of horses may have influenced her decision a little, for even St. Monica, the patron saint of patience, would require a reprieve from her mother's company on occasion. And no one had ever accused Lana of having the patience of a saint. So, it was with a light heart that Lana arrived at Irvine Castle dressed in her emerald green riding habit with her best friend by her side.

She barely had time to notice her surroundings before Lady Gabrielle bounced over to her and Phoebe. A beaming smile lit the beautiful girl's face.

"Miss Hillary, you've arrived. I have most exciting news. Mama is allowing me to accompany everyone on the ride. Please say you'll be in my group, so we might catch up."

Lana glanced sideways at Phoebe. Gauging from her friend's open mouth, she knew nothing of her sister-in-law's early coming out.

Phoebe placed a delicate hand on the girl's arm. "Gabby, I'm afraid Richard is unable to act as chaperone today. He has joined the hunt this morning. I would happily volunteer if not for..." She glanced down at her pregnant belly and blushed.

Gabby patted her hand. "I understand, Phoebe. But you needn't worry. Drew volunteered to fulfill the role."

"Drew? Oh, Gabby, I think that is a bad idea."

"Did I hear my name?"

Lana swung toward the sound of Lord Andrew's voice and her heart stopped. *Heavens above!* He moved toward them with grace and determination. His buckskin pants hugged his hips and thighs with precise accuracy, revealing how sleek and muscular he was.

His wild toffee-colored locks were reminiscent of the majestic lion's head mounted on Lord Eldridge's wall at his country estate. When Lana had stared into the lion's hungry eyes some years ago, fascination and terror had surged through her blood. A different hunger lurked in Lord Andrew's eyes, but the effect on her senses was the same.

He flashed his dimpled smile. "Phoebe and Miss Hillary, how lovely to see you."

Phoebe's brow wrinkled. "Gabrielle informs me you're to act as her chaperone for the riding excursion."

"That's correct, Pheebs. And Mother informed me of my duties as well as the consequences should I fail to fulfill them, so there is no cause for alarm." Lord Andrew offered his arm to his sister. "Shall we make our way to the mews before the best horses are claimed?"

As Lana made to follow, Phoebe detained her with a soft touch to the arm. She nibbled her bottom lip, as she was prone to do when worried. "Lana, be cautious with Drew. He means well, but..."

"Please don't fret for me, dear Phoebe. I'm aware of what Lord Andrew is." And what he would never be.

He would never be one to fall in love. He'd never settle for one woman. Lord Andrew would never endanger her heart, because he would never try to win it. "I'll be fine, really."

Phoebe's expression didn't ease with Lana's reassurance, but she held her tongue.

At the stables, Lana's gaze strayed to Lord Andrew while he assisted Lady Gabrielle with mounting a pure white horse. He glanced up too quickly, caught Lana in the act of ogling him, and grinned. She spun around and pretended to study the horseflesh before he noticed her flaming cheeks. Without any thought, she selected a gray gelding closest to her and waited for the groom to give her a hand up.

A moment later prickling sensations at the back of her neck prompted her to look up. Lord Bollrud's ice-blue eyes followed each movement she made, triggering a rush of bashfulness. Lana's gaze dropped to the dirt beneath her boots.

There was no doubt her mother approved of the gentleman and wished her to make a match with him, but Lana didn't know what to think after their dance last night. He had been polite enough and seemed to have honorable intentions, but his lack of experience navigating the *ton* had been awkwardly apparent.

The gentleman offered a slight smile before dismounting his horse. Her stomach flipped when he secured the reins of his chosen mount and made to approach.

A light touch at her elbow caused her to jump. "Miss Hillary, you need a more spirited ride," Lord Andrew murmured into her ear. His soothing voice and warm breath on her neck created pleasurable shivers.

"I-I do?" He did refer to a horse, didn't he?

"Indeed. Leave the docile gray mare for one of the

more seasoned ladies. There's a lovely chestnut this way that will suit you nicely."

Lord Andrew offered his arm and directed her away from Lord Bollrud. She glanced over her shoulder in time to witness the other gentleman grimace. Concerned that he might see her action as a cut direct, she offered an apologetic smile, but all thoughts of Lord Bollrud vanished the moment she saw the chestnut.

"Oh, Lord Andrew. How beautiful," she said on an exhale.

He smiled broadly, showing his dimples again. "I thought you would like her. She's an Andalusian. The breed is docile, but you'll notice a difference in her gait, more energetic than other horses. Andalusians tend to be intelligent and respond to the lightest of hand."

"I see." Lana cared little for the specifics of the breed, but she enjoyed how animated Lord Andrew became when speaking of the horse. She ran her hand over the mare's gleaming reddish-brown coat. "Are you an expert on horseflesh?"

He grinned wickedly. "Among other things."

Such as pleasures of the flesh? Heat engulfed her body and she fidgeted with her gloves.

"Allow me the honor of assisting you, Miss Hillary."

Lord Andrew linked his fingers to form a step in which she placed her boot. With her hand resting on his shoulder for balance, he lifted her as if she weighed nothing. A whiff of sandalwood teased her senses. The easy movement of unyielding muscles under her fingertips sent her heart racing again. She had never been as aware of any man as she was of Lord Andrew, nor as flustered by his presence.

"Th-Thank you, my lord." She fussed with her skirts to allow herself time to recover from their contact.

"My pleasure, Miss Hillary." He held her gaze several seconds longer than necessary before a tantalizing grin spread across his lips. He spun around to return to the black stallion he'd chosen for himself.

Lana gripped the reins to hide the tremor in her hands and exhaled, wishing the butterflies in her belly would cease their agitated flutters.

Only eleven guests had chosen to participate in the ride around the lake, mostly young women and their chaperones, while the more adventurous guests participated in the hunt. As the group prepared to leave, raucous laughter floated on the air, and six young men rounded the side of the stables.

"Prepare six more mounts," Lord Brookhaven called as the men wandered into the stable yard. "We wish to join the riding party."

"Forest, we heard you had attached yourself to this group," Mr. Collier said with a twinge of amusement in his voice. "Thought you must know what you're about."

The head groom glanced toward Lord Andrew in askance. A flash of irritation crossed Lord Andrew's countenance, but he gave a sharp nod indicating the groom should provide the men with mounts. The servant issued brusque orders to the other grooms, who scrambled to outfit the additional horses.

Lord Andrew jerked his mount's head around and tapped his sides. "Let's go. They may find their own way to the lake."

Lady Gabrielle followed behind her brother. "Are those men your friends?"

"Acquaintances," he answered sharply and urged his horse into a faster walk. "No one to earn your notice."

Once out on the trail, Lady Gabrielle and Lana rode

side by side while Lord Andrew lagged behind. The young woman fired question after question at Lana about the London season. How nice it was to be in a position to provide guidance to Lady Gabrielle, especially with Phoebe unable to accompany her. She enjoyed the younger woman's discourse until the mob of latecomers to the riding party galloped their horses past, upsetting Lana's mare.

Her horse danced sideways and issued a soft whinny while she clung to the reins.

Lord Andrew urged his horse alongside hers and grasped the bridle. "There, there, girl." His rich voice soothed the skittish mare but sent Lana's pulse racing again.

Lord Bollrud rode up on Lana's other side. "Are you all right, Miss Hillary?"

"I'm a bit out of sorts," she admitted, "but suffer no harm." Not yet, at least, although her body's response to Lord Andrew warned of the precarious nature of their continued association.

Lady Gabrielle had stopped her mare in the middle of the path and studied her with a troubled frown.

"Please, let's continue our ride," Lana said, not wishing to hamper the younger woman's enthusiasm.

Two of the gentlemen who had galloped past a moment earlier doubled back and approached Lady Gabrielle. She smiled sweetly and called out a greeting. The men took this as encouragement to flank her mount and make introductions.

"Hell's teeth," Lord Andrew grumbled.

Lana and her two gentlemen followed behind Lady Gabrielle and her apparent admirers.

For a time, Lord Andrew stared holes into the backs of his sister's companions, his posture rigid, but as the gentlemen conducted themselves with utmost propriety, he seemed to relax his guard slightly.

Lord Bollrud cleared his throat. "Is not the country-side beautiful, Miss Hillary?"

"Very beautiful, my lord."

"And the weather is perfect for a ride, wouldn't you agree? The sun shines its radiance upon us this fine day."

Lana kept her eyes trained ahead, attempting to hide her amusement. "Indeed. It is a fine day."

Lord Andrew chuckled under his breath. "Surely, you are not suggesting the radiance of the sun is any more beautiful than one smile from the charming Miss Hillary."

When Lana looked in Lord Bollrud's direction, he winced, as if he experienced a sharp pain in his gullet. "Well, no. Of course not, Miss Hillary. I wasn't implying... Not even the *sun* can compare to your... your radiant beauty. I've never seen anyone more radiant. Not the sun... even."

The poor man. He didn't realize Lord Andrew teased him.

"Thank you, my lord." Lana made certain their companion couldn't see her cross her eyes at Lord Andrew.

"And her *eyes*," Lord Andrew gushed. "They shine brighter than the stars in a midnight sky. Wouldn't you agree, Bollrud?"

"Oh, well. Yes, yes, they do." Lord Bollrud sounded confused by the direction of the conversation but eager to please. "Miss Hillary's eyes are quite—um, *shiny*. I suppose."

Lord Andrew was being quite incorrigible, mocking the gentleman as he was. Lana playfully stuck out her tongue in his direction.

"And those lips," Lord Andrew raved. "Ah, lips like—"

Lady Gabrielle glanced over her shoulder and grinned, apparently eavesdropping on their conversation. "Cease your nauseating rhapsody, you besotted ninny. We're having lunch soon and you are spoiling my appetite."

A giggle escaped Lana. The two siblings' playful exchanges reminded her of the relationship she shared with Jake. A twang of remorse sobered her mood. Jake had warned her to avoid Lord Andrew, but she hadn't listened. Perhaps he knew her better than she knew herself. One day in Lord Andrew's presence and she was dangerously close to developing a fondness for the scoundrel.

Eleven

At the end of the ride, Lord Andrew and Lady Gabrielle took up position on each side of Lana and accompanied her to the picnic set up on the grounds. The younger girl wandered off a moment to retrieve a beverage, leaving Lana and Lord Andrew in the queue for the buffet.

As they gathered food on their plates, Lana leaned toward him and lowered her voice. "Do go on about my lips, my lord."

"Why stop with the lips when I can wax poetic over every inch of your body?"

Lana drew in a sharp breath. She had only meant to tease him for playing the foppish suitor in Lord Bollrud's presence.

He gave her a covert wink. "What's the matter, my little muse? Did I finally leave you speechless?"

She made a face, trying to hide her pleasure over engaging in such inappropriate banter with such a handsome scoundrel. In spite of her resolve to marry a respectable gentleman, a roguish one still possessed the power to turn her head, especially one as charming as Lord Andrew was.

"I'm sure you are accustomed to leaving women

breathless," she replied as smoothly as possible. Lana might be an innocent in the strictest sense, but two years in society didn't leave her naïve. Nevertheless, flirting in such a manner was a bold action for her, and thrilling.

Lord Andrew led her to a spot under a shade tree and held her plate while she lowered to the grass. As his sister approached, he called out, "You have no grapes on your plate, Gabby. You must go back for some. Oh, and try some of the melon."

Lady Gabrielle scowled but slowly turned and plodded back toward the buffet table.

"Miss Hillary, were you trying to seduce me in the queue?"

Lana's eyes rounded. "No. I wasn't trying—no."

He chuckled and handed her the plate. "I see."

They sat in silence while Lord Andrew satisfied a healthy appetite and Lana picked at her food.

Oh, for heaven's sake. Must her curiosity always be satisfied? "Why do you ask, my lord? Was I succeeding at seducing you?"

He cocked one eyebrow. "You're an amateur, but close to irresistible."

Lana pressed her lips together and narrowed her eyes. *An amateur? An amateur!*

"Don't be angry, Miss Hillary. You asked. I thought you sought my advice."

"Advice?" She almost screeched the word. Searching to see if anyone overheard and finding everyone else engaged in his or her own tête-à-têtes, she lowered her voice. "I do not require your assistance, sir. I'm more than capable of... of... *handling* gentlemen."

It was a bold lie, but her pride demanded as much.

He shrugged. "If you insist." Leaning back and

bracing himself with one hand, he bit into a pear he held in his other. "Maybe you require more practice. I don't mind lending my assistance."

"I do *not* need more practice," she whispered angrily.

He held up his hand in surrender. "All right, all right. And everyone believes I'm up to no good. Allow me to pose this question, Miss Hillary. Has anyone pulled you aside and demanded you to stay a hundred feet from me?"

Jake hadn't exactly specified a particular distance. She shook her head.

"Apparently they should, because it's obvious you seek to *handle* me." His lopsided grin injured her pride. Why must he mock her? "And though I'm certain you possess two of the best hands in England, regretfully, I must resist your advances."

Her head lowered, her cheeks burning with mortification. Not only did the proper gentlemen of the *ton* find her lacking, the wickedest libertine in London didn't want her, even when she wantonly threw herself in his path. Lana may be no beauty, but Lord Andrew could at least have the good manners to pretend he found her desirable.

She studied her plate and fought back tears of humiliation. "You needn't mock me."

"What is this? Have I truly upset you?" The toe of his boot brushed her ankle. "Look at me, peach."

How could she resist his request when his rich voice flowed over her like a lover's caress? Lana reluctantly lifted her gaze to meet his smoky blue eyes.

"You could tumble me in a heartbeat if there were not extenuating circumstances."

Lana's heart leapt and then sped to an unnatural pace. "Wh-what circumstances?"

"I gave my word to Rich that I wouldn't touch you."

She frowned, displeased by Lord Richard's interference. Lana was a grown woman and didn't require her host's protection.

"Why would you make such a promise, my lord?"

Lord Andrew grinned. "I can only claim a moment of insanity, my sweet."

❧

After a full day of dangling after Miss Hillary, Drew needed a distraction. His plan to rid himself of his craving for her had failed. Evidence of her mutual desire hadn't released him as he had expected. If anything, it stoked the flames of his lust, but a night of cards and a romp with a beautiful woman should cure him. It had to or else he would go insane.

Drew placed a marker on the spaded Knave, his lucky card, and the Queen of Hearts, Lady Love. *Lady Love.* He scoffed. Gambling should take his mind *off* the enticing Miss Hillary, not play into his fanciful imagination. Yet, her image, her smell, and her voice had become his obsession, following him even into his domain. And devil take it, he ached. Badly. He'd not had cause to experience the painful sensation since being ushered into manhood.

Drew's gaze swept the small room of the east wing parlor crowded with the more adventurous guests. His parents pretended ignorance as long as the guests confined their activities to this area of the castle. Alluring women, less virtuous than the debutantes in the ballroom, dotted the vast room. Most were widows, but some married women traveling without their husbands had straggled in as well.

Drew never passed judgment on anyone. It was no secret many ladies of the *ton* entered into loveless matches for the sake of prosperity. He'd not begrudge them a passionate tumble now and again. He himself preferred less complicated liaisons, but perhaps he could make an exception. He was quite desperate to banish Miss Hillary from his thoughts.

A beautiful brunette hovered on the fringes of the crowd, her full figure capturing Drew's notice. An unmistakable invitation lingered in her stare, and he allowed a seductive smile to spread across his lips. The lady would do nicely to soothe the dull throb in his trousers. She inclined her head and returned his smile. After this round, he would go to her and be done with the matter. His grin widened as he rose from his seat, prepared to make his departure.

"Queen of hearts," Norwick called out. "Forest, you lucky bugger, looks like Lady Love is with you tonight."

Drew gaped at the board. The Queen of Hearts won?

He pictured Miss Hillary, her cheeks pink from riding this morning, her eyes shining with amusement then later with desire.

Devil take it!

His agreeable partner for the evening wouldn't do at all. Only one woman could ease his torment, and Lana Hillary remained off limits. Pummeling his interfering brother probably wouldn't help matters, but why dismiss any alternatives?

Drew scooped up his winnings and pushed from the table with a screeching of chair legs against the stone flooring.

"Forest, you can't leave," Norwick protested.

"Of course he can," Radcliff argued. Several other gents chimed in with their opinions.

"Let him go."

"He must allow us a chance to win back our blunt."

Drew tossed the pot on the table. "Split my winnings."

A scuffle followed as the down-and-out gamblers jostled for their take.

The dark-haired beauty trailed Drew from the room. He turned and lowered his voice where only she could hear. "Please forgive me, my dear. You are quite divine, but I would make for lousy companionship tonight."

The lady parted her lips as if to argue but must have reconsidered and pressed them back together in a slight pout. No doubt, her action was designed to entice. "Perhaps another time, my lord?"

"I'll be a lucky gent when the time comes, love."

Drew didn't intend to surrender to his ridiculous longings without a struggle. Once he discovered a way to banish Miss Hillary from his mind, he would dive back into his usual activities with gusto. Until then, there seemed little point in remaining at Irvine Castle, not if he couldn't engage in his favorite pastimes. If Rich was still awake at Shafer Hall when Drew arrived, he could receive his beating early.

❦

Lana gazed out at the moonlit grounds of Shafer Hall. Her body was weary after the festivities of the day, but her thoughts refused to quiet. Had Lord Andrew tried to save her feelings by saying he would bed her in an instant? He'd actually used the word tumble, which always sounded like wrestling to her, only minus any clothing from what she understood. She covered her fluttering heart with her hand. A nude Lord Andrew would be a remarkable sight. He was so very beautiful. Maybe everyone reserved that particular term for women, but no one with sense would debate the description. Lord Andrew was ungodly beautiful with his sculpted face and mesmerizing eyes the color of the sea in the distance. The man couldn't possess a single place on his lean frame where any blemish resided. He was...

"Perfection," she grumbled. And Lana could never measure up. Blasted spots dotted her skin all over, and her hair flamed like orange fire. Was *this* the reason Lord Andrew called her a peach?

She sighed. What did it matter what Lord Andrew had said earlier, or how exquisite he was? He remained at Irvine Castle when her party left and likely shared a bed with some other lady. And Lana didn't like it one bit.

She snatched up her wrapper. This was madness. Maybe she could find a good book in the library to occupy her thoughts. She wouldn't remain in her bedchamber and torture herself with thoughts of Lord Andrew, a man who could never be what she needed. Perhaps Mama was right. Sentimentality had no place in the selection of a mate. On the morrow, she would turn her attentions to the only gentleman with promise, Lord Bollrud. He seemed a nice enough gent.

A shiver rippled through her and she drew the wrapper snug around her body as she slipped into the darkened corridor. No one moved about the house, so she could get what she wanted and return to her chambers with no one the wiser.

As stealthily as possible, Lana descended the stairs. A soft gasp slipped from her lips when her bare feet touched the cold marble floor in the entrance hall. She hurried toward the library on her toes to minimize her contact with the floor and wished she had sought out her slippers before leaving her chambers. Inside the library, she felt her way along the furniture before locating the lamp she had seen earlier, along with the match and flint lying on the side table.

The room sparked to life for a second as she lit the oil lamp, casting the area around her in a warm glow. She stood and stretched her arms overhead, considering where to start.

"Can't sleep, peach?"

Twelve

Lana squealed and spun around to discover Lord Andrew resting in a wingback chair. "You scared me to death."

"I had no idea you startled so easily, my sweet."

A thrill of excitement accompanied his use of the endearment, but Lana knew "my sweet" meant nothing to a man like Lord Andrew.

Her hands landed on her hips with a huff. "Who wouldn't be startled given the circumstances? What are you about, lurking in the dark?"

His warm chuckle made her knees wobble. She had never been one to require smelling salts, but she became a blasted ninny in Lord Andrew's presence.

He sampled the amber liquid from the tumbler he held. "Am I lurking? I thought I was enjoying a nightcap."

Lana pulled her wrapper tighter around her middle, painfully aware of her thin attire and the man's intense inspection. "I-I didn't expect anyone would be sitting in the dark. I'm surprised to see you returned tonight."

His gaze strayed to her bare feet and back again. "Why wouldn't I return, Miss Hillary? Shafer Hall boasts beds as good as any at Irvine Castle."

"Oh," she said. The scoundrel teased her. She could tell from his lopsided grin. "Yes, well. I was under the impression the beds at Irvine Castle might hold greater appeal for you."

"As did I," he muttered, scowling. "But there's nothing of great appeal to me anywhere except here, it seems. I did happen upon a game of faro, but unfortunately the cards didn't play out as I had anticipated."

Now she understood his soured expression. "Oh, dear. I do hope you didn't lose an excessive amount, my lord."

"Just my senses. Nothing to fret over."

"Jake always feels rotten after a rough evening at the tables."

Lord Andrew rose from the chair and sauntered toward her, brushing past to reach the sideboard housing the decanter of spirits. "Your brother is a sore loser, Miss Hillary."

Lana whipped around, gasping with outrage. "How dare you speak ill of Jake? Why, he's a wonderful man with no faults deserving ridicule from anyone, least of all you." She looked down her nose at him as she'd witnessed her mother do when chastising her father. "You, on the other hand, are a scoundrel."

He didn't appear insulted in the least by her comments. Instead, he smiled then poured himself another drink. "I admire your honesty. And your loyalty is commendable."

Why did Lord Andrew have to compliment her? It was easier to stand before him in her nightrail with anger emboldening her. "I-I call things as I see them, sir."

He sloshed liquor into a second tumbler and handed it to her. "You evaded my original question, as you are wont to do. Are you having trouble sleeping? Perhaps a few sips of this will help."

She sniffed the strong concoction but didn't sample it. "Thank you, but I find occupying my mind is usually an effective remedy. I'm seeking a book. Do you have any recommendations?"

"Does reading typically result in slumber for you?"

She shrugged. "Not always. Sometimes I get swept into a story and find I cannot put it down. I'll read into the wee hours on occasion."

"I see." He returned to his chair and lowered into the cocoon it provided. "Care to join me in conversation instead?"

"Are you insinuating your discourse will cure my insomnia?"

He cocked a brow. "If not, I'm sure I could employ other methods."

Other methods? Her breath hitched. "I'll find a book. Thank you."

"What if it keeps you awake all night? Surely, you don't wish to be worthless during tomorrow's activities." He gestured toward a chair. "Come on. I'll be good."

No doubt, Lord Andrew would be good at anything he tried. Being on his best behavior, however, likely wouldn't be one of those things.

She remained standing, rolling the glass back and forth between her hands. "I've always wondered… How does one play faro?"

"You want me to teach you faro? *That* is a novel request." He sounded much too pleased.

"Oh, never mind. I'll simply go to bed." She prepared to scoot from the library before she got into trouble, but Lord Andrew bolted from his seat and grasped her elbow.

"I'll teach you, Miss Hillary. Come, have a seat at the table while I locate a deck of cards."

He guided her toward the table, sat down his drink, and pulled the seat out for her.

She placed her own glass on the table and folded her hands onto her lap while he foraged through side table drawers. Waving two decks in the air, he returned to the table.

"Now, I have to arrange the cards like so." He stood beside her and sorted through the deck, setting aside the spades. Once he had the king through ace cards, he laid them out in two rows. Then he reached for a small paperweight, turned her hand over, and placed the paperweight in her palm, closing his fingers around hers so she gripped the object. "Use this as your marker. Decide which card you think the dealer, that is me since we have to improvise, will turn up first and place your marker on it."

She balked. "There is no skill involved in this game at all?"

"Of course not, peach. Faro is all about chance, though a good memory does afford some advantage. Never knowing what might happen. It's exciting."

"Foolish is more like it," she scoffed.

He pulled a chair close and sat, bumping his knees against hers, but she didn't shift away as she should. The scent of sandalwood filled the air, leaving her light-headed and trembling. "May I ask a favor, Miss Hillary?"

Her breath caught in her chest and her heart galloped. She nodded as if in a trance, feeling powerless to deny him anything he requested.

"Will you please stop referring to me as Lord Andrew?"

"Oh." She had not expected this to be his request. "But that *is* your name."

"I prefer Drew. Would you do me the honor of calling me Drew?"

"It would be improper, my lord. What would people think?"

"I didn't take you for one who worried about convention, but nonetheless I understand your concern. Perhaps only in *private* you will call me by my preferred name. Could you do that for me?" He brushed a strand of hair behind her ear, the warmth of his fingers branding her skin.

"Yes," she replied, breathless from his touch, "all right, *Drew*." She didn't point out they shouldn't be sharing private moments.

"My God, peach. Your hair—"

They both heard the slap of a slipper on the foyer floor at the same time. Drew launched from his chair and dove behind the couch a heartbeat before a noise sounded in the doorway. Lana twisted around to find Lord Richard hovering on the threshold of the library.

The poor man jumped and tugged his dressing gown snugly around his body. He appeared to sport scarlet cheeks, probably as red as Lana's were. "Miss Hillary, it's you. I saw a light… I thought maybe you were…"

"My apologies, my lord. I'm afraid I couldn't sleep."

"I'm sorry to hear that." A slight crease lined his forehead as he craned his neck to inspect the table. "Are you playing faro?"

"Oh, dear heavens. Am I?" Lana hoped she sounded sufficiently scandalized. "But my brothers said this was a form of Patience."

Lord Richard attempted to suppress a smile. "My mistake, Miss Hillary. Please stay as long as you like." He made to leave, but his gaze landed on the two tumblers in front of her and he frowned.

Lana shrugged, supremely embarrassed to have him

think her possibly foxed. "I hope you don't mind, my lord. I thought a splash of brandy might help my insomnia, but I overestimated the dose required. I believe one will do the trick after all."

He cleared his throat. "Very well. Just leave the other on the table. The staff will dispose of it tomorrow. Carry on with your game of Patience, Miss Hillary."

Once Lord Richard disappeared from earshot, Drew sprang from the floor, came to her, and squeezed her shoulder affectionately. "Sorry to have deserted you, peach, but I fear my continued presence would have led to your ruin."

"Indeed. A prudent choice." She forced a shudder of revulsion. "How horrid that would have been."

He smirked. "I suppose I should be thankful you don't wish to marry either. Perhaps you would have given up my location otherwise."

"Don't be silly, Lord Andrew. I have no desire to be forced into marriage any more than you."

She tried to ignore the lump forming in her throat. She truly did not wish Lord Andrew forced into marriage with her. Such a match would lead to her heartbreak. Blast it! What was she doing playing with fire again? Had she learned nothing from her failed betrothal?

"I believe I shall retire, my lord."

"We do have a demanding day ahead of us tomorrow." Lord Andrew squeezed her shoulder once more. "That was a magnificent performance, peach. Run along to bed."

Lana whisked from the library without a book, but it didn't matter. Sleep would evade her. She would think of nothing but Drew's touch and what a foolish girl she was.

Thirteen

DREW STOOD ON THE LAWN OF IRVINE GARDENS WITH Gabby. He searched the perimeter and, seeing no one stood close enough to overhear him, he bent forward to meet his sister eye to eye. "You know the plan, correct?"

Gabby huffed and crossed her arms. "Must you treat me as if I'm an imbecile? Of course, I know the plan. You *just* shared it with me."

He patted her head. "That's a good little girl."

She slapped his hand away and glared.

"Remember, I'm doing a favor for you, too. Mother is almost convinced you are ready to come out next season."

Gabby's face brightened and she clutched her hands to her chest. "Oh, do you speak the truth? Please, tell me. What might I do to sway her?"

"Stay out of trouble, especially when I'm not around to chaperone you for this short time."

Drew had several misgivings about leaving Gabby unsupervised, even for a short while, but he spotted none of the worrisome rakehells wandering about the grounds at this hour. Likely, they would not wake from their drunken slumber for several hours.

"Perhaps I should call a halt to this," he said.

Gabby's eyes rounded, and she spoke in a harsh whisper. "No. Miss Hillary hasn't given you a second look these past four days. I fear she has set her sights on that deplorable Lord Bollrud, but the man is an embarrassment."

He frowned, disliking his fears validated by his sister. He'd thought he and Miss Hillary were getting on nicely in the library, but now she spent most of her time with that bumpkin Bollrud. For a lady who claimed a distaste for matrimony, she seemed much too amenable to Bollrud's clumsy courtship. Perhaps Drew could talk some sense into her, if she stopped avoiding him.

"Very well, but I mean it, Gabby. Stay out of trouble."

Drew gave her the sternest look he could muster, but found the glower difficult to maintain when she bubbled with undisguised excitement.

Gabby's innocent eyes glittered with adoration. "I promise to behave, Drew."

"Goodness, princess. I almost believe you."

His sister howled in protest and swatted his arm.

"Gabrielle," their mother sang out from the veranda where she conversed at an outdoor table with two other women.

Drew chucked her under the chin. "Don't ruin everything with your temper, princess."

Her gray eyes narrowed, but she didn't strike him again.

Drew peered beyond her shoulder. "I see Bollrud. Keep your eyes open for Miss Hillary while I speak with him." He hugged her on impulse. He would have to be sincere in his campaign on her behalf with their parents. It seemed only fair given the lengths she would go to in order to help him spend time alone with Miss Hillary.

Lord, help him. His obsession with the woman was worse than the pox, and probably more lethal.

"Thanks, Gabby. I mean it."

Her frown melted, and she tossed her arms around his waist and squeezed. "Drew, will you help me distract Mama when I want to be alone with the man *I* love?"

Not on your life. "Of course, princess."

"You *are* going to profess your love to Miss Hillary, aren't you?" Gabby beamed and her voice jumped an octave. "Will you offer for her today?"

Gabby's high-pitched squeal made him cringe. What in the devil's name had given her the impression he intended to offer for Miss Hillary? Either his ability to orchestrate situations had reached perfection, or his sister truly wasn't ready for society.

"I would prefer to speak directly with Miss Hillary on the matter. I'm certain you understand. If you will excuse me."

One last task and his plan would be in place. Drew approached his target.

Bollrud hunkered over a plate loaded with pastries, eggs, and thick slices of ham. The man shoveled food into his mouth as if he didn't know when he might partake of another meal. How he remained thin was a mystery.

"Mind if I join you?" Drew asked.

Bollrud's cheeks bulged with food. His eyes narrowed to slits, but he gave a sharp nod.

Drew flopped into the chair facing him. "Thanks, chap."

"I'm not your friend." Bollrud spewed crumbs as he spoke.

"I'm certain the fault lies with me, old man. May I ask a question?" Without waiting for a reply, Drew continued, "Do you fancy Miss Hillary?"

"What do my affairs concern you?" His voice resembled a growl, reminding Drew of a hound with a bone.

"I'm a close friend of Miss Hillary's brother," he lied.

"We attended Oxford together. Of course, Hillary is laid up with a broken leg, so I promised to help look after his sister."

Bollrud clamped his lips together and glared.

Damnation, the man had no cause for such hostility. Drew didn't intend to steal the lady out from under him. He simply wished to borrow her for a time, and if she didn't wish to return to Bollrud, how could Drew be to blame?

"Miss Hillary has grown close to my sister," he said, "so I'm certain you can understand my protective instincts. I can't bring myself to disappoint Hillary or my dear sister."

Did he spread it on too thick? Bollrud gave no outward signs of awareness that he might be the victim of a deception.

Drew leaned forward, his jaw hardening. "Now, sir, I will ask you once more, what are your intentions with Miss Hillary?"

Bollrud's gaze shot around the terrace.

"Are your intentions honorable, sir?"

The man's eyes flicked back to hold Drew's stare. "Not that it's any of your concern, but I will marry her."

Drew bolted upright. Hearing Bollrud say these words aloud sent a bolt of anger to his core. The man must be incredibly dense if he thought Miss Hillary would accept his proposal. Bollrud wouldn't suit her at all. She hadn't given her promise yet, had she? Drew might become sick at the thought.

"In case she hasn't told you, sir, the lady is set on remaining unwed. I'm afraid you are fighting a losing battle."

The gentleman balked. "She never mentioned she has no intentions of wedding."

"Has she indicated she will marry you?"

Bollrud's mouth thinned and a glower darkened his face. "Not in so many words."

Drew repressed a show of relief. "Yes, well. Why would Miss Hillary confide in you? She has barely made your acquaintance. Unless you've declared your intentions, she would have no cause to speak of her wishes. It's a pity. She'd make someone a lovely wife some day." *Just not for this bugger.* Drew drummed his fingers against the tabletop. "You wouldn't want the chit refusing your proposal outright. A man does have his pride. Listen, Bollrud. I might be able to assist with your dilemma."

The man scoffed. "Why would you help me?"

"I wouldn't. I barely know you. Nevertheless, Miss Hillary doesn't realize the foolishness of her decision. She needs to make a match before it's too late, so essentially I'm helping *her*. At this point, her prospects are dwindling."

Trickery had become a way of life for Drew. It was useful at the gaming tables. Yet, he didn't know if he could pull off this particular lie. Anyone with eyes could see Miss Hillary would have no trouble attracting a mate, aside from the impediment of her mother. But Drew hardly viewed Miss Hillary's relations as an insurmountable obstacle. He cared nothing about her mother's eccentricity, and his only point of contention with Mrs. Hillary was the lack of attention she paid to chaperoning her daughter. Of course, her distractibility worked to Drew's advantage at the moment.

Bollrud still regarded him through slits. "What are you proposing, Forest?"

"If you intend to offer for Miss Hillary, you need to find another way to win her approval. I say you should go through her mother."

"Her mother?"

"Miss Hillary will be unable to resist the pressure her mother will surely put on her if she has a serious suitor."

"You suggest I go through her mother?"

Drew nodded slowly, fighting to keep his expression neutral.

"How would I go about such a task?"

"Spend as much time with Miss Hillary's mother as you can, and show her what a charming husband you would make for her daughter. No mother wants her daughter to marry a scoundrel or a ninny. Show her you are an upstanding member of the *ton*."

Would Bollrud take the bait? If this toad-eater occupied Mrs. Hillary, Drew could spend more time with her charming daughter, and all without arousing the woman's suspicions, possibly resulting in an unwanted match between Miss Hillary and him. It was perfect.

Bollrud scratched his head, appearing more perplexed than usual. "You're sure this is the way to proceed?"

"I realize things may be done differently in Bavaria, gent, but in England everyone knows to court the mother first. It's the only way to get what you desire."

Bollrud pressed his lips together and nodded as if this argument made perfect sense. "Courtship is much different than I had been told." He crammed another bite into his gaping mouth.

"It's a complicated maze to navigate. I wish you luck." Drew pushed from the table. Everything was in place.

Fourteen

LADY GABRIELLE CLAIMED LANA'S ATTENTION AS SOON AS she arrived at Irvine Castle, linking arms and dragging her toward the maze.

"How about a lovely stroll, Miss Hillary?"

"P-perhaps Lady Phoebe would like to join us." Lana glanced over her shoulder but couldn't locate Phoebe.

"I highly doubt it. Phoebe complains of swollen feet all the time. I never knew babies could affect a woman so. Her ankles resemble plump sausages."

"Lady Gabrielle," Lana reprimanded with a giggle.

"I speak the truth, Miss Hillary."

They entered the lush maze arm-in-arm. Lana had walked the hedge corridors almost daily on her last visit two years ago. "I do feel bad for leaving her alone. Perhaps I should forgo the walk."

"Don't be silly. Phoebe enjoys her solitude." Lady Gabrielle tugged Lana's arm. The young woman was stronger than she appeared. "This way."

Lana furrowed her brow. "As you wish, Lady Gabrielle."

"Call me Gabby. We're practically family."

Family? What a strange young woman she'd become

in the last two years. "Very well, Gabby, but I insist you call me Lana in return."

The towering hedges closed out almost all outside sounds as they strolled deeper into the maze. It was quite peaceful. "Ah, this was a nice idea, Gabby. I'd forgotten how much I enjoyed our strolls."

"We walked this path many times in the past. How well do you remember the layout?"

Lana accessed the mental map she still carried, surprised by her recall. "Fairly well, I believe."

Gabby darted a look behind them. "It appears no one followed us."

Lana reflexively looked as well. What did it matter if anyone joined them?

"Do you recall where the Cupid statue is housed?" she asked.

"I believe I do. It's a dead end, correct?"

Gabby leaned close. "Drew is waiting for you there," she whispered. "I'll create a distraction, but don't be missing for long."

"Lord Andrew?" Lana's heart pounded out of control. This was beyond the pale. Why, she had gone to great lengths to avoid him the last several days, resigning herself to a match with Lord Bollrud, and Drew wished a clandestine meeting with her? What could he want?

Dizziness engulfed her, and she gripped Gabby's shoulder to regain her equilibrium.

Blast it, Lana, breathe already. She gulped in a deep breath, filling her lungs and slowly banishing the dizziness.

"Please, hurry, Lana. Someone might discover us any moment. He will think you didn't wish to meet him."

Lana snapped out of her daze and broke into a running walk.

Left. Left. Right. Left. Right. Right. Dear heavens, the Cupid statue would be around the next corner. Lana stopped and worried her bottom lip. Perhaps she should turn back. If discovered with Lord Andrew, her reputation would be ruined beyond repair.

Before she could change her mind and run in the opposite direction, he stepped into the opening.

He offered a glorious smile. "You came." His sudden appearance determined her course. Like a sleepwalker, she moved toward him.

"Lord Andrew, what is the meaning of this?"

A tiny crease formed between his brows. "I thought we'd established you are to call me Drew when we are alone."

She glanced around to see they were very much alone. "I shouldn't be here, my lord."

"Here in Cupid's room? Have you lost your way, my sweet?"

She had lost *something*. Perhaps her God-given good senses.

Drew smiled like an innocent choirboy, which they both knew was a fabrication.

"I should return before Mama realizes I'm no longer with your sister."

He offered his arm. "I promise not to keep you long, Miss Hillary. Please, stay a moment."

She hesitantly placed her hand in the crook of his elbow, her acceptance bringing another radiant smile to his face.

"If I'm to call you Drew in private, then perhaps you would like to refer to me as Lana?" She forced a frown so as not to give him a false impression. "But don't expect we will continue to meet privately. My mama would be crushed if I sullied my name."

He led her farther into the Cupid room. "I have no intentions of ruining you, Lana. I only wish to speak with you for five minutes without incurring the wrath of my kin."

"Five minutes then," she conceded.

"Splendid." Drew dropped her arm and walked to the hedge wall, feeling along the edges. "Here we are." He held out his hand. "This way, please."

"Have you gone mad?" Despite her protest, she took his hand.

"There's an opening here. You'll have to shimmy through, but you'll meet with no impediments."

Lana detected the narrow passage now that she stood close. "Is this supposed to be here?"

Dropping his hand, she moved carefully to avoid snagging her dress.

"It's a hidden exit from the maze. My father added it years ago."

"Wh—?" Her question was lost on an intake of breath. They stood on the edge of an open field dotted with millions of wildflowers. The sun saturated the field, making the purple and yellow flowers even more radiant. "Oh, Drew. How beautiful."

A huge smile spread across his lips. "I thought you would appreciate the view. If you want to come back with Gabby to pick some, you approach from that direction," he said, pointing to their left. "It comes out by the stable yard."

"That would be lovely." She walked farther into the field until a blanket of purple, yellow, red, and white surrounded her in every direction. With a giggle, she turned in circles to see them all. "Truly magnificent."

Drew chuckled.

She stopped mid-pirouette. "Do I amuse you, my lord?"

"I only now realized how truly untouched you are, Lana, watching you spin 'round in a field of flowers." He held out his arm. "Allow me to escort you back to the maze."

She pulled at his sleeve. "Nonsense. We just arrived. Walk with me farther."

He didn't budge and instead shoved his hands into his pockets. "I realize now I can't. Have you no care for my reputation?"

Lana tossed her head, her laughter carrying on the breeze. "What harm could I do to your reputation, my lord? It's already atrocious."

Drew's forget-me-not eyes sparkled with merriment. "Yet, you would tarnish my reputation by drawing attention to my sensitivity? Have a heart." He took her hands in his and coaxed her back toward the maze. "We can't allow anyone to discover us, peach."

Although he made light of the situation, his warning sobered her. What was she thinking wandering off with a scoundrel like Lord Andrew? They both had much to lose, Lana's reputation and heart, and his freedom. She tromped toward the maze, wishing she had an excuse to ignore her good sense.

"Heaven forbid anyone should discover *you* possess a soft spot," she grumbled.

"Apparently I do."

Reaching the hedge, she whipped around to face him. They stood inches apart, his heat infusing the space between them. "Did you really bring me here to view the flowers?"

He held her gaze without wavering, his blue eyes darkening and sending a rush of desire to her belly.

"I wish I were that noble, Lana."

Her eyes trailed to his lips. Oh, how she wanted to taste him. A scrumptious blend of sandalwood and seduction wafted across the short distance between them. Never had Lana met a man who emitted sensuality from every pore.

She licked her lips. "I wish you were *less* noble, my lord, like that night in the Eldridge's garden."

His dimpled smile stole her breath. "Why, Lana, I do believe you are trying to seduce me again."

His voice washed over her, filling her with warmth and tingles from head to toe, even in her unmentionable spot. Unable to resist temptation any longer, she grazed her mouth over his, flicking the tip of her tongue across his bottom lip to satisfy her curiosity. Heavens, he tasted sinful.

Tentatively, she threaded her arms around his neck and pressed her lips harder against his. When his soft hair touched her fingers, she buried them into his locks then leaned into his firm chest.

Drew groaned against her mouth. "You have no idea what you're doing, do you?"

Pardon?

She fell back a step and released him. Hurt shook her to the core. She didn't know how to kiss a man properly?

Drew's fists were shoved to his sides, and a grimace marred his handsome face. His eyes fluttered open. "Is something wrong?"

Good heavens above! He hadn't been kissing her back, had he? She repulsed him. A scoundrel who had kissed hundreds of women, and she, Lana Hillary, repulsed him.

Clamping her lips tightly, she fled toward the maze. No lady should have to endure such humiliation.

"Where are you going, peach?"

She stopped long enough to glare over her shoulder. "Stop calling me that, you scoundrel."

"Lana, wait."

Before Drew could reach her, she wiggled through the secret passage and dashed for the maze exit.

Fifteen

DREW WRESTLED WITH THE URGE TO RUN AFTER LANA. As much as he wanted to discover what went wrong, he couldn't risk her reputation by chasing after her. Though he didn't want to see her married to Bollrud, he wouldn't stand in the way of her making a match with a decent gent if she wished to reconsider matrimony.

What in the devil's name came over her? One moment she nearly sent him over the edge with the start of a sensual kiss—Good God, what a kiss that could have been—and the next she took off in a fit of anger. Lana Hillary was as predictable as a tempest and twice as destructive. His body was in shambles, thanks to that woman. What type of lady stoked a man's passion then left him in misery? She was a cruel chit, indeed.

Shoving his hands in his pockets, he stalked around the outside of the maze. If he hurried, he could cut through the house and intercept Lana on the veranda. He would demand she explain her outburst.

Drew had faced many angry women over the years, but at least he usually knew the cause of their ire. And if he didn't know the reason, he didn't bother finding out. He'd always considered it fortuitous if the woman stomped away, leaving him to consider his actions, at least until now.

As soon as he passed through the double glass doors, he spotted a small crowd of women huddled together, distracting him from his mission for the moment. The ladies clucked over a figure slumped in a chair. His curiosity piqued, he moved closer only to discover the crumpled figure was Gabby.

Lady Eldridge vigorously fanned his sister while their mother clutched her hand. Lana loitered right outside of the circle, her expression troubled.

He trotted over to them, his heart accelerating. "What happened to Gabby?"

His mother's watery eyes fixed on him. "Oh, thank heavens. I need you to carry your sister to her chambers."

"There, there, Lady Gabrielle," Lady Eldridge cooed.

"Oh, my poor, poor darling." Worry etched his mother's forehead.

"What in God's name happened to her?" he demanded. His furious gaze shot around the veranda. He'd kill the blackguard who'd dared to touch his sister.

"Drew, please watch your tongue," his mother scolded. "There are ladies present. I need you to carry your sister to her chambers right away. She must stay abed the rest of the day."

"No," Gabby protested a little strongly, but then repeated in a much weaker voice, "I'm better, Mama. I simply overheated. That's all."

Drew's eyes narrowed. The air was pleasantly warm, but not hot enough to cause problems for a young woman her age. She lied. "Overheated you say?"

His sister's eyes bore into him. "Yes, *Drew*. I overheated while playing a game of hide-and-seek with

Miss Hillary in the maze. I'm afraid I was forced to stop searching for her after five minutes passed with no sign of her. I felt faint, you see." Gabby swooned again, eliciting shrieks from the older women around her. With a weak smile, she blinked up at Lana. "Miss Hillary, I'm sorry to have left you waiting in your hiding spot. Thank heavens you didn't become lost."

Drew unsuccessfully tried to capture Lana's eye.

Their mother stood and shook his arm. "Drew, *please*. Carry your sister inside where she may recover."

"Yes, Mother." What a little pretender. Drew scooped Gabby into his arms and toted her into the house.

On the stairway and out of the center of attention, she scowled. "Why didn't you return her when you said? I didn't know what to do when Mrs. Hillary cornered me outside the maze."

"I'm sorry, princess. I hadn't intended to keep her."

Gabby's gaze narrowed. "What did you do to Lana?"

Her intense accusation startled him. "Nothing."

"I don't believe you, *Andrew*. Lana is obviously upset. Thank goodness *my* plan worked. Everyone attributed her troubled expression to worry for me." She poked her finger against his chest. "You promised not to hurt her."

They made it to the top of the stairs before he dropped Gabby to her feet. Grabbing her shoulders, he met her accusing stare. "I did *nothing* to Miss Hillary. I was a perfect gentleman. She was fine one moment then without warning, she stormed away."

Gabby wrinkled her nose. "Did you pat her on the head? I hate it when you pat me on the head."

"No," he answered, unable to suppress a chuckle.

"What about an insult? Did you call her a silly name?"

"Absolutely not. Princess, this line of questioning is

ridiculous. I don't pat grown women on the head or insult them, not if I wish to get anywhere."

"Aha!" Gabby poked him in the chest again. "You tried to seduce her. I *knew* it. I never should have trusted you. You're a scoundrel *and* a rogue."

"That's practically the same thing, princess."

"Oh, be quiet. You—you roguish scoundrel." His sister flounced into her chambers and tried to slam the door, but he jammed his palm against the hard surface.

"One angry lady is more than any man should have to contend with in a day. I swear to you, I didn't touch Miss Hillary." A grin stretched his lips. "*She* touched me."

His sister's mouth fell open, but no sound came out.

"Believe me, Gab, I wanted to kiss her, but she caught me quite by surprise."

His sister yanked him into her bedchamber and slammed the door. "Oh, my goodness. Tell me. What did *you* do?"

"I already told you, I did nothing inappropriate. I stood there, trying my best to maintain control—"

She thumped his chest hard this time. "You dolt."

"For the love of—Gabby, control your temper."

She hit him again.

"Ouch! I said stop it."

She marched across the room, the Oriental carpet cushioning her steps, and then whipped around to throw her hands in the air. "I can't believe this. And you're supposed to be a connoisseur of women."

"Gabrielle Forest, where did you learn such language?"

She tossed her head. "You truly *are* an imbecile. I possess two ears, dear brother. I hear the scandalous things the ladies say about you. How can you be ignorant to the fact that when a lady kisses you, you are expected to kiss her back?"

Heat crept up his neck to the tips of his ears. Gabby knew of his liaisons? "I was *trying* to be a gentleman," he mumbled.

She punched her hands to her hips. "Why start now? Miss Hillary is a thousand times more perfect for you than any of those ninny hammers. It's no wonder you never offered for any of them."

He cleared his throat. "Yes, well, Richard demands I leave Miss Hillary alone."

She gawked as if he belonged in a carnival sideshow. "So Richard is allowed the woman he wants, but you're not. How is that fair?"

Gabby made a valid point. Why *should* Rich be the only one satisfying his desire? Of course, his brother married his lady, and Drew was certain that was Gabby's implied meaning.

He rubbed his hands over his face and heaved a sigh. "What if our brother disowns me? Then you'll be stuck with me always instead of half the time," he warned.

She tossed her head. "Perhaps I'll disown you as well. Let Lizzie and Katie deal with your foolishness for a change."

Why couldn't Rich be as understanding as Gabby? Drew gathered his sister in a hug and kissed the top of her head. "Thanks, princess."

Halfway to the door, he turned back. "Great performance, by the way, although you might wish to be a tad less melodramatic next time."

❦

Drew's place at dinner was too far from Lana to converse with her, but he noticed she picked at her meal. He sat next to Amelia, much to his displeasure.

"Lord Andrew, what a pleasure it is to see you, at last." Her greeting sounded accusing.

"I've been here several days, Lady Audley. Have you been enjoying the festivities?"

The lady fidgeted with her napkin. "Very much, my lord, although I'm puzzled as to the reason I'm here."

"It's a house party. I'm certain you were meant to partake of the activities offered."

His gaze strayed to Lana again, and he suppressed a sigh. She concentrated on manipulating the peas on her plate as if she recreated an edible Mona Lisa.

Amelia's knee brushed against his. Drew jumped and banged his leg on the table.

"Oh, dear. Are you all right?" Amelia's nervous laughter rose above the garbled conversations at the table.

The loud noise grabbed Lana's attention, and she glared in their direction.

Hell's teeth. Why did she make him feel as if he'd done something to deserve her glower? He stared back without wavering.

Lana's eyes dropped to her plate again, and she studied it with an even greater intensity while her face flushed an attractive pink.

He tossed a distracted glance at his dining partner. "My apologies, Lady Audley. I'm a little out of sorts tonight."

"I didn't mean to startle you," Amelia whispered. "Perhaps we could slip away after the last course is served. We should talk."

He smiled as graciously as possible. Amelia happened to be a perfectly nice lady. Her beauty had gained his notice one evening at the opera. Widowed for a year, she had seemed ready to dabble in pleasure. Unfortunately, Drew had misread her.

Amelia seemed to desire a replacement for her husband, but Drew wasn't the one to fulfill her wishes, so he ended their association, or he had tried to end it.

"I couldn't ask you to miss the ball, Lady Audley. All the gentlemen will be searching for you."

"I see," she murmured and turned her face away.

He looked toward Lana again. Her apparent misery invoked the worst pain in his chest, and he longed to ease her suffering, if only she would allow him.

Sixteen

LADY AUDLEY'S TINKLING LAUGHTER MADE LANA GRIT her teeth. If there were a subtle way for her to crawl under the table, she would do it, just to see if Drew's hand rested on Lady Audley's thigh. The blasted scoundrel offered an insolent smile, and Lana turned away to speak with Lord Henley on her left. There was no need for Drew to flaunt his proclivities at the dining table or taunt her from afar.

Was she too inexperienced for his tastes? Her cheeks heated. Only a fool would fall for a rake, and she had never considered herself a member of that organization, at least not until now.

When the torturous dinner concluded, Lana heaved a great sigh. She must find a way to bow out of the ball to follow. If Drew attended, she'd be as jittery as a cat in a room full of booted men, as Papa always said. But if he was absent… Lana shook her head, forbidding all thoughts of kissing and beautiful widows.

Outside the dining hall, she glanced around for Phoebe. Perhaps Lana would allege a headache and return to Shafer Hall.

"Miss Hillary, there you are." Lady Gabrielle claimed

her, whisking her to the drawing room. Really, the young woman's habit of clinging reminded Lana of a parasite.

Phoebe approached them with a wary smile. "Gabby, do you mind if I speak with Lana alone?"

"Not at all, Phoebe." The young woman bounced away, unaffected by the dismissal.

Lana hugged her friend. "Thank you, Phoebe. Your sister-in-law seems to have taken an unexplained interest in me."

"So I noticed," she replied with a giggle. "Will you sit with me?"

Lana followed her friend to a seating area for two. Phoebe awkwardly lowered herself into a chair. Despite her increasing bulk, she remained beautiful.

"Pregnancy is a nice accessory on you, my lady."

Phoebe waved her hand to dismiss the compliment. "I feel like a fatted calf."

"Well, you appear as glorious as a fertility goddess."

"I happen to find those idols quite hideous, but I'm sure you meant it as a compliment, so thank you." Her friend's smile radiated warmth. Phoebe always reminded Lana of sunshine. "Back to Gabby... It appears she is with you often."

Lana sank into the brocade Queen Anne chair. "Yes, Lady Gabrielle seems rather attached to me. It's puzzling, because I barely recall interacting with her when we met a couple of years ago. Yet, she acts as if we are the best of friends."

"I noticed as much. Of course, that also means Drew must spend time with you as well if he's Gabby's chaperone." Phoebe's brow wrinkled, and she tapped her fingers against the armrest. "Lana, I know you probably think you know him, but Drew can—"

Lana held up her hand. "Please stop, Phoebe. You mean well, but—how can I say this delicately—I don't want you to meddle in my affairs."

Phoebe drew back with rounded eyes. "Oh, I see—"

"Please don't misunderstand. I appreciate your desire to protect me, but I'm a grown woman. I don't require anyone intervening on my behalf." She smiled and folded her hands in her lap to convince Phoebe she remained unaffected by Lord Andrew. "I have no interest in Lord Richard's brother, and he has none in me."

At least the latter part of her assertion was true.

"Lana, I must persist in discouraging you. Drew can be charming, and... then later he..."

Lana grasped Phoebe's hand and gently squeezed. "Thank you for caring for me as you do. You are my dearest friend. But, rest assured, I'm not in any danger." She would have to be desirable to be in danger, and clearly, she wasn't. Lana mentally cringed recalling how rigid Drew had held himself, as if he found touching her distasteful.

She suppressed a sigh of despair. She wouldn't be a source of amusement for Lord Andrew any longer, not without suffering dire consequences. Her mother was correct. It was time to secure a husband before the last opportunity slipped through her fingers. And Lord Bollrud had something to offer her besides a broken heart. Mama said he wanted to make her his bride. So why did the prospect feel like a boulder dropped on her shoulders?

A footman entered the drawing room to announce the time had come to move to the great hall.

Lady Gabrielle linked arms with Lana and Phoebe. "I do so love dancing."

How wonderful for the young woman. Lana dreaded

the coming dance with the same intensity as an encounter with a guillotine.

Hundreds of candles twinkled in the chandeliers and wall sconces inside the great hall. Opened French doors allowed easy access to the veranda, and the scent of roses wafted on the air. It was a night designed for romance.

Lord Bollrud caught her eye and meandered her way. A horrible churning began in her stomach, and she drew in a slow breath to quell her nerves. Must she always experience that sick feeling when gazing upon the man she would eventually marry?

"May I have the first dance, peach?" Drew's warm breath brushed the edge of her ear, sending shivers racing along her skin. She willed her heart to stop its incessant pounding. She'd not make a cake of herself any longer. Better to put an end to their association and salvage what she had left of her pride.

Ignoring Drew, Lana forced a gracious smile for the gentleman who had just reached her. "Lord Bollrud, what a pleasure to see you this evening."

His shocked expression almost brought her to genuine laughter. She supposed the man had never received anything other than a distantly polite greeting from her in the past.

"Uh, may I have this dance, Miss Hillary?"

"Of course, my lord." Lana glanced back at Drew before allowing the most uncoordinated man on the premises to escort her to the floor, the man destined to become her husband. May God have mercy on her toes.

⤞⤝

Drew never took his eyes from Lana as Bollrud jerked her around the ballroom floor. How could she be interested in that simpleton? He paced back and forth, his muscles tensing with each step, as he waited for the dance to end.

Lana wore an apricot-colored dress that, from a distance, made her appear as if she wore nothing. Although Drew liked the illusion, his fists tightened with a desire to pound Bollrud for his part in appearing to touch her nude body.

As soon as the music stopped, Drew pounced. He reached Lana at the edge of the dance floor in four strides. "Excuse us, Bollrud."

Lana's lips parted in surprise. "I've promised the next dance to—"

"He begs your forgiveness, but he had to leave." Drew placed his hand on the small of her back and guided her back to the floor.

Lana bestowed a resentful glare. "You didn't even give me a chance to name the gentleman. How do you know he has left the ballroom?" Still, she took position for the waltz as the music began to swell.

Drew pulled her close, no longer caring what his brother or anyone thought. If the *ton* believed he desired Lana Hillary, they wouldn't come close to guessing the intensity with which he longed for her. "That wasn't nice, peach, the way you cut me."

Lana's graceful movements seemed rote, as if she'd received extensive instruction in dance. "I asked you to refrain from referring to me in that manner, *my lord*."

His lips turned up into a half smile. She made his courtesy title sound downright disrespectful, and he admired her gall. "What's wrong with my pet name for you, peach?" Drew grazed his lips against her ear.

She slanted her head away from his mouth. "It's not clever. I would think you could come up with something more creative. Peach isn't much different from the other names I've been called all my life. Let's see… there was carrot, pumpkin, and tangerine. It's always a food."

"You think I'm mocking you."

"What else am I to think? I have orange hair. Ha, ha. I comprehend your reference. I look like a peach."

He twirled her, drawing her as close as he could without actually making love to her on the ballroom floor and scandalizing everyone. "I think you smell delicious like a peach, and I'd love nothing more than to devour you."

Lana's sharp intake of breath made him smile. There were a thousand ways he could leave her breathless. "You're my forbidden fruit, Lana, and I don't like that I can't have you."

"Why… why can't you?" The way she boldly met his gaze in spite of the quiver in her voice sent his blood rushing. "And wasn't the fruit in question an apple?"

"I don't care for apples." The music ended and he led her from the floor to a settee in a quiet corner.

They sat in silence, his bouncing leg betraying his agitation. Lana had shown a preference for Bollrud, snubbing Drew. Had she misled him in her attitude toward matrimony? Did she want to marry Bollrud, to grant him issue? The very idea made him want to thrash the man. "You and Bollrud make a dashing couple, what with your eyes all shiny and his dull as a lump of coal." He smirked to give the impression the answer to his next question didn't matter. "He intends to make an offer for you. Do you plan to accept his proposal?"

She wrinkled her nose, a reluctant grin on her lips. "It's not my desire to marry Lord Bollrud."

That wasn't a complete denial as Drew had hoped. "Hmm. That's reassuring. Have you set your sights on some other poor chap?"

Lana swiveled to face him and grimaced. "I'd rather not have this conversation. Can't we leave it be?"

"Marriage would bring you security, and perhaps you would be happy with the *right* gent. It's possible. Just look at Rich and Phoebe." Drew wanted to kiss Lana in the worst way, but he forced himself to keep distance between them on the settee. "Good God, Lana, any man would count his blessings every day if you agreed to be his wife. What are you thinking settling for Bollrud? You can do much better."

She studied her hands. "You mention your brother and Phoebe. They are made for each other. It's unfair to use them as an example. Their happiness is a fluke."

"Don't you believe in love?"

She nailed him with a glower and crossed her arms under her bosom, distracting him from their conversation. "Do you?"

When he didn't respond, she shook her head as if giving up on him. "Tell me the reason you avoid marriage, Lord Andrew. No, wait. Allow me to contemplate."

"By all means, Miss Hillary, take your time. I'm anxious to hear your thoughts."

She tapped her finger to her bottom lip several times. "*You* hate women." She sounded so proud of herself, Drew couldn't help but chuckle.

"*That's* what you think? I hate women? Quite the opposite, Miss Hillary. By history, I've loved women too much to select only one."

"I don't believe you," she stated with a defiant tightening of her jaw.

"What's not to believe? I surround myself with women at every opportunity."

"Clearly, it is untrue you take advantage of all women," Lana challenged. "I'm a woman."

Drew couldn't hold back a grin. "An undeniable fact."

"And you have been nothing but a gentleman in my presence. I believe your renown as a rake is overstated. Besides, I haven't seen you talking to any woman for more than a few minutes at most, aside from Lady Audley, but I get the distinct impression that association has ended."

He cocked a smile. Cheeky and beautiful. How was a man to resist her? "Is that so? You do realize discretion is essential in any liaison."

She gasped. "Are you saying…? No, never mind. I don't want to know." She catapulted from her seat, but sat back down just as abruptly and glared. "Why did you promise to keep your hands off me?" she whispered.

Drew's jaw dropped. "Good heavens, woman. The things that come from your mouth…"

Lana's shoulders slumped forward. "Seriously, my lord, if you are a scoundrel, why did you agree to leave me be? Am I lacking in some way?"

"You lack nothing, my sweet. You're beautiful."

How could she think otherwise? Didn't she view her image in a looking glass? But beauty aside, Drew couldn't have Lana, and this knowledge caused a wrenching in his chest. She belonged with someone who would love her forever, not bed her once and toss her aside.

"If you must know, Miss Hillary, I do have standards, although low they may be."

Her arched brows shot upward. "A scoundrel with standards? I like that in a scoundrel. Do tell."

He wanted to wipe the adorable impish grin from her face with a passionate kiss, but that would violate his rules completely. "I never seduce an innocent, Miss Hillary, *never*."

Her merriment vanished, and she lowered her voice to a whisper. "What makes you think I'm an innocent?"

"Virgins are off limits," he replied bluntly. "They always fancy themselves in love, and I don't wish to bring heartache to anyone. No virgins. It's an unbreakable rule."

"Again, Lord Andrew, *what* makes you think I'm a virgin?"

The impudence. This entire conversation was inappropriate for mixed company, yet Lana Hillary didn't blush, swoon, or exhibit any other typical reactions he would expect. Perhaps he had pegged her incorrectly.

"For starters, you're a respectable young woman from a good family."

She rolled her eyes. "Oh, and I'm certain *that's* written in stone. Are you telling me you've never met a respectable young lady from a good family who behaved a bit recklessly?"

"No," he admitted with a smirk. "I suppose all young ladies don't fit the same mold."

"Then I rest my case," she stated triumphantly, a smile lighting up her face.

Drew clapped. "Bravo. Excellent argument, Miss Hillary. Enough of this nonsense. As much as I want to monopolize your time engaging in impolite conversation, I better allow you to dance with some of the other gentlemen." Just not that bugger, Bollrud.

"I don't want to dance with other gentlemen," she grumbled as he propelled her back toward the crowd.

It was Drew's turn to feel triumphant. He didn't want any other man near her either, even though he was loath to admit it.

Seventeen

RICH AND PHOEBE HUDDLED TOGETHER BESIDE THE mahogany desk, waiting for Drew when he entered the study. Drew groaned. He was in for another lecture, an undeserved one given he'd restrained himself with Lana yesterday.

Phoebe stood with arms akimbo. The weight of the baby growing within her caused her to arch her back.

Drew crossed the room and bent down to speak directly to her tummy, which allowed him to avoid eye contact with either of them.

"How's baby today? Uncle Drew can't wait to teach you all sorts of fun things."

When he finally looked up, Phoebe's face had softened and her hands instinctively caressed the top of her stomach.

"I've never seen you look more beautiful, Pheebs," he said and meant it.

Rich cleared his throat. "Do you mind removing your hands from my wife?"

Drew wandered to a vacant chair and collapsed onto the soft cushion. "Funny how you're always telling me what I *cannot* touch, old man. You're worse than Mother when we were little boys and weren't allowed to finger the figurines."

"And you never learned the lesson."

Drew rested his right foot on his left knee and slouched in the seat. "Shall I start the lecture for you? Let's see… I'm acting irresponsibly. I'm a threat to all young women. I'm a disgrace to the family. What is it today?"

Phoebe's eyes clouded with disappointment, making him feel like a cur. "Oh, Drew, you are not a disgrace. We all love you very much."

"Speak for yourself, love," Rich groused. "Drew, you know why we're talking to you. I asked you to stay away from Miss Hillary, but instead she is the only female receiving any of your notice."

"And you're worried a riot will break out amongst my jealous admirers?"

His brother's face darkened. A tirade would soon follow, but Phoebe intervened to keep the peace again.

"We are worried about Lana. We don't want to see her hurt."

"Neither do I, Pheebs." He didn't, so he had used every ounce of his willpower not to bed her. She would be easy prey, but the thought of manipulating her, using her for his pleasure, sickened him.

"But all this attention…" Phoebe argued. "Surely she will come to the conclusion your intentions are honorable."

Drew's hands gripped the armrests. "Are you implying I have dishonorable intentions?"

"That's not what she is saying," Rich said. "You are sending the message you want more from Miss Hillary, and an innocent young woman will assume that is marriage."

"You don't know anything about Miss Hillary's thinking." Neither did he, for that matter, but surely he had been clear with her. "She is not expecting a marriage proposal from me."

Phoebe drew in her breath. "You and she… You didn't… Oh, Drew. Please, tell me you didn't."

Had his sister-in-law lost her mind? "Rest assured, our association is purely platonic. Nothing more."

Richard snorted. "When have you ever regarded a woman as anything other than a conquest?"

Drew shot out of the chair. "For starters there's Mother, then Gabby, Liz, and Katie." He slapped his hand down in his upturned palm with each name to emphasize his point.

"Family doesn't count," Rich said.

"Don't forget Phoebe." Drew stalked to the door. "And I'm telling you Lana fits in that category."

"Lana? You're on a first-name basis now?" Rich started after him, but Phoebe grabbed his arm.

"Let him go," she murmured.

Rich spun to face her. "Why?"

"Just let him be, Richard."

Drew didn't need any other invitation to leave their company. He bolted from his brother's study and slammed the door behind him.

On his way to Irvine Castle, Drew slumped in the saddle, blindly staring at the rutted lane. What if his brother and Phoebe were correct and Lana expected an offer of marriage? He had rarely met a woman who didn't hope for something more than a wild romp.

Perhaps God created females too differently. Even when they thought they wanted nothing, a part of them couldn't help contemplating the future. Either that or the women Drew had known had hoped to change his mind over time, but it had never happened.

A groom met him in the stable yard. "Will you be joining the hunt today, my lord?"

"Not today."

Drew joined the other guests milling around the buffet tables inside the castle. He and Lana had formed an easy camaraderie. Granted, she stirred his lust often enough, but he found her amiable as well. She deserved better treatment than he seemed capable of doling out. Lana had a right to love, to have a home, a family if she wished. She would never have any of those things with Drew.

Pushing his plate away with a loud exhale, he stood a beat before Lana glided through the doorway. Her flaming tresses fell from her coiffure already, and tendrils framed her pretty face. She'd donned a green walking gown but had removed her bonnet. A dazzling smile lit her features, and she wandered toward him.

"Good morning, my lord." Her ever-changing eyes were green this morning, and they sparkled with delight. "I believe you're slowly abandoning your corrupt habits. Early to bed *and* early to rise. Don't tell me you are becoming respectable." She feigned a shudder.

"Would that bother you overmuch, Miss Hillary?" He studied her countenance for signs of optimism and detected a flicker of what he believed to be hope.

"To each his own," she responded, a teasing gleam in her eyes. "Do you have any covert meetings planned for us today, my lord?"

His gut clenched with regret. Lana was his for the taking, but he couldn't bring himself to collect his prize. Drew must end what he'd set into motion.

"I'm afraid you must proceed without me, Miss Hillary. I'm joining the hunt. Good day." He brushed past her in his haste to escape before he changed his mind.

"It's your *turn*, Miss Hillary." Lady Audley's impatience showed. This was the fourth time one of the ladies reminded Lana to play her hand since she'd sat down for a round of whist.

"My apologies." Lana absentmindedly tossed a card on the table and lost the hand. Thoughts of Drew and his cool greeting preoccupied her mind. What could have transpired between last night and this morning to change his manner toward her? As far as she recalled, she hadn't said anything remotely upsetting.

Lana shifted on the chair. She had spoken freely with him, but he had to know she teased, didn't he?

She threw another card at random before lying her cards face down on the table. "I'm afraid I am not much challenge today, ladies. Perhaps you would excuse me from the game?"

Lady Benton offered a gracious smile. "Certainly, Miss Hillary."

"I believe I will concede as well," Lady Audley announced and stood when Lana did. When Lana moved away, the widow fell into step with her. "Would you care to stroll through the gardens, Miss Hillary?"

Lana wanted to decline, but she didn't have the energy to create an adequate excuse. She followed the widow through the glass doors and down the stone stairs to the garden.

They walked in silence for several minutes until Lady Audley disturbed the peace. "You seem rather glum, Miss Hillary. I hope all is well."

"Thank you. I'm feeling a little under the weather, but I'm certain I shall be fit again soon."

They wound their way through the purple and

white phlox-lined path. Lana glanced sideways at the widow. She was breathtaking, more beautiful than Lana could ever hope to become. And yet, Drew had ended their relationship.

Lady Audley's soft voice broke into her thoughts. "He does that. Makes you feel like your feet will never touch the ground again before sending you crashing back to earth."

She stopped and stared, trying to determine her companion's motivations. Lady Audley returned her gaze with sadness shining in her blue eyes.

Lana didn't pretend to misunderstand. It seemed too unkind. "My heart goes out to you. I believe Lord Andrew has hurt you more than he realizes."

Why didn't the widow notice how Jake held her in such high esteem? Lana's brother would cherish the lady if given the chance. They fell into step again as Lana debated broaching the subject of her brother.

"I know your assessment of Lord Andrew is correct, Miss Hillary."

"Please, call me Lana."

The corners of the lady's lips curved gently. "Thank you, Lana. I would like it if you referred to me by my given name as well. Out of curiosity, are you familiar with the tale of the lamb and the snake?"

"I believe I might have heard it long ago. Please, remind me."

"A lamb discovered a snake while walking in the field. He had been trampled, and he gasped for breath, his body broken. Feeling compassion for this dangerous creature, the lamb gently carried him to safety. Day and night she tended the injured serpent and grew to love him."

Lana bit her lower lip. She recalled the tale with more clarity, and it did not have a happy conclusion.

"The lamb was pleased with her efforts to nurse the snake back to health, and one day the snake regained his former strength. As the lamb reached to tend him, he mortally struck her. The lamb felt such deep betrayal. 'How could you strike me? I've nursed you back to health. I've loved you and treated you with such kindness. How could you do this to me?' With no malice, he said—"

"I'm a snake," Lana finished, a frown on her face. "Do you truly believe it's Lord Andrew's nature to hurt anyone who tries to love him?"

"I think it's within the nature of women to hope otherwise, but history suggests men like Lord Andrew are incapable of love or fidelity." Amelia stopped to rub her fingers over the petals of a red rose before breathing in the light scent. "Miss Hillary, you are a beautiful, intelligent woman. Your future awaits you. Don't toss your chances of securing a match by dallying with Lord Andrew. He will hurt you in the end."

In the face of Amelia's sadness, Lana couldn't help but to feel sympathy. "I suppose you are warning me he is not worth it."

The lady's hand dropped back to her side. "I wish I could convince myself this is true. But it isn't too late for you. At least I don't think it is."

Her response didn't bring Lana peace. Amelia obviously believed Drew had been worth the heartache. How was Lana to turn away from her heart's desire?

Eighteen

DREW BERATED HIMSELF FOR HAVING AGREED TO CHAP-
erone his sister for the duration of the stay at Irvine
Castle, but he couldn't bow out. Gabby had kept her
part of the agreement. Just because Drew had changed
his mind about Lana didn't mean he would break
his word.

His sister dragged him to the great hall where their
mother had planned *another* dance. Women were always
anxious to dance, but he supposed a waltz provided the
only proper excuse for a lady to get close to a gentleman.
The double standard hardly seemed fair.

Irritation swelled within him as no less than five
gentlemen, those bloody rakehells Brookhaven and
Fielding included, raced to reach Gabby first without
trying to look too conspicuous. On second thought,
the rules governing ladies' behavior worked well. He'd
not like any of the men touching his sister outside of
the ballroom. He didn't especially appreciate their eager
attentiveness in the ballroom either. Drew crossed his
arms and glowered, imitating the look his brother often
bestowed on him.

The lucky gentleman to reach Gabby first beamed,

but one glance at Drew tempered his enthusiasm. "My lord, might I request your sister's dance card?"

Drew deferred to Gabby. He would not assume his sister wished him to make her decisions, given her strong opinions on certain matters.

"I would be honored, Lord Holt."

One by one the gentlemen made the same request until her card had filled. Gabby didn't turn away a single suitor, much to Drew's discontent.

Before her first dance, he drew her close to murmur in her ear. "Make Brookhaven and Fielding behave, princess, or else I will settle the matter on the morrow."

Her face paled. "You wouldn't dare challenge either gentleman. I'm telling Mama."

"Mama couldn't stop me, or Rich for that matter, if any gent treated you improperly. Now, make them behave and save me an early wakening. You know I don't care for mornings."

Gabby rolled her eyes. "Cease your fretting. Mama watches me like a hawk. I'll not do anything to make her swoop down and snatch away my chance to be presented next season. Go dance with Lana. I'm properly chaperoned."

She nodded toward an alcove where both parents vigilantly stood watch. So much for having his parents' trust. It was just as well. Perhaps he could leave the ballroom early and put these past several days behind him. He could return to London on the morrow and forget all about Lana and his ridiculous yearnings.

Misleading her had been cruel. When he had set out to prove to himself he could bed her, he hadn't considered her feelings in the matter. Self-loathing churned in his belly, and he turned on his heel to escape the ballroom, but he glanced over his shoulder before he reached the double doors. He wished to see Lana one last time, before she belonged to another. He scanned the crowd, his heart skipping when he located her.

Lana sat along the outskirts of the room as if she wished to go unnoticed. Longing flooded through him, and that horrible emptiness that had plagued him these last few weeks returned. He'd hated every minute of hunting today. The one occasion when he glimpsed the fox all he could think of was Lana's fiery locks falling around her face. Staying away from her had ripped his insides out, and he didn't want to walk away now.

This evening she wore an emerald and cream gown that displayed her assets to great advantage. Drew's breeches tightened, and he forced his gaze from her. *Hell's teeth*. He was a man of four and twenty, not a green boy without mastery over his body.

He stalked to the refreshment room. Requiring something stronger than punch, he poured a glass of port, downing it in one gulp. He poured another and attempted to conjure the least arousing things he could imagine—dividing 476 into 8,982; sitting on the church pew next to Mother; rolling dice with Norwick.

His mind refused to cooperate with the distractions, and his thoughts strayed back to Lana. What if he *could* love her? Perhaps his interest wouldn't wane as he feared. He had held no desire for any other woman since his arrival in Northumberland, since the Eldridge ball if he were to be honest. Was it outrageous to believe he possessed the same capacity to love as his father loved his mother and Rich loved Phoebe?

When he gained better control over his body, he returned to the ballroom to seek out Lana where he'd spotted her earlier, but the chair was empty. Alarmed, his gaze darted around the ballroom until he discovered her in Bollrud's arms. She tilted her head and bestowed a flirtatious grin upon her dance partner.

Fire raged in Drew's belly, and he shoved his fists to his side. He had no right to rip her from Bollrud's arms, but he would bloody well like to make it his right. When the dance ended, Drew weaved through the guests loitering around the dance floor, attempting to intercept her. Before he could claim Lana, another gentleman approached then led her on the floor. She beamed at him as well when they moved into position.

Bollrud sauntered over to Drew, looking extremely confident. "I have to thank you, Forest. It appears your advice to court Miss Hillary's mother is working to my advantage. The young lady's manner toward me has warmed considerably. I believe the time has come to offer for her hand." The bugger chuckled as he moved past.

When the music ended, Drew practically sprinted to Lana before anyone else could reach her. Taking her arm, he escorted her back onto the floor.

"This dance is mine, peach." He didn't leave any room for misinterpretation. He wasn't making a request.

"Of course, Drew," she purred, catching him off guard. He had expected her to respond with anger, or at least irritation. Instead, she smiled and glanced at him from beneath her lashes. "I thought you would never make your way to me tonight."

Lana's eyes darkened to the color of a lush forest as she snuggled closer to him. Hell's teeth! She had deliberately made him jealous.

"You know exactly what you're doing to me," he growled.

"Do I?" She fluttered her lashes like the most experienced coquette. "You are difficult to read sometimes, my lord. Please, enlighten me. Tell me what it is I'm doing to you."

Challenge rang clear in her words. How could his unspoiled peach behave in such a brazen fashion?

Her lips brushed his earlobe. "Maybe it is better if you show me," she whispered.

His body sprang to attention again, and there would be no way to tamp down his passion with her in his arms.

"Meet me outside by the maze entrance in ten minutes. We have much to discuss." He led her to the sidelines then darted from the hall.

❧

Lana gaped at Drew's back as he stalked from the ballroom. Had she just agreed to meet him in the garden or had he simply assumed her a willing partner?

Double drat, what have I done?

Following her discussion with Lady Audley, thoughts of Drew had absorbed her afternoon. Lana had mentally debated the merits of a continued association with Drew. She had even confiscated a sheet of foolscap and found a quiet corner to create a list of pros and cons comparing him to Bollrud before burning it in a grate.

At the conclusion, Bollrud's cons outnumbered those in Drew's column, but Drew's one negative was insurmountable. He didn't want a wife. In her mind, she had thought the matter decided. She would accept Lord Bollrud's offer when he made it. Yet, when Lana had dressed for the evening, she'd chosen a gown to please Drew.

Their encounter last evening left no doubt in her

mind Drew desired her, but he had also been honest. He would never settle for one woman, and Lana would never settle for heartache. It had been silly to incite him to jealousy. There was nothing to gain.

She wrung her hands, her body burning with shame. The other evening Lana had teased Drew when she had suggested she was impure, but after her behavior tonight, he would believe her ruined for certain.

Scanning the room, she found her mother occupied by Bollrud and made an instant decision. She would meet Drew and explain her flirtation had been an act, impulsive and appalling. Lana remained an innocent. She must turn her attentions toward finding a husband, and Drew must focus *his* attentions on someone more suited for his type of play.

Her gaze dropped to the floor as she maneuvered through the crowd, praying no one took notice of her departure. Once in the hallway, Lana hurried toward the blue parlor. An alternate route should keep anyone from witnessing her exit. She would discourage Drew once and for all and return to the dance before her mother noticed her absence.

She stepped into the crisp darkness and shivered. Fog hovered along the ground so that she could barely make out the maze from the veranda. She descended the stone stairs with caution and wandered to the entrance of the hedge maze. Wishing she'd remembered her shawl, she moved farther into the enveloping blackness.

"Drew," she whispered. Lana rubbed her hands up and down her arms for warmth. "Drew?"

Charming by day, the gardens were menacing in the darkness. The topiary dragons flanking the maze entrance transformed into sinister monsters leering through the mist. Her knees knocked. Perhaps she should return to the house. She could explain her mistake as easily in the light of day. Spinning around to dash back to the house, Lana released a strangled cry. A tall figure approached, his features obliterated by the fog and darkness.

"Where are you going, peach?"

Drew's warm voice wrapped around her and she melted with relief. "Blast it, Drew. You scared the life out of me."

"Your body has more sense than you do apparently." Wicked amusement resonated in his words.

Lana pictured him smiling in that way he had. The smile he had bestowed on her the night he had rescued her from the Eldridge's tree, the one that left her trembling with anticipation. "I'm surprised you came. It's not too late to go back, Lana."

"I'm… I'm not afraid of you."

She accepted his arm when he joined her at the entrance and followed him into the maze. They stopped after a few steps. Drew released her arm and backed away, placing distance between them.

"I don't want you to fear me, peach, but you need to understand the risk involved with your choice."

Choice? Her stomach plunged. She *had* made a choice, hadn't she? Knowing what Drew expected of her, she had chosen to follow him outside. Lana risked everything by sneaking away to the garden. She was alone with a notorious rake, and she was contemplating surrendering to him.

In the ballroom, desire had darkened Drew's eyes to a stormy blue sky, and his body had vibrated with need. God help her, Lana needed him too. Drew offered her passion, an experience she would never know with Lord

Bollrud. Giving herself to Drew would violate everything she valued—her integrity, her family's trust, her mother's hope for a match with Lord Bollrud. If she gave in to temptation, she would never fulfill her duty to marry for she could never betray her future husband's trust.

Her hands shook and she swallowed over the lump in her throat. "I do understand the choice I have made."

"What do you want, Lana?" Drew's strangled voice jarred her. "Please, make this easy on me. Go back to the house."

She stepped toward him, reaching out to touch his forearm. "I don't wish to go back, Drew. I want to be with you."

He lifted her hand to his lips and placed a tender kiss on her exposed wrist. "For how long do you wish to be with me?"

Forever. Lana could never speak the truth, or Drew would bolt like a frightened stallion. He quivered under her touch and her heart squeezed. When had she fallen for Andrew Forest, the most unavailable, disreputable man in England? If anyone should run, it should be her.

Drew blew out a long breath. "I don't wish to hurt you, and I fear I'm only capable of bringing you heartache."

A flash of disappointment had her blinking back tears. So, it was true. He desired nothing more than a night of passion. She intended to turn away, but her will was weak. "I don't believe you will hurt me. Please, Drew."

His fluid movements startled her. He captured her around the waist and pulled her against him. A frisson of apprehension stirred in her belly. Nonetheless, she stood toe-to-toe with him, trying to shore up her courage.

His thumb brushed her bottom lip. "So fearless, my little innocent."

No. Lana wouldn't allow him to turn her away, not with his arbitrary rules for seduction. "I told you I'm not…"

Drew's fingers nestled into her hair. Their bodies fused as his supple lips possessed her mouth, his tongue tracing the inner circle of her lips. Their sighs of pleasure merged, expressing the one word repeating in Lana's head. *Yes.*

With almost imperceptible movement, he drew her mouth flush against his and dipped his tongue into the recesses. The port on his breath was more intoxicating than the alcohol itself.

Lana's arms encircled his neck as she pressed herself against him, wanting—*needing*—to be closer. Was it possible to absorb him, allow his essence to flow through her, making them one? His rapid withdrawal from her embrace left her in daze. Lana sought his warmth again, but Drew held her upper arms to maintain the distance.

"Not here, my sweet." His words brushed across her like a caress. "I want to do this properly."

She giggled. How did one go about properly doing the improper? Her eyes had adjusted enough to the dark to see the gleam of white as he grinned.

"I mean I wish to take my time making love to you without risk of discovery," he amended.

She attempted to concentrate over the rat-a-tat of her heart sounding in her ears. "Where do you suggest?"

"It is early yet. We'll take the carriage to Shafer Hall and return it before Rich and Pheebs need it."

"What if someone notices our absence?"

"You shall pen a note for your mother informing her you're feeling unwell and have retired early. I'll have the footman deliver it when the carriage returns. I could be any place. No one will guess we are together."

The weight of his implication slammed into her. He could as easily be in any lady's bed as hers.

"Lana." Drew captured her mouth again and kissed her until she almost forgot his words. When he pulled away, he didn't release her. "I'm not with anyone else. I'm yours, peach."

For now. Lana wouldn't fool herself into believing otherwise, but she still thrilled at his admission.

She walked toward the maze entrance. "Let's be off then."

"We can't be seen together. I'll go to the stable yard first to chat with the groom and coachman. They know to be discreet, but I'll make certain they have additional motivation. I won't have them bring the carriage around to the front, so come to the west side of the castle. I'll wait for you." Drew enfolded her in his arms and rested his cheek against hers. "You can still change your mind," he whispered.

She shook her head, loving the security of his embrace and sensation of his skin against hers.

"Don't dismiss the possibility too hastily. Think about it." He kissed her temple. "If you don't come to me, I'll understand."

"I won't keep you waiting." Lana kissed him once more before he walked away. Their fingers were the last to break contact. "I will be there, Drew. I promise."

She breathed in deeply and ran her hands along her upper arms as he disappeared into the fog. She wouldn't change her mind. She would never forgive herself if she didn't go to the man she loved, and she did love him. At least she could be honest with herself if no one else. And even though Drew didn't return her love, her sentiment remained the same.

The west side of the castle. Lana stepped from the maze and stopped to get her bearings. Drew's shadowed frame appeared out of the fog again.

"Did you change *your* mind?" she called out.

"Quiet, ya worthless whore."

Her body convulsed and she stumbled backwards, barely maintaining her footing. "Y-you should remember your place. I'm a close friend of the duke and duchess. They shall hear of your transgression."

The hulking form advanced. "Ya think I *work* for 'em, bitch." Hatred dripped from the unfamiliar male voice. His guttural accent and vulgar tongue separated him from the guests at Irvine Caste. "The bloody toffs ain't 'ere to save ya."

Nineteen

LANA DASHED INTO THE MAZE. IF THE CUR THOUGHT SHE would subject herself to his abuse willingly, he was even dumber than he sounded.

"Bloody hell." The man's heavy footfalls pounded as he gave chase, but she had gotten a good lead.

Thick fog inside the hedges made it impossible to see more than a few inches ahead, but she barreled on, less concerned about falling than being captured.

"You can run, bu' ya cain't 'ide," the man sang out, taunting her.

Frantic, Lana scooted to the edge of the maze and skimmed her hand along the manicured hedges to orient her to the trail. If she found the secret passage again, maybe she could escape.

Think, Lana. Think. At the first intersection, the directions to Cupid's chamber flooded her memory. *Left. Left. Right. Left. Right. Right.*

She hurried her pace, repeating the directions. *Now a left.*

"I 'ear you, ya li'l slut." He spit out the venomous words. "And yer gonna pay for makin' me chase ya."

Lana's hand flew to her mouth to hold back the

scream building in her throat. No one would hear her except her pursuer, not in the thick hedges.

Another left. She shuffled along, the branches scratching her arm. *Right.* She listened to determine the man's location, but the only sound she heard came from her own breathing and pounding heart. *Go left. Hurry.*

A sharp crack echoed close behind, and she ran blindly into the mist. *Go right. One more turn. Almost there.* Bursting into the open area, she smothered her cry of despair. She had gone the wrong way.

Panicked, she lurched into the room in search of a place to hide. Five steps in and the Cupid statue loomed into sight. She stumbled into the hedge and flailed her arms, searching for the gap that marked the secret passage.

"Ya like 'ide-an'-seek, do ya?" His voice sounded close. The crescendo of his bootfalls indicated he approached the area where she hid. "I got sumptin to 'ide, inside ya. Aye, a good time you'd 'ave."

Dear lord, she was going to lose her dinner. Her movements became frenzied as she batted at the hedge. When her hand encountered the small open space, she almost sobbed with relief. Lana shimmied through the hedge just as she detected the man's heavy footsteps entering the clearing.

Once through the opening, she lifted her skirts and dashed for the stable yard. She had to reach Drew. Perhaps the stranger knew of the secret passage too and pursued her still. Staying focused on her goal, she pushed herself harder, her side stitching painfully.

As she rounded the corner of the castle, the bulky shapes of the carriages rose out of the fog. *Where is the Forests' coach?* If the man had eavesdropped on her conversation with Drew, he knew where she was headed. She darted to the first carriage several feet away and pressed her face close to the door in search of the correct insignia.

She heard voices somewhere close to the castle and the groom speaking softly to the horses. Likely, the drivers and footmen gathered near, but with the thick fog hiding them, the servants seemed miles away. Should she yell out for help? She had no way to explain her presence in the stable yard and didn't wish to draw notice unless she had no choice.

Thudding footsteps rounded the corner of the castle. A scream lodged in her throat and she hurried around the back of the carriage to race to the next one. The door bore the Foxhaven coat of arms. Easing the door open, she scrambled inside.

"Peach, you came."

Lana dove across the carriage and covered Drew's mouth. "Be quiet," she whispered fiercely. She cocked her head and held her breath. The man's footfalls ran past the back of the carriage. Once she could hear him no more, she released a whooshing breath and dropped her hand. She looked up, and her heart stopped. She was kneeling between Drew's legs with her hand resting scandalously on his lower belly.

❦

Lana's hand lying against Drew's abdomen scorched him. When she hadn't appeared after a while, he thought she had become frightened and returned to the ball. But here she knelt between his thighs, her hand only fractions of an inch from his rapidly growing firmness. He had severely misjudged her. Lana Hillary was no innocent young maiden.

She shifted her weight, brushing against his length. Drew sucked in a sharp breath. He hadn't bedded a woman since his arrival at Shafer Hall, and her touch was a blend of pain and ecstasy.

Lana's gaze lifted from his breeches to lock eyes with his, and she trembled. "There was a man…"

Drew had heard the bugger too, but he hadn't discovered them together. They were safe. He entwined his fingers with her glorious ginger locks and bent forward to kiss her, hoping to quell her anxiety. No one knew of their clandestine activities.

Lana clambered from the carriage floor and threw her arms around him with a whimper.

"I was so frightened."

"You're all right, peach. You are safe."

He dropped his mouth to hers, testing her receptivity. When her lips parted beneath his, he groaned and swept his tongue inside her sweet little mouth, greedily consuming her kisses. She pressed her supple body against his harder one, clutching him tight.

Dear God, she was a passionate one. Drew couldn't wait any longer. With frenetic movements, they tore at each other's clothing. She tugged at his cravat, loosening it in no time. He gently grasped her hair, tilting her head back so he could nibble along her elegant neck. When his lips trailed to the swells of her breasts, Lana rewarded him with a delightfully lustful moan that made him even harder.

Shoving her skirts around her waist, Drew deftly untied her drawers to rid her of the unnecessary hindrance before hauling the front of her bodice down. One at a time, her pert breasts burst free. Cupping the soft flesh, he grazed his thumb over one nipple while his tongue stroked across the distended tip of her other mound. Her cool skin heated under his fingers.

She murmured her pleasure as he arched her backwards, supporting her weight with his arm and swirling his tongue over her breast before closing his mouth around her nipple. Lana dug her fingers into his hair, her nails lightly scraping his scalp, and urged him to take more of her.

Lily of the valley coiled around him, reminding him of their first encounter and heating his blood. Drew had dreamed of making love to Lana the first night in the garden. Now that he held her, he couldn't believe he'd waited this long. Everything about her aroused him, her smell, her taste, those erotic little noises she made.

His free hand slid up her silky thigh.

"Oh," she responded as if surprised when he explored the opening between her legs.

She was creamy and hot beneath his fingers, the discovery causing a husky groan to lodge in his throat. He gently stroked her pleasure spot, and she bucked against his hand with a strangled cry.

"Oh, Drew."

He loved the breathy quality of her voice and his name on her lips. When he grinned up at her, she kissed him with a wildness he matched. Their tongues wrestled until the drive to become part of her overwhelmed all else.

"I want to be inside you, Lana."

"Yes," she whispered, her slender fingers unfastening his breeches. Pushing the front fall down to release him, she ran the backs of her fingers along his hardened length. Waves of lust engulfed him, the intensity sudden and staggering.

"Come here." He captured her wrist to end the

exquisite torture before he shamed himself, and then lifted her to straddle his lap. As she lifted her skirts, he probed her luxurious softness. Positioning himself at her entrance, he clutched her hips and roughly pulled her down on him in one swift movement.

A tiny whimper broke through the blinding haze of lust that gripped him. Lana's body had resisted his entrance.

He didn't move, his breathing ragged as he fought the urge to plunge deeper. "Lana?"

She cupped his face with both palms and kissed him tenderly. When she pulled back, her beautiful eyes held his. "Please, don't stop." She adjusted her weight and gasped as the change of position sheathed him to the hilt, her nubile body gripping his shaft tightly. He'd never experienced anything as divine, never.

Withdrawing from her only made him desperate to bury himself deep again. A few thrusts sent him soaring. His release hit him like a tidal wave, unexpected and powerful. His breath came in pants and his heart beat a heavy rhythm against his ribs. He hugged Lana close as her body held him snug inside her. He loved the feel of her and the sweet scent of her perfume combined with her own essence.

He caressed her back up to her neck and down again until his world righted itself. Lifting Lana, he placed her across his lap and cradled her against his chest. He kissed her, slowly, tenderly. "Your turn, my little peach."

He gingerly caressed the curls between her thighs, careful to bring her no more pain. Lana's head lolled back, a sensual moan escaping her parted lips. Devil take it, she was receptive to his touch. His fingers glided along her luxurious skin, stealing their way inside briefly before withdrawing to stroke her pleasure bud. He did this again and again, slowly at first then gradually increasing speed as her excitement grew. The tensing of her muscles and sudden outpouring of moaning sighs signaled her own moment of satisfaction. How exquisitely pleasurable to observe as she surrendered to ecstasy. Drew's chest filled with tenderness for his lovely forbidden fruit.

Lana allowed him to hold her for a long time without moving. Had he hurt her? If he had known with certainty she had been pure, he would have been gentle. But she'd led him to believe she wasn't a virgin.

"You lied to me, Lana Hillary. You insinuated you were experienced."

Her spine stiffened and she pushed herself to a seated position. "What difference does my lack of experience make?" She reached down to gather her drawers from the carriage floor and stood to pull them on again.

Drew frowned. "It makes all the difference in the world."

She stared for an endless moment before adjusting her dress. "Not to me, so why should it matter to you?"

"How could you believe your virginity would make no difference to me?"

"You needn't bother yourself on my account, my lord. I *was* an innocent. I am no longer, and you are free to go your merry way."

Did their lovemaking mean nothing to her? Anger coursed through his veins. "Go my merry way?"

"Yes, Drew, you're in no danger. I haven't fallen in love with you, so do not fret over breaking your *unbreakable* rule."

"Lana—"

The carriage lurched and she tumbled into his lap.

"Drew, we're moving." Her panic rang out in the enclosed space. "We're moving. We'll be discovered."

What was the blasted coachman doing? Drew hadn't given the signal to leave.

"Please, stop yelling. Let me think." He could jump from the carriage, but they might pass the front door in seconds. He could leap into a crowd of guests for all he knew. Besides, with Lana's mussed hair and disorganized clothes, it would be obvious she had been tumbled. He wouldn't leave her to face the consequences alone.

"Drew, my mama will be heartbroken." Her tears flowed and the pain in her voice broke *his* heart.

"We'll have to marry, peach. That is all there is to it."

Her outraged cry startled him. "Marry? We don't *have* to marry, you blackguard. I would rather be ostracized." The carriage stopped and she flew out the door.

"Lana, wait." Drew raced after her, fastening his breeches at the same time.

The look of shock on Phoebe's face as she and Rich wandered out the front door of the castle fleetingly grabbed his attention. Lana ran up the stairs where Phoebe gathered her into her embrace.

"*Andrew,*" his brother growled and tore after him, but Drew's focus remained on Lana. Her shoulders hunched and her frame shook as she sobbed onto Phoebe's shoulder. Rich's fist slammed into Drew's cheekbone, landing him with a thump on his backside. Stunned by the blow, he remained on the ground until Rich lifted him by his lapels and dragged him away.

"Phoebe, you and Miss Hillary step into the carriage before anyone else comes outside," his brother ordered.

The realization that his brother intended to take Lana away woke him from his stupor. Drew struggled against Rich's hold. "Let me go to her."

"You've done enough damage. Leave her be."

He continued to fight against Rich and almost broke free of his grip. "I need to speak with her. Take your hands from my person."

Rich slammed Drew against the castle wall, knocking the wind out of him. "We need to get her out of here. Stay the night at Irvine then come speak with her in the morning. Think of someone besides yourself, Drew."

He rubbed his face with his hands, weary. All the fight drained from him and he sagged against the wall in defeat. "Will you tell her...? Tell her I..."

"I will apologize for you, but you must make everything right tomorrow." Rich glowered. "And you *will* correct your mistake. Do I make myself clear?"

His brother could be a self-righteous prig when he chose to be. "I make my own decisions." He shoved away from Rich and lost himself in the fog.

Twenty

LANA SLUMPED NEXT TO PHOEBE ON THE CARRIAGE bench, allowing herself to be coddled. Fresh tears sprang to her eyes, but she swallowed her cry of anguish. She would never allow Drew to marry her out of obligation. He would resent her for the rest of his life. And even worse, she would grow to resent him when he continued to carouse about London. He had made it clear he loved his carefree bachelorhood and had no intention of abandoning his wicked ways.

She would rather live in isolation than have her heart broken time and again. She could heal this once. Maybe not without scars, but she would survive this encounter with Drew. Her soul, however, would wither if forced to witness his indiscretions.

Phoebe moaned softly.

"Phoebe, are you all right, love?" Lord Richard's anxiety alerted Lana that something was wrong.

"Just a little tightening," Phoebe answered. "It has passed."

Lana twisted toward her friend. "Is it the baby?"

Phoebe patted her hand. "I'm sure it is nothing. Richard's mama said it's common to feel as if the baby is coming long before the actual time. She said it is the body's way of getting used to the idea. I still have six weeks."

"Mother is not a doctor or midwife," Lord Richard argued. "We are returning to London first thing in the morning before it's too late."

Phoebe sighed. "Darling, you're overreacting. I am fine."

Lana's gaze darted to Phoebe's stomach. Good heavens above. If anything happened to her dearest friend... "Perhaps you should listen to Lord Richard. It's best to be close to good doctors. I'll travel to London with you, if you don't mind." Getting away from Drew was in *her* best interest and the sooner, the better. Her mama might want to stay and finish her visit, preferring to avoid London, but Lana could travel without her since she would be in good company.

Phoebe groaned once more and held herself stiff. Once the pain had passed, she released a weary sigh. "I suppose you are both right. But I *won't* leave at the crack of dawn."

"You will if I command it," her husband answered.

"Of course, I won't, my lord." Phoebe's argumentative tone shocked Lana. She held her breath, fearful of the gentleman's reaction, but she needn't have worried.

Lord Richard chuckled. "You are going to be fine, love. Fate wouldn't dare cross you."

At Shafer Hall, he assisted Phoebe from the carriage and escorted her inside while Lana trailed behind them. Her friend appeared as weary as Lana felt. She would rather drop into bed and forget the events of the evening, but there was an important matter to discuss with her host. And it couldn't wait for morning.

"My lord, might I have a word with you?"

Phoebe glanced over her shoulder, her eyebrows raised in question.

Lord Richard looked between his wife and her. His wrinkled forehead betrayed his worry for Phoebe and Lana, and his indecision on which lady needed him most.

Lana would take the burden from him. "After you settle Lady Phoebe, my lord."

Phoebe waved her hand as if to dismiss both of their concerns. "I'm fine, really. Joanna will assist me. Please, Richard, give Lana an audience now. I will wait in the bedchamber for you."

"If you're certain…"

Phoebe stepped into his embrace and placed a chaste kiss on her husband's cheek. "I am certain."

A profound sadness enveloped Lana like a heavy quilt. She would never experience love like the one they shared. If she had ever held out hope for a love match, it was shattered now. What a horrible fool she had been tonight.

"This way, Miss Hillary." Lana followed Lord Richard into the study. "Perhaps you should pull the door closed behind you."

She did as he directed and tentatively took a few steps into the room.

"Miss Hillary, may I offer my deepest regret over my brother's ill treatment of you?"

"I don't wish to discuss Lord Andrew." She flinched in response to her sharp tone. "Please forgive my disrespect, my lord."

Lord Richard chuckled and filled a glass with port. "If I took offense every time someone censored me, I would walk around in a black mood all the time. Would you like to take a seat?"

Lana lowered herself to perch on the edge of a chair and folded her hands in her lap. "I have distressing news to share, Lord Richard. Tonight a rough character accosted me in the gardens. He didn't appear to be a guest, because he spoke with a vulgar accent, much like the street vendors in London."

Lord Richard moved closer. "What did he do? Did he harm you?"

"No, my lord, but I believe he would have if I had not escaped."

"No doubt he would have robbed you." A worry line formed between his brows. "I will send word to my father immediately to search the grounds and post guards. Perhaps their presence alone will frighten the thief away, so no one else is at risk."

He stared for a long time as if contemplating saying something more. She couldn't bear it if he reprimanded her for being outdoors alone. Being outside in the dark was the least of her sins this evening.

"I'm grateful you were unharmed, Miss Hillary." His sympathetic expression nearly brought her to tears again. They both knew his statement to be untrue. Her harm was beyond repair.

Her eyes dropped to her lap. "Thank you, my lord."

❧

The bloody toffs ain't 'ere to save ya. Lana gasped and jerked awake. Her damp nightrail clung to her body, and she trembled as her mind flashed back to her harrowing run through the maze. Just as quickly, she recalled the warmth and security of being in Drew's arms. Her hands covered her chest as if she could hold the broken pieces of her heart together.

Several moments later, she tossed aside the covers and swung her legs over the edge of the bed. Dwelling on her encounter with Drew wouldn't change anything. He had offered to marry her last night, but only because they had been discovered together. Drew didn't want a wife, and she didn't want a rake. Tears welled in her eyes again. She also didn't want the pain that came from loving a rake, but it was too late to remedy the situation.

Sunlight streamed through the windows. She had best get dressed and ready herself to leave for London. After donning her travel gown with the assistance of Phoebe's maid, Lana made her way to the breakfast room to find Lord Richard dining alone.

"Good morning, Miss Hillary. I see you are dressed for travel, so I take it you haven't changed your mind about returning to Town."

Lana slipped into one of the armless chairs at the table, leaving her hands in her lap while a footman served her poached eggs and ham. "No, my lord, I am determined to leave today."

He checked his watch and frowned. "Will you be ready for travel within the hour, Miss Hillary? It's a long ride, and I will want to find an inn before nightfall where Phoebe may rest comfortably."

Lana spread the napkin over her lap and lifted her fork. "I'll be ready."

"I hope you don't mind, but I took the liberty of speaking with your mother."

The fork slipped from her fingers to clatter against the china dish.

"It's not what you think, Miss Hillary. I explained that you left the ball early to tend to Phoebe. I also suggested your presence on the return journey would be helpful."

"Thank you, my lord. Has she departed for Irvine Castle already this morning without saying good-bye?"

A flush crept up his neck. "She seemed in a hurry to return after learning of the potential thief on the grounds. I did not inform her you were the victim."

Lana's cheeks heated too, and she dropped her gaze to her plate. Her mother was eager to be the first to share the gossip, most likely, not realizing how close Lana was to being a participant in a mortifying scandal.

"Mrs. Hillary would like to stay in Northumberland until Mother and Father leave next week. Father is allowing her full use of Shafer Hall."

"That is kind of His Grace."

Lana's mind drifted to Drew. Was he still abed upstairs? Would he bid her farewell before she left? "Has your brother arisen yet?"

Lord Richard's lips set in a firm line. "He did not stay here last night, Miss Hillary, and I've not seen hide nor hair of him this morning."

"Oh." She forced back the sadness that threatened to spill over and reveal itself. "I will go ready my belongings for travel."

Twenty-one

SOMETHING TICKLED DREW'S NOSE AGAIN AND HE swatted it away. It came back. Growling his discontent, he slapped his face.

"Ow," he moaned.

Giggles broke through his dream state. Opening his eyes, he discovered a feather duster advancing toward him and yanked it from his tormentor's hand. More tittering followed.

"Lord Andrew," one of the downstairs maids teased, "you've outdone yourself this time."

"What happened to your face?"

He palpated his sore cheekbone. Thanks to Rich, he probably looked a fright. Three young maids gathered in a semicircle around the settee where he sprawled. His back ached and his head hammered.

"Where am I?" His voice sounded scratchy as if he had consumed half a bottle of broken glass instead of brandy last night. He pushed himself to a seated position and groaned. If he had eaten anything recently, he might spew it all over the pristine carpet.

"You are in the west parlor, my lord. And you're lucky no one comes here except at night. Why are you not in a bed?"

"I don't have a bed at Irvine."

More snickers assaulted his senses. "We've never known that to stop you, my lord."

Hell's teeth. "I need to locate the facilities."

"This way, Lord Andrew." One of the taller maids reached under his arm and helped haul him to his feet. She pressed her body against his side as she draped his arm over her shoulders.

"I can walk, love, but thank you."

She hesitantly stepped away. "Of course, my lord."

"What time is it?"

"It is nearing two o'clock," the maid he thought they called Sheila said. "We allowed you to sleep as long as we could, but you are sure to be discovered soon if you continue to slumber."

Devil take it! He needed to get to Shafer Hall and speak with Lana if she hadn't arrived at the castle already. "Could one of you lovelies arrange a bath for me?"

"As you wish, my lord." The small blonde raced to do his bidding.

The taller maid stepped forward. "If you need help washing…"

He sighed. "Thanks for the kind offer, but I am able to manage that on my own, too. You may check to see if Miss Hillary has arrived if you would like to be of assistance."

Disappointment clouded her expression. "Yes, sir."

In another thirty minutes, Drew lowered his battered frame into a steaming tub of water. He didn't know how they had done it, but the chits had come through for him. They had also procured a bar of sandalwood soap and a tumbler of scotch to ease his suffering. By the time he finished his bath, he felt almost human again.

One of the maids found a change of clothes for him too. He didn't dare ask from where, but in case she had pilfered them from another guest, he slipped out of the castle as quickly as he could. As he had expected, Lana hadn't come to the castle this morning, and he couldn't blame her. He had behaved like a beast, allowing his lust to override his good sense.

The groom noticed his approach and went into the stables to ready a horse. He led the black stallion by the bridle. "Your horse is ready, my lord."

On the ride to Shafer Hall, he considered his hurried conversation with Lana last night. He could see how his fumbling proposal might upset her. A lady expected romance and eloquent words. *We will have to get married.* Drew shook his head at his ineptitude. In his defense, he'd never once believed he would propose to anyone, so he hadn't practiced how he might go about it.

A broad smile spread across his face. How absurd to have believed he would be able to forget Lana once he'd bedded her. She plagued his mind more than ever this afternoon. He anticipated making love to her again once he had properly offered for her and announced their intentions. On second thought, perhaps she wouldn't insist on waiting until their betrothal was official; at least he could hope.

When Shafer Hall came into view, his stomach twisted and he urged the stallion into a canter. His desire to see her again was almost unbearable. A footman met him outside to take the horse while Drew jogged up the steps.

"Lord Andrew," the butler greeted.

"Good morning," he replied happily. "Please inform Miss Hillary she has a caller requesting an audience." He continued toward the library. That would be the perfect place to propose. He'd almost kissed her for the first time there, and would have if his lousy brother had not intruded.

The butler cleared his throat. "My lord?"

He swung around to face the servant, irritated with the delay. "Yes, what is it, man?"

"I'm afraid Miss Hillary left for London this morning with Lord Richard and Lady Phoebe."

"Pardon? You say she's gone?"

"They departed several hours ago, my lord."

Bloody hell. She left me? Drew growled his frustration. What manner of woman bedded a gent then took off without a by-your-leave? He stormed from Shafer Hall, startling the footman outside.

"Collect my horse," he commanded. He would show Lana Hillary she couldn't dally with him then toss him aside like an old hat. She would marry him, by God, and she would be happy. He wouldn't accept her refusal. Mounting his black again, Drew urged him into a gallop toward London.

Hours later, Drew's horse plodded along the muddy lane as he huddled in the saddle attempting to stay warm. A bone-chilling rain poured down on him.

"Bloody idiot," he muttered.

To think he could catch up to Lana with the lead they had was lunacy. He should have taken the time to pack some clothes. And perhaps a carriage would have been wise, but no, he had to race after the chit half-cocked. Either way, whether traveling by coach or on horseback, drenched clothing was the least of his worries.

"What has she done to me, Demetrius?" He spoke aloud to the horse, having decided to give his patient listener a name. "Fools run after ladies all the time, but only a truly besotted bugger would give no thought to clothing before giving chase." He didn't even carry a firearm and here he traveled after dark.

"We'll stop at the next village with an inn and find a warm place to sleep. Perhaps the mews will have a filly that pleases your eye." The horse deserved a little recreation after this harrowing day. "I have sworn off ladies myself, but my abstinence needn't affect you, old chap."

Demetrius had stopped responding with a shake of his head twenty minutes earlier.

In the morning, Drew would hire a coach to take him the rest of the way to Town, and then he would deal with Miss Lana Hillary.

He traveled perhaps another hour at least before reaching the next village. Soaked, starving, and irritable, he deposited Demetrius at the stables and slopped through the puddle-filled streets until he located the Oak Barrel Inn. Rainwater ran down his cloak in rivulets when he stepped inside the establishment, leaving large wet spots on the floor.

The innkeeper greeted him with a slight nod. "You need a room, sir?"

Drew tossed a purse on the desk. "Locate a change of clothing for me also, and you may lay claim to this entire purse."

"Yes, sir." The man turned to a barmaid. "Beatrice, show the gentleman to 'is room, and find some clothes for 'im."

The barmaid eyed Drew's wet clothing and smiled. "Of course. Perhaps ye would like a warm bath too, sir?"

"Brilliant suggestion." He followed the wench upstairs. If he rose early on the morrow, maybe he could catch up to Rich. How far had they traveled today? His brother couldn't travel too quickly with a child and ladies accompanying him.

The maid opened one of the doors off the hallway and preceded Drew into the room. She lit a lamp with the candle she carried before starting a fire in the fireplace.

"Billy will bring up water for ye're bath when it's ready. If ye want to take off yer wet clothes, I can take 'em wit' me to wash." She stared unabashedly, waiting for him to strip.

"I'll wait for the bath, but thank you." He didn't care to stand around in the nude nor did he want this Billy walking in on him while he didn't wear a stitch of clothing.

Beatrice curtsied then left the room.

Drew meandered to the fire and held his hands toward the warmth. His gaze strayed to the bed. Too bad his little peach wasn't here to share it with him. His body stirred immediately to memories of her silky skin.

A scratch at the door signaled when his bath water arrived. After several trips between two lads, the tub filled to the halfway point. He tossed them each a shilling before they walked out, and then set to peeling off his wet garments.

Drew sank into the warm water and his mood improved a great deal. "Dear God, yes." After his bath, he would seek out nourishment and feel more like his old self. Plunging his head under the water, he quickly emerged and shook his head. A giggle rang out in the room.

Drew snapped his head around to discover Beatrice had returned with a towel and the most hideous clothing he could imagine.

"Where did you find that atrocity? I asked for clothing, not a horse blanket."

Her lips narrowed to a firm line. "It is all I could find, sir. We ain't a fancy clothier. These belong to me older brother."

"If I leave the funds, will you purchase something decent for the poor man?"

She dropped a hand on her hip. "They ain't that bad. Ye must be one of those dandies that stop through 'ere on your way to fancy places I'll never see."

Drew chuckled. "Didn't mean to offend, Bea. Just leave everything on the bed, and thanks for your efforts. I'll make sure you are rewarded later."

Beatrice didn't move. "I think I'll take me brother's clothes back. And maybe the towel can go too."

"You wouldn't dare."

She raised her eyebrows, challenging him to do something about it. She took one step toward the door. "Ye better come and get 'em if ye want 'em, my lord."

Drew had grown accustomed to the female gender propositioning him, and he had to acknowledge Beatrice's efforts were less blatant than some offers he received from proper ladies. "If you think I won't take the garments from you, you are mistaken, love."

She took two more steps toward the door. "Ye'll 'ave to be quick about it."

He shot out of the water and clambered over the side of the metal tub. The maid squealed and threw the towel. Drew snatched it with one hand and wrapped it around his waist before pursuing the mischief-maker.

Beatrice opened the door and ran into the hallway, but he captured a handful of her skirts.

"Come back here, you little vixen. You aren't getting away that easily."

The maid giggled and struggled to break his hold.

"Uncle Drew, can I play chase too?"

Drew froze in the corridor. *Bloody hell*. Finally daring to look up, he met Lana's furious green eyes. His brother and Phoebe also stood in the hallway, gaping as if he'd gone barking mad.

"Uncle Drew isn't playing anymore, Stephan," he mumbled.

"Ah, but you caught her."

"That's enough, Stephan," his mother said, hauling the lad closer to her side.

Drew dropped the maid's skirts and stepped away from the chit.

Beatrice's face glowed red. "My apologies, my lord." Shoving the clothes at him, she curtsied then dashed down the corridor.

Lana glared, sparks shooting from her deep green eyes. He took a step toward her, and she flinched.

"It's not what it seems, peach. I have no dry clothes and…"

She lifted her nose and sniffed. "*If* you will excuse me, Lord Richard and Lady Phoebe, I'll wait for you downstairs." She rushed by Drew, pressing herself as close to the wall as possible to avoid touching him.

Rich frowned. "Phoebe and Stephan, please accompany Miss Hillary to the dining room. I will meet you in a moment."

Phoebe shook her head as if to say, "Oh, Drew," as she and Stephan brushed past.

Drew pulled the towel tighter around his waist and hung his head. Scolded like a young boy.

Once they had disappeared down the stairs, Rich followed Drew to his room and closed the door.

"Where were you this morning?" he asked. "I expected you to present at Shafer Hall to offer for Miss Hillary. What the hell are you doing here dallying with the maid?"

Drew gritted his teeth. "I arrived at Shafer Hall this afternoon to discover you had absconded with Lana."

Rich lowered himself onto the simple wooden chair by the hearth. "I couldn't tarry all day, Drew."

"Last I had heard you hadn't planned to leave Shafer Hall until after the babe was born." Drew dropped the towel to the floor and grasped the borrowed trousers, shoving his legs into the garment one at a time.

Rich's brow creased. "Phoebe started having pains last night. I want her in London where we can access a doctor if needed."

"Oh. I didn't know." He pulled the shirt on over his head and fastened the buttons. "How is she today?"

"Phoebe claims she hasn't felt anything out of the ordinary today. Just the baby kicking."

"That has to be a good sign, wouldn't you agree?"

Rich smiled ruefully. "If she is telling the truth. I shan't rest easy until we are safely ensconced in Town."

Drew searched the floor for his boots. He didn't relish putting on soggy footwear, but he had little choice. "You didn't travel far today."

"We stopped early. The journey is uncomfortable for Phoebe."

"It beats riding in the rain." Drew tugged on a boot. "I should join you in the carriage tomorrow."

His brother held up his hand. "Not on your life, Drew. I can't participate in Miss Hillary's suffering. Have you forgotten you've ruined the poor girl?"

Drew scoffed. "I've ruined *her*? I was perfectly content before Miss Hillary came along and mucked up my life. She plagues my thoughts morning and night."

Rich cocked an eyebrow, sending a jolt of irritation through Drew.

He jabbed a finger in his brother's direction. "And I'll have you know I proposed last night. She turned me down." He pulled on the other boot as he reconsidered his statement. "Well, I didn't *exactly* propose. But I suggested we marry, which is the same bloody thing, if you ask me. It's not like I have ever considered shackling myself to anyone else."

Rich regarded him with an amused grin.

"What are you smirking at, you pompous arse?"

"Which horse died and left you his clothes?"

Drew glanced down at his ensemble. "It's hard to believe I chased the poor wench for this monstrosity." The threadbare gray plaid trousers sagged on his frame and the billowing yellowed shirt had enough extra fabric drooping on him to sew a sail. "I seem to have left Shafer Hall without giving much thought to anything other than catching up to you. I had nothing but the clothes on my back."

Rich chuckled. "Welcome to my world. Love drives a man insane."

Love? Why, he didn't *love* Lana. Granted, he thought about her every minute of every day. But that proved nothing. He did long to hold her, but again he couldn't put much credence into that either. There was that warm sensation in his chest when he thought of wedding her, but—

"Devil take it." He loved her. He loved Lana Hillary. Drew collapsed on the bed and cradled his head in his hands. "How... how did this happen?"

Rich came over and slapped him on the back several times. "You'll survive, I promise."

Drew suspected his brother mocked him, but only witnessed understanding in his demeanor. "But I never thought it would happen to me."

"Bound to happen eventually. I shall loan you some clothes," Rich offered. "You can't court Miss Hillary in *that* outfit."

"Does that mean you've reconsidered allowing me to ride in the carriage?"

Rich adopted a stern expression. "Andrew, do you swear you were not planning to bed that maid?"

"Honest, Rich. It never entered my mind."

"Odd that I should believe you," he responded with a slight frown. "I must explain everything to Phoebe first."

Drew cringed. "Must you tell her everything? Pheebs doesn't need to be privy to all my indignities."

"It's nonnegotiable. Otherwise, you may secure your own transportation to Town."

"Very well." Drew stood to follow his brother from the room.

"Where are you going?"

"Downstairs to dine."

"Not with us. Keep your distance tonight until I have spoken with my wife. And gather some decent clothes from my room." He pointed to a door at the end of the hall. "Until tomorrow."

"I'm still planning to eat," Drew grumbled.

Twenty-two

LANA YAWNED FOR THE FOURTH TIME SINCE CRAWLING from bed that morning. Her sleep had been fitful with her waking every half hour it seemed. The horrible scene with Drew in the corridor had preoccupied her dreams.

Thank goodness she had refused his impulsive offer of marriage. She couldn't tolerate this type of heartache every day. To possess the knowledge that Drew was a man of the town had been upsetting, but to witness him in nothing but a towel, grabbing the young maid… She shuddered with revulsion. He should have driven a dagger into her chest instead. It would have been less painful.

The sooner her party reached London, the quicker she could forget Andrew Forest. If she was lucky, they wouldn't cross paths this morning, and she would never have to see him again.

Last night, without intending to do so, she had scanned the main room of the inn to see if she could locate Drew when she and her traveling companions left their private dining room. The tavern stood empty except for one old man. Unbidden images of Drew in bed with the maid hit her like a punch to the gut, and Lana's stomach had threatened to evict her dinner.

How could Drew bed another so soon? Lana's face flushed as memories of their intimacy flooded her senses. Her body thrilled as it recalled his gentle caresses, which only made her want to cry. Lovemaking meant nothing to Drew. Lana had been nothing more than a willing partner, one of many.

She brushed away the tears she hadn't realized ran down her cheeks until that moment when a light knock sounded on her door. "Enter," she called in a small voice.

The door creaked open, but it was taking the person a long time to enter her room.

"I said come in," she repeated.

The maid from the corridor debacle peered through the crack in the doorway. "Are ye certain I may enter, miss?"

Lana wanted to rescind her offer, but figured the girl had to attend to her duties. She waved her inside. She didn't blame the maid anyway. The girl had likely been as susceptible to his charm as Lana had been.

"Um…" The girl stood inside the closed door, not moving to stoke the fire or do any of the other things Lana expected were her responsibilities.

"Is there a problem?" Irritation was heavy in Lana's voice.

The maid scuffed the toe of her boot against the floorboards. "No, miss. I come to offer me apologies for last night is all."

"I'm sure *you* have nothing to apologize for. Lord Andrew should be the one offering his regrets for flaunting his corrupt habits in such a public manner."

The girl's cheeks flamed a bright red. "About that, miss. It wasn't milord's doing." She glanced up from the floor, her eyes round and as innocent as a fawn's. "Honest, I didn' know 'is lordship traveled with 'is intended. I never woulda—"

"I'm *not* his intended," Lana protested, her voice rising to a near yell.

The girl's face scrunched. "But I 'eard the older gent'lman talking 'bout yer marriage to Lord Andrew."

So, Lord Richard thought to interfere in her life again and insist Drew marry her. What role did Phoebe play in the whole affair? As well-intentioned as her host and hostess might be, Lana wouldn't allow her companions to force a match between her and Drew. Forcing him into marriage would be nothing but a disaster, and she would be the casualty.

"Obviously, this will not come about," Lana answered curtly.

"Oh, miss. Please don't break yer betrothal 'cause of me. I shouldn't 'ave teased his lordship. I just thought… Sometimes…"

"Say your piece and be done. I haven't the patience to listen to any more."

Lana hadn't thought it possible the girl could turn a darker shade of red, but she managed it until her face almost appeared purple. "You see, miss. Sometimes I make a few extra coin by… Um, I thought his lordship might be game for a little… Well, the gent'lman was dressed all fancy like 'e 'ad money. But 'e wasn't biting, so I shoulda known 'e wasn't avail'ble."

"Lord Andrew turned down your… *offer?*" Had she heard the girl correctly?

"The gent'lman never gave me a second glance."

Lana crossed her arms and narrowed her eyes. "Did Lord Andrew request you speak with me on this matter?"

"No." The maid's appalled expression told her Drew wasn't involved in this particular encounter.

"Nevertheless, he didn't appear to be pushing you out

the door," Lana said. "As a matter of fact, he was pulling you back inside."

The girl wrung her hands. "I told ye I was teasing 'im, miss. I took 'is only clothes. The gent'lman 'ad nothing with 'im like 'e left in a rush. I'm terribly ashamed."

Lana studied the maid. Although she believed in the girl's sincerity, Drew couldn't be trusted. The likelihood of him perpetrating some distasteful act remained high, so Lana wouldn't lose more sleep just because she had arrived at the wrong conclusion about him.

"You may go about your duties," Lana said. "I must dress for the long journey."

The maid curtsied then hurried to stoke the fire and add another log. She walked out of the room but returned within five minutes with warm water for the basin before disappearing again for good.

Lana met Lord Richard, Phoebe, and Stephan in the private room for breakfast before they continued their journey. She sank onto the chair in relief when she saw no sign of Drew.

"Good morning, Lana," Phoebe greeted. "Did you sleep well?"

She offered a smile rather than lie to her friend. "And you?"

"Not so well." A worry line creased her brow. Was something wrong with the baby? "I have something I must tell you—"

"Good morning." Drew's annoyingly cheerful greeting made Lana cringe.

"Uncle Drew." Stephan bounced up and down on his seat in his excitement. "Ride with me today."

Lana gaped at Phoebe. "You wished to inform me Lord Andrew will be joining us?"

Her friend blushed prettily.

Drew slid into the seat beside her. "Come now, peach. No need to stand on formality," he murmured.

Lana glowered, but adopted a sweet tone for Stephan's sake. "Yes, Uncle Drew. I believe you should ride with your darling nephew in the *other* carriage."

Drew laughed good-naturedly, as if he found her greatly amusing, and then addressed Stephan. "Maybe later in the day, little one. But I promise to play with you when we stop to change horses."

This seemed to pacify the boy, but his answer disturbed her.

Lana sat with her back rigid. Although she had been hungry when she came downstairs, she found nothing appealed to her anymore. Five days in a carriage with Drew? *This has to be the worst punishment ever.* Her cheeks heated again as she remembered they would be in the *same* carriage where they had been intimate.

"I beg your pardon, but I no longer have an appetite." Lana pushed from the table and hurried upstairs to gather her wits before being forced to endure Drew's company.

Drew stood beside the carriage waiting for Lana and grinned. He had five days to press his suit. With his brother lifting the ban on her, Drew would court her with vigor. He'd win over his little peach before the first day ended, and Lana would share his bed that night.

His heart faltered a moment when she stepped outside into the sunshine. She wore her auburn hair knotted at the nape, a jaunty yellow bonnet framing her pretty face. A strip of creamy skin peeked out from her collar and begged for his kisses.

He winked as she whisked to the carriage with her head held high. "Miss Hillary, you look ravishing this fine morning. In fact, I would go as far as to say you are more radiant than the sun itself."

Rich and Phoebe moved at a slower pace behind her. She ignored the hand Drew offered to assist her into the carriage and clambered up the stairs. Rich handed Phoebe inside and followed, leaving Drew to climb in last. He sighed as he dropped onto the bench beside his brother. Setting off down the lane, he glanced at Rich and found him gazing at Phoebe, never taking his eyes from her.

Drew suppressed a chuckle. Lana didn't stand a chance against both of them. Rich would find a way to sit beside his wife before noon, and Drew would be that much closer to winning Lana.

Approximately two hours later, they stopped to change horses. Phoebe had been squirming and looking uncomfortable for quite some time. Rich assisted her outside and hovered like a mother hen. Drew resisted the urge to roll his eyes. His brother's worry was for naught. Nothing could happen to Phoebe and the baby. Drew refused to believe otherwise.

His gaze settled on Lana's middle. What if she carried his child? Similar thoughts would have sent him into hiding not long ago, although he had taken precautions never to leave any woman with child; at least he had until now. A slow smile spread across his lips.

He fell into step with Lana as she strolled around the outer perimeter of the coaching yard. "Do you fancy children?"

She gave him the evil eye and kept walking. "I have nothing against them."

Drew chuckled. "Such enthusiasm speaks for you, Lana. Do you truly want no children *and* no husband?"

"I don't see how this is of interest to you, my lord."

He blew out a deep breath, moving the hair on his forehead. "It's quite ridiculous to revert to addressing me in such a manner. You had begun to call me Drew even before we were intimate."

She gasped and hurried her step, but Drew whirled her around to face him. "I'm not going to pretend it never happened, peach."

"If you were any kind of a gentleman, you would."

"I believe I established from the start of our association that I was no gentleman. And it *is* my concern if you like children or not since you could be carrying mine."

Lana's pallor drained of color, and he caught her around the waist to keep her from crumpling to the ground when her knees buckled.

"I insist upon taking the honorable path. Marry me before anyone is the wiser."

She recovered enough to bear her own weight, but he kept his hand on the small of her back.

"I believe I have established I am uninterested in becoming your wife. Nothing has changed."

Lana's stubborn streak ran deeper than he'd thought.

Drew's hand brushed over her round little bottom before he stepped away. "I refuse to give up, Lana."

Twenty-three

LANA SUPPORTED HER WEIGHT AGAINST THE ROUGH BARK of an old oak, waiting for the driver and footman to change horses before continuing their journey.

What have I done?

Her legs trembled as she contemplated the possibility of carrying a child. She would never forgive herself for being so foolish. How would she raise a child alone?

If she found herself with child, she would have to reveal her compromised state to her parents. A hard, icy knot of shame settled in her belly. She would disgrace her entire family.

She would need to hide away until the babe was born, and the prospect of being away from everyone she loved destroyed her. But what other option would she have if she remained unwed?

In the distance, Drew played with his nephew, the lad joyfully squealing as he chased his uncle. Drew allowed the youngster to tackle him to the ground, where they wrestled, and Stephan hopped up and down on his uncle's back with delighted screams. Lana giggled at their antics in spite of herself.

Perhaps she should consider Drew's proposal, even

if he only made his offer to save her reputation. Lana might be able to cope with the shame associated with an illegitimate issue, but asking a child to bear the stigma seemed exceptionally cruel. Yet, Drew was little more than an overgrown child himself. He'd likely make the worst of husbands and fathers.

With fresh horses hooked to the carriage, the party readied for departure. Phoebe wobbled down the stairs of the coaching inn with Lord Richard's arm around her waist. Fine lines of discomfort formed at the corners of her lips. Once she had safely navigated the stairs with her husband's assistance, Phoebe drooped with exhaustion. Lord Richard hurried back inside the coaching inn for a moment to conclude whatever transaction required his attention.

Lana sighed with resignation. She couldn't ask her friend to endure such obvious suffering because of Lana's injured pride. "Phoebe, you should seek comfort from your husband. Perhaps you should sit beside him for the remainder of the journey."

"No, I couldn't ask you to—" Her friend bit her lip and regarded Lana with troubled blue eyes. "Really, I'll be fine."

"Please, I insist." What difference did propriety make now? Lana was ruined.

"You should pay heed to Miss Hillary," Drew said from behind Lana. "This journey is taking a toll on you, Pheebs. If nothing else, think of my brother."

Lana glanced back to see if he gloated, but Drew's expression seemed sincere, as if he too had noticed the hardship on Phoebe. She looked uneasily between them, but at their encouraging nods, she consented. "Thank you, Lana."

Lana threw a grateful smile Drew's direction, unsure if her gratitude stemmed from his part in convincing her friend to see to her comfort or for not making Lana feel like a cake for her concession.

The little boy ran up to Drew and tugged on his jacket. Drew scooped the lad and swung him over his shoulder, prompting more squeals from the youngster. "Allow me to return this monkey to his cage, and we may resume our journey."

"I'm not a monkey, Uncle Drew."

"Quiet, little monkey," he teased as he carried him to the second carriage to rejoin his nanny. "Are you aware monkeys don't speak?"

More peals of laughter floated on the air. "I'm *not* a monkey."

When Drew jogged back to their carriage and offered his assistance traversing the stairs, Lana accepted his help. He graced her with one of his heart-stopping smiles and sent her senses reeling. How was she to remain strong when he unscrupulously used his arsenal of seductive weapons against her? If she grew weak in the knees from a simple smile, what would happen if he chose to employ more persuasive means?

Drew squeezed her fingers before releasing her hand. Joining her on the bench, his firm thigh pressed flush against hers. The contact inspired vivid images of her straddling those thighs in this same carriage. Scooting away, Lana flattened herself against the side of the coach and scowled her displeasure. Drew rewarded her efforts with a wicked grin, inflaming her even more.

Phoebe grunted as she settled against the squads. The poor dear had grown large with child over the last couple of weeks, although she had hid it well with billowing high-waist gowns. Lord Richard's arm went around his wife, and she rested her head against his shoulder. A short while later Phoebe slumbered as her husband rested his cheek against her hair and closed his eyes. Their affection caused a pang of envy.

Lana shifted uncomfortably and averted her gaze out the window, watching the passing landscape until her eyelids grew heavy. With the road proving uncommonly smooth, the carriage swayed gently, lulling her.

❧

Drew watched Lana with amusement. Her eyelids had finally dropped, and her head bobbed every so often, startling her into a brief semiconscious state before she surrendered to sleep again. After the fourth head bob, he inched closer and cradled her against his chest.

He sighed with relief when she didn't wake and push him away. Grazing his lips across her silky hair, he breathed in her sweet scent, a hint of lily of the valley with an added trace of Lana's unique essence. Her fragrance was irresistible, and he hugged her closer. Drew could hold her like this for the rest of his life, if only she would allow him.

He couldn't say he regretted bedding her. In fact, he anticipated making love again—soon. Yet, he hated how their relationship had changed, how guarded she had become. Over the last few weeks, he'd grown fond of Lana's tendency to blurt whatever thoughts skittered around her charming mind. Her quick wit proved razor sharp and challenged him unlike any woman he had ever encountered. He missed her carefree spirit and laughter, and part of him feared they might never regain the intimacy they had shared as friends.

Lana snuggled against him but still didn't wake. His arms tightened around her as a smile pulled at his lips. *So, this is love.*

A moment later Rich woke, took in their intimate embrace, and raised an eyebrow. Drew simply grinned like a besotted fool and cared not what his brother thought.

❧

"Lana, wake up."

Warmth pressed against her forehead, and she nestled her cheek against her pillow, breathing in the light fragrance of sandalwood-scented sheets. She didn't want to abandon the warmth of her bed or her wonderful dreams just yet.

"We're arriving at our next stop, peach."

Peach? Her eyes flew open. She wasn't lying comfortably in her own bed, but rather in Drew's arms.

Oh, dear Lord. Her whole body sagged with disgrace. Shoving away from his cozy embrace, Lana smoothed her skirts while keeping her gaze on the floor. She didn't dare sneak a peek at her traveling companions for fear she would crumble if she saw censorship on their faces.

"They are still sleeping," Drew whispered, his breath warm against her neck.

Her gaze flicked to Phoebe and her husband, relieved to discover them both sound asleep. Turning to Drew, she whispered, "Did—did you just kiss me?"

A smirk played about his lips. "Were you having naughty dreams about me again?"

Lana crossed her arms and slumped low on the bench. "More like a nightmare."

Her sharp retort only served to widen his smile and

deepen his dimples. "Ah, there's my little peach. I've missed you."

Familiar warmth infused her body despite Lana's determination to remain immune to Drew. She could easily have inappropriate dreams about the scoundrel, although one typically referred to them as fantasies while still awake. A fleeting memory of Drew buried inside her made her center pulsate with excitement. Her body seemed ready to surrender, but Lana willed herself to stay strong. Neither her body nor her heart could be trusted, as history had shown. She needed to rely on her common sense, although even it had failed her most times in Drew's presence.

To hide her embarrassing state of arousal, she wrinkled her nose and frowned. "I asked you *not* to call me peach."

Twenty-four

LANA FORCED EACH BITE OF ROAST BEEF DOWN HER CON-stricted throat. Drew's scrutiny made her uncomfortable. It was as if he followed her every movement. To battle the riotous beating of her heart, she drained her glass of wine. Drew refilled her goblet the moment it touched the tablecloth, earning a suspicious glower from her. Yet, halfway through the second glass, waves of warmth washed over her and her nerves dissipated some.

Several minutes later, Phoebe groaned as she struggled to her feet with the assistance of her husband. "Lana, please forgive me, but I must retire early."

Lana swallowed against her rising panic. "Oh, of course. I'll be all right."

Drew placed his arm on the back of Lana's chair. "I will see that she makes it safely to her room." A seductive glint in his sea blue eyes made Lana's stomach flip.

"I-I might retire early as well," she said.

"An even better idea," Drew murmured where only she could hear.

"See that you do get her back safely, Drew," Phoebe said. "It's horrifying to consider what might have hap-pened the other night."

Drew met Lana's gaze and his eyebrows shot upward. "What does she mean? What happened the other night?"

Lana cringed. If Phoebe weren't pregnant, she might tackle her to the ground and cover her mouth. Lana stole a look at Drew and found his lips had settled into a firm line.

Phoebe's hands landed on her hips. "Lana was accosted in the gardens the night you and... She and you... Well... She did tell you about the incident, did she not?"

"Come, love. Miss Hillary can apprise Drew of the details." As Lord Richard led his wife from the private dining room, Lana considered making a dash for the door.

When they were alone, Drew's eyes bore into her. "What details, peach? Someone accosted you after I left the gardens?"

Lana fidgeted with the napkin lying across her lap. "Likely a thief after my jewelry. I managed to get away. Truly, it's of no consequence."

"Allow me to judge the seriousness. Tell me what happened."

Her hands trembled, and she breathed deeply to slow her racing pulse as memories of that night threatened to overwhelm her. "A man... He appeared out of the fog. I thought he was you at first, but his speech... I knew I was mistaken. He was vulgar and threatened to—"

Drew leaned forward, a dangerously dark look transforming him. She had only known Drew to be the jovial sort, and his graveness disconcerted her. "Did he hurt you?"

Lana's fork clattered against the plate as she set it down. "No. I ran into the maze and escaped him."

"And you never thought to mention this to me? He followed you to the carriage?"

"I tried to tell you, but then——" She choked back tears.

"Come here, Lana." Drew lifted and settled her on his lap. Her limbs flopped ineffectively as if her entire backbone had turned to mush. She couldn't have stopped Drew if she wanted. To have him holding her in his protective embrace, cradling her body against his chest, released a myriad of emotions. Tears filled her eyes, making everything blur together. Finally, Lana allowed herself the luxury of letting go, surrendering to her vulnerability.

Drew rocked her back and forth. "There, there, my sweet. You are safe."

His tender voice and soft caresses rent soul-wrenching sobs from her. She cried until she couldn't shed another tear while Drew continued his gentle ministrations.

When her sobs subsided, he kissed her cheeks where they were still wet. "No one will ever hurt you again, peach," he promised. "You're no longer in danger."

Lana disagreed. She was in dire danger, because she had fallen hopelessly in love with Andrew Forest.

❧

Drew escorted Lana to her room. He desired her as a man addled by opium craved his drug. He needed her, and he *could* have her. She hadn't pushed him away when he'd gathered her to his chest in the private dining room. She hadn't protested as he had walked her to the room. She hadn't barred him from her room even though his presence in her private lodgings was highly improper.

Yet, even with the bed in his line of sight, Drew couldn't take advantage of Lana's vulnerability. When he made love to her next, she would be an active participant in the decision.

He couldn't resist kissing her, however. He wasn't a damned saint. Cupping her head, he urged her to meet his lips. Lana's rosebud mouth tasted as sweet as ever, like fruit and minted tea. She returned his kisses, leaning into him and brushing against his shaft.

He stifled the moan ready to escape his lips. Leaning his forehead against hers, Drew called upon every ounce of his willpower. If he didn't leave soon, he would toss her on the bed and do all kinds of inappropriate things.

"Until next time, Lana," he whispered. Drew broke contact and moved toward the door.

"You're leaving?"

He glanced over his shoulder to discover Lana wide-eyed with disbelief. Perhaps her emerald eyes even held a hint of relief. "Not for good, peach. You won't rid yourself of me that easily."

⤜✦⤛

Lana bristled when the traveling party arrived at the inn for the last night of their journey. It had been three days since Drew had treated her with anything other than polite respect. No flirting, no subtle innuendos, and no more marriage offers. One would think she was his blasted sister for all the interest he showed now. And to think, Lana had considered accepting his proposal.

The driving force behind her decision may have been the possibility of carrying Drew's child, but after he had exhibited such compassion when she told him of the thief in the garden… Well, it hardly mattered *now* that her stance on his suitability as a husband had wavered.

Lana rubbed her forehead to ease the pounding behind her eyes. Oh, what cause did she have to complain? Drew had remained a perfect gentleman. He had stood in her room three strides from her bed, and he hadn't attempted to seduce her.

She marched into the White Stag with Drew on her heels. Throwing an angry look over her shoulder, Lana didn't notice Phoebe had stopped and nearly plowed into her.

"Are you all right, Miss Hillary?" Drew reached out to steady Lana.

Miss Hillary? Tension spread from her shoulders up her neck and into her jaws as she clenched her teeth. Again, he behaved as a perfect gentleman. And *that* was the blasted problem. He had become the proper gentleman she'd sought all along, except, drat it, she liked the scoundrel he had been and mistrusted his newly acquired manners. Obviously, he no longer fancied her, so he hid behind detached politeness. He probably couldn't wait until their arrival in London so he could return to his whoring ways.

Lana jerked her head around to glower once more, but he seemed oblivious as he searched the interior of the room. His entire face lit as his sight landed on something across the tavern. She turned to seek the object of his attention and almost cried out in agony.

Across the room, with arms laden, stood the most voluptuous woman she had ever seen. As the barmaid leaned over to place drinks in front of the patrons, her unbound breasts jiggled, drawing the hedonistic interest of every man at the table. A quick glance at Drew revealed he wasn't immune to her charms either. A sensual smile spread across his lips.

As the woman's head lifted, she spotted him. "Lord Andrew." Sparing Lana a fleeting glance, the barmaid returned her full notice to Drew as she approached. The erotic sway of her hips had Lana fidgeting and burning red hot. She spun around and stomped away before she overheard whatever salacious arrangements they were surely making.

"Our chambers have been prepared," Phoebe announced as she joined her. "Is everything all right? You look flush."

Lana nodded curtly. "I'm ready for rest is all. I think I will retire to my room until dinner."

It was taking forever for her companions to move toward the stairwell. Lana shifted her weight from foot to foot and kept her eyes trained on the stairs rather than ogle Drew and that *harlot*. As she reached the stairs, she involuntarily glanced over her shoulder and clamped her lips together.

The woman leaned close to Drew with her hand lightly resting on his chest. Her head tilted to the side as a seductive smile spread across her full lips. Lana marched the rest of the way up the stairs and fought the urge to slam the door to her room.

Twenty-five

DREW WATCHED LANA STOMP UP THE STAIRS, HIS EYES glued to her perfectly formed derriere. If he played his cards right, he would get his fill of her gorgeous body tonight.

"Lord Andrew, you are bad," Ann admonished with a laugh. All flirtations ceased. "The poor girl doesn't stand a chance."

He smiled broadly at the barmaid. "I see you received my message. Thanks for playing along."

Ann moved to a vacant table and swiped it with a wet cloth before offering him a seat. "If I were not happily married, I wouldn't dare play with fire. I prefer to avoid a serious burn."

Drew smiled warmly at the woman. "How is the lucky bugger?"

"He's as wonderful as ever." Ann lowered her voice, stealing glances toward the kitchen. "Marcy's upset you are traveling with a woman."

Marcy? He tried to conjure a face to go with the name but failed.

"She won't cause any trouble, my lord." Ann slid into the chair closest to him. "Are you going to reveal the reason you need my assistance in persuading the lady? I see you have lost none of your former allure."

Drew shrugged. Although he appreciated Ann's assistance, he saw no need to divulge details of his relationship with Lana, not that they had a relationship to discuss. The morning after he had comforted her—fighting the urge to bed her, he might add—she had greeted him as she would a stranger. Lana resisted his attempts to melt her icy exterior, and after a couple of days of rejection, he'd had enough. Drew never begged women for attention, and he wouldn't beg Lana Hillary.

Unfortunately, he couldn't walk away from her either. She held some unseen power over him, and he wanted her as he had never wanted anyone or anything. And not just in his bed. He wanted Lana sharing his table at mealtimes. He wanted her riding beside him in the park. He wanted her involved in every aspect of his life. Yet, to make that happen, he needed to burst through the wall of indifference she had erected, because she cared for him whether she wished to admit it or not.

His plan to force Lana into facing her feelings was risky, but hopefully his scheme would reap rewards. Making her jealous didn't settle well with his conscience, but Drew had run out of ideas. They would reach London on the morrow, and his chances of success would plummet once she was under her brother's protection again. Jake Hillary wouldn't allow him anywhere near her.

"Will you be around for dinner?" he asked the barmaid.

Ann stood. "I don't believe you will need additional help judging from the look on the lady's face. I best return to work. Good luck with your endeavor. She is a lovely young woman."

Drew grabbed the barmaid's hand and discreetly pressed a coin into it. "Thanks, Ann."

She frowned and opened her palm to gape at it. "I've never made a living as a trollop, Lord Andrew, and I do not intend to start."

Heat rose up his neck to the tips of his ears. "I don't wish to insult you, Ann. Would you please accept it as payment for retrieving an ale for me?"

She stared for a moment, then sighed and replaced her injured expression with one of friendliness. "Of course, my lord."

Later that evening Drew took extra care with his appearance before speeding downstairs in anticipation of being late for dinner. But when he burst into the private dining room, the space was empty. Where the hell was everyone? He dropped onto one of the spindle chairs and tapped his fingers against the wooden slat table.

He ordered a carafe of wine and waited some more. A shuffle at the doorway drew his notice and he whipped around in his eagerness to see Lana.

He frowned at his brother and sister-in-law. "Where's Miss Hillary?"

Phoebe trudged into the dining room, her womb seeming to have expanded exponentially in the last day. Her sallow complexion set off warning signals. For the first time, Drew worried she might deliver his brother's child while on the journey. Rich should have kept her at Shafer Hall as planned rather than dragging her to Town.

"Are you well, Phoebe?"

"I'm first rate, Drew. And you?" Her smile was weary, but the spark in her eye reassured him a little.

"You will make it to Town before the baby comes, won't you?"

Rich assisted as she lowered into a chair. "If the Virgin Mary could travel to Bethlehem and give birth in a stable, I can surely travel in luxury to deliver my child in my own bed. Both of you, stop fretting. I have a few weeks to go." Phoebe snatched her napkin, shook it out, and laid it across her lap. "For heaven's sake, you men act as if birthing has never been done. Yet, you both stand here."

Drew chuckled. If her spit and fire were any indications, she was quite well, albeit ill tempered. "Splendid. Then I apologize for inquiring. Where did you say Miss Hillary is this evening?"

Rich assumed the spot next to his wife. "She has chosen to take her meal in her room."

Drew scowled and sipped his wine. "Our last meal together, and she chooses to barricade herself in her room."

Phoebe shot a dirty look in his direction. "Can't say I blame her after your little performance with the barmaid."

"Pardon?" His tone of voice spoke of his offense. Of all people, he wouldn't expect Phoebe to judge him.

Rich shook his head slightly, pleading with his eyes for Drew to be quiet.

Her jaw set firmly. "*Pardon?* Was I unclear, Drew? You have ruined the poor girl and now you flaunt your dalliances. I am beyond put out with you. You deeply disappoint me."

Drew flinched. His mouth opened and closed several times. He hadn't meant for it to seem he had tossed Lana aside. He only wanted her to own up to loving him as he loved her. He had to repair things, and quickly.

He shoved from the table. The chair legs screeched along the floor in protest. "I think I'll retire early," he announced and bounded from his seat.

"Wait a moment, Drew."

He ignored his brother's call and hastened to the tavern to find Ann. She regarded him warily as he closed the distance in a few strides.

"One more favor, love."

"Yes, my lord?"

"Miss Hillary is taking her meal in her room. I want to make the delivery."

Twenty-six

LANA PACED AT THE FOOT OF THE BED, ANGER AND JEALousy shaking her to the core. She had never been so afflicted by any emotion. Yanking the covers from the bed, she threw them on the floor. Something primal propelled her, made her want to scream.

Calm down. Just calm down.

She forced slow, deep breaths, but that helped minimally. Visions of Drew with that woman drove her insane. She grabbed a pillow, placed it over her mouth, and screamed her frustration. After several good bloodcurdling screams, the tension eased a little.

A knock on her door made her jump. *Blast.* Did someone hear her screams?

"One minute, please." She glanced at the mess she had made. Embarrassed by the evidence of her tantrum, she scurried to lift the covers from the floor and tossed them on the bed.

There was another knock, louder and more insistent. Suddenly, she recalled she had ordered the delivery of her meal to the room.

"Uh, wait one more moment." She raced to remake the bed, but didn't bother with perfection. The servant would deliver her meal and be gone in a matter of a few moments, not long enough to evaluate her bed-making abilities, or lack of abilities.

Taking one more calming breath, she smoothed her skirts and opened the door.

"Egads, peach. What took you so long?"

All of Lana's anger returned when she discovered Drew in the corridor holding a tray of food. She snatched the slice of apple custard pie and smashed it into his face.

Oh, drat, drat, drat. She gasped and stumbled back a step. What had she been thinking? She had gone too far this time, assaulting a member of the nobility, and with a pie, no less.

Drew kicked the door closed before placing the tray on a side table. He wiped a dollop of pie from his chin with his index finger. "For the love of God, Lana. I told you I don't care for apples." His lopsided grin was contagious, and she chuckled in spite of the horrid circumstances.

"I-I'm sorry, my lord. I don't know what came over me." She hurried to the washbasin and saturated a cloth before carrying it to him.

He didn't accept her offering. "You do it. Hardly seems fair I should have to clean your mess."

Drew plopped into a chair and pulled Lana to stand between his legs.

"Oh." She wiggled to remove his hands from her backside but only succeeded in providing a thorough tour of her derriere. "Lord Andrew."

"Yes, Miss Hillary?"

"Kindly remove your hands from my person."

Drew dropped his hands to his knees. "My apologies, Miss Hillary. I quite forgot myself."

Lana's face heated and she swiped at the pie stuck to

his cheek. *He'd* forgotten himself. She concentrated on removing all evidence of the sweet from his face, trying her best to ignore the bulge pressing against her thigh.

"There. All clean. You may leave." She scooted away and dropped the cloth into the basin.

Drew remained seated as if she hadn't dismissed him. He glanced around the room, taking in the disheveled bedclothes. "You've been rumpling the bed without me? Now, that's not very gracious."

The scoundrel was back, and the heat in his gaze served as evidence of his desire for her.

"If memory serves, you have never suffered from a lack of willing bed partners."

Drew frowned and rubbed his chin. "True, Miss Hillary."

She gritted her teeth. Rage boiled under her surface, ready to explode again.

"Of course, there is only *one* partner who interests me, but she continually pushes me away. I've even offered for her hand, but she refuses me."

Lana busied herself with straightening the covers. "She sounds like an intelligent young woman."

"Brilliant, I'd say. 'Tis her suitor who has proven dim-witted."

Her head shot up.

"And desperate," he added. "We cannot ignore the fact the gentleman has grown desperate, especially since he and the lady reach London tomorrow. She may be forever out of his reach."

Gone was all of his teasing and bravado. His eyes locked with hers. Her hands shook and she clasped them together to hide her reaction. "H-how so, my lord?"

Drew raised himself from the chair. "Lana, I simply

wanted you to feel jealousy like I experienced when you chose Bollrud over me. I thought perhaps you would realize you desire me if someone else seemed interested."

Lana sniffed and shook her head slightly. He had no idea how badly she wanted him, but not just for a bed partner. "It is best that our association ends here. An affair would be foolhardy."

Drew advanced, his movements languid and reminiscent of the leopards prowling the Royal Menagerie. "I don't propose an affair, my sweet. I wish to marry you."

Lana stepped back, but her legs butted against the bed. "Y-you don't have to marry me. Lord Richard should tend to his own affairs."

Drew caressed her hair. "I don't give a damn about Rich. I want to be a husband to you, a father to our baby." His other hand covered her stomach.

Every nerve in her body zinged. She willed herself to be strong even as her knees turned to jelly. "W-we don't know if there is a baby."

"Then we could make one."

His mouth claimed hers, his hot lips searing and delicious. Drew's essence was wild and intoxicating, and Lana lost her ability to think clearly. She moaned as his tongue delved into her mouth and tangled with her own.

He broke the kiss, still clinging to her, their foreheads pressed together. "Peach, you keep making noises like that, and I won't last long enough to undress you."

Her eyes flew open. "Y-you want me to be quiet?"

"Hell, no. It's highly arousing." He lightly tossed her on the mattress then flipped her on her belly to loosen the fastenings down the back of her gown. Untying the straps of her chemise, he pushed the garment down as he went. "No corset," he noted. "Very nice." His lips burned a trail down her back as he nibbled her exposed skin.

After releasing the last button, Drew worked her skirts over her hips and untied her drawers in a matter of seconds. His warm hands grazed her buttocks and down the backs of her thighs as he removed them.

A cool breeze replaced his heat, and she pushed up to her elbows to look over her shoulder. Drew seemed to be feasting on the view. "Mmm, mmm, mmm," he muttered, shaking his head. "The most perfect derriere ever."

Lana gasped and her face blazed at the inappropriate compliment. She buried it in the covers to hide her mortification but gasped a second time when he nipped her cheek. "Drew."

"Yes, dear?" He kissed her other cheek before turning her to face him.

Drew removed his jacket, cravat, and shirt then towered over her, bare from the waist up. Leaning to caress her thighs, his honed torso rippled with each movement. He epitomized excellence in the male species. Why would he choose to commit to her when he would have women throwing themselves at his feet?

She dropped her eyes and crossed her hands over her chest, but he captured her wrists, holding them gently against the bed.

"No, Lana. Look at me." His hardness pressed against her core, and her gaze skittered around the room. "Do not push me away. Tell me what's wrong."

She shook her head. Drew could have any beautiful woman he wanted, as evidenced by the buxom barmaid earlier, so why would he stay faithful to her?

His guttural growl snapped her out of her contemplative state. "Lana, please don't do this to me again."

Her eyes shot to his face and his pained expression almost broke her heart in two. "I don't mean to push you away. It is just… I don't understand…"

When she didn't continue, he took a deep breath then spoke with more patience. "You don't understand what, love? You can tell me anything."

She should speak up. Once she made love to him again, she would be completely his. This was her last chance to extricate herself from Drew's grasp, although the timing was quite horrible. "I don't understand how a man as exquisite as you could forsake all others for someone like me."

The strained look slid from his face, and he dropped his head against the pillow of her breasts. His warm breath wafted across her skin as he chuckled.

"Someone like *you*?" He lifted his head, his blue eyes clouded with passion. "You mean someone with kissable rosebud lips that make me hard just looking at them?" He bent down to kiss her deep and slow, taking her breath away.

His eyes twinkled when he pulled back. What mischief had he planned? Drew released her hands to grab a fistful of her dress and chemise. He dragged the fabric of both garments lower to expose her breasts. The dress and undergarment bunched around her waist. Her nipples puckered as he blew across each of them, and her heart sped to an unnatural rate, thumping hard.

"Or perhaps you mean someone with luscious breasts begging to be lavished with attention?" His tongue lapped at her hardened tip, circling it several times before drawing her flesh into his hot, wet mouth. She arched and moaned as pleasurable heat radiated to her core. She loved it when he did that, delighted in his labored breathing when he touched her.

"They… they are not full," she disagreed, playfully goading him.

Again he pulled back to view her face with lustful eyes. "Your breasts are exactly how *I* like them."

"Oh." She shuddered as his mouth closed around her other nipple and lightly tugged. He licked and suckled until she throbbed with need.

When he had gotten his fill, he placed kisses down her chest and stomach until he reached the barrier created by her clothes. Growling his displeasure, he yanked her garments over her hips and down her legs, leaving her completely nude.

Drew lifted her ankle to his lips and licked the sensitive flesh.

"And lest I forget, your legs are divine, sweet, so long and shapely." Lana trembled as he kissed a trail along her calf then inner thigh. She jumped when his lips touched her mound of curls.

"What are you doing?" Uncertainty made her voice high-pitched and loud.

Drew knelt between her legs, slipped his hands under her buttocks, and tugged her to the edge of the bed. "I'm pleasuring you."

"But… but… *Drew*…" She lost all thought as his tongue ran along the ridges of her sex and flicked across her sensitive spot.

Oh, dear Lord in heaven. Lana allowed him to hook her knees over his shoulders and lift her hips so her heat met his mouth.

She became lost in a whirlwind of sensation unlike

anything she had ever experienced. Her body tingled in every imaginable spot. She floated on a cloud of ecstasy higher and higher and higher until she thought she might leave her body entirely.

His loving kisses to her most private place left her writhing against the counterpane. Threading her fingers through his gorgeous locks, she held him tight, fearful he might stop his exquisite torture. Her breath hitched and came harder, faster until she shattered into a million blissful pieces and cried out.

As her muscles released and she dissolved into the bed, Drew's head popped up. He grinned expectantly and she couldn't help smiling back.

"That was amazing," she conceded.

"That is just the beginning." He stood over her, gazing with adoration.

The dull ache between her legs started again as Drew unfastened his trousers and released his length. She examined him, her eyes rounding, and a shiver shook her limbs. The darkness of the carriage had kept him hidden from view their first time, but the soft glow from the fire in the grate hid nothing; not his chiseled stomach, solid thighs, nor the surprising sight of his enlarged member. Drew was beautiful, unlike anything she had been able to imagine with her limited knowledge of male anatomy.

Standing between her legs, he bumped against her center before guiding himself inside. Lana sighed, her body welcoming the divine feel of him. He caressed her inner thighs, closing his eyes and drawing in a deep breath as he slid in and out with elongated strokes. Over and over, he coaxed sensual sounds from her like a talented musician gliding his bow across the strings of his instrument.

The fiery lust in his eyes beckoned to her and even if she perished in the flames of their desire, she couldn't resist her fate. Lana surrendered all of herself—her body, soul, and heart.

"Take me," she whispered.

"Lana." He grasped her hips and pulled her flush against him, plunging deeper.

Lifting her hips, she met his every thrust. Drew grazed his thumb over her sweet spot while filling her, stoking her passion until she exploded, her body gripping his hardness and encouraging his own release. Drew threw his head back with a lustful moan and ground against her once, twice, three times.

For a long time he gripped her hips, buried deep inside her, staying connected. When he finally withdrew, he climbed on the bed to lie beside her. Gathering her into his embrace, he brushed his lips against her forehead. "How could I want anyone but you, Lana?"

Twenty-seven

LANA'S LIPS ENGROSSED DREW AS HE FED HER A SLICE OF pear while they lounged propped up against pillows holding hands. How she could be oblivious to her charms dumbfounded him, but he had learned over the years most women didn't recognize their allure. They all had something beautiful about them, but rarely did they see themselves as he did when they gazed in the mirror.

He hadn't falsely flattered Lana when he'd worshiped her body. He had always preferred her body type, slender, long-legged, nice bum, but she possessed more than physical beauty. He loved her quick wit, sincerity, and lack of inhibitions. He loved all of Lana. Drew inclined his head and kissed her jaw before sliding his mouth down her gorgeous neck.

She laughed and angled her head away, only providing better access. "Drew, I thought you wanted me to eat."

He hauled himself upright and leaned against the headboard. "You're right, I do. I cannot have you fainting on me."

Lana smirked. "My, you do think highly of your skills, Andrew."

"I didn't hear any complaints."

"No, I suppose you didn't." She squeezed his hand. "I'm not ready to return to London. Could we extend our trip another day?"

He drew her close to lay her cheek against his chest. "Would you like to stay this way forever?"

She nodded, making him smile.

"I think we could arrange something, my sweet."

Lana placed her hands on his biceps and pushed away. "Oh, I don't think that is possible, Drew. My family would eventually notice I'm missing."

Jake Hillary would be furious once he learned of Drew's courtship of his sister, but damn the man if he thought to get in his way.

He rubbed his hands together in mock delight. "I never considered how riled your brother will be over everything. Even more reason to be happy."

"You cannot say *anything* to Jake. He can never know."

"Won't he be suspicious? Granted, Hillary can be a bit slow, but even he has to know husbands tumble their wives."

Her eyes grew big and she licked her lips. "Oh, yes... Well, are we back there again?"

"Hmm, I thought I had made that part clear *before* I had you writhing on the bed with pleasure."

"The first or second time?"

The wicked twinkle in her eye had him tossing his head back with laughter. He definitely loved this woman.

"Apparently, I didn't make it as clear as I imagined." He swung his legs over the side of the bed and walked to her side then tugged her into a seated position. "I have to admit I never pictured doing this, and if I did, I am fairly certain I wasn't buck naked." His smile widened. "However, this somewhat resembles a few nightmares

I have had, but I can assure you today is more like a favorite fantasy—"

"Will you get to the point?"

Drew dropped to one knee. "Lana Hillary, I would be honored if you would become my wife."

"Drew—"

"Before you say no *again*, at least hear me out. We are perfect together, as I believe we have demonstrated the last few hours."

Lana wrinkled her nose, but a smile tugged at her lips.

"I want us to raise our child together." He placed his hand over her abdomen. Could she truly be carrying his offspring? His chest grew tight. "I want you in my bed every night. I—"

"Drew—"

He held up his hand. "Wait. *And* I—"

"If you would be quiet, I could tell you I accept."

He blinked in surprise. "Truly?"

"Truly."

"But I had sound arguments prepared." He shrugged and lifted her from the bed. She wrapped her legs around his middle and clung to him, while his hands cupped her bottom. "Rather disappointing you didn't allow me to present them."

"No arguments are required. I considered your proposal, and marriage presents the best solution. If I'm with child, it is unfair to expect the babe to be raised without a father."

He kissed her as he walked her backwards to press her back against the wall. "I had hoped for a less practical reason," he murmured, feeling himself becoming aroused again, "but if you promise to wrap these gorgeous legs around me every day, I will overlook your lack of romantic sentiment."

"I give you my promise, sir."

"I'm having that added to the vows," he warned before plundering her mouth.

❧

Lana rubbed her gritty eyes as she climbed into the carriage for the last leg of their journey. She couldn't stop gazing toward Drew and smiling, despite the amusement she detected on his brother's face.

Before, she would have been horrified if anyone even suspected what they had been doing all night, but Drew had worked some kind of magic on her. His spirit pumped through her blood, and he filled her thoughts. Their lovemaking entwined her with Drew forever. She had no hope of ever breaking away, but no desire either.

Her worries were not gone, however. What if he changed his mind once they returned to London and never offered for her? Lady Audley had warned of his ability to make a woman believe she was special, only to crush her hopes in the end. Lana bit her lower lip and glanced at his profile. Had Drew ever suggested marriage to Lady Audley?

Perhaps sensing she stared, Drew met her intense gaze. His face softened and his eyes lit. She smiled tentatively and he beamed in return. No, he loved her. She could see it in that one glance.

Her anxiety turned to her family, in particular Jake's reaction. Lana didn't relish telling her brother she had fallen in love with Drew, not when it might bring Jake pain simply being in his presence. At a minimum, everything would be awkward, at least for a while. How could it not be when her brother held a torch for Drew's former lover?

She swallowed over the lump forming in her throat. Drew had a lover before her. In fact, he'd had many. It might be awkward wherever they went. Did she really wish to cope with facing the other women?

Of course, as soon as Jake learned of their engagement, he would probably assume Drew compromised her. Surely, her brother wouldn't challenge Drew. Lana linked her fingers and tapped her hands against her bottom lip. Jake's leg wouldn't have healed yet, and he wouldn't stand a chance in a duel with Drew.

Her heart constricted. Even if he could best Drew, she would lose her love. No, she must find a way to prepare Jake for the inevitable. She would be Andrew Forest's bride, and her brother would have to live with it. Dying wasn't an option for either man in her life.

Drew leaned forward slightly and raised a questioning eyebrow. Lana likely presented a worried picture and dropped her hands to her lap, offering a reassuring smile. He drooped against the squabs again.

When they stopped a couple of hours later, Drew offered his arm and took her away from everyone where they could speak in privacy. "What's going through your mind, Lana?"

"You are sounding more and more like a woman," she teased and noticed a flush creep up his neck. "I'm thinking about home."

"Let's go to your father as soon as we arrive. If my father procures a special license, we can marry immediately."

Tightness squeezed her chest and her head spun. "I-I think we should wait, just a little while."

Drew's lips parted slightly as if contemplating her answer.

"Please, I need time to prepare my brother," she added. "I'm sure Papa will be delighted with the match, but I fear Jake's reaction."

His chin jutted forward and he wrapped her in his embrace "Your brother can go to hell. I can't be away from you. I want you now."

Lana's eyes darted around the area to reassure herself they were alone. "You are behaving like a spoilt child."

"Don't toy with me, peach." His voice held a subtle warning. "If you're having second thoughts, tell me."

She met his riveting gaze. When immersed in his adoration, her concerns receded, though they weren't gone. "I'm... I'm not. I want to be with you, too."

"Then it's settled." His seductive smile left her breathless before he lowered his lips to hers.

Lana lost any remaining willpower the moment his mouth claimed hers. She returned his kiss with passion. Every thought vanished except for how much she loved the man holding her. When Drew released her at last, her head slowly cleared again.

Drew's body had grown lax under her hands, and his frown had disappeared. "I apologize, Lana. I shouldn't speak that way about your family. Jake is an honorable chap, but I won't allow his sense of duty to keep us apart."

"You... You cannot keep doing that," she said. "It is unfair to use kisses to muddle my thinking."

He rewarded her statement with a dimpled grin. "Peach, love and war are all one."

❧

Lana had insisted the first stop be at the Forests' town home. Her friend had raised an argument, but her lack of energy translated into a brief debate. Once Lana and Drew were alone, he pulled the drapes then hauled her onto his lap to nuzzle her neck.

"Let's take a detour," he suggested.

"And go where?"

He frowned, irritated with his lack of foresight. He had no place to take her aside from his rented rooms, but they were unfit for a lady. He would have to employ men to make repairs to the town house Overton had left him.

"I'm not ready to give you up yet," he admitted, "but I have nowhere to take you."

Lana kissed the tip of his nose. "I need to return anyway, Drew."

He hugged her against him. What if he absconded with her? Closing his eyes, he breathed in her familiar scent. Parting would be a struggle, but he couldn't ruin her name. There would be damage enough if anyone spotted them together, and he didn't wish to harm her. He could as easily begin a life with her while following the proper steps, despite the agony of wanting her beside him each night.

Lana cradled his head and met his gaze. "We must speak before we arrive at Hillary House. Please listen and understand."

Drew frowned, unhappy with her tone, but he wouldn't deny her if she had need of anything.

"You cannot interrupt or distract me, because this is important."

He sighed. "Out with it, peach. I'll wait until you have finished speaking before responding."

"I love you, Drew," she said, sincerity shining in her eyes. "And I want to be your wife."

He liked the direction of the conversation thus far.

"But…"

His heart stopped beating for a split second before taking off at a gallop. Why must there be a caveat? "Continue."

"I'm worried for Jake." She held up her hand to stop his retort. "I realize he can go to the devil as far as you're concerned, but he is my brother, and *I* cannot dismiss him as easily."

"What cause would there be for upset? I intend to court you properly and offer for your hand." Jake should concentrate on *his* life. He obviously pined over someone, though Drew didn't know her identity. The last few times he had been around Jake, the man had become maudlin under the influence of spirits, which generally meant a gent experienced troubles of the heart.

"Jake is serious about his responsibility to me. He views himself as my protector, and... he warned me away from you after the Eldridge ball. He said I would get hurt if I allowed myself to get involved..."

Drew caressed her soft cheek with his knuckles. Her perfume filled him with longing. "Do you believe I want to hurt you?"

She turned her face into his palm. "I know you don't *want* to hurt me, although I am afraid it could happen in the end."

He embraced her and placed a kiss on her hair. "Lana, I'm a different man than I was before Northumberland."

She giggled. "Oh, come now, you haven't changed overmuch. Your appetite for lusty pursuits remains unabated."

"You would ask a leopard to change his spots?" he teased. "If anything, peach, my appetite has increased with you, but you are *all* I crave. You have nothing to worry about in that realm or any other."

"Either way, Jake won't believe in your transformation without proof, which brings me back to my request. Will you please postpone the audience with my father until I have spoken with Jake? I'm terrified he will call you out if he guesses what has transpired between us." Her voice broke and tears welled in her eyes. "I cannot abide losing either of you."

No matter how irksome he found Jake, Drew had no cause to harm the man, and he had no doubts Hillary would be on the losing side. But to glimpse the damage that would come to the woman he loved if he injured her brother... How could he deny her request? "Convince him soon, Lana. I won't wait forever."

She threw her arms around his neck and hugged fiercely. "Thank you."

"We shouldn't wait too long. If there is a baby on the way, we don't want to be fodder for the gossips."

Her face transformed with a somber expression. "Indeed."

Hating to see her dejected, he infused some cheer into his voice. "Enough speculation. Tell me. When will I see you again?"

She licked her lips. "I must resume my usual activities unless I wish to rouse suspicion. You wouldn't want to begin attending dinner parties and such, would you?"

Drew groaned, loath to rejoin polite society and the mindless conversations that flowed too freely at these gatherings. Yet, if attending such affairs meant seeing Lana, he would brave it. "How will I know which events you plan to attend?"

"My lady's maid will carry messages between us. But, Drew, you cannot be too familiar when we cross paths. It won't be like up north. Jake watches me much closer than Mama."

The carriage pulled up to Hillary House, and Drew took a deep breath. "If I am forbidden from stealing kisses, then you had best give me my fill." She complied with his request, but he would never get his fill of Lana.

Before she climbed from the carriage, a worry line creased her brow. "Drew, you won't... You don't plan to return to *everything* again, do you?"

He would have teased her about not wanting to rouse suspicions, but he feared she might believe him. "I'll be too busy scheming ways to get you alone, my sweet. I won't have time for frivolous pursuits."

Lana's countenance lit with a beatific smile more valuable than any winnings at the hazard table.

"Send word to me soon, Lana."

Twenty-eight

Lana experienced mixed emotions as she entered Hillary House. She had always possessed a lighter spirit upon her return when she'd been away a long while. This time, however, loneliness swept over her.

The butler stepped forward to accept her bonnet. "Welcome home, miss."

"Thank you, Hogan. Where might I find my brother?"

"I believe he has retired to his chambers."

She offered a wan smile before plodding up the marble staircase. At Jake's door, she knocked once before barging inside.

Jake perched on a wingback chair, his splinted leg propped on a stool. He barely glanced up from his book. "Lana, I have directed you to never enter my chambers without permission." Despite his gruff tone, he sported a delighted smile.

She swept across the chamber and hugged him. "Indeed, you have. And where are your toy soldiers? If I recall, you forbid me to touch those as well." Jake's greeting had been all in fun, and he returned her enthusiastic hug.

"How are you, dear brother?"

"It has been terribly dull without the hassle of keeping you from mischief."

She dropped onto an adjacent chair. "You need your own life, I fear. How much longer are you out of commission? I thought you would be healed."

Jake grimaced. "As did I. Do you tire of Mother's chaperoning? I can navigate decently with a crutch." A wry smile twisted his lips. "Has Mother secured a husband of her choosing for you, or are you destined to become a bitter spinster?"

"And why must I be bitter? I should think a spinster light of heart given she has no husband to order her about."

"Enough," he conceded, snapping his book closed. "I can't endure another heated round on this topic."

She feigned a scowl. "Because you have no leg to stand on."

"I still have one and can hop over there and whip you if need be."

She stuck out her tongue.

Jake settled against the chair with a satisfied sigh. "Do tell. Was there truly no one of interest at Irvine Castle or have you brought a gentleman up to scratch?"

"You *must* be bored to solicit gossip like a dowdy old aunt." She hesitated. Should she blurt everything and deal with his reaction? Fatigue left her reluctant, but perhaps introducing the subject could prepare him for her revelation.

"I was surprised to see Lord Andrew Forest in Northumberland. I had been under the impression he never traveled north."

Lana's eyes widened as red spread up her brother's neck.

"Did the scoundrel bother you?" he asked.

"Of course not. Why would he?"

"I should've insisted Father cancel the visit." His gaze narrowed. "Forest must have known of my injury, and he sure as hell knew I wanted him nowhere near you. He traveled north to spite me."

She balked. "How ridiculous. The gentleman has more important things to do besides scheme ways to make you miserable."

"What do you know of Forest or his habits?"

She shrugged. "Nothing, but I know you are acting paranoid."

Jake crossed his arms over his chest. "I have been acquainted with Forest since Eton. He is a manipulative reprobate and powerless to back down from a challenge."

"How is any of this relevant to his presence at Irvine Castle? And people can change, you realize."

"Forest will never change." His jaw tightened stubbornly. "He traveled north simply to prove a point. I saw him at Brook's the night I broke my leg and demanded he stay away from you."

Lana huffed. "Might I add you are completely ridiculous?"

"I should have known better than to wave a red flag in his face." A look of great intensity crossed his face. "Lana, please tell me he didn't get to you."

"Do you take me for a fool?" she managed to eke out.

Jake was wrong about Drew. He loved her. It was ludicrous even to suggest he had bedded her in order to rile Jake. "I'm retiring for the evening. The journey has left me weary."

"Understandable." A moment later, his severe expression eased into a smile. "I am pleased you're home."

"So am I," she responded automatically although she lied. The conversation with Jake illustrated the challenge she faced in choosing Drew. She wished they could go back to last night and stay there.

❧

Lana gripped her brother's arm to steady his gait as he escorted her into the theatre.

"I'm not an invalid," Jake protested, but she didn't loosen her hold. Lana fretted over his wobbling ascent of the stairs. Her brother might not be up to the task despite his claim.

Lana had been in Town almost a week and had received no word from Drew. Although this had been her request, she was disappointed he hadn't attempted contact. He could be resourceful when he chose to be. Without the reassurance of his affection, doubts wiggled their way into Lana's heart. Seeing Drew this evening would restore her confidence, or at least she hoped.

Her lady's maid had carried a message to Drew earlier, but Betsy hadn't waited for a response. Lana didn't know whether to expect his attendance or not.

Settled into their box, Lana lifted her glasses to scan the crowd. Her stomach plunged when she located the Foxhaven's empty box.

It's still early. Lana studied the theatre, noting several fellow Irvine Castle guests had also returned to Town, although most of the *ton* wouldn't return until the spring. Her family chose to reside in London year-round with the exception of a few holidays Mama enjoyed in the country. Lana lowered her glasses. Of course, her mother's holidays were simply a ruse for when she needed to convalesce. Apparently, it had fallen to the eldest son to provide safe haven when Mama suffered one of her spells.

Lana checked the Foxhaven box again, but there was still no sign of Drew.

As the lights extinguished and the first strains of music rose on the air, tears of disappointment pricked the backs of her eyes. She blinked to hold them back. Leaning toward Jake, she whispered in his ear. "I must visit the retiring room."

"At this moment?"

"Please, stay seated. I will return posthaste."

He frowned but didn't stand to escort her from the box. Lana suppressed her tears as she whisked down the hallway. Only presumptuous ninnies cried over minor disappointments. She sniffled.

"You are the worst of the ninnies," she mumbled.

She was surprised to find no attendant in the retiring room, but the silence relieved her. She didn't want to engage in the pretense of happiness when her stomach tangled into knots. Plopping in front of one of the dressing tables, she cradled her head in her hands. Unbidden thoughts of Drew invaded her thinking. She hated being ignorant of his whereabouts or what entertainments earned his attention.

The soft clicking of the door opening and closing reached her. She averted her gaze. Hopefully the lady would see to her needs and be off without paying Lana any mind.

"Alone at last, peach."

Lana spotted Drew's reflection in the mirror. His dimpled grin melted her heart. She leapt from the seat and launched herself into his arms before lavishing his entire face with enthusiastic kisses.

Drew chuckled. "And I had hoped you would have missed me a little." Her lips silenced his. He cupped her buttocks and slid his tongue into her willing mouth. Lana sensed his arousal when he pulled her against him. Vaguely, it occurred to her how recklessly they behaved. Nonetheless, she returned his kisses with vigor.

Drew gently broke the kiss but kept her secure in his arms. "This separation is killing me, Lana."

She held him tight. "I missed you, too."

"I need you."

He kissed her deeply until her thoughts scrambled. Would he make love to her here, in the theatre?

The soft click of the door and an audible gasp jerked her from her lustful stupor. She and Drew swung toward the entrance to find Lady Audley gaping in disbelief. Her bottom lip trembled as she hovered inside the gilded room, viewing their embrace. Tears washed over her cheeks, and the hurt on the other woman's face wrenched Lana's heart. She must have looked the same when she had discovered Drew with that barmaid.

Turning her back to them, the lady fumbled with the door handle.

Lana reached toward her. "Amelia, wait."

The door flew open and Amelia dashed into the hallway.

"Drew, give chase," Lana urged. "You must talk to her. Please."

He appeared to wrestle with the decision.

"Hurry while you might still catch her."

With a determined set to his jaw, Drew bolted through the doorway.

Twenty-nine

Drew caught Amelia by the elbow at the theatre entrance. Her cheeks glistened with tears, and she struggled to break free. He had never been present to witness the aftermath of his careless affairs. The destruction he'd left behind had been easy to deny. Amelia's obvious humiliation shamed him.

"Shh, Amelia." He threaded her hand through his arm and held it firmly. "Could we speak in privacy? I'm overdue for an explanation... and an apology."

Her shimmering blue eyes regarded him warily. He had never before realized how young Amelia was. He'd always considered her older given her widowhood, but there couldn't be a vast difference in age between Lana and the widow. Amelia nodded once and dabbed her tears with a handkerchief.

"Very good. We shall take my carriage. Do you have a shawl?"

"I left it in my box."

"Are you here alone?"

"I arrived with guests, but I will make my excuses."

While Amelia returned to her box, Drew ordered his carriage brought round. He kept watch for Lana, but the lobby remained deserted. When Amelia returned with her shawl and reticule, he escorted her outside before anyone discovered them together.

Drew assisted her into the carriage and gave the driver instructions before taking the seat opposite. Shadows obscured Amelia's face, but he sensed her watching him. She reminded him of a porcelain doll, feminine, innocent, and beautiful. Her outward appearance could never explain his lack of enthusiasm toward her. He simply hadn't fallen in love with her.

Now he knew his heart had belonged to Lana, even before their encounter in the Eldridge gardens. He was unapologetic over loving Lana. Yet, he had brought pain to the young woman across from him, and he regretted his actions. Perhaps for the first time in his life.

When the carriage stopped in front of Amelia's Park Lane home, Drew followed her inside. She directed him to the drawing room, settling into the role of gracious hostess.

"Would you like a drink? I have port, brandy, or scotch."

"I'll have a scotch, thank you." Drew waited for her to pour his drink and take a seat before selecting his own. He swigged the fiery liquid, welcoming its familiar warmth. Amelia demurely held her glass to her delicate lips and sipped, watching him over the rim.

Setting his drink aside, he took a deep breath. "There is much I should say to you. Words I should have spoken long ago."

She gripped her glass with both hands.

"I am profoundly sorry for the treatment I bestowed on you. I'm shamed by my selfishness."

Tears moistened her eyes again. "You never misled me, my lord. You warned our association would be fleeting, but I chose not to listen."

He winced. It had been clear from their first encounter Amelia still loved and missed her deceased husband. Yet, Drew had selfishly convinced himself she would escape an association with him unscathed. Had he even used the knowledge of her loneliness to press his cause? Shame slammed into his gut. He gulped his drink, hoping to chase away his guilt.

"I was wrong to suggest such an arrangement. You deserve to be cherished, not treated like a passing fancy."

Amelia puckered her lips, a spark of anger lighting her eyes. "What about Miss Hillary? Doesn't she deserve the same?"

Drew met her direct gaze. For once, he cared what another person thought of him. He needed Amelia to understand Lana was special, that he wasn't toying with her. "I have offered marriage."

Amelia started. "I see." She stood and wandered to the fireplace. "I wasn't privy to your betrothal."

How could he explain so this made sense? "Miss Hillary has discouraged me from speaking with her father yet."

"Indeed? Why? I'm assuming from her receptiveness this evening she is amenable."

Drew blew out a weary breath. "Lana is concerned how her brother will take the announcement. It's no surprise Jake considers me an unacceptable match."

A slight frown marred her features. "Yes, well. Mr. Hillary can be unpredictable. What will you do?"

"I'm attempting to remain patient while Lana delivers the news gently. In the interim, I will attend the usual events to be close to her."

Amelia closed her eyes and uttered a deep sigh. "You cannot know how relieved I am."

Drew furrowed his brow. Amelia's reaction puzzled

him even as it lessened some of his guilt. "Could I ask you to explain?"

A half smile graced her lips. "I had thought myself a fool for believing you capable of love, but it seems I detected something redeemable in you after all."

"I beg you not to spread such vicious rumors about my person."

She chuckled and lowered to the settee. "Your secret will be kept in the strictest confidence." She leaned forward, her smile fading. "Don't be anxious about tonight. I won't repeat what I saw. Mrs. Hillary has been kind to me since Audley's death. I have no desire to bring her grief."

Amelia's friendship with Mrs. Hillary seemed an odd match, but he appreciated her discretion, whatever the reason. "You are a good woman, Amelia. Some man will be fortunate to discover you one day."

Sadness flickered in her eyes but disappeared as quickly when she hit her hands against her knees. "Goodness. You have no home of your own, do you? Where do you plan to keep your lovely bride?"

"I have the town house in Piccadilly, but as I am sure you are aware, it isn't fit for habitation. Lord Overton let it sit vacant for the past four years."

"Your godfather, correct?"

The question passed across her face, the same one he noted any time someone spoke of his inheritance. Why would the Earl of Overton leave his fortune to Drew? Lana had been the only one with the nerve to ask him outright. Overton, the last of his line, had taken a liking to him practically from his birth, but even Drew had been surprised by the contents of the earl's will.

"Yes, my godfather's town house. A complete remodel is being undertaken."

"Well, I never thought I would see the day. Allow me to congratulate you."

He grinned like a child at Michaelmas. "It's a surprise for Miss Hillary."

Drew would love to have the home completely refurnished and decorated when he brought home his bride.

Of course, he had no interest in taking on the task, unlike Rich who insisted on having a hand in every decision when preparing Phoebe's chambers for her use. He glanced around Amelia's drawing room with an assessing eye. He hadn't noticed until that moment, but the room looked quite nice. Amelia had excellent taste.

"Lady Audley, I'm wondering if you might grant a favor? You have a beautiful home. Since the Piccadilly home requires extensive redecorating and I possess no talent in this area, would you refer me to your decorator?"

"My decorator?" she squawked. "Good heavens. I didn't employ a decorator. All of these choices were mine."

"My apologies. I meant no insult."

She waved her hand. "I will do better than a referral. Allow me to assume the task. I have grown quite bored and need something to fill my time."

He narrowed his eyes. Was this a ploy to keep him close?

Amelia appeared to be the picture of innocence with her hands folded in her lap.

"I'm unconvinced it's a good idea to involve you."

Her jovial mask slipped, revealing an underlying sadness. "Please, allow me to assist. The second anniversary of Audley's death is next month. I would be grateful to have something occupying my mind."

Amelia didn't owe him forgiveness, much less gratitude. Hell's teeth, when had he become such a tenderhearted fool? He hoped he wouldn't regret this. "I would be honored to accept your assistance, my lady."

He collected his hat. "Please forgive my abrupt exit, but I must return to the theatre before the performance ends."

※

Lana resumed her place beside Jake in the darkened theatre box.

"What delayed you?" he whispered then added, "Never mind."

His attention drifted to the stage, and she suppressed a sigh of relief. Lying to her brother didn't come easily. She had trusted Jake with all of her secrets since she was old enough to have any. In addition, Jake was perceptive. He always had been. Even when she wanted to keep things from him, he knew something was amiss, so she was grateful for the dark and the distraction of the play.

Unfortunately, Lana couldn't focus on the actors when her mind replayed the true-life drama she had just experienced. Had Drew reached Lady Audley in time to apologize? Whether he had intercepted her or not, he should occupy the Foxhaven box by now.

Lana held her glasses up again and discovered it remained empty. She tipped forward slightly and gazed at Lady Audley's box. Only one seat was empty. Lady Audley hadn't returned either. A jolt of uneasiness rattled her nerves. Had she made a mistake in sending Drew after the widow?

She laid the glasses in her lap and threaded her fingers, twisting them back and forth. She checked four more times over the next half hour, but neither Lady Audley nor Drew appeared in their respective boxes.

The widow was incredibly stunning, the most beautiful

woman Lana had ever seen. What if Drew realized he had made a mistake in ending their affair? What if the two of them were making love at this moment?

Lana's gut twisted. She shook her head to dislodge the notion. Drew wouldn't treat her that poorly. Just because he had engaged in disreputable behaviors in the past didn't mean anything. Drew had changed. Why, many reformed rakes led perfectly respectable lives, although their names escaped her at the moment.

She peeked at Jake, who didn't believe in Drew's reformation. In fact, he hadn't hesitated to discount the idea of reformation. Perhaps she had been too hasty in rejecting Jake's opinion. After all, he possessed more experience with Drew than she did.

Blast! Had she truly sent Drew after his former lover? She groaned under her breath.

Jake's forehead wrinkled in puzzlement. "Lana, are you in distress?"

She didn't trust her voice not to betray her, so she nodded.

He turned his whole body to face her, his demeanor growing more anxious. "Are you ill? Should we return to Hillary House?"

"Could we?" Her voice came out as a pitiful squeak.

He struggled to his feet, and she handed him the crutch. This time he didn't complain when she grasped his arm to help him descend the stairs. She searched the area once they reached the lobby, nearly running into a column from lack of attention to where she walked.

In the carriage, Jake broke his silence. "Your behavior is rather odd. *Are* you ill?"

"It's nothing, Jake."

"*Nothing*? You dragged me from the performance for

no reason?" Anger laced his voice and raised her hackles. "Tell me what troubles you, Lana. I'm not an imbecile."

"Everyone says the same, yet it is obvious some are mistaken given the number of imbeciles overpopulating the world."

"Lana." His voice held a subtle warning.

"I *said* it's nothing. Please, cease your badgering."

Jake glared, probably regretting his solicitous behavior a few moments ago. Lana should feel more remorse for her words. But blast it. If her brother were less stubborn, she wouldn't have to keep her love for Drew a secret. Lady Audley wouldn't have discovered them together. And *Lana* wouldn't have sent Drew away with another woman.

After a while, the tense silence began to grate on her. Jake might continue his silent treatment for days unless she gave in and supplied an answer. She crossed her arms and huffed. She hated when he punished her in such a way. His reticence often spoke louder than words.

It would take no time for her father to notice Jake's silence and begin to question them both. She loved that their father was sensitive to his surroundings, unlike their mother, but she didn't wish to undergo an interrogation.

"If you must know, I'm having *female* issues," she lied.

"Oh." She knew Jake's face burned red-hot under the mask of darkness, and she turned away with a smirk. Her brother had developed an arsenal of weapons over the years to get at what he wanted, but she had developed her own counterstrategies. And they proved effective at shifting his attention.

Thirty

LANA WOKE EARLY THE NEXT MORNING AND WANDERED to the breakfast room.

Her father lowered his newssheet. "*Bonjour, ma petite bébé.*"

"I'm not a baby anymore, Papa." Lana's reprimand was playful as she kissed his cheek.

He set the newssheet aside. "You are awake early after a night at the theatre."

Lana slipped into a chair to her father's right. A footman stepped forward to place a napkin on her lap. "I'll take eggs and toast with marmalade," she said then returned her attention to her father. "We didn't wait for the performance to end."

"I wondered if it was too soon for your brother to venture out." Lana didn't correct his assumption. "What are your plans today?"

The footman returned with a plate and placed it before her. "I'm considering a ride in the park, if a footman can be spared to accompany me."

"A ride sounds delightful, but no need to call for a servant. I'll join you."

Outside, the air had grown cooler over the last three

days, but it felt good against Lana's cheeks. Exercising her horse warmed her and eased her anxiety a little.

"I love a morning ride," she spoke aloud before flushing from her toes to the top of her head. She had echoed Drew's words from the last time they had been together. How mortifying to have such memories in her father's presence.

"Nothing beats an autumn morning," Papa agreed, unaware of her discomfort.

The last of summer's bountiful leaves had fallen from the towering trees. Several other riders also took advantage of the last bits of good weather before winter.

Her father nodded toward another rider. "Isn't that Foxhaven's son?"

As they came closer, Lana spotted Drew on the black stallion he had brought from Irvine Castle. "It is Lord Andrew, the duke's youngest."

Drew nudged his horse in their direction. She had never encountered him in the park any other morning and hadn't expected to see him today. Her heart fluttered as she smoothed the back of her hair and wet her lips. My, he looked dashing in his buckskin breeches, navy coat, and top hat. Why couldn't she be immune to him? It would make her life a lot simpler.

"Lord Andrew," her father called out.

"Mr. Hillary." Drew's gaze landed on Lana and he offered a slight smile.

"Have you been introduced to my daughter, Lana?"

"I *have* had the pleasure, sir. It's nice to see you again, Miss Hillary. I hope all has been well with you since your return to Town."

She acknowledged his greeting with a nod and polite smile.

"Would you like to join us, my lord?" her father asked.

He seemed uncharacteristically oblivious to her discomfort. She breathed in deeply and tried slowing her racing pulse.

Drew walked his horse next to hers, so that both men flanked her.

"I hear your parents will return with my wife sometime today or tomorrow. Mrs. Hillary sent word last week."

Drew raised his eyebrows. "Indeed? I would have thought my parents would travel directly to Belle Lora rather than return to Town this time of year."

"Mrs. Hillary's letter indicated your parents are performing a service for her. I suppose she preferred having companions for the remainder of the trip."

Lana attempted to hide a yawn behind her hand. Waking early after a tumultuous night was taking its toll.

Her father grinned. "I dare say this conversation is boring my daughter. I'm afraid she is difficult to entertain as of late. Apparently she found the theatre boring last evening too."

Lana's eyes widened. "Papa."

"Is that true, Miss Hillary? I found the performance quite enjoyable. In fact, I would venture to say it ended too soon."

She scowled. How enjoyable and which part?

"Lord Hollister," her father called out to the gentleman standing under a tree chatting with two other men. "If you will excuse me, I have a matter to discuss with him."

Lana halted her horse to wait for her father.

Instead of moving on as she expected, Drew stayed with her. "Were you bored at the theatre, peach? I must work on my technique."

She skewered him with a fierce glare. "Papa is correct. I don't find you entertaining in the least."

Drew rewarded her huffiness with a dimpled smile that made her melt. "What have I done to earn your disapproval today, my sweet?"

She nudged her mare forward, and Drew's horse fell into step. Simply looking at Drew could lead to her downfall, and she must be strong. Otherwise, he would have her back in his bed and too addled to remember he had left the theatre with another woman.

She lifted her nose. "How was Lady Audley when you left her this morning? Quite sated, I hope."

He laughed.

Lana gripped the reins as heat flashed through her body. "Do not laugh at my expense, sir."

The cocky smile slid from his face. "Are you serious? You think I stayed the night with Lady Audley?" He grasped her reins and halted both horses. "I returned to the theatre, but you had departed before intermission."

She wanted to slap his hand away but didn't dare draw added attention to them. "Kindly release my horse."

"Not until you tell me you don't believe I dallied with Lady Audley."

Dallied. That word tore through her, leaving her trembling. "Just because you didn't stay the night doesn't mean anything."

"Lana, you urged me to go after her. I only did as you bid and comforted her."

"B-but, I didn't want you to… to *comfort* her overmuch."

He chuckled again, his face brightening. "I should be angry with you for casting doubt on my honor, but you are adorable when you're jealous."

"I'm not jealous."

"Of course you are, peach. Just like that night at the inn."

Fury erupted in Lana. "You are a rakehell," she whispered furiously, "and I have been a fool to love you."

She tried to jerk the reins, but his grip was too tight. "But you still love me."

She grimaced and tugged sharp on the reins again, releasing them. "I... I feel all shaky and frightened when I'm with you... and giddy... as if I could sprout wings and fly over a rainbow." She sighed and shook her head. "Good heavens. I sound like a madwoman."

His eyes sparkled. "I love you too, Lana."

"Oh, Drew." She loved him to her own detriment. "Why couldn't you have left me alone from the beginning? This cannot end well."

"I'll make you happy if you will allow me."

He seemed sincere, but how could he change what he was? Lust flowed through Drew's veins. She had witnessed it firsthand, and she grappled with believing in his innocence with Lady Audley. How could she live with the worry he might be with another woman at any given moment?

"I'm unsure you are capable of making me happy."

Her heart caught in her throat when his face fell.

"I apologize for taking so long." Her father's voice startled her, and she wondered how much of their conversation he had overheard. "Thank you for keeping my daughter company, Lord Andrew."

Drew smiled, but no spark of liveliness lit his features. "It was an honor, sir. I wish you both a good day." He urged his horse forward without looking back.

Lana's father lowered his brows and observed her before glancing in Drew's direction. She held her breath as a knowing look crossed her father's face.

"Lord Andrew, might I detain you one moment?" Her father caught up to Drew, but she couldn't hear their conversation. Drew glanced in her direction, nodding several times as her father posed questions to him. Finally, he accepted her father's handshake then rode off.

"Very good," her father said when he reached her again, but he said no more.

After a few seconds of silence, curiosity was killing her. "Papa, what did you say to Lord Andrew?"

"I invited him to dine with us this evening."

"Dinner? Why would you invite him to dinner?"

"Have you another engagement this evening, my dear?"

"N-no. I am simply surprised by your desire to extend an invitation to Lord Andrew."

Lana's father tipped his hat to Lady Banner and her companion, smiling politely. "I wasn't thinking of my wishes. I believe Lord Andrew holds a *tendre* for you. If you do not return his affections, I shall send a message bowing out of the invitation."

Lana swallowed hard. "Papa, I'm uncertain it is wise for me to welcome Lord Andrew's attentions."

"Perhaps you should give him a chance. It's obvious he has a fondness for you."

She forced a laugh. "Oh, Papa, you have a wild imagination. Lord Andrew is a—how can I put this delicately? He is fond of *many* women."

"Listen to me, my dear." Her father's voice reverberated with tenderness. "Men often sow their oats when they are young, but that does not render them incapable of love when the right lady presents herself. Don't hold Forest's past against him."

Drew's present concerned her more, but she wouldn't admit this to her father, who appeared sad all of a sudden.

"Papa, what troubles you?"

Her father started and forced a smile. "I was simply woolgathering."

"You look sad."

"Sometimes I feel sad," he admitted, to Lana's surprise, "and then I remember the blessings in my life—you and your brothers. That cheers me quick enough."

He hadn't mentioned her mother.

Lana lowered her head to hide the tears gathering in her eyes. How horrid to be a witness to her parents' painful marriage. How could she be certain she wouldn't be in their position in a few years if she married Drew? Yet, the thought of losing him sent her sliding into an abyss of misery. Whether she ended their association or waited for him to do the deed, Drew had ruined her heart forever.

Thirty-one

DREW GRASPED THE BOUQUET OF FORGET-ME-NOTS AND reached for the knocker with his free hand. He knew Lana loved wildflowers, but he had been at a loss as to what to choose. Phoebe had suggested forget-me-nots, which would adequately express his love, but he'd had no idea what the flower looked like.

Fortunately, his sister-in-law had pulled out her book of botanicals. Drew had pointed to a flower he thought were forget-me-nots, but apparently, he would have been sending the wrong message. The *last* thing he wanted to convey was that Lana should beware of him.

Drew rubbed his head. Why couldn't a flower be nothing more than a flower?

The butler answered, his neutral glance taking in the bouquet and giving Drew no indication of how his offering compared to Lana's other suitors. Drew would have appreciated some sign from the servant, but he proved uncooperative in this venture. The man would make a hell of an opponent at the gaming table.

Settled in the first-floor drawing room, Drew perused the chamber filled with opulent furnishings and priceless art. He shifted the bouquet from one arm to the other, unsure of what he should do with the flowers.

How would Lana react to his presence in her home? She had been adamant about handling her family, but Mr. Hillary's invitation presented an opportunity he couldn't easily dismiss. Drew had wrestled with accepting, given Lana's doubts about him. He'd nearly fallen from his horse when Mr. Hillary, inferring that Drew held tender feelings for his daughter, extended the invitation. Despite his initial shock, he had recovered and assured Mr. Hillary nothing would keep him from dining with his family.

"What the devil are you doing here?"

Drew spun round to find Jake in the doorway. Lana's brother glowered and hobbled forward, proving his leg had not completely healed.

"I asked you what the hell you're doing here, Forest."

A bolt of anger rushed through Drew. His muscles tensed. He would love nothing more than to jerk the crutch from under the jackass and beat him with it. Wanting to please Lana, he resisted his impulse and instead offered a friendly smile. "Your father invited me to dinner."

"The hell he did."

Had Jake disliked Drew when they had attended Oxford? The man hadn't uttered a civil word to him for months.

"Shall we call a truce? For Lana's sake?"

With a reddened face and bulging eyes, Jake staggered across the room and stood so close Drew wasn't certain if he intended to draw his cork or kiss him.

"Stay away from my sister," he hissed.

"Ah, Lord Andrew, you made it."

Jake jumped, taking a wobbling step backwards. Drew reached out in the event he needed assistance, but he recovered and glowered, obviously taking offense.

Mr. Hillary senior strode into the room. "I see you have been greeted already. Jake, did you offer our guest a drink?"

Drew stepped around him. "Thank you for the kind invitation, sir." Just to needle Lana's brother, he added, "I'll take a scotch, Jake."

"Get your own damn scotch," he mumbled in reply and maneuvered to sink down into a chair with a hiss of breath escaping through his clenched teeth.

Mr. Hillary frowned at his son, a touch of color flushing his cheeks, but he didn't say anything. Moving to the sideboard, he poured the tawny liquid into three tumblers. Drew willed the churning in his gut to cease, but his body had its own thoughts.

Mr. Hillary passed a drink to Drew and his son. Jake gulped a fair bit of his before either man had a chance to lift the tumbler to their lips.

Drew sipped his drink before accepting a seat. "Sir, before your daughter joins us, I have a matter I would like to discuss. I had the honor of furthering our acquaintance at Irvine Castle, and I have grown fond of her. I would like to request permission to court her."

"Go to hell," her brother said.

"Jake, that is enough. Lord Andrew is a guest in my home. If you cannot act civilized, you may leave."

Jake banged his glass on the side table. He wore a murderous scowl. "But, Father, do you have any idea the type of scoundrel Forest is? Lana deserves better."

She did deserve better, so Drew had changed his habits. He avoided his usual haunts. The gaming hells and bawdy houses no longer held appeal. Lana lived in his thoughts at all times, and he yearned to be with her, even if it meant living a respectable life.

Drew measured his words before he spoke. "Sir, your son has good reason for protesting. My behavior up to the point of meeting your daughter could only be described as decadent, but she inspires me to be a different man."

Jake snorted before snatching his glass and draining it.

Mr. Hillary regarded Drew as if assessing his worthiness. His eyes dropped to the flowers still clutched in his hand. "What are your intentions with Lana?"

"I wish to wed her, sir."

"Over my dead body." Jake struggled to launch himself from the chair, but the slower reaction time gave Mr. Hillary a chance to speak.

"Have you gotten yourself into debt, young man? I am sure you're aware my daughter possesses a hefty dowry."

Drew's grip tightened on the tumbler. "With all due respect, sir, you may keep your money. I'm capable of caring for your daughter once we have married. She needn't bring anything to the marriage other than herself. If you wish it, the money may pass to our children."

Her father studied Drew for a long time. "I've known your family for years, Lord Andrew, but I cannot be too careful. My daughter is dear to my heart, and fortune hunters have approached me many times. Not one has cared a whit for the woman she is or spoken of her happiness. You can understand my skepticism."

"I would expect no less," he admitted and let go of his ire. Lana's father had every right to protect his daughter.

"Regarding your past, I wish you the best of luck, Lord Andrew. You have my blessing, but Lana must freely give herself in marriage. If she doesn't agree, I will not apply pressure."

❧

Lana hovered outside of the drawing room, straining to hear the men's conversation.

"The duke excels at selecting bang up prime," her father said.

Disappointment washed over her as she realized they spoke of horseflesh.

She licked her lips, held out a trembling hand, and considered claiming illness and escaping to her chambers.

Taking a deep breath and steeling herself against seeing Drew again, she entered the drawing room. "Good evening, gentlemen."

Her father and Drew quickly gained their feet while poor Jake struggled to stand.

"Papa. Jake. Lord Andrew." She greeted each with an incline of her head.

An awkward silence followed while she stared at the bouquet gripped in Drew's fist. As if snapping from a trance, he bolted forward and held out the bundle.

"Forget-me-nots, for you."

Lana accepted the flowers with a nervous giggle. Their color matched Drew's adoring eyes.

Behind her, a footman announced dinner.

Drew ignored the servant and kept his gaze on Lana. His dimpled grin sent her pulse racing. He offered his arm. "You look lovely."

A thrill jolted her like a bolt of lightning as she placed her hand in the crook of his arm. She cradled his beautiful gift in her other arm and allowed him to lead her from the room. Once out of the line of sight of Jake and her father, Drew covered her hand with his. She stifled another giggle. If they had been alone, she might have teased him about looking like a lovesick pup, but his reaction warmed her heart.

Lana lifted the flowers to her nose before reluctantly turning them over to a servant. "Place these in my bedchamber."

Behind them, Jake grunted, and she stole a look at Drew to assess his reaction. Since he appeared unaffected, in fact he seemed to be fighting a full-out grin, she allowed herself to relax.

After dinner, they retired to the drawing room. Jake took up sentry in the most comfortable chair close to the fire. Her father spoke with Drew about horses again until she thought she might die from boredom. She entertained herself by watching her brother's eyelids grow heavy until they closed completely. When his head began to bob, she couldn't help smiling.

"I hope the two of you will excuse me," her father announced, "but I think I will take up the book I was reading earlier." He moved to a different chair and reached for the book on the side table.

"Would you like to play cards, Lord Andrew?"

"It would be my pleasure." The wicked twinkle in his eye returned and lifted the burden she had carried since their conversation at the park. "I hear you know several versions of Patience. Perhaps you could teach me."

She smiled sweetly. "I'm sure you know much more than I when it comes to cards. Do you play whist?"

"I'm a bit out of practice, but I'm sure I can pick it up again."

They moved to a table away from her family, and Lana dealt the cards. Drew allowed his knee to bump against hers. Her gaze shifted to her father and then Jake, but neither paid notice of them.

"Let's make this interesting," he whispered. "If I win, you will agree to a ride in the park tomorrow."

"A ride?" Her voice sounded breathy. Blast him for affecting her so.

He winked. "I love how your mind works, peach. But I meant I would like you to accompany me in my curricle."

"Oh." Her face blazed, and she chastised herself for allowing her thoughts to drift to the inappropriate. "And what if *I* win? What's my reward?"

Drew flicked an appreciative glance over her gown. "Whatever your heart desires, Miss Hillary, I will gladly deliver."

She smiled in anticipation. "Then I shall let you know my price when I am the victor."

"I'm impressed by your confidence." His knee bumped hers again and maintained contact for a moment before he turned his attention to his cards.

Lana easily beat him every hand until she began to doubt he put forth any effort. "You let me win, didn't you? Why?"

"Curiosity over what reward you will demand, of course. Perhaps you will reveal it to me on our ride through the park?"

"But you didn't win," she protested.

"Why must either of us lose?"

Why indeed? She could argue the point, but Drew always managed to make her head as foggy as London and logic abandoned her. The man had a way of bending her to his will, or perhaps revealing what she desired all along.

"Very well, I will reveal my demands tomorrow in the park."

The next afternoon, Drew hid his smile as Lana scooted closer on the carriage seat. Her body heat warmed his hip, and his trousers began to feel crowded. He would love nothing more than to pull off the path and gather her to him, but he had declared his intentions honorable. He wouldn't go back on his word to her father.

"How long will you make me wait, Lana?"

She blinked several times. "Wait? I don't know your meaning."

"Don't be coy," he said. "You must know the suspense is killing me. You won last night. What are your demands?"

"Oh, that." She fiddled with her reticule and demurely batted her lashes.

Little coquette. He had only been teasing at Irvine Castle when he'd told her she needed practice. She had bestowed the same beguiling look on him their first meeting, and his heart had quickened. Of course, he hadn't wanted to admit the effect she had on him, not when he was accustomed to leaving women breathless. It had never been the other way around.

"Oh, that," he echoed. "To what else would I be referring?"

"I didn't know your meaning."

She pressed her lips together and remained silent until Drew couldn't stand it any longer. He pulled the curricle off the path. "Lana, must you torture me?"

She laughed. "It's not as if I must do it to live and breathe, but it is a bit fun. I don't want to tell you at the moment."

"When?"

"When you take me home. I will tell you then.

Besides, I'm still deciding." When she smiled, her face glowed and he'd never seen a more beautiful woman. "Can't we enjoy the park?"

He brushed a strand of hair from her eyes. "I cherish any time I have with you." He wanted to kiss her but knew he couldn't in the middle of Hyde Park. Instead, he picked up the reins and signaled the horses to begin walking again.

"I thought Jake was rather well-behaved last night," she commented.

"Hmm." Drew's gut tightened. He didn't care for the direction their conversation headed.

"I know he wasn't friendly, but he didn't call you out."

"Wise," Drew countered. "He heard me declare my intentions to your father. He has no reason to challenge me."

"You spoke to my father? Drew, I thought we agreed—"

"No, *you* agreed. I told you I wouldn't wait forever."

Lana studied her hands resting on her lap. "I misunderstood."

He stopped the carriage again and placed his hand on hers. When she didn't speak, he prompted her. "What did you think, Lana?"

Her eyes appeared bluer today when she held his gaze. "I thought… When you said you wouldn't wait, I thought maybe you wouldn't wait for me."

He wanted to kiss her. He needed to show her how much he loved her, how he would wait his entire lifetime for her. Yet, he didn't relish the idea of waiting another day, so he didn't care to plant the notion in her mind. "You are first in my thoughts when I wake and the last one I think about when I go to bed at night. Then you're on my mind constantly throughout the day.

I don't know how to let you go, and I don't want to live without you."

Her eyes filled with unshed tears. "When will I no longer be enough?"

"Never." His finger caressed the bare skin of her wrist, wishing he could hold her close and reassure her of his constancy. "I cannot envision a time when I won't love you, Lana."

She offered a half smile. "You still love me after the way I treated you yesterday?"

"Hmm, now that you remind me…" He squeezed her hand. "Of course I still love you, silly girl."

"Drew?"

"Yes, peach?"

"You should take me home."

The abrupt change in topic caused him to draw back. "You want me to take you home?"

She nodded.

He picked up the reins with a sigh. Neither of them spoke as he drove them back to Hillary House. Once in front of the town house, he climbed from the carriage to assist her. He escorted her to the door but stopped at the threshold, loath to let her walk away from him again.

Lana moved inside but then turned back. "Are you not following?"

"Oh, you want me to come with you?"

Her grin made his heart skip. "I won, remember. You must pay your debt."

She grasped his hand, led him into the library, and closed the double doors. Drew had a feeling he had won as well.

"I prefer to collect my winnings in kisses," she announced and wrapped her arms around his waist.

"Then I shall always let you win." He pulled her close and covered her lovely lips with his own, the scent of lily of the valley filling the air. He had missed her sweet kisses. The combination of her soft lips, supple body pressed against his, and contented sighs made him light-headed.

The stolen moment with Lana and her promises to see him again the next day preoccupied Drew's thoughts as he left Hillary House. Bounding through the front door, he collided with Jake. The man stumbled back and Drew's hand shot out to grasp his waistcoat to steady him.

"Sorry, old chap," he offered.

Jake sneered. "You're back? I thought you would have tired of my sister by now."

His fist gripped Hillary's waistcoat tighter. "Don't you dare disrespect my future wife."

"Let go of me, you prick." Lana's brother pulled away and Drew released him. "If you hurt her too, I'm going to kill you." Jake's eyes blazed with unrestrained hatred.

"I won't hurt your sister. And you have my permission to kill me if I do."

"I won't require your permission."

Drew blew out an exasperated breath. "The way I see it, we have a lot of years where we must endure each other's company, because I'm staying. Do you really want to continue this animosity?"

Jake made to move around him, but Drew stepped into his path. "Do you think Lana will go unscathed if two people she loves are at each other's throats?"

"I'm unconvinced she loves you, or that you love her."

"You are mistaken," Drew stated, staring him down. "I can appreciate your doubts, but you are dead wrong. She is the *only* woman I have ever loved."

"That makes you an even more contemptible bastard."

Drew's jaw dropped, and Jake took advantage of his shock to slip inside Hillary House.

Thirty-two

After leaving Lana, Drew met Amelia at the house in Piccadilly to allow her access so she might draw plans for the redesign. She wandered the first floor, stopping every few minutes to jot something on a sheet of foolscap while bracing it with a book. Since Drew had apologized, his guilt had lessened, but he still had an itch to escape her company. His gut bound itself into a tangle of nerves as if he betrayed Lana by being alone with Amelia, *Lady Audley*.

Drew scoffed. Everything he did was for Lana. He had no cause to feel guilt.

"It is a charming town house, Lord Andrew. I'm positive your betrothed will love it." He followed at a distance as she continued her tour. "The natural lighting in the drawing room is wonderful. I picture a pale yellow on the walls."

Drew paid little attention to what she said, his mind preoccupied with fantasies of his life here with Lana. He had never believed himself capable of love, yet here he stood in a house he wished to make a home for the one woman who had captured his heart.

Lady Audley's voice cut through his musings. "And

then," she said, sweeping her hands in a grand gesture, "a gilded mirror to the ceiling flanked by huge bouquets of peacock feathers in Ming vases."

Drew recoiled. *Feathers?*

Lady Audley's hearty laughter brought a smile to his lips. "Lord Andrew, you didn't hear a word I said. Woolgathering, I take it?"

He shrugged and grinned. "My apologies. All this discussion of color and fabrics isn't my cup of tea. I trust in your judgment. Please make whatever changes you deem appropriate."

"Are you certain you trust my choices?"

He handed her a key. "Explicitly. Just no feathers, please?"

"Agreed." She accepted his offering with a smile, appearing happy for the first time since he had met her.

Leaving Lady Audley to wander the residence and make her drawings, he left for Talliah House. As soon as he entered his father's home, he knew his family was back. Gone was the oppressive silence that had bothered him since his return. The house vibrated with liveliness as maids rushed around the ground floor carrying vases of flowers and throwing open draperies while the footmen set about building fires in the grates.

"I take it my parents are back?" he asked a passing maid.

"Yes, my lord. They arrived twenty minutes ago, and with a guest."

A guest? Drew scratched his head. Whom would his parents invite to stay with them? His father was likely livid with this additional disruption to his routine.

He went to his mother's chambers and knocked on her door.

"Enter." He swung open the door and watched as his

mother buzzed about the room directing the servants, before he walked inside. "I wish for my evening dresses to be placed in the larger wardrobe this time. My day gowns can go in the other."

"Mother, it's great to have you in Town before Easter for once."

"Oh, darling, I wish your father felt the same. He has been grumbling the whole trip." She bustled across the room, stood on her tiptoes, and kissed his cheek. "I am sure you will get your ears blistered over taking his horse. It's all he has talked about for days."

Drew returned her kiss and took a seat to watch her in action. He had missed her constant chatter. For a woman who barely reached five feet in height, and that wearing heels, she commanded with the confidence of a general. "Trish, take those gowns on the bed and have them ironed."

"Yes, Your Grace." The girl curtsied and hugged the bundle, her arms barely encircling the load. He wasn't sure she could see over the pile and hurried to open the door for her.

"Why the change of plans?" he asked once he and his mother were alone.

His mother collapsed into a chair. "Several reasons. For one, my newest grandchild will be born in a matter of weeks, and I have no intention of missing the blessed event."

Drew smothered a chuckle. He could imagine his mother attending the birth, shoving the midwife aside and shouting orders. *You, baby, we haven't got all day. It will be teatime soon, and we have the Hollisters' ball tonight.*

"Then there are preparations to be made for Gabby's coming out."

He sat up straighter. "Indeed?"

His mother's cheeks flushed pink. "I considered our conversation, and conceded your argument may have merit. I don't wish to alienate my daughter. And she behaved herself at Irvine Castle." A slight smile graced her lips. "Besides, your father has agreed he will not grant permission for her to marry until her second season, but this way we both get our wishes granted."

"A nice compromise." Of course, Gabby might not abide by the agreement.

"Your sister will need an entirely new wardrobe, so we'll visit the modiste right away. And something else..." She tapped her jaw with her index finger. "Oh, yes. A much less important reason for coming to London, but a reason all the same. Lord Philip Bollrud has returned from Northumberland as our guest."

Drew lightly shook his head. He couldn't have heard her correctly. "Bollrud, you said?"

"Yes, Lord Bollrud. He has been out of the country and has no residence in London. He intends to search for rooms to rent, but in the meantime, he will stay as our guest."

"What of Lady Dohve's residence?"

His mother frowned. "According to rumor, Lady Dohve has fallen on hard times and was forced to sell her town house, although I am uncertain if Lord Bollrud is aware of her financial hardships. He mentions nothing of offering his assistance to his aunt, but it is a private matter and Lady Dohve's pride is legendary."

Another reason to dislike the prig. If he possessed the means, he should assist his aunt, though Drew suspected the count didn't have two shillings to his name. "Haven't you extended enough hospitality in the last several weeks?"

His mother heaved a great sigh as if she had already explained herself several times. "As I have tried to tell your father, this is a favor to Susan Hillary."

"A favor? What kind of favor?"

"She is discouraged by Miss Hillary's lack of interest in securing a husband."

Drew clutched the arms of the chair until his knuckles turned white.

"Susan has promised Lord Bollrud he may have Miss Hillary's hand."

He jumped from his seat. "Pardon?"

"Darling, I'm not certain Susan is thinking clearly."

"Mother, how is it you are friends with that woman? She seems quite dotty."

Disquiet flitted across his mother's features. "Our connection goes back many years." She offered no other explanation. "Susan hasn't spoken with James, and I fear he will be in a temper when he learns of her promise. I'm afraid he will disapprove of the young man, even if Miss Hillary seems fond of him, but perhaps when he sees the two of them together at dinner tonight—"

"Bollrud is *not* marrying Miss Hillary."

His mother startled. "*Andrew*, what has gotten into you? You are bellowing like your father."

"Miss Hillary—Lana—is marrying me."

"*You?*"

"Yes, *me*. Mother, what have you done?" There was no official agreement between them to marry. What if Lana changed her mind? She had shown a preference for the dolt before Drew laid claim to her, and even though he was somewhat confident in her feelings for him, he didn't need any competition for her hand.

"Darling, how was I to know? I thought I was assisting

a friend. And you have always maintained the position you would never marry." A happy glow lit her face and she clapped her hands. "My youngest son is getting married? We'll have the grandest wedding celebration."

"Mother, could we please keep everything quiet for now?"

"I suppose we must make it through tonight's dinner first." She bit her lip. "I must rearrange the seating. I couldn't possibly expect Miss Hillary to sit beside Lord Bollrud given the circumstances."

"Lana goes by me tonight," he demanded, "and every dinner until the end of time."

His mother scoffed. "And to think you used to be my most pleasant child."

❧

Lana alighted from the carriage first when they reached Talliah House and wrapped her pelisse closer to deflect the chill from the wind.

Inside the Foxhaven town house, the butler led them to an exquisite plum drawing room draped with intricate tapestries. Lana adored the duchess's excellent taste in furnishings. She perched on the edge of a plush chair that provided a view of the doorway. Drew treaded heavily into the room with the oddest expression. She might describe him as dour, which contradicted his nature.

Lana stood as the duke and duchess entered.

"Splendid of you to come, my dear friends," Her Grace gushed. She glided to Lana's mother, lightly pecking each cheek before moving in front of Lana and gathering her in an exuberant embrace. "Miss Hillary, what a pleasure to see you again, my dear."

The woman's enthusiastic welcome made her giggle.

An observer might think them the best of friends separated for years. Speaking of friends, Lana noted Phoebe's absence.

"Do you have word of Lady Phoebe?" she asked.

The duchess spoke in low tones. "The baby may be on its way. Phoebe suffers pains on and off."

"Oh, dear. It is early still."

Drew's mother patted her hand. "I believe they miscalculated. Phoebe appears to have swallowed a small pig, not that my grandchild will be anything less than perfect."

Lana giggled again as she sought out Drew. The Forests produced gorgeous children, and with Phoebe's added beauty, the baby would be the *most* perfect in all of England.

Her Grace squeezed Lana's hand. "I await many more grandchildren, my dear."

Drew's mother knew of their association? Lana nervously licked her lips. Was she also aware Lana could be with child?

A prickle at the back of her neck alerted her to the presence of another person. Turning toward the doorway, she suppressed a gasp.

"Please forgive my late arrival." Lord Bollrud stood in the threshold, one corner of his mouth slanting upward and a gleam in his eyes.

"Oh, dear," she murmured.

❧

Drew's hand brushed discreetly over Lana's knee under the table. Happiness shone in the green depths of her eyes, mirroring his sentiment.

"Miss Hillary, what entertainments would you recommend for a gent new to Town?" Bollrud asked.

Lana tensed beneath Drew's fingertips. "I suppose that would depend on your interests, sir." She sampled her soup and offered nothing further.

A flicker of irritation crossed Bollrud's features. "And what interests *you*, Miss Hillary? We must share similar likes."

"Do you enjoy needlework, my lord?"

The man's mouth formed a thin line, but he persisted despite Lana's discouragement. "What about carriage rides? I haven't visited Hyde Park since I was a child."

"It's rather cool this time of year, but a slight chill shouldn't deter you. Solitary reflection on childhood memories can be an enlightening experience."

Drew hid his smile in his glass of burgundy. Bollrud was no match for his peach.

"There's not much activity off season," Jake said. "I fear you arrived in London too late."

Drew appreciated the emphasis on the words *too late.* Perhaps Jake was coming to accept him after all.

Bollrud threw a disgusted look at Jake before refocusing on Lana. "I am to understand theatre productions continue. Do you enjoy the theatre, Miss Hillary?"

"I prefer the companionship of a good book." Her innocent smile was most convincing. "Do you enjoy reading, sir? Perhaps the circulating libraries interest you."

He flicked his hand. "I care nothing for books."

Lana shrugged one delicate shoulder. "My apologies, but not being a gentleman, I fear my recommendations fall short. Perhaps Jake would be so kind as to offer his suggestions."

Bollrud's glower could fell a man.

Mrs. Hillary cleared her throat. "Do not be discouraged,

my lord. My daughter receives many invitations. Perhaps she will allow you to escort her on occasion."

"I would be honored." Bollrud smirked.

Drew's jaw hardened. It would be a cold day in Hades before the blackguard accompanied Lana any place.

Mr. Hillary changed the subject, albeit to one that only interested Drew's father. "How was hunting this season?"

For the remainder of dinner, the duke inundated them with tales of foxes and hounds. The only thing more tedious than hearing hunting stories was hunting itself. Drew suppressed a sigh when the women adjourned to the drawing room. He would much rather join the ladies than endure more of this insipid conversation.

He removed himself to a corner and observed Bollrud. His awkward manner suggested he didn't attend many dinner parties. When it was time to rejoin the ladies, Drew trailed at a distance, adopting Jake's slower pace.

"Who *is* that pompous prick?" Lana's brother mumbled.

"Philip Bollrud is Lady Dohve's nephew."

"Why don't I know him?" Jake frowned as if Drew held some responsibility for his lack of familiarity.

"His parents moved to Bavaria when he was a child. Bollrud only returned to England recently."

"Why doesn't he have an accent?"

Drew shrugged. "He is English and born to an English mother."

"I like him even less than I like you."

"Finally, we have discovered common ground."

Jake frowned. "At least Lana appears happy when she's in your presence." His admission seemed grudgingly given. "This Bollrud gent makes her nervous. I don't care for him at all."

He suspected Lana's brother would disapprove of

anyone courting her, but he agreed with Jake's assessment of Bollrud. "Shall we put our differences aside long enough to oust the gentleman?" Drew asked.

"I believe an alliance is prudent in this instance. Do not think, however, my opinion of you will alter."

"Of course not. Please, feel free to continue your blatant animosity as soon as we dispose of Bollrud."

Jake almost grinned. "Agreed."

Thirty-three

"HOW KIND OF YOU TO EXTEND AN INVITATION TO US this evening, Mrs. Murphy," Lana's mother greeted their hostess.

Mrs. Murphy returned her mother's false smile. "It is always a pleasure, Mrs. Hillary. Did you bring that charming young man you spoke of earlier?"

Lana did her best to hide her irritation as she waited on Jake's arm.

"She is referring to me, correct?" Jake whispered.

Lana appreciated his attempt at levity, but humor couldn't soothe her frayed nerves. Thanks to her mother, she would spend the evening attempting to avoid Lord Bollrud while Mama orchestrated enforced encounters. How she had finagled a last-minute invitation for the man stumped Lana.

"We should be so fortunate," her mother answered, "but Lord Bollrud will arrive with Her Grace."

Clearly, her mother had relied on the Duchess of Foxhaven's popularity and influence to encourage their hostess to invite Lord Bollrud.

Mama moved past their hostess to mingle with the other guests.

Mrs. Murphy clasped her hands together. "*Miss* Hillary, I hear there are exciting things happening in your life."

Lana could only imagine what her mother had told her. "I'm afraid nothing out of the ordinary. Although I must say, I find charades an exciting prospect. Thank you for the kind invitation."

Their hostess beamed. "It is our pleasure, my dear. So nice to see you up and about, Mr. Hillary."

Jake exchanged pleasantries before they joined the other guests. Lana scanned the faces for Drew but didn't see him. Fortunately, Lord Bollrud remained absent too. Was it evil to wish a mild stomach ailment might keep Bollrud away? Lana sighed. What a horrible thought. She should be ashamed of wishing an ailment upon the gentleman.

Soon the duchess's effervescent chatter carried on the air. Butterflies flittered about inside her. Drew had arrived. She craned her neck to catch a glimpse. The duchess swept into the parlor followed by Lord Bollrud, but Drew never trailed in behind his mother.

The duchess strode to Lana and gathered her in a bone-crushing hug. For such a small woman, she had the strength of Hercules. "Miss Hillary, you look lovely, dear," she murmured in Lana's ear. "Drew is running behind schedule but asked me to extend his love."

Lana sucked in a full breath to inflate her lungs when the duchess released her. "Thank you, Your Grace."

A small frown formed on her face. "We will need to address this 'Your Grace' nonsense at another time."

Lord Bollrud stepped forward to capture Lana's hand and placed a kiss on her knuckles. "Miss Hillary, what a pleasure."

She tugged her hand from his grip. "Thank you, Lord Bollrud."

Jake loomed beside her, and a spark of satisfaction warmed her belly when Bollrud backed away. Her brother could be intimidating, even with a bum leg.

"Bollrud." Jake's rumbling voice was laced with unmistakable warning. She adored her brother at this moment.

Mrs. Murphy floated around the room arranging dining partners for the promenade. Lana breathed a grateful sigh when their hostess paired her with Jake. Unfortunately, Lord Bollrud would take position on her right. As Lord Bollrud hadn't offered for her, she didn't feel comfortable broaching the topic with him. She would like to avoid wounding his pride, so she must be studious in her attempts to discourage his courtship.

Drew sauntered into the parlor and approached their hostess with a charming smile and an apology for being late. Lana's thoughts of Bollrud evaporated.

Her gaze often strayed to Drew during the dinner. He seemed mesmerized by whatever Lady Chickering told him. In fact, she wondered if the countess had hypnotized him with the way his eyes had acquired a glassed-over look.

"This soup is superb," Lord Bollrud announced beside her.

She did her best to ignore his deplorable manners, but his slurping drew more than a few horrified glances.

"What is this delicious concoction?" he asked.

Lana's stomach turned as broth dribbled down his chin. "Mulligatawny. It is an East Indian recipe." She set down her spoon, her appetite lost.

Her mother stared in dismay. Laughter bubbled inside of Lana, but she pushed it down. It would serve her mother right if Lana pretended interest in the boorish man.

The gentleman insisted on conversing with a full mouth of food throughout the meal. She provided head nods and verbal acknowledgements when he spoke but couldn't stomach looking at him. In fact, she tried blocking the entire experience.

"Splendid. I shall call tomorrow."

Lana snapped from her daze. "Tomorrow?"

"Yes, for our stroll through the park."

Blast! Had she given her consent without realizing? "Oh, tomorrow…" She pretended to contemplate her schedule. "I am afraid tomorrow is no good."

"Very well. The day after then."

"Hmm…" She could feign illness the day after, although conjuring thoughts of his eating habits might bring on an actual stomach ailment. Lana released a resigned sigh. "Very well, sir. Come by the day after tomorrow."

Better to be direct with Lord Bollrud and encourage him to seek out another. Perhaps she could suggest a nice young lady and assist with his efforts.

The guests moved to an adjoining room after dinner. A moment later, a footman approached Drew's mother, passing her a folded piece of foolscap. She perused the note then waved for Drew. A wide grin indicated she had received good tidings. Drew's dimpled smile followed his reading of the note. His head snapped up to search out Lana.

"Pheebs has given birth," he said in a low voice as he reached the spot where she and Jake stood.

Lana issued a tiny squeal. "How wonderful. The baby is all right? How is Phoebe?"

"Both are well. Mother and I must excuse ourselves from charades, I'm afraid." Drew hesitated a moment. "Would you like to accompany us?"

"Oh, do you feel that would be proper? I'm not family."

Jake nudged her. "You should go, Lana."

"But what about you? I dragged you here when you hate charades. I cannot abandon you."

"I'll manage," he said. "Go before Mother harangues you into spending more time with that dullard Bollrud."

No further prompting was required.

In the landau, the duchess prattled about the baby. "I cannot believe Richard sent no word when Phoebe began labor."

As soon as they rolled to a stop in front of the Forests' town house, Her Grace darted through the carriage door.

Drew offered a lopsided grin and closed the door against the cooler evening air. "I promise to follow Rich's example and keep Mother far away during the birthing of our babe."

Lana's heart overflowed. Good heavens. How she longed to bear Drew's children. Struggling to push aside her earlier misgivings, she exhaled. "I'm ready, Drew."

He started. "Of course, shall we go inside? Phoebe will be pleased you came."

"You misunderstand me. Do you—" She took a deep breath. "Would you still like to wed me?"

Drew jerked the curtains closed, blocking out the night, and moved to sit beside her. The dim glow of the carriage lights created a cozy sanctuary.

"Are you accepting my proposal a second time?"

She licked her lips then nodded.

"And you will not change your mind in the morning?" His teasing tone relieved her anxiety.

"That depends on how well you convince me I have made the correct decision."

"I see." Cradling her face, he met her lips. His heated fingers warmed the sensitive skin of her jaw line as his smooth lips pecked at hers. Lana dissolved against him, never wanting the kiss to end and whimpering when he stopped it.

He leaned his forehead against hers and sighed, a hint of mint jelly on his breath. "I wish I could make love to you. But I suppose we best go inside before someone searches for us."

She groaned. "When did *you* become so proper?"

"Since I promised your father I would be a proper husband." Drew gathered her against him. The contoured muscles of his chest twitched against her palm, heating her blood.

"A proper husband knows when to bed his wife."

Drew's heart beat heavily under her hand. "It has been a long time, hasn't it, peach?"

Lana didn't trust herself to speak. *Eleven days, twelve hours, forty-two minutes, and thirty seconds.*

With her sight adjusted to the dim light, she caught the naughty sparkle in his eyes before he hauled her on his lap.

"Drew." She giggled as he showered her neck and shoulders with playful kisses.

"Yes, my sweet?"

"What are you doing?"

Cupping her breast, he gently rolled her nipple between his fingers and nuzzled her neck. "Practicing being a proper husband."

"What if… we…?" She lost the thought on a sigh. Goodness, Drew knew how to rattle her mind.

"What if we are found?" he completed her thought.

"Indeed." Lana closed her eyes and leaned her head back, breathing in deeply as he nibbled her earlobe and slid his fingers into her hair.

"Do you think we should stop?"

"Probably," she murmured. "But don't you dare."

Chuckling, he tugged the bodice of her gown low and captured her nipple with his lips, wetting her chemise. The unique sensation thrilled her. Drew was unpredictable and exciting. "Lift up, peach."

Lana stood, slightly bent over to keep from hitting her head on the rooftop of the carriage, eager to engage in whatever improper behavior he had in mind. Gathering her skirts around her waist, Drew untied her drawers and smoothed his hands over her bottom as her undergarment slithered to the floor. He freed himself before seating her on his lap again, this time facing away.

"Wh-what are you doing?"

"So very inquisitive tonight, my dear." Her skirts slowly slid up her thighs as Drew bunched her silk gown in his fists. "Allow me to satisfy your curiosity."

Pushing with his knees, he spread her legs, delving his fingers into her curls. His free hand found her breast while his fingers stole inside her before swiping across that special spot that gave her pleasure.

Lana gave a throaty moan and soon rocked her hips to match his tempo, losing herself in the ecstasy of his touch. His hardened length pressed against her bottom, sending her heart into an erratic rhythm.

Drew's lips brushed the rim of her ear. "Take me inside of you, Lana."

Her eyes popped open. "How?"

Grasping her waist, he urged her to rise before pulling

her down. A shuddering sigh shook her as Drew entered her. She had no idea they could make love in such a way.

He didn't move immediately, taking a moment to nuzzle her neck, creating delicious shivers along her skin. "I've missed you, Lana."

She closed her eyes and reveled in the delightful tingles he created with his fingers. Instinctively, she tilted forward slightly and placed her hands on his knees.

Gripping her hips, Drew guided her movements, hauling her flush against him. Lana quickly mastered the lesson, feeling decidedly wicked and exhilarated.

When he withdrew, Lana uttered a cry of protest, which earned a chuckle. "We aren't finished, you little vixen. Turn around. I want to see your face when you reach your pleasure."

She maneuvered in the crowded space to straddle him, and he filled her immediately. She rocked forward, riding him, pleasuring them both. The power was heady.

"My God, you are beautiful," he said on a heavy breath.

Lana stilled. She had never felt attractive and desirable until Drew. Leaning to kiss him once again, she whispered, "I love you."

His breath hitched and his head dropped against the seat back. A few deep thrusts sent him over the edge, his husky moan signaled his release. Moments later, Lana cried out as bliss swept through her, hard, sudden, unexpectedly.

Holding her close, Drew stroked the length of her spine as her heartbeat slowed. "You've ruined me, peach." His breath blew across her ear.

She laughed and pushed away from him. "Oh, Andrew, you were ruined long before me."

"No," he replied, still running his hands along her back. "I am quite hopelessly in love now."

Thirty-four

DREW ASSISTED LANA WITH PINNING HER HAIR AND straightening her clothes.

She nibbled her bottom lip, an action he found adorable. "What will the servants think?"

He knew what they would think. The men had grown accustomed to his habits, much to his chagrin. "Don't worry, peach. They won't suspect anything other than a stolen kiss or two."

Some lies were meant to be told, especially if they protected loved ones. Drew exited the carriage and found the driver feigning sleep on his perch while the footman had wandered from his post. He would adequately reward the servants for their discretion later.

Scanning the grounds first and finding the area deserted, he reached inside to assist Lana down the steps. "Hurry," he whispered. "No one is around."

She grasped his hand tightly and scrambled from the carriage before rushing inside his brother's home. With no one lingering in the foyer, Drew ushered her to the water closet where she could freshen.

"I will wait in the drawing room, three doors down," he whispered.

Color brightened her cheeks, and she gave a brief nod before disappearing inside the water closet.

Drew sauntered toward the drawing room, wondering if he had time for a drink before Lana joined him.

"It's a boy." His father's booming voice startled him. Raising a glass in salute, his father grinned from ear to ear. "Your sisters are upstairs, and I detected a flash of skirts dashing up the stairs a while back. I assume that was your mother."

"And why are you down here?" Drew asked. "Have you seen your grandson yet?"

The duke shook his head, flushing pink. "Don't misunderstand. I am proud."

Drew moved to the sideboard to pour a celebratory scotch for himself. "You should be most concerned with how Rich interprets your absence."

"Your brother must know I'm pleased." His father paused and took a gulp of his drink. "But Richard has produced two sons already while your oldest brother hasn't even taken a wife."

Poor Luke would never hear the end of it once Drew married Lana and produced issue. Perhaps their firstborn would be a boy as well.

"Don't fret over Luke. He will marry once he finds the right match."

"He isn't even bloody looking," his father grumbled.

Drew sipped his drink to hide his smile. "Forget Luke. Today is a joyous occasion. Come upstairs to welcome the new family member. Miss Hillary will join me in a moment and then we will go up."

His father frowned. "You've brought a guest? This is highly irregular, Drew."

"No need to be high on the ropes, Father. Miss

Hillary enjoys a close friendship with Pheebs. Besides, she will be part of the family soon."

"You mean to adopt her?" His father's confused expression left him tongue-tied. If the question had come from his mother, he would have known she had asked it in jest. Yet, his father's show of humor was rare and delivered with such absence of expression, Drew never knew if he joked or not.

Finally, a smile spread across his father's face. "Your mother and I do speak, Drew. Congratulations."

Drew accepted his father's handshake and backslapping hug. "Thank you. I couldn't be more pleased."

"Your mother is fond of Miss Hillary, although I'm troubled by her relations."

"But you are friends with the Hillarys."

His father frowned. "Remaining on friendly terms is important to your mother. I simply accept her feelings on the matter."

Drew lowered his brows, trying to make sense of his father's words.

His father waved his hand. "Never mind the history. That's unimportant. You've already offered for Miss Hillary, so you must follow through with your word."

Drew rubbed his chin. His father was an odd chap at times, but another thought was foremost in his mind, so he didn't contemplate his sire for long. "Father, do you think you might be able to procure a special license?"

He flinched in response to his father's rapid change in demeanor. His fierce glare reminded Drew a lot of his brother. "What have you done, Andrew? Do not tell me you've compromised the girl."

A flash of anger heated his blood. "My relationship with Miss Hillary is none of your concern."

"You've gotten her with child, haven't you?" His father's pink complexion changed to a dark red. "How many times have I warned you about your reckless behavior? How am I to correct your mess?"

Drew clenched his teeth, furious with his father's insulting assumptions. "I don't need you to correct my mess. Can you procure the license or shall I seek help elsewhere?"

"I'll see what I can do." His father downed his drink, a glower still on his face. "I always knew with your indiscriminate bedding of wenches one day, you would make a mistake. Indeed. You're marrying the chit… I'll stand for nothing less."

Drew opened his mouth to correct his father's belief that Lana was a mistake, but she appeared in the doorway at that moment. He forced a smile, not wishing to alarm her. "Miss Hillary, there you are. Shall we offer our congratulations to Rich and Phoebe?"

He would set his father straight later, and demand an apology. His relationship with Lana was the only intelligent decision he had made in his life.

Lana stood at the threshold with uncertainty clouding her wide green eyes. Had she overheard their conversation?

Drew stepped forward with an easy smile, hoping to reassure her. He weighed the wisdom in mentioning the incident later. If she wasn't privy to his father's insults, he didn't want to upset her.

"I'll send a footman to announce our arrival," he said.

"Very good." Lana's tentative smile didn't reassure him, but he would watch her the rest of the evening for signs of distress before broaching the topic.

Several moments later, the servant rejoined them. "Please, follow me."

"I know the way." Drew held Lana's hand and pulled her up the stairs while his father followed at a slower pace.

⬦⬥⬦

Lana did her best to push her doubts aside as they neared Phoebe's chamber door. She hadn't meant to eavesdrop. Her heart squeezed. The duke had demanded Drew marry, that he'd made a mistake—their child was a mistake.

She didn't know if there was a child yet, but there would be before long if she continued to surrender to her lust. Lana was no better than Drew. Perhaps she was even worse, behaving like a trollop.

She blinked against the tears threatening to make an appearance. Drew hadn't corrected his father. Did he see her as nothing more than a huge misstep?

Stop it.

Drew had professed his love in the carriage. If a baby came a few months after they spoke their vows, he or she would simply be a beautiful addition to their family.

Drew rapped on the door before entering his brother and sister-in-law's private chambers. Phoebe sat in the middle of the rich cherry canopied bed, reclining against luxurious silk pillows, Lord Richard on one side and their firstborn, Stephan, on the other.

All Lana's concerns evaporated the moment she laid eyes on the bundle in Phoebe's arms. She could think of nothing but the miracle her friend cuddled close to her heart. The Forest women perched on the edges of the bed, cooing to the baby and expressing their wonder.

Phoebe's face glowed with happiness, and she appeared fresh, as if she had just woken from a full night's sleep, which seemed quite unfair.

She reached toward Lana. "You came."

Lana hurried to the bed to take her hand.

"Please, sit."

The two youngest girls moved aside to make room, and Drew sat beside her. The baby's dark hair stuck up from his tiny head, and sooty lashes lay against his pink skin. He resembled Lord Richard.

Gabby caressed the baby's cheek with her small finger. "Isn't he handsome? He'll grow into a proper gentleman with all of us women to guide him." From the opposite side of the bed, she shot a pointed look in Drew's direction. "Too bad all men can't boast the same advantage."

Drew rolled his eyes before turning his full attention to his newest nephew. "Good thing your father wasn't proper or you wouldn't be here," he mumbled under his breath. Phoebe must have heard, because her cheeks changed to bright red while Lord Richard beamed with pride.

"What is his name?" Lana asked, hoping to ease her friend's embarrassment with a change of topic.

"Samuel Richard. Sam," she answered.

"Stephan and Samuel; what do you think of that?" Drew asked his nephew who was snuggled against his mother's side.

"Both start with the same letter," he answered with confidence. "Sam doesn't know that yet, because he's a baby. I'll have to teach him, since I am the big brother like my papa."

Lana couldn't help but marvel at the beautiful picture they presented. Was it possible for her and Drew to be as happy?

"Would you like to hold him?" Phoebe passed the baby to Lana.

"Oh." His weight settled in her arms, as light as a cloud. And he was tiny, frighteningly small, as if one rough movement might break him. Just as she thought to hand him back, he puckered his lips, making the most heavenly mewling sounds and capturing her heart. Smiling, Lana hugged him close and gently rocked.

Before passing him to the duchess, she placed a tender kiss on his forehead. She had never guessed the joy a baby could bring. The soft glow on Drew's face made her chest swell with love.

After several more moments, Lana reluctantly bid them farewell. Drew insisted on escorting her home and dragged Gabby along to quell any possible rumors. It seemed a poor choice, but Lana wouldn't ask the duchess to leave her grandson's side.

When the carriage arrived at Hillary House, Drew frowned at Gabby. "Do you mind?"

"Why did you ask me along if you planned to ruin her anyway?" She sighed as if world-weary and covered her eyes with her hand. "Happy?"

Drew pulled Lana across the carriage and placed a brief kiss on her cheek. "Very."

❧

James Hillary sat at his desk reconciling his accounts when a servant tapped at the door. "Enter."

The butler approached his desk and leaned down to speak discreetly. "Mr. Hillary, there is a gentleman here to see you."

He tossed his quill on the desk with an exasperated sigh. Who could it be now? Andrew Forest left only thirty minutes prior. He had barely gotten anything started and here he had another interruption.

"Where is the gentleman's card?" He thought he sounded more patient than he felt.

Hogan shifted uneasily. "He doesn't appear to have one, sir. He said I'm to tell you he is Lord Bollrud, great-nephew to the Dowager Lady Dohve."

James squeezed the bridge of his nose. Perhaps he could deny him an audience, but then again, it wouldn't do to insult Foxhaven, and the man was the duke's guest. "Show him to the formal drawing room. I will join him in a moment."

Hopefully, Bollrud hadn't come for the reason he suspected. Susan had been excessive in her praise of the young man, having met him at Irvine Castle. She had hinted of his interest in Lana, but to hear his wife talk, Bollrud spent most of his time doting on *her* rather than his daughter. If the gentleman offered for his wife, he might consider giving his consent.

James grimaced, ashamed of his uncharitable thought, but living with Susan was challenging. He found it easiest to avoid her. Unfortunately, when it came to their children's welfare, he couldn't keep his distance. He must interact with her, and if things didn't go as well as she anticipated, he was to blame. In fact, he was responsible for every ill that befell his wife, and she never allowed him to forget it.

Perhaps the match with Lord Andrew would please her. Warmth infused his face. He should have already told her of Lord Andrew's offer and his acceptance.

James reached the doorway to the drawing room and studied Bollrud. He seemed unaware of James's presence as he snooped around the room, picking up objects as if weighing their worth. He stood with shoulders slumped in ill-fitted clothes. How could his wife think this buffoon would be a good husband for Lana? A title did not make him worthy of their daughter. He wouldn't allow his wife to use Lana to gain status. Lord Andrew inspired James's confidence. He believed in the young man's promise to make his daughter happy, especially after witnessing Lana's reaction to Lord Andrew at dinner the other night. She was smitten. She reminded him of the joyful little girl she once had been. How could he deny her the happiness he had lost?

He cleared his throat. "Lord Bollrud, to what do I owe this pleasure?"

Bollrud jumped and fumbled the Limoges figurine his wife cherished. James held his breath as he waited for it to crash to the floor, but the man recovered and placed it on the sideboard.

James ambled into the room. "You demonstrate an aptitude for juggling. What other talents do you keep hidden?"

Bollrud turned on his heel. "I'm here to finalize the agreement."

"Indeed? And to what agreement do you refer?"

The man sank into a chair without an invitation. "To marry your daughter, of course."

"I see. And has my daughter indicated any desire to wed you, sir?"

Bollrud frowned and rubbed his temple. "Miss Hillary... I believe she will accept me." He shook his head as if to clear cobwebs from his rarely used head. "May I be direct, Mr. Hillary?"

"By all means." The sooner he dismissed the man, the quicker he could return to his books.

"I spoke with your wife, and I am aware of your situation. Miss Hillary hasn't been receiving offers of marriage despite her obvious attractiveness. I'm here to take your daughter off your hands."

James's fists clenched at his sides, and he ground his teeth. "It is unnecessary to relieve me of my daughter's company." He spoke in clipped words.

The man blinked. "But Mrs. Hillary said—"

"My wife spoke out of turn. She is in no position to arrange anything for our daughter. Lana is my sole responsibility." He started for the door. "I'm sorry for your trouble. I will have Hogan show you out."

"If she doesn't find a husband next season, which seems doubtful since she hasn't found one in two seasons, will you put her on the shelf?" Bollrud rested his foot on his opposite knee and picked his teeth with his thumbnail. "There is no need. I'll marry her."

"So, you will rescue my daughter from a life of spinsterhood?"

The man nodded. "Exactly. We understand each other. I want to marry your daughter."

Another fortune hunter. None of them proclaimed to love his daughter. No one ever spoke of her happiness or what he could bring to the union. This was the true reason Lana remained unmarried. James had received many offers after his daughter's broken betrothal with Paddock, but not one of her suitors had struck him as sincere, until Lord Andrew.

"I'm afraid my daughter doesn't want to marry *you*, Bollrud. If you will excuse me, I have matters that require my attention." He stalked from the room without a backward glance.

Thirty-five

As Lana came down the staircase, angry voices drifted from the vestibule. Curious, she made her way toward the front of the house.

Lord Bollrud stood at the entry, his words coming out in a furious hiss. Lana couldn't decipher what he said, but his demeanor communicated everything. His face contorted into an ugly mask of fury and he advanced on her lady's maid.

Lana hurried forward. "Is there a problem?"

Her maid jumped and spun in place. Betsy's face glowed red, and she cast her eyes downward. "N-no, miss. I… uh… ran into the gentleman. Almost caused him to fall. I should watch where I'm going."

Lana blinked. Her mild-mannered maid had been arguing with a nobleman. What had Bollrud done to evoke such a strong reaction from the young woman?

Lana waved the maid from the vestibule. "You may go, Betsy."

"Yes, miss." The maid brushed past her, keeping her gaze on the floor. Perhaps she expected a scolding in private, but Lana didn't doubt the man deserved whatever sharp words Betsy had delivered after witnessing the encounter.

Yet, he was a member of the nobility, and to disrespect him would be foolish. Lana adopted a penitent stance, lowering her eyes and clasping her hands at her waist. "Please accept my apologies, my lord. Such behavior is inexcusable, and I shall speak with her immediately."

Lord Bollrud sniffed. "No need. I made myself clear to the clumsy chit."

Lana bristled. *Of all people to call another clumsy.* She'd had quite enough of his toe treading at Irvine Castle to last a lifetime, and almost couldn't believe the gentleman's gall. He was nothing like the man she had thought him to be.

"Lord Bollrud, what are you doing at Hillary House? I thought you planned to call tomorrow."

He glanced beyond her shoulder, fiddling with the hat in his hands.

She turned to see if someone stood behind her, and finding no one, she returned her attention to him.

His lips stretched into a strained smile. "I apologize, Miss Hillary. I thought we agreed upon today. Perhaps you would indulge me with a stroll in the park today after all, since I traveled all this way?"

Lana should send him away with no explanation after his ill treatment of her maid, but perhaps settling the matter would be best. He deserved the courtesy of knowing he should pursue other prospects in his search for a wife, especially since she had accepted Drew's proposal.

"Unfortunately, my lord, I must decline, but if I might request a brief word with you."

He grinned, smoothing his newly sprouted mustache with his thumb and index finger. Truly, the man was oblivious to fashion. No respectable gent sported facial hair. "Shall we move to a private area, my dear?"

Drat.

Her body quaked. Given her experience with delivering unwelcome news to a suitor, she wouldn't place herself in the same precarious position.

"I must insist on an escort, my lord, to protect against rumors."

Anger flashed in his eyes even though he produced a strained smile. "I understand, Miss Hillary. I'm sure propriety is important to you."

Lana turned away before he noticed her blush. Given her behavior with Drew, propriety must be last on her list of values. "Allow me to locate a servant."

She found a footman and instructed him to stay with her until the gentleman left the premises. Returning to the vestibule, she led Lord Bollrud to the first floor formal drawing room, which boasted uncomfortable furnishings with the hope visitors taken there wouldn't stay long.

He followed in his lumbering gait.

Before he could close the door, Lana stopped him. "Leave it open. Truly, this won't take but a moment. And you needn't bother sitting."

His expression turned to stone. "As you wish."

Lana wiped her wet palms on her skirt as her stomach churned, leaving her slightly nauseated. Even with the servant present, the situation mirrored her encounter with Paddock too closely for her comfort.

She drew in a shaky breath. "Lord Bollrud, I believe your intentions to be honorable—"

"Very honorable, Miss Hillary," he said, rushing forward.

Lana held up her hands and scooted behind a chair to create a barrier between them. "Please, my lord. I have something to say, and I would be grateful if you allowed me to finish." She bit her lip to fight against blurting everything before dashing from the room. She refused to allow her past to turn her into a skittish kitten.

"You look pale, Miss Hillary. Are you ill?"

Lana would like to jump on the excuse he offered, but then she would have to deal with him again. Better to put a stop to his courtship immediately.

She cleared her throat. "I don't wish to cause you any inconvenience, but I am unable to encourage your courtship. In fact, I must cancel our appointment for tomorrow. I'm afraid my affections lie elsewhere. Just last evening I accepted an offer of marriage, and the marriage contract is under negotiation."

He frowned, his face flushing scarlet. "You can't possibly mean Forest."

She lifted her chin. "And why *not* Lord Andrew?"

"I know men like him," he growled, baring his teeth. "Forest is nothing more than a mongrel sniffin' round a bitch in heat."

With a loud gasp, Lana's hand flew to her chest and she stumbled backwards. Never had anyone insulted her as he had. The gentleman had essentially labeled her the most insulting thing anyone could call a lady. "You should leave, sir."

The footman stepped forward to remove him from the room.

He sneered. "You are making a huge mistake. Jus' wait and see." The blackguard whipped around and stalked from the room, slamming the door as he went.

"Please make certain he leaves Hillary House."

The footman offered a quick bow and trailed him.

Lana's legs shook and she collapsed on the settee. A strong tremor wracked her body, and she hugged her arms around herself. She was uncertain how long she sat there—the clock may have chimed twice—but it seemed her shaking might never cease.

Once she recovered enough to walk, she escaped to her chambers.

Betsy was hanging pressed gowns in her wardrobe, but she stopped to stare when Lana entered. "Miss, please forgive me for upsetting the gentleman."

Lana's wobbly legs carried her to the dressing table, and she plopped into the chair. She took a fortifying breath, chiding herself for allowing her unpleasant encounter to affect her as it did. "No need for apologies, Betsy. The man is deplorable."

Her lady's maid fidgeted with her apron. "Be that as it may…" Betsy slowly returned to her task, but a moment later, turned back. "Miss Hillary, do you not welcome the lord's courtship? He appears a good choice given…" She trailed off and dropped her eyes.

Lana clenched her teeth, a surge of irritation heating her body. "You mean given I've completed a second season without an offer of marriage?"

Betsy had the decency to blush.

"I'm not so desperate as to accept Bollrud." Lana yanked pins from her hair to relieve the slight headache beginning at the base of her neck. "You may be surprised to learn I have received another offer."

Betsy balked. "Is it the duke's son? The one you sent a message?"

Despite her annoyance with her maid's impertinent questions, Lana's expression in the looking glass softened as she thought of Drew. "Lord Andrew is the one."

"Congratulations, miss." Betsy sucked her bottom lip, a pained expression creasing her brow.

"Speak up, Betsy. Something is troubling you."

"No, miss." She positioned herself behind Lana and assisted with removing the pins before picking up the brush and pulling it through her auburn locks. "Please don't think me rude, miss, but are you certain it is wise to marry Lord Andrew? I have heard the gentleman is a scoundrel. Wouldn't Lord Bollrud present a better choice?"

Lana's contentment was short-lived. She held her hand out for the brush. "You may tend to your other duties," she snapped. Her affairs didn't concern her servant, and she would not answer to her.

Her chamber door swung open, and Lana almost groaned when her mother's image reflected in the mirror.

"You never uttered a word." Her mother's statement sounded like an accusation, and she planted her hands on her slender hips. "You kept a secret from your own mother."

Lana didn't stop her toilette. She couldn't be certain what she had kept from her mother, but took a guess. "Lord Andrew and I only recently decided we would suit, Mama."

Her mother marched to the dressing table, shooting a look toward Betsy. Her lady's maid placed the last dress in the wardrobe and dashed for the door. Lana wished she could make her own escape with as little effort.

Her mother clutched Lana's hands, her demeanor grave. "Sweetheart, why didn't you tell me of Lord Andrew's courtship?"

Lana tried to slip her hands from her mother's grasp without making it too obvious. "You were in Northumberland."

Her mother captured her wrists again, holding tight, while her eyes bore into Lana's. "Tell me this is *your* choice. I must know you aren't marrying Foxhaven's son because you have to."

"Don't be silly." Lana tried to pull her hands away, but her mother's grip tightened.

"You didn't answer me. Do not marry this man because you believe you have no other choice. I made that mistake, and I have lived to regret it."

"Mama. You can't mean—"

Her mother released Lana's wrists and stepped away. "Nothing like that. Your father never touched me before we spoke our vows." She scoffed. "He was a paragon of morality."

Lana winced at the bitterness in her mother's voice. "Do you truly hate him?" She had wanted to ask this question for a long time, but now that it was out, she didn't know if she could cope with her mother's answer.

Her mother covered her mouth, and tears flooded her eyes. Swiping at them, she fluttered her lashes, as if trying to stanch their flow. She sank onto an armless Queen Anne chair and leaned against the emerald green cushion with a shuddering sigh. "I don't hate your father. Perhaps everything would be easier if I did."

Lana's stomach quivered. Hadn't she thought something similar of Drew not long ago?

Her mother's gaze locked on her again. "Lana, does Lord Andrew love you?"

She pictured his marvelous azure eyes, so expressive. Immediately, Lana's misgivings evaporated. "Yes, and I love him."

Her mother released her breath in a whoosh as if she had been holding it. "I never would have pushed that awful Lord Bollrud on you if I had known."

Indignation straightened her spine. "Lord Bollrud is

only awful if I have another option available? Someone with more prestige?"

"Now you are the silly one. I didn't realize how horrendous the man was until last night." She scrunched her face. "His manners are atrocious, darling. Did Her Grace never serve soup at Irvine Castle?"

Lana giggled in spite of her annoyance. Leave it to Mama to find soup slurping the most heinous of Bollrud's crimes. "You must have missed his dancing as well," Lana said. "If one would even call his stomping of toes dancing."

Her mother grimaced. "Another reason to scratch Bavaria from my future travel plans. All that toe smashing and noisy eating. I think I would feel out of place."

They both laughed, the tension in Lana's shoulders melting away.

Her mother folded her hands in her lap and pressed her lips together as if considering what to say. "Will you tell me about Lord Andrew?" Her voice trembled as if Lana might deny her request.

"You know him already, Mama." Lana would have liked to keep her complete adoration a secret, but her huge smile betrayed her. Then she twittered like a harebrained debutante. If she didn't feel elated, she would be disgusted with herself. "He is amazing," she finally admitted, leaning forward. "Too incredible for words."

Her mother clapped her hands and leapt from her seat. "Lana, how wonderful. Wonderful, wonderful, wonderful."

"One might think *you* are newly betrothed," Lana teased, delighted by her mother's dramatic reaction.

"I might as well be." Her mother grasped Lana's hands to encourage her to stand. "I couldn't be more excited if I *were* the bride-to-be."

She twirled Lana around the room as she had done occasionally when Lana was a young girl. They hopped the steps of a country-dance while her mother hummed a lively tune. Laughing with joy, they collapsed onto chairs to catch their breath.

Lana studied her mother, some of her happiness dissipating. This lighthearted creature she called Mama often made an appearance right before she left on one of her trips. Lana enjoyed this mother and didn't want her to go away again.

"Mama, I need you right now."

Her mother's smile faded as she gazed at Lana. A heavy silence hung in the air. "I won't go anywhere, my darling."

Thirty-six

SEATED FOUR SEATS DOWN ON THE OPPOSITE SIDE FROM Bollrud, Lana tried her best to ignore his glowers. The gentleman's barely concealed anger made her hands tremble. Her engagement should be a happy occasion, but instead of overflowing with joy, her chest was heavy. She never should have consented to extending an invitation to him. Even though he was a guest of her future in-laws, she didn't want him at her celebration.

Drew's hand brushed against hers as he reached for his water goblet, and she returned her attention to him.

"You appear to be woolgathering," he murmured. "I suppose you are thinking of ways to make amends."

Her gaze snapped up to meet his amused expression. "And for what should I make amends?"

"For the horrible lack of attention I've received over the last few days." He smiled rakishly, sending her pulse racing. "I could supply several ideas if you are short on them."

She spoke in a soft voice. "I'm never short on ideas since meeting you, Lord Andrew. You've quite inspired a side of me I didn't know existed."

He chuckled and raised his goblet in salute. Drew's

banter took her mind off Bollrud, and she found herself enjoying the rest of the meal. Yet, when her father stood to offer a toast, she watched the man's reaction. Bollrud gave no hint of distress as her father announced their engagement, and Lana allowed herself to revel in the wonder of the moment.

❧

Drew waited on the sidelines as Lana danced with her brother but claimed her as soon as Jake led her from the floor.

"This next dance belongs to me." Drew gathered her close to touch his lips to her ear. "And every set after."

Lana pressed against him for a moment before creating a less scandalous distance between them. "I've missed you."

She spoke what had been echoing in his heart all night. He breathed in deeply, filling his lungs and savoring her lily of the valley perfume. "You smell as scrumptious as always, peach." Her shivers reminded him of her response when he had placed kisses along her neck. "Is there any chance we might slip away?"

Her green eyes lit with mischief. "If only there was a way, but I'm afraid we have more eyes on us than usual since we are the guests of honor."

"True, but I had hoped to speak privately with you. Instead, I must press my case on the dance floor."

"Then please get on with it. The waltz may not be long enough as it is."

"Father has procured a special license, and I want to marry tomorrow."

Her eyes rounded. "Tomorrow?" she whispered. "That's so soon."

He brushed his finger across the soft skin of her inner wrist. "Not soon enough for me."

"I-I don't think my parents will agree."

He guided her from the floor before the dance ended. "Let's speak to them."

"No," she whispered furiously. "Wh-what if they ask the reason for our hasty decision?"

"I'll tell them I can't wait to bed you, so either allow us to marry, or I will toss you over my shoulder and run away with you, ruining your reputation."

"That isn't funny."

"And I'm not laughing, peach, at least not on the outside." He winked, bringing an attractive blush to her cheeks. "Your father knows I have waited a long time, at least by my standards. I think he will understand."

"It's not as if you waited," she grumbled, but he knew from the twinkle in her eye, she didn't mind too much.

As he steered her toward Mr. Hillary, Lana clutched his arm with both hands, her eyes wide with apprehension. "Drew, please. Not here."

He stopped and faced her. She trembled by his side, and he offered a smile meant to reassure her. "I'll wait until tomorrow to speak with your father, but I need to know if you are in agreement. I have contacted Vicar Dunlevy already, but I can send word to him if you aren't ready."

She sagged with relief and released his arm. "Thank you for understanding," she murmured.

The stab of disappointment caused him to draw in a jagged breath. How could Lana be uncertain about them still?

"Of course, Lana. Shall I retrieve two glasses of punch?"

She offered a small nod.

Drew looked at her once more before seeking out the refreshments table.

"Lord Andrew," she called, "I shall look forward to tomorrow."

His heart skipped and a huge smile spread across his face.

⁂

Jasper Hainsworth, the Earl of Norwick, stumbled along the sidewalk on his way to White's. His luck had run dry at Brook's, but perhaps a change of scenery would end his losing streak. He supposed he could skip the hazard tables all together and visit his mistress, but he had grown tired of her harping on his sloppy appearance.

He glanced down at the buttons straining to hold his rotund belly inside his overcoat, a sign of good fortune he had always thought. But perhaps he should lay off the desserts and wine. Come to think of it, maybe he should cut back on his meat consumption, too. And then there were the heaps of mashed potatoes and gravy, not to mention the chunks of bread dripping with butter. All contributed to his rather robust appearance, he supposed.

His stomach growled. The mention of food made him hungry. Perhaps he should eat a bite before returning to the gaming tables and, with his winnings, he could purchase a man's stays. Yes, that sounded like a much better idea.

He walked a few more weaving paces and recognized he was close to Madam Montgomery's. He hadn't visited in a while, not since that wicked little sprite with straw-colored hair giggled at him. How could he perform after such taunting? And when she had regarded him with pity and offered to return his money? That was more humiliating than being lobcocked to begin with. He would never step foot in that establishment again.

A carriage pulled up to the curb, sporting the Foxhaven crest on the door. There was that bugger, Forest. Jasper hadn't seen his friend since Northumberland, despite the messages he had sent. Forest had been absent from the clubs although everyone knew he'd returned to Town weeks ago.

It was also common knowledge Forest was diddling the widow Audley, and his prolonged preoccupation had Jasper worried. He had a lot of money riding on the outcome of the affair, but he could breathe easier since it appeared he wouldn't lose the bet after all.

He hurried to reach Forest as his friend exited the carriage, but Jasper lost his footing and careened into him.

"Watch yer step, you fool."

Jasper drew back and blinked, trying to focus his blurry vision. "Forest, what happened to you? You look like hell."

"What are you mumbling, you drunken idiot?"

Jasper blinked, unsuccessfully clearing his vision. He could see he'd made a mistake, however. The man, more akin to a street thug, couldn't be his friend. Jasper examined the crest again then he returned his attention to the man's face. "You're not Andrew Forest, are you?"

The man sneered. "Are you blind as well as cork brained?"

Forest had never insulted him in such a manner. Clearly, this man was... Jasper had trouble completing his thought, but he knew the coach belonged to the Duke of Foxhaven.

He craned his neck to see inside the carriage. "Have you abducted the duke and duchess?"

The man bumped him as he tried to pass. Jasper

stepped aside, but they moved in the same direction. This happened a few times until it appeared they engaged in a clumsy dance of sorts.

"I should have known you weren't Forest," Jasper complained. "Ever since he took up with that widow lady, no one sees him anymore."

The man froze in place. "What widow lady?"

"I felt certain it was a sure thing. Now, it appears I'll lose the bet."

"Tell me what you're talking about," the man shouted and Jasper drew back. The burly fellow spoke again, but in a softer tone. Jasper appreciated his lowered voice since he was developing a headache. "I beg your pardon. Please tell me what widow you mean."

"Well, Lady Audley of course. I placed my bet at White's. Forest is only diddling the lady again, but a few fools want to part with their money and insist he plans to marry her." He leaned close to the man. "Don't take that bet, sir. I've known Forest for years. He'll never get leg-shackled. He would chew his own limb off first."

The man wrinkled his nose in disgust and moved away. "I think you may be right, sir. Maybe wedding bells aren't in his future."

Jasper poked his finger against the man's chest. "You may count on it." Squinting, he tried to make out the man's identity. "Who are you again?"

"No one important." The man stalked toward Madam Montgomery's, disappearing through the front doors.

Thirty-seven

LANA STRETCHED IN BED AND SMILED AT THE CEILING, not seeing the lengthening rays of late morning sunlight so much as picturing Drew's glorious mane. She couldn't wait to run her fingers through his unruly locks upon waking every morning once they married, if he ever allowed her to sleep. A giggle bubbled from her chest.

Today she would become Drew's bride, forever entwined, and forever loved. *And well loved.* Her scandalous thoughts made her blush. With no wedding breakfast or other celebration to attend, nothing would delay consummation of their marriage. No doubt, this was Drew's plan. She appreciated a man with a sharp mind.

There was a light knock. "Enter."

A chambermaid bustled inside. "Pardon me, miss, but there is a gentleman requesting an audience with you. He says it is urgent. A Lord—"

Lana squealed and threw the counterpane aside. "Tell him I'll be there in a moment."

"Very good, miss. He waits in the blue drawing room." The girl swept from her chambers as quickly as she had entered.

Lana yanked the bell pull to summon Betsy. Why,

Drew had arrived earlier than she had expected. She should've started her toilette already. Her lady's maid came in to the room.

"I need your help dressing. I have a visitor."

"So early?"

Lana smiled in response and lifted her arms, waiting for her maid to remove her nightrail. They raced through her preparations. Lana caught her reflection in the mirror. Her cheeks boasted a rosy glow. Pinching them was unnecessary. She licked her lips before dashing for the door.

She skipped to the drawing room and pulled up short. "Lord Bollrud, what are you doing here?"

She backed toward the doorway, but he dashed between her and the door, blocking her path.

"I have a matter of importance to discuss with you, Miss Hillary."

She offered a stern look to hide her uneasiness. "I'm sure nothing you have to say is so important it cannot wait until a decent hour."

He closed the door and leaned against it. "It is of vital importance, I assure you. Please, Miss Hillary, hear me out."

She crossed her arms and tapped the toe of her slipper against the Oriental carpet to mask her quivering limbs. "Do make it quick. I have much to do today."

Lord Bollrud's eyes narrowed for a fraction of a moment before his face reverted to a neutral expression. "I'm afraid I discovered something distressing last night."

Lana frowned. What made the gentleman believe any news affecting him would interest her?

"I crossed paths with a good friend of Forest's." He took a step forward. "I'm sorry to be the bearer of bad tidings, Miss Hillary, but your betrothed is involved with another woman. He is playing you for a fool."

Lying about Drew having an affair was low. "Hmm, and did the gentleman indicate which female is the object of my betrothed's affections?"

"It brings me no pleasure to tell you this, my dear. Please, believe me." He moved closer again and spoke in a soft voice. "It's Lady Audley. And this isn't their first liaison."

Lana's eyes widened. "W-why would the gentleman say that about Lady Audley?"

Lord Bollrud captured her hands and squeezed. "Everyone is saying the same. There is even a bet on the books at the gentlemen's clubs. Some are betting Forest will marry the lady while others believe it is nothing more than a dalliance. Either way, everyone is certain of their involvement."

She jerked her hands from his grip. "There is no proof in what you've said. Those men are nothing but drunken imbeciles who will place a bet on anything."

"I thought the same, so I did some investigating this morning. I learned Forest owns a town house in Piccadilly where he has been meeting his lover every day for the past few weeks."

"A town house?" Drew had led her to believe the house was uninhabitable. Why would he lie? Did he intend to keep a place without her knowledge? A place for clandestine meetings? She shook her head. No, this was a ridiculous rumor.

"My darling." Lord Bollrud swept her against him, capturing her chin between his thumb and index finger while his other arm encircled her back. His rough finger scraped against her sensitive skin. "I would never abuse you as Forest has, my love."

"Let me go." Lana pushed against his chest with both hands, struggling to break his hold. "Let me go at once, or I'll scream."

She almost fell when he released her. "Forgive me, Miss Hillary. I... I became... overwhelmed, by my passion... for you." He rubbed his face with both hands. "Bloody hell."

Lana hugged herself, unable to control her shaking. "Lord Bollrud, I think it is best you leave and never come back." When he moved aside, she raced past him to wrench open the door and run.

Once Lana had escaped, she paused outside of Jake's chamber door. Uncertainty was a difficult place to be. Should she ask about the bet? Surely, the odious Lord Bollrud made up the entire story in a feeble attempt to win her.

Jake would be able to calm her fears. She raised her hand to knock on her brother's door just as it flew open. "Oh."

Jake jumped back. "Blast it, Lana. The only time you actually knock before entering and you frighten me."

Lana's cheeks warmed. "It's still morning. I couldn't be sure if you were decent."

He scrutinized her face, before stepping aside. "Would you like to come inside? I was going down for breakfast, but I can wait."

"Thank you." She wrung her hands and walked into his chamber to sit on the edge of one of his chairs.

He followed and sat too, watching her quietly for a long time. "Won't you tell me what is troubling you?"

She released a pent-up breath. "I'm sure it is nothing, but..."

Jake's brows drew together with worry, but he didn't

rush her. In fact, he exhibited great patience and didn't speak at all.

"I had a visitor this morning. Bollrud."

Her brother's jaw clenched. "What did *he* want?"

"Jake, I need to ask you something. And I want you to be honest. I believe Bollrud is lying, but if he's not..."

"Tell me what he said. I'm always honest with you."

"I know you are." And he always had been. Yet, part of her feared he might fly off in a rage. "You have to promise to remain calm when I tell you."

His eyes narrowed. "Now I *know* it's something bad. I can't make any such promise."

"Then I cannot confide in you," she replied and stood.

"Wait, sit down." He reached out and grabbed her hand. "I promise to do my best. I *promise*."

Lana sank back onto the Chippendale chair and cleared her throat. "Bollrud said he crossed paths with one of Drew's friends last night. He said there is a bet on the books at the gentlemen's clubs." She swallowed, embarrassed to say the words. "They are betting on whether or not Drew will marry or if he is just dallying again."

He scoffed. "Well, the fools will know soon enough. Word of your betrothal is likely making the rounds this morning."

"Jake, they don't mean *me*."

"Then who? Forest has been here most evenings for near a month."

Perhaps this was a bad idea. "Indeed, Bollrud must be lying."

The scowl on Jake's face showed his displeasure. "Lana Hillary, tell me whose name is linked with Forest."

"It's Amelia, Lady Audley." She winced as soon as the name left her lips.

"Pardon?" He sat up straight, his knuckles turning white from gripping the arms of the chair. "What proof do they have?"

"It is rumored she and Drew have been meeting daily, at Drew's house. He told me it was unlivable." Her stomach churned until she feared she might be sick. "You haven't heard anything?"

"I haven't been to the clubs in a while, not since my injury. But I'll get to the bottom of this rumor." He launched from his chair and stalked from the room.

"Wait." Lana scrambled after him. "Don't do anything foolish."

"I'm doing something I should have done long ago," he snapped. He moved faster with his leg healed, but his size alone wouldn't have allowed her to stop him anyway. He stormed from the house and left her with her heart in her throat.

❧

Jake marched to his destination, ignoring the increasing ache in his leg. When he reached the town house, his anger hadn't dissipated in the least. He reached the door and pounded on it with his fist. He banged on it a second time before the door swung open to reveal a very displeased butler.

"Sir, do you have any idea of the time?"

Jake pushed past the man, knowing he could be intimidating. "I'm a personal friend."

"Bradford, what is the commotion?" Amelia's soft voice made his heart skip a beat.

Jake swallowed hard. Amelia's golden tresses tumbled around her shoulders and bounced as she moved. He had never seen her hair down, and he winced as his groin tightened painfully.

The butler made to leave the room. "I'm sorry, my lady. I shall have him tossed out immediately."

"That is all right, Bradford." Amelia, his lovely Mia, frowned. "Mr. Hillary, what brings you by this morning?"

"I'm sorry to barge in like this, my lady. Perhaps I should come back later."

"Don't be ridiculous. You are here, so come in. You may leave us, Bradford."

The butler hesitated as if weighing the wisdom in leaving his mistress alone, but he eventually followed her orders.

She waved her arm toward another part of the house. "I was having breakfast. Would you care to join me?"

"No, I don't wish to be a bother, my lady."

She smiled sadly. "Jake, you may drop the formality. It's not as if we are mere acquaintances. Please, join me."

Her blasé attitude cut him deeply, but he followed her to the breakfast room, trying not to stare at her curvaceous figure but having little success. God, he still wanted her after everything. He couldn't stomach the thought of her with Forest, nor any man besides himself.

"What are you about, Amelia?" His voice sounded gruff and accusatory.

She whipped around with wide eyes, her mouth formed into a perfect O. Her pink lips begged for kisses, but he smothered his impulse.

He forced his gaze away from her. "Have you no respect for your husband's memory? Running about like a wanton woman."

Amelia fell back a step. "A wanton?"

Jake reached out to steady her when she wobbled. She recovered and slapped his hands away.

A fresh wave of anger swept over him. "How long before you allowed Forest to bed you?" he asked. How long had Jake been in Sussex?

"How dare you question my morality?"

"Tell me the rumors are untrue, Amelia. Please, tell me you aren't involved with Forest again."

Her hands settled on her hips, sparks shooting from her large blue eyes. "I don't owe *you* any explanations. You are not my husband."

Her argument knocked the wind from his sails, and he heaved a great sigh. "Indeed." He wasn't her husband, nor did she wish him to be. She hadn't even extended the courtesy of answering his letters from Sussex. "I'm sorry to have bothered you. I'll take my leave."

He limped toward the entrance, his leg bothering him even more now that his anger was subsiding.

"What rumors?" Her quiet voice surprised Jake. He hadn't realized she had followed.

He turned to study her countenance as he delivered the news. "People are talking. They say you and Forest are engaged in an affair. You've been meeting daily at his town house in Piccadilly."

Her eyes widened momentarily before glistening with unshed tears. "I suppose everyone believes the worst about me. You obviously do."

His heart lurched at the sight of her crying. "I don't want to believe anything untoward about you, Mia."

"It isn't true." She brushed away her tears. "At least not as the gossips are insinuating. The home is a surprise for Lana, a wedding gift. I'm simply overseeing the remodel. I needed something to occupy my mind."

Jake cringed. He'd made a complete cake of himself. "I see."

"You must know I would never do anything to hurt your sister. I know how you care for her."

"Well, my apologies. Sorry to have disturbed you."

He gripped his hat in his hand and hurried through the open front door.

"Jake, wait."

He didn't stop. He was too humiliated to look back.

Thirty-eight

DREW BOUNDED FROM THE CARRIAGE AS SOON AS IT stopped in front of Hillary House. He only needed to convince Lana's father to allow them to marry today, and she would be his by the afternoon.

Inside, he handed his card to the butler and requested an audience with Lana first. He wanted to approach her father with her by his side.

The butler showed him to the drawing room, and he positioned himself where he could spot her as she approached the room. The clicking of heels moving in his direction made him smile with anticipation, but one glimpse of Lana's somber expression caused it to fade.

"Peach, is something wrong?"

She hesitated inside the door, looking as if she might turn and run. Instead, she dashed across the room and threw herself into his arms. "Oh, Drew. I was so frightened."

Her cheek nuzzled against his chest, and his arms tightened around her. He sensed her heart pounding, causing his own to race in alarm. "What frightened you?"

"I thought Jake might have found you. He left in a temper. I was afraid…"

Trying to soothe her, Drew rubbed his hands along

her back and kissed the top of her head, drawing in her sweet scent. "Everything is all right. I'm certain he'll calm once he has had time—" He held her at arm's length. "Pardon? Your brother is angry with *me*?"

Lana dropped her arms from his waist and licked her lips. "Drew, I must ask you something unpleasant."

He propped his forearm on the chair back, curious as to what she might ask and clueless as to the nature. "Ask whatever you'd like."

The worry line between her brows softened. "Is it true about the property in Piccadilly?"

He blew out noisy breath. "Who ruined the surprise?"

"Surprise?"

"The place was in shambles. I couldn't ask you to reside in bachelor quarters or with my kin. A gentleman should provide for his wife."

"I don't understand. Is the house in Piccadilly inhabitable or not?"

"Only halfway, I'm afraid. I had hoped to have the remodel completed before our wedding, but I don't wish to wait any longer."

She collapsed in a chair like a rag doll. "But rumor has it you meet Lady Audley there daily. Drew, please tell me if you still have feelings for her."

"I don't…" He went to Lana, lifted her, and then sat in the chair with her on his lap. "As depraved as I know this will make me sound, I've never had tender feelings for anyone except you. I would do nothing to jeopardize what we have."

"You haven't been meeting Lady Audley?"

Drew dropped his head back against the chair and groaned. "Not in the way you think. Lady Audley has been in charge of remodeling the residence. I had no idea it would spark these rumors, although I should have anticipated it." He frowned, unhappy with his own stupidity. "It's been two years since her husband died. Lady Audley confesses this is a difficult time of the year." Drew held her gaze. "Lana, I'm sorry. I wanted to pay her a kindness, to make peace with my past. I never meant to cast a shadow over us."

Lana's wide smile eased his worries. "So, it's untrue. You aren't *involved* with her."

Chuckling, he kissed her cheek. "I'm only involved with you, and I plan to keep it that way until my last breath."

"Oh, Drew." She tossed her arms around his neck. "I knew the rumors had to be false."

Thank the heavens he hadn't ruined everything with his foolishness. "Will you still marry me today?"

"Nothing could stop me."

At first, Lana's mother protested the sudden nuptials based on Lana having no wedding gown or celebratory breakfast planned. Yet, when Drew promised to buy Lana any gown she desired to wear to any celebration her mother chose to host in the near future, she had given her hearty blessings. Papa hadn't been resistant in the least, and Lana was grateful neither of them questioned their haste to join in matrimony. She hadn't wanted to disappoint them by revealing the necessity of a rushed wedding, but it seemed quite necessary given her cycle was a few days late. Her stomach somersaulted when she considered motherhood.

"I'll be back at four o'clock with Vicar Dunlevy." Drew dropped a chaste kiss on her cheek while her parents pretended not to notice.

Lana escorted him to the front door.

Drew flashed a roguish grin, looking for all the world as if he wished to devour her on the spot. "You haven't forgotten your special vow, have you, my sweet?"

Her cheeks flamed as she recalled his wicked teasing about adding a promise to wrap her legs around him every day to her wedding vows. "Perhaps the nature of the agreement between you and my legs should remain a secret."

Drew planted a less virtuous kiss on her lips. At this moment, she would promise him just about anything he desired.

She eased from his embrace. "You best leave so I have time to make myself beautiful."

"You require no time at all, my sweet."

With arms linked, they approached the front doors.

Jake barreled inside, nearly knocking them over in his rush. She held her breath, silently begging him not to cause a scene.

"Forest." Her brother nodded before handing his hat and cane to Hogan as if nothing was amiss.

"Hillary." Drew raised his eyebrows in askance.

Lana shrugged.

He lifted her hand to his lips and pressed his lips to her glove. "Until later, Miss Hillary."

Once she and Jake were alone, he cleared his throat. "Later? What exactly does the scoundrel have planned for later?"

"We're exchanging vows. Today." She studied her brother's blank expression. "Where have you been?"

He evaded eye contact. "I needed to speak with someone. But you needn't worry about Forest. The rumors are untrue, but I suppose you already discovered the truth."

"Drew denied any involvement with Lady Audley, but I'm glad for the confirmation."

"Happy to be of service," he mumbled as he headed toward the staircase.

⁓

Lana chattered as Betsy arranged her hair. She couldn't recall ever being this excited about anything, except maybe Michaelmas when she was a child.

"And I learned today he is remodeling the town house in Piccadilly for us." She grabbed her maid's hand and squeezed. "I never thought I would see the day I'd become a bride."

Her maid offered a half smile. "I knew it would happen, miss." She twisted Lana's hair and pinned it up. "Perhaps you would like a glass of wine to calm your nerves?"

"My nerves?" Lana giggled. "I'm not nervous. This is me *ecstatic*, Betsy. I know I'm usually a stick-in-the-mud when you're preparing me to go out, so I don't blame you for being confused by my current demeanor."

Her maid placed her hands on Lana's shoulders and leaned down to view her face in the mirror. "You are glowing, miss. I can clearly see your excitement. Maybe you would like tea and biscuits instead. It's best to have something in your stomach. You wouldn't want to faint at your wedding like my cousin did."

Lana pressed her lips together and searched her memory for what she had eaten that day. She couldn't recall having had anything, but she doubted she could sit still long enough to eat. "Perhaps some tea, Betsy. Thank you."

"Of course, miss. I will inform the kitchen staff."

While Betsy was out of the room, Lana surveyed her

bedchamber. She would miss her home. Yet, the time had come to move forward in her life. She welcomed the change with open arms.

Finally, her maid returned with a tea tray loaded with a white tea pot and plate of lemon biscuits.

"Why didn't you have the footman carry it up?"

Betsy shrugged. "Everyone seems busy with preparations for this afternoon. Mrs. Gibbons is buzzing around the kitchen shouting orders. It seems a feast is to be served after the vows."

Betsy held out the tray and Lana plucked a biscuit from the porcelain plate before she placed the refreshments on a side table then poured a cup of tea and handed it to Lana. Taking a sip, Lana wrinkled her nose. "It's strong. I believe it steeped too long."

"Should I add more sugar and cream?"

"Please."

Betsy doctored her tea, then handed it back, her hand shaking and causing the china to clatter. "I hope that is better."

"Why don't you have some, too?"

Her maid shook her head. "Oh, no, Miss Hillary. I have too many tasks to complete still. I have yet to pack your gowns and I haven't finished laundering your undergarments. I must see if they have dried on the line downstairs." Her maid dashed from the room.

Lana shook her head and chuckled. Maybe *Betsy* could benefit from a glass of wine to settle *her* nerves. Poor girl. Lana had never seen her as frantic. It must be disconcerting for her maid to contemplate leaving Hillary House for good.

Lana sipped her tea and found the bitter taste less noticeable. After finishing her cup, she drank a second one, but decided against another biscuit. She didn't wish to spoil her appetite before dinner.

With a contented sigh, Lana rose to examine her two gown choices again. Should she wear the apricot one Drew had complimented her on at Irvine Castle, or should she wear green, his favorite color?

As she took a step forward, she teetered off balance and caught herself against the dresser. Her head spun as she clutched the highboy to keep from tumbling to the floor.

Good heavens. Perhaps she should have a second biscuit after all. It would be mortifying to swoon at Drew's feet. He would never allow her to hear the end of it. Instead of her body righting itself as she expected, Lana stumbled into her dressing table. Why, she was as uncoordinated as Lord Bollrud on the dance floor.

Pinpricks of blackness started at the outer edges of her vision until all she could see was a narrow point in front of her, and her limbs hung heavy as if made from rock. Then she was falling, only vaguely aware when her head bounced on the intricately patterned carpet.

Drat. Betsy would have to rearrange her coiffure.

Thirty-nine

DREW ARRIVED WITH THE VICAR AT FOUR O'CLOCK SHARP and discovered the butler had already shown his family to the drawing room. Their early arrival didn't surprise him as his mother was beside herself with excitement. Her only lament was not planning another large celebration as she had done for Rich and Phoebe, but a more intimate gathering suited Drew.

Mr. Hillary joined everyone in the drawing room first, followed by his wife who greeted Drew's mother and sisters with hugs.

"Lana should be down soon," Mrs. Hillary said. "I sent a servant to announce your arrival."

"Thank you, Mrs. Hillary."

Everyone took a seat except Rich, who paced the room on Drew's behalf, a habit his brother had developed when anxious. Jake entered next, taking a seat close to Drew, but still there was no sign of Lana.

Fighting back his impatience, Drew attempted to engage her brother in conversation. Jake wore that somber expression he often sported when he was deep into his cups. Drew discreetly sniffed to see if he detected alcohol. Nothing appeared out of the ordinary.

"Is everything satisfactory, chap?"

Jake swiped his hand across his brow. "It's nothing. Just a personal matter on my mind." Then he amazed Drew by offering a slight grin. It was a poor effort at gaiety, but it was an effort all the same. "Lana is happy. Do not foul it up."

"Agreed."

Jake accepted Drew's handshake.

After a long while, the butler approached Mr. Hillary and murmured in low tones Drew couldn't make out.

He scooted to the edge of his seat and rested his hands on his knees, ready to jump up and go to Lana. If she was having second thoughts, he could change her mind again. With any luck, she kept a lock on her door, for his powers of persuasion worked best without uninvited guests barging in.

Lana's father moved outside of the drawing room to speak with the servant, but his voice carried. "What is the meaning of this? Have you searched everywhere? Look again."

Drew bolted from the chair and stalked from drawing room. "Something has gone awry."

Lana's father scratched his head. "Hogan reports my daughter is not in her chambers."

Mrs. Hillary bustled into the corridor. "James, what is it? Where's Lana?"

Soon every member of their combined families gathered outside of the drawing room, asking for explanations.

"I'm sure she's fine," Mr. Hillary said. "The servants are searching the house."

"She has to be here somewhere," Lana's mother stated. "Where would she go?"

"Perhaps she came to her senses," Gabby mumbled.

Drew ignored his precocious sister.

The pinched-faced butler returned. "Sir, I'm afraid Miss Hillary is not in the house. The staff searched every place imaginable."

"We'll see about that," Jake said and sprinted toward the staircase.

Drew liked his initiative and followed on his heels. They dashed through the open door of her chambers, but no one was inside.

"Check under the bed," Drew said.

Jake took two steps then halted and threw a harassed look over his shoulder. "She's not hiding under the bed, you dolt."

Drew crossed to the mahogany bed and checked anyway. Not finding her, he hurried to the wardrobe to throw open the doors. She wasn't there either, not that Drew had expected she would be, but he didn't trust the servants to have checked *every* conceivable hiding place. He glanced toward the window then dismissed the idea.

"Would she have gone for a walk with her lady's maid?" he asked.

Her brother pulled a watch from his pocket and checked the time. "Not bloody likely. She knew the time of the nuptials. I can't fathom she would leave the house."

Truth, the blasted rounder, delivered a gut-punch. "Hell's teeth. She has changed her mind again. I knew I shouldn't have left to change attire."

"Lana is too stubborn to cry off." Jake shoved the watch back in his pocket. "She has vowed to make me miserable ever since I pulled off her dolly's head when she was four. Now that she has found a way to make good on her promise, she isn't going to leave it go." Jake moved toward the staircase. "I'm searching outside."

"Not without me."

Jake, Rich, and Drew huddled on the front steps to form a plan of attack before each of them took off in a different direction. They would search the surrounding neighborhood while servants combed the gardens and fanned out to search Hyde Park. Two hours later, no one had seen any sign of Lana nor found a clue to hint at her whereabouts. Drew refused to give up the hunt. He expanded his search, praying she *had* come to her senses and was crying off. This seemed the better scenario than any other he imagined.

◈

Faraway voices broke through the blackness, but Lana only caught a word or two before sliding back into a dream state. Her arms and legs refused to budge. She tried to swallow against the grit in her mouth, but she couldn't produce any saliva. Something rough pressed against her cheek, and she thought to change her position, but sleep overtook her before she could put thought into action.

"'Ow much did ya give 'er?"

"I don't know." A high-pitched whine broke through her drowsiness. "I just poured it into the teapot."

"Is she dead?"

Dead? Well, that would be a dratted inconvenience.

Ice-cold fingers touched her forehead, unpleasant in the extreme, but reassuring her that she was well and alive, and a mite irritated to have been left lying on the floor. The delicate hand settled on her chest for a moment before withdrawing. "She's warm and still breathing."

Footsteps clomped toward her. "I should kill 'er *now*. Get it over with."

Goodness, Vicar Dunlevy was on a tear today. The delay in their nuptials seemed a minor inconvenience at best, but the man had always been a bit of a malcontent.

"I only fainted," Lana tried to say but her words came out garbled.

"She is only good to us alive," the woman said. "How do you expect to get the money otherwise?"

As Lana slowly returned to full consciousness, she blinked into the darkness. Where was she? She wasn't at Hillary House, at least not in her lavender-scented bedchamber. Her lip curled. What was that stench? It was like rotten onions and sheep. Lana turned her head away from the smell.

Moonbeams poked through the grimy glass of a window, doing a poor job of lighting the space. This had best not be Drew's idea of a decent home in which to raise their family. Men should never be entrusted with a woman's task.

The small room amplified every sound, the shuffling of feet, the gurgling of the woman's stomach—or was that *her* stomach? She really was ravenous now.

"Wake 'er up."

"Quiet, Reg, and speak proper like I taught you," the woman scolded. "This is your fault. You had one task and you bungled it."

A deep roar reverberated through the air followed by a crash and the sound of splintering wood.

Lana's heart leapt in surprise.

"It was a damned stupid idea," he said. "I shoulda taken 'er when I had the chance. It was a waste of my time."

"It wouldn't have been necessary to take her at all if you had done your part, and we wouldn't be reduced to criminals. The plan would have worked," the woman repeated. "I know it."

An involuntary sigh escaped Lana's lips as her body worked to revive itself, to recover from whatever plagued it.

"I think she's waking." Lana recognized the speaker's voice.

"Betsy?" It came out as a croak.

"Get her something to drink."

The man grumbled as his footfalls retreated. There was a rustle then more stomping back into the room. "'Ow long do ya think we can keep 'er 'ere? Are ya sure no one can find us?"

A flash of light alerted Lana to the flask in his hand when he thrust his arm toward Betsy.

The maid accepted the flask and slid her arm under Lana's shoulders. "How would they know to look here? You have to sit up, miss."

Lana struggled to lift her shoulders from the ground, finding the movement made her head spin. Betsy supported her weight and raised the cold metal container to rest against her lips before spilling the liquid into Lana's mouth. Fiery alcohol scorched her tongue before blazing a path down her throat. She gasped and sputtered, coughing until she doubled over on her side.

"I take it you have no lemonade?" she asked when she could breathe normally again.

"I know it's hard to get down, miss, but it's all we have."

"Where am I?"

"It don't matter," the man growled. "Don't get no ideas."

Lana could see his outline in the dark, but she couldn't distinguish any of his features. Nevertheless, his voice struck a familiar chord and the hair on the back of her neck stood on end. "It's you," she whispered, but neither seemed to hear. The man from Irvine Castle. The one who chased her in the maze. "Wh-what do you want?" Her dry lips stuck together in the corners.

"Why don't ya shut up?" the man barked.

"Reggie, allow me to explain. I'm certain she will assist us."

Lana's eyes had adjusted to the darkness, and she could visualize parts of Betsy's face. Her maid sat by her side, still holding the flask. The man called Reggie snatched the alcohol from Betsy's hand before walking away with it. Lana caught a brief glimpse of blond hair, but nothing more. The man grunted before opening a door, allowing a gust of cold air to steal into the space and sweep over her body, then slammed the door as he left.

She recalled her maid mentioning a brother once when she had started her position. Was it three years ago? "Reggie? Isn't that your brother's name?"

"You should keep your observations to yourself, miss," Betsy whispered. "He won't be happy."

"A bit of a curmudgeon, is he?" she muttered.

Lana had no idea why the man was angry with her, but he spoke with such hatred, she didn't question Betsy's assertion. She struggled to sit, realizing for the first time that they had bound her hands and ankles. Hearing her maid's voice upon waking had lulled her into feeling secure, but panic surged through Lana as she recognized the actual danger of the situation.

Her breaths came rapid and shallow as the sound of blood swished in her ears. She fought against the ropes, writhing on the floor and scraping her knuckles against the wood in the process. Papa always complained about the difficulties of finding good help. Now she understood his dilemma.

"Really, Betsy. I'm afraid I must terminate your position."

The door slammed again. "Keep 'er quiet, or I'll quiet 'er for good."

Betsy's hand cupped Lana's forehead, and she leaned close to speak softly in her ear. "Please be still, miss. Once your family pays, this will be over and you can go home. But we need something from you."

Lana forced her breathing to slow and she swallowed. "What do you want from me?"

"It's easy, Miss Hillary. We simply need you to write something for us, that's all."

"*Write* something?" She must have misunderstood. Why sedate and abduct her to have her write something? And what? A letter? "I hope you don't expect me to pen a letter of recommendation."

Reggie took several threatening steps in their direction. "You'll write wot we tell ya, or else."

Lana suspected she could write *Hark, Hark the Dogs do Bark* twenty times and he would never know the difference. "But I have no writing materials, and my hands are tied."

Betsy scrambled up from the floor and moved into the shadows. The sound of crinkling paper reached Lana's ears followed a few moments later by the scratch of a match and pop of its spark. The maid's face lit to reveal her features while shadows hid the rest of her body. She put the match to the candle, catching the wick. The room glowed around her and Betsy while the man retreated into the blackness of an adjoining room.

"I packed a sheet of foolscap from your desk, miss, and a quill and ink."

How thoughtful. Lana held her bound hands in front of her. "I must be freed to write."

The maid sat the candle and holder on the floor and worked the knots that held her wrists together.

"Don't get any ideas," Reggie said, reinforcing his warning with the click of a pistol. He seemed to have a peculiar aversion to *ideas*. Perhaps because he had none of his own.

Once the rope fell away, Lana grasped her right wrist and rubbed.

Betsy held the foolscap out, and she took it with a shaking hand. "Do you wish me to write on the floor?"

The maid held out the ink jar and quill. "It will have to do."

Lana settled the paper on the floor to her side. With her ankles still bound, she had no choice but to stretch her legs out in front of her. She rolled to the left to brace her elbow by the paper and reached across her body with her right hand to dip the quill in the ink.

"I'm ready."

"Let's see… Start with, 'Dear Mr. Hillary,'" Betsy began.

"Not *dear*. She ain't invitin' 'em to tea."

"Let me handle this, Reggie." Her maid returned her attention to Lana. "Actually, since this letter is from you, Miss Hillary, you may want to start it with, 'Dear Father.'"

"Do you expect me to write my own ransom note?" Lana took a wild guess. "Because having one compose one's own ransom note seems rather lazy."

"Jus' do it," Reggie snarled.

"We've already written our demands, Miss Hillary. This will provide proof that we have you."

Lana licked her lips and dipped the quill once more.

She touched it to the paper and scribbled as Betsy instructed. "What more do you wish me to write?"

"Tell your family you are safe and will remain unharmed."

"Am I... safe?" She held her breath waiting for the answer.

Betsy patted her shoulder. "Of course you are, miss. There's no need to be frightened. No one will hurt you."

That was a relief, if she could believe her maid. Unfortunately, Betsy had just recently proven herself to be untrustworthy.

Lana composed the note as requested, tempted to ask Betsy how to spell numbskull out of spite, but thinking it unwise to antagonize the armed numbskull standing in the shadows. She held the letter up to proofread.

"Jus' take it," Reggie snapped at his sister.

Her maid took the letter and glanced at it. "Thank you, Miss Hillary."

Lana cleared her throat. The gnawing pain in her belly was almost more than she could bear. "Betsy, do you have any food?"

"Tie 'er 'ands, then get back to the 'ouse. Leave the notes and don't let anyone see you."

When the maid moved to bind her again, Lana grasped her sleeve. "Please, don't leave me with him," she whispered.

Betsy pried Lana's fingers from her arm. "The sun will rise in a few hours. I cannot wait any longer."

"But I have need of the necessary."

"Devil take it!" Reggie stomped to the door. "I ain't helpin' with no necessary."

Lana cringed when he slammed the door.

Betsy untied the rope at her ankles and assisted her

to her feet. Lana's belly cramps returned. As the maid helped her on the chamber pot, the intensity of her cramping doubled her over. She panted as a wave of pain washed over her, leaving her shaky, cold, and ready to toss up her accounts. Closing her eyes, she waited for the pains to recede.

"I am finished," she murmured at last. Her eyes stung and her throat ached. The discovery that she did not carry Drew's child should have given her a sense of relief, but instead it produced a flood of tears. Betsy hauled her to her feet. Sniffling, Lana roughly wiped away the evidence of her disappointment with the backs of her trembling hands.

Betsy patted her shoulder in a misguided attempt at comfort. "You have no cause to fret, Miss Hillary. I will return posthaste, just as I promised. I'm sorry, but I must bind your feet and hands again."

Lana thrust her hands forward, wrists together. "Forgive me for doubting your sincerity."

Reggie returned as Betsy tied the last knot. She wheeled around to face him. "You *will* feed her, Reginald."

Lana's hunger was the least of her concerns when it came to being under the man's care. An evening of snarls, snaps, and barks sounded exceptionally unpleasant. And she remained unconvinced Reggie didn't bite.

Forty

IT WAS A TORTUROUSLY LONG TIME AFTER BETSY AND HER brother left Lana alone before heavy footsteps approached the cottage. The door swung open on a blast of wind. The candle flickered and blew out, leaving Lana in darkness with her captor. Moonlight cast a bluish glow over his body, but there was not enough illumination to see his face.

The door creaked as it closed. He loomed within the threshold, silent. Prickles chased along her skin. Could his eyes penetrate the blackness? The idea that he might be able to observe her like some nocturnal creature while he remained hidden increased her disquiet. Maybe he knew this and intended to torment her. She refused to allow him the satisfaction of knowing how he frightened her.

"C-care to play a game of whist?" she asked, trying to control the tremor in her voice.

He stayed frozen in the dark. The only sound in the cramped room was her rapid breathing. She closed her eyes and attempted to slow her heart's pounding. She must survive this night, just this one, and then she would be home again, safe with her family and beginning her life with Drew.

Reggie's sudden move made her jump. "Never learned," he said at last.

"I-I could teach you. Do you have a deck of cards?"

He clomped through the cottage, the sound fading as he entered another area. She would take that as a no. A few moments later, a glow filtered into the room where she curled on the floor.

His body filled the doorway, blocking most of the light, his features cast in shadow.

"Eat this." He crossed the room in two steps and bent to shove something into her hands, something hard and crusty.

Lana sniffed his offering. It was bread. She devoured the stale hunk in three bites and longed for more, but she wouldn't request a second course. At the end of this ordeal, if her kidnappers were to comment on her person, she would not be known as the disagreeable captive.

Reggie approached again and when he thrust the metal flask into her hands, she was prepared for the burning pain of the alcohol. Lana sipped only enough to wet her tongue and ease the rasping dryness in her throat.

"Thank you."

When she passed it back, Reggie screwed on the top then yanked her bound hands with terrifying speed to haul her from the floor. With her legs lashed together, she couldn't get her feet under her, but he was undeterred. He dragged her across the rustic floor, ripping her stocking above her ankle.

Blast and damn. That was the last time she would waste courtesy on the likes of him.

Lana quivered and bit the inside of her jaw to keep from screaming out when he tossed her on the bed, if one could call the lumpy thing a bed. Shoving her hands

above her head, he secured her bindings to the iron bed
rail. He tugged the ropes then climbed from the bed.

"That ought ta keep ya from runnin' away."

Lana bristled. The cottage housed a bed this whole
time and the idiots had dumped her on the floor?

Without another word, Reggie spun on his heel and
left her alone without a fire or even a blanket to keep
her warm.

Lana frowned. Her kidnappers had much to learn
when it came to hospitality.

The sky began to wake with shades of pink and purple.
Drew sighed. He was weary from walking the streets of
London most of the night. The odds of finding Lana in
the overcrowded city had been slim, but he couldn't sit
and do nothing.

Jake had joined him for the first four hours, but with
no sign of Lana, they had returned to Hillary House to
see if there was any news. There was nothing, so instead
of pacing a trench in Mrs. Hillary's floors, Drew walked
the streets.

When he rounded the corner, Hillary House stood
lit like a beacon in the gray dawn light, guiding him
back. Hope flickered inside him when he entered the
house, but extinguished as soon as he saw Mr. Hillary's
drawn face.

He stepped forward, waving two sheets of foolscap.
"We've received word. A ransom note and a message
from Lana."

Drew raced to grab the papers from his grasp. Never
was one object so despised and welcomed at the same time.
He scanned the contents of Lana's letter first. She promised

she was safe and would remain unharmed. Nevertheless, the kidnapper's demands provided little comfort.

"The cemetery? Is this an ill-conceived joke?" He tossed the notes on a side table. "I'm delivering the money."

Lana's brother bolted from the overstuffed chair where he had been slumped. "Now wait a moment, Forest. We are her family. We'll decide how to handle the situation."

Drew stalked across the room to stand toe to toe with him. His fist itched to bloody Jake's lip. "Lana belongs to me as much as anyone. I'll not rest until I have her back safe."

Mr. Hillary placed a firm hand on Drew's shoulder. "We all want the same thing, Lord Andrew. We want Lana back, and we'll get her back. But not if we fight each other."

Drew backed up a step and dropped his raised fist. Lana's father was right. Jake wasn't his enemy. His enemy, the man holding his peach captive, was in for a thorough beating, and Lana's brother might be just the chap he wanted on his side. He possessed a wicked right jab.

"My apologies, Hillary."

Jake nodded. "We are all wound tight."

Drew scooped up the letter and read the demands again before handing it to her father. "I have most of the funds, sir."

Mr. Hillary shook his head. "Save your money, my lord. You will need it to care for my daughter. She has exquisite taste in gowns, or so the shopkeepers inform my man of business when he settles the bills."

Lana could have a ballroom filled with gowns, for all Drew cared. He just wanted her home.

"We've come up with a plan," Mr. Hillary announced. "I will be the one to drop the ransom."

Before Drew could protest, Mr. Hillary held up his hand. "That's not all. You and Jake will go to the cemetery several hours before the appointed time and wait. If the damned blackguard shows without Lana, I want you to follow."

"You won't be involving Bow Street?"

Mr. Hillary's jaw twitched. "The fewer people who know of her disappearance, the better."

Drew cared nothing for society's acceptance, but he was glad to hear Lana's father intended to follow her abductor's instructions not to involve the runners. Besides, he had more faith in Lana's brother and himself.

Mr. Hillary glanced at Drew and his son. "You should leave within the hour to find a spot to observe the ransom exchange. I'll leave the money at the grave of Carter Daniels, as directed."

Drew raised his brows. "A man of your past acquaintance?"

Mr. Hillary shook his head. "I'm assuming he's no one of importance. I sent a man earlier to locate the grave. It lies in a secluded area on the south side. Once I drop the money, I'll leave the cemetery as I entered, in case he is watching."

It seemed foolish to recover the ransom in daylight, but perhaps the kidnapper thought it would be easier to detect someone waiting to give chase.

At the cemetery, Drew and Jake chose a spot behind a crypt partially hidden by mature trees and settled in for a long wait. The crypt was a distance from the gravesite, but this section of the cemetery was open with the gravestones coming no higher than Drew's hip. It would have been preferable to split up and take positions closer, but there was no help for it.

They sat in silence. Drew's muscles tensed and twitched with every sound, preparing to chase the blackguard.

"There's Father," Jake murmured.

Drew craned his neck. When Mr. Hillary reached the grave, he dropped the full bag in front of the tombstone and moved away. Then they waited.

A flash of movement caught Drew's eye. "Someone is coming."

"It's just a boy. Stay down."

Jake was correct. A small youth tugged his hat over his face and glided through the cemetery, appearing to have a destination in mind. Perhaps he visited a relative's grave. Yet, instead of moving past the designated grave as Drew expected, the boy stopped.

"Could that be him?" Jake whispered. "He appears too fragile to capture a kitten, much less hold Lana." He shifted his position, cracking a small stick under his boot.

The boy's head shot up to scan the area before he bent to retrieve the purse and took off at a run.

"He has taken it. Catch him."

The lad had at least twenty paces on them, but they both flew after him. Jake's footfalls pounded the ground close behind Drew. Gaining on their quarry, Drew increased his efforts, but a heavy thump followed by a sharp cry of pain made him glance over his shoulder.

"Keep going," Jake's muffled voice commanded.

Where the bloody hell had he gone?

Drew forgot Lana's brother and pushed himself harder, but his hesitation had allowed the boy to escape the cemetery and head for the streets of London.

He reached the street as the boy darted into traffic, taking no notice of a carriage barreling down the opposite side of the road. A high-pitched scream pierced his ears. The driver jerked the reins.

The boy's abrupt appearance spooked the greys, causing one to rear up. The boy crumpled to the cobblestone road.

More screams rippled through the air.

"I didn't see 'im, on my honor," the driver wailed. "Came from nowhere, 'e did."

Drew shoved his way through the pandemonium, kneeled beside the boy, and turned him to his back. Hell's teeth. The lad must receive merciless teasing, for he looked every bit as delicate as a girl.

"It's Betsy, Lana's maid," Jake stated, limping toward him. Dirt covered him head to toe.

"What happened to you?"

"Some blasted idiot left a hole in the cemetery."

"And you didn't see a hole large enough for a man?"

Jake sniffed. "I saw the hole fine. It was the shovel I failed to see. Is the girl alive?"

Drew checked for breathing and shook his head. Standing, he dusted off his trousers. A servant in the Hillary household had betrayed them. Who else might be involved? He turned on his heel and started back to Lana's home.

"Where are you going?" Jake asked.

"The maid wasn't working alone. I intend to find out who has Lana."

Forty-one

DREW NAILED THE BUTLER WITH A GLARE AS SOON AS THE doors to Mr. Hillary's study closed. "Get every servant down here at once."

Jake tossed the bag of money on his father's desk. "Every single one of them, Father."

Mr. Hillary gave a sharp nod. "Do it, Hogan."

"Yes, sir." The butler hurried to do his master's bidding.

"Tell me what transpired." Mr. Hillary drummed his fingers against his desk as Drew retold the events of the last hour.

A timid knock sounded at the door. Lana's brother half-hopped, half-walked to the door and yanked it open. A hair-raising, spine-shivering screech ripped through the air.

"Hellfire and damnation!" Jake leapt backwards, knocked his elbow against a marble pillar, and careened into side table.

The young maid slapped both hands over her mouth, her eyes as round as shillings.

"Why were you blasted screaming?" Jake's dark brows lowered dangerously.

"I don't know," she mumbled from behind her hands.

"Well, stop it." He rubbed his elbow. "You'll take ten years off a man's life running about shrieking like a banshee."

She dropped her hands from her mouth and curtsied. "Forgive me, sir. My nerves are a bit frazzled, what with Miss Hillary and all."

"Yes, well, try to contain yourself." Jake waved her inside. "My apologies for my lapse in manners. Enter."

The maid ducked her head and scurried into the study.

Jake grumbled as he limped to the settee and lowered his battered frame.

"Come here, girl," Mr. Hillary said.

She shuffled to stand before her employer with her hands clutched.

Lana's father crossed his arms and leaned against his desk. "What do you know of Betsy March?"

"Not much, sir." Her voice quavered. "She mostly kept to herself."

Drew stepped forward. "Did she mention any family or friends?"

"Not to me, my lord." With a shaky hand, the maid tucked a wayward curl under her cap. "Is she in trouble, sir? She seems like a nice girl."

Further questions revealed nothing of importance, and the scullery maid was dismissed.

The next interview ended with the same results, and then the next and the next. No one knew anything about the reclusive Betsy March.

"Damnation." Drew rammed his fingers through his hair.

Jake leaned back against the settee cushion and closed his eyes. He had removed his boot before elevating his leg and now sported an ankle the size of a Goliath-sized yam. Drew shook his head. He'd never met a less graceful chap.

He turned to Mr. Hillary. "Someone has to know something. Bring them in again. Someone is hiding something. How could the kidnappers get her out of the house without anyone noticing?"

"Everyone was engaged in preparing for the wedding feast," Jake said. "Given the time of day, none of the chambermaids were cleaning the rooms. It's difficult to believe, but not impossible."

"Does no one know of Betsy's past? How did she come to be here, Mr. Hillary?"

Lana's father rolled his neck and blew out a long breath. "She answered the advertisement in *The Times*, and she arrived with a first-rate letter of recommendation from—Wait. Can that be accurate?" Mr. Hillary strode around his desk, tugged open a drawer, and rifled through papers until he found what he sought. "Yes, here it is. Lady Dohve vouched for her."

He passed Drew a piece of parchment marked with the elaborate looping letters often favored by females.

"Bollrud's aunt," Drew said. The man was like vermin, impossible to drive away.

"I will summon the gentleman from Talliah House," Mr. Hillary said. "He might know something of the maid's past."

Drew's fingers curled into a fist. "You won't find him at Talliah, sir. He left Town yesterday after he learned of our intentions to wed."

Jake swung his leg off the settee and sat up straight. "Do you believe Bollrud is involved?"

It wouldn't do to malign another gentleman without proof. "I'm unsure, but as your father said, maybe he knows something of value pertaining to Betsy March." Drew handed the letter back to Mr. Hillary. "I believe I will pay a call to Lady Dohve and her nephew."

"Perhaps I should go with you," Mr. Hillary said.

"It isn't far to Lady Dohve's estate. I can be there and back by sundown. You should stay in the event the kidnapper sends another communication."

Jake winced as he tried to stand. "Just let me get on my boot."

"You aren't in any condition to travel. Rest your ankle. I may need your assistance tomorrow."

Jake hesitated, but then lowered to the settee. "Return with your findings posthaste."

"Of course." Drew bid farewell to the gentlemen before retrieving Demetrius from the Talliah mews.

Lady Dohve's estate was an hour out of London by horseback. The manor house stood in the distance, grand and almost desolate. Although the grounds suffered neglect, evidence suggested they had been well-tended at one time. The mature hedges had grown ragged and the topiary appeared more like a grotesque version of a hare, but Drew could discern the gardener's original intent.

As he rode Demetrius up the lane to the Tudor manor, no servant came to greet him or lead his horse to the stables. The home suffered the same neglect as the gardens. Apparently, the rumors of the baroness's depleted fortune had not been exaggerated.

Leaving Demetrius to graze on the overgrown lawn, Drew hurried up the steps and knocked. The wait seemed extraordinarily long, but as Drew raised his fist again, the door creaked open.

A hunched-over relic hobbled outside, shaking his fist in the air. "No, no, no. The horse cannot be on the lawn. Lady Dohve strictly forbids it."

With the overgrown grass, Demetrius was providing a service to the lady, in Drew's line of thinking, but he didn't care to debate the issue.

"So sorry." Drew returned to Demetrius and gathered his reins. "Perhaps you could summon a groom to take him to the stables."

"There is no groom, sir. It's only me and me grandson left in the baroness's employ, and a housemaid for indoor work. What affairs do you wish to discuss with her ladyship?"

Drew sought out a place to secure his horse then returned to stand before the man. "Inform Lady Dohve that Andrew Forest, the Duke of Foxhaven's son, requests an audience."

The man's narrowed gaze swept up and down Drew. He supposed his ruffled appearance engendered suspicion. Fortunately, he carried one of his cards and offered it to the servant. "I shan't require much of her time."

He held the calling card close to scrutinize it before lowering it to inspect Drew again. "Very well, you may wait in the drawing room, Lord Andrew."

The elderly servant shuffled around and struggled up the stairs leading inside, his muddling gait agonizing. Drew fought against the urge to tote him inside like a sack of grain and be done with it. One couldn't go any slower if one stood still.

Once they passed into the house and neared the drawing room, he thanked the servant and whisked inside to wait for Lady Dohve. He hoped the grandson was fleeter of foot and would carry his request to her ladyship in place of his grandfather. Otherwise, Drew couldn't be certain he would return to London before the year's end.

Lady Dohve joined him in the drawing room after several minutes. She beamed her pleasure. "Lord Andrew, how nice of you to call. What brings you to my little spot of heaven?"

Drew returned her gracious smile, recalling he'd met the baroness in London a couple of years prior. "Lady Dohve, I hope you are well."

"Yes, as well as can be expected at my age. Thank you for asking. May I offer you some refreshment?"

"I apologize, my lady, but I am unable to stay for long. Please, don't go to any trouble."

"It would be no trouble, my lord, but I don't wish to delay you."

Lady Dohve selected a Chippendale chair with a worn brocade seat, and Drew slipped into its twin.

"Your graciousness is appreciated. I pray you will please excuse my impatience, but I have an inquiry to make pertaining to a former employee of yours."

Lady Dohve folded her hands in her lap. "Oh, I do hope I'm able to assist you, Lord Andrew. My staff has dwindled over the last few years. I'm uncertain if I can recall them all."

"You wrote a letter of recommendation for her, a young woman named Betsy March."

Lady Dohve's lips lifted at the corners. "Yes, my darling little Betsy. She moved to London a few years ago to search out employment as a lady's maid. She was more suited for that line of work than as a chambermaid. How is my dear girl?"

Drew drummed his fingers against the arm of the chair.

He hadn't expected the lady might hold the girl in esteem. "I fear I must be the bearer of unfortunate news, my lady."

"Oh?" Her smile slid from her face.

"There was an accident involving Betsy."

"Oh, dear." Lady Dohve snatched a fan from the side table, flicked it open, and fanned herself. "Is she all right?"

"Betsy didn't survive her injuries, my lady."

Lady Dohve's hand clutched her chest. "Wh-what happened?"

He debated revealing the truth, but she would likely find out at some point and realize he had withheld information. "Apparently she didn't see the carriage coming toward her."

Lady Dohve's wide eyes swam with tears. "Oh, dear," she repeated, creating a windstorm with the rapid waving of her fan. "Oh, dear me."

"I'm sorry for your loss." Drew had no reason to believe Lady Dohve was involved with Lana's abduction, and he did feel bad for her.

"Maynard will be crushed," she said.

"Maynard, my lady?"

"My manservant. You met him when you arrived."

Drew nodded as if he understood the reason the information would trouble Maynard, or Lady Dohve for that matter.

"How he doted on his granddaughter. He had high hopes for her. We both did."

Drew reached for his handkerchief and offered it to the baroness. She accepted with her thanks.

"Betsy was your manservant's granddaughter?" he prompted.

"Yes, Maynard raised her and her brother when his daughter died from the pox."

Drew's mouth dropped open in shock. Lady Dohve was much too candid by half. "The *pox*, you say?"

She nodded as she dabbed at her tears. "Yes, the poor dear contracted smallpox in '98."

"Oh." Well, that was a horse of a different color, wasn't it?

"Betsy was like my child. I could never have any of my own, though Lord Dohve, bless his soul, gave a jolly good try." Her smile widened and revealed several missing back teeth.

"I see." Though he wished he could strike the disturbing image from his mind. "I can't tell you how sorry I am. I wish I could have called under better circumstances."

"I'm glad you came, Lord Andrew. How thoughtful of you to personally carry notice to us." She wrung her hands. "I don't look forward to informing Reggie. He's unlikely to take it well."

Drew's brows lifted. "If I may ask, my lady, who is Reggie?"

"Betsy's brother. He just returned from visiting her in Town. I was surprised by the length of his visit, but they always were close. I'm glad he took the time. Hopefully, he will have fewer regrets this way."

Drew sat up straighter, his heartbeat doubling in speed. "Is Reggie here now?"

Lady Dohve shook her head. "I'm sure he has returned to the caretaker's cottage. I do hope he won't stay away long. He will want to receive the report as soon as possible, but Maynard and I are in no condition to go to him."

She blew her nose into his handkerchief, folded the linen square, and tried to pass it back.

Drew waved it off. "I have another. Please, enjoy."

"Thank you, my lord. I have no inkling where my handkerchiefs have gotten off to."

Drew scooted to the edge of his seat.

This man, Reggie, lived in a secluded cottage, one where he wouldn't be disturbed. "Lady Dohve, would you like me to carry word to Betsy's brother?"

"Would you do me such a kindness? You've done so much already. I hate to impose."

"It's no trouble, my lady."

"I would very much appreciate your assistance. Poor Reggie will be beside himself." She sighed. "The cottage is north a little past the family cemetery."

Drew extended his sympathies once more and bid her farewell. Outside, the sun hovered lower in the sky. Sunset would be on him in a few hours. He swung into the saddle and directed Demetrius north.

He rode until the house was out of sight. Around the first bend, he spotted iron fencing surrounding a plot of land. The names on the headstones became visible as he rode closer. He urged his horse to pick up the pace, but a name jumped out at him from a fresh marker. He eased back the reins and dismounted then hopped the fence. He blinked, distrusting his eyes.

PHILIP BOLLRUD
BELOVED GREAT-NEPHEW OF
LORD AND LADY DOHVE
AUGUST 5, 1786 – JUNE 6, 1816

"Hell's teeth." It hadn't been Bollrud at Irvine Castle at all, which left one other likely scenario. Bollrud was really Reggie March. And he had come for Lana. Unlucky for him, she belonged to Drew.

Forty-two

LANA CURLED INTO A BALL, SHIVERING AS SHE DREW HER bound feet toward her middle. Her fine wool morning dress provided little warmth in the frigid cottage air. Perhaps if she'd had advance notice, she would have dressed more appropriately for an abduction.

She had been alone in the cottage for what seemed like hours, but considering Reggie's ill-mannered company was all that was available, solitude was preferable. Her stomach had finally stopped rumbling sometime around dawn, and the hunger pangs had ceased, but she still wouldn't turn away a plum pudding if someone happened by with one.

In the slanting rays of sun barely penetrating the grimy windows, she examined the ropes binding her feet. *A double butterfly knot.* What a novice. She could untie the knot with her eyes closed, if her hands were free.

Lana thought back on the lessons from her brother Daniel to keep her mind occupied. Her brother had spent hours patiently teaching her how to tie sailor's knots while he waited to sail back to the West Indies. And Lana had practiced for weeks perfecting the skill. Of course, she hadn't played with her ropes for several years, but the construction remained familiar. She ran through all the knots she could recall to pass the time.

Lana shifted but couldn't roll from her right side with her hands above her head. Her muscles had burned in the beginning. Now they were heavy with numbness, and she wiggled her fingers to encourage blood flow.

Footsteps sounded outside. Splendid. *He* was back. Where was Betsy? It was taking a dratted long time for her to return. Lana had stomached more than enough of their nonsense.

She listened to the bumps and bangs outside the cottage, as if her captor stacked wood against the wall, which seemed a much less logical place for logs than ablaze in the hearth.

In the distance, a horse approached, and all banging ceased. She almost cried with relief. *Betsy.* The girl deserved a thorough dressing down for delaying Lana's release, but at least she would be going home at last.

A thud sounded as the rider dismounted, followed by footsteps too heavy to belong to her slight maid. Did she dare hope the new arrival was a rotund cook bearing a turkey? Her mouth watered at the thought of food.

"Lana?"

Drew! Her heart raced. She tried to answer his call, but her dry throat croaked an indecipherable sound. The door swung open, and Drew entered with his pistol drawn. Blinding light invaded the dark interior of the cottage.

"Lana, where are you?"

"Here," she managed to eke out.

"Peach." The word rushed from him on a relieved breath. "Thank God, I found you." He placed the firearm on the bed and moved to untie her hands. One quick kiss then he went to work on the ropes.

"Drew," she whispered. "He's out there."

"Reggie? Or should I say Bollrud?" He dropped his hands from her bindings and reached for his firearm. Before he could react to her warning, a sickening clunk reached her ears, and his pistol clattered to the floor. Drew's body pitched forward to land on Lana, knocking the air from her.

Good heavens above. What were men eating these days? Iron anvils?

Lord Bollrud stood with legs planted wide, lightly smacking a thin log against his palm. A triumphant smirk twisted his lips, revealing his jagged teeth. He reminded her of an animal, and reeked just as bad.

"*You* are Reggie?"

His gleeful cackle turned her stomach. Either that or it was the spittle he had just shared with all.

"'Ow did 'e figure it out?" Reggie scratched his cheek where a patchy beard had begun to grow. The man was hopelessly without a sense of fashion.

Grabbing Drew by the back of his jacket, he hauled him from the bed to land on the floor with a thump.

"Be gentle with him," she scolded. Though her darling would look just as dashing sporting bruises, there was no need for carelessness.

Reggie kneeled beside him. "Still alive," he muttered.

A rush of gratitude swept over her and tears welled in her eyes. Reggie pushed from the floor and tromped outside only to return moments later with more rope and a knife. He tossed both on the ground. Bending, his face flushed as he put all of his strength into lugging Drew to a post. He grunted as he strained to lift Drew to a seated position.

The rope coiled on the floor, and Reggie held up a long length before hacking through the fibers with the knife. He cut an equal length and used the two ropes to tie Drew's hands behind him, most likely employing a full carrick bend. That would be her choice.

"I suppose it is safe to say Betsy is not returning." Reggie—or was he Bollrud?—reverted back to the way of speaking to which she'd been accustomed during his stay at Irvine Castle.

"Who are you exactly?"

Reggie jeered. "I'm the one in control, Miss Hillary. You may address me as *sir*."

Not blasted likely, though she knew a few other choice names to bestow on him.

He stretched his arms above his head, arched his back, and groaned. "I have to figure out what to do with the two of you."

The glint in his eye dampened any hopes she might have had of him hosting a ball in their honor. They wouldn't survive this ordeal if he had his wishes.

Something cold and wet engulfed Drew, jerking him awake. He tried to move, to wipe the water from his eyes, but rope bound his hands behind his back.

Good Lord. What had he gotten himself into this time? He didn't recall indulging in a single drink, though the ache in his head disputed his recall.

He blinked to clear his sight, the glare from the oil lamp making him squint, and focused on a man standing over him holding a bucket.

"Good, yer awake."

That was a matter of opinion, decidedly not Drew's. His vision blurred and his head pounded a rhythm in time with his heartbeat. "What happened?"

"Drew, are you hurt?" Lana's urgency broke through his haze, and his memory returned in broken pieces.

He gave her a slight smile to ease her worry when he spotted her lying on the bed. "I've been worse, love."

"Quiet. Both of ya," the man snapped. Reggie was his name. Drew remembered that much.

He held his tongue, assessing his adversary, not wanting to taunt the man while he retained the more prestigious position. Perhaps Drew could beat him with one arm tied behind his back, but not two.

Reggie ambled toward the bed where Lana lay. She met her captor's gaze without wavering. Only the tremble of her bottom lip revealed her fear. His peach was every bit as good at holding her cards close to her chest as any gambling man.

"Pretty little chit, ya are," Reggie said and reached for her.

Lana shrank back. Lunging, he grabbed her hair, twisting and pulling until a small cry escaped her lips.

The ropes cut into Drew's wrists as he strained against the knots. His threats to kill the blackguard stuck in his throat when the man turned to study his reaction. Reggie's motivation became clear. He sought to defeat Drew. He wanted domination. Kent's own Little Corporal.

Drew forced himself to project neutrality when Reggie traced a finger down Lana's silky cheek and over her full lips. Fury blazed in her beautiful eyes, and for a moment, Drew thought the man might lose a finger.

"Not bad." Reggie licked his lips. "Not bad at all. A peppery wench, I think."

Drew refused to blink. He had been a gambler all of his adult life, and the one thing he had learned was never to reveal weakness to an opponent.

"Hmm," Drew responded with a shrug. "I've had better."

Lana's eyes flew open as an outraged gasp escaped her lips. Hell's teeth. He would pay for that lie later, he could see that now. He focused on Reggie's ugly face, afraid if he looked at Lana again, he might tip his hand.

Reggie's lip curled. "Then ya don't mind if I take some more?" He tried to push Lana onto her back, but she couldn't move the way he had her tied. With a growl, Reggie worked the knots at her wrists to release her hands, but quickly captured them and shoved them over her head.

Rage ate at Drew. He wanted to rip the man's arms from her person, but words were his only weapon. "Personally, I don't believe she's worth breaking a sweat over. But, as you wish."

Reggie's head whipped toward Drew. "I seen ya wit' her. Yer lyin'."

Drew caught Lana's eyes and held her gaze. *Please forgive me, peach.* "Then I was better at the pretense than I thought. Of course, I had little choice in the matter. You've been carrying a torch for her all these weeks. You can have her."

Reggie released her hands and moved a step toward Drew. "It was Betsy's addle-brained idea, 'aving me court 'er. She thought the chit'd be easy pickings, being a spinster. Whadda ya mean about 'aving no choice?"

Drew tried to look chagrined, which, given the horrible things he knew he had to say, wasn't a stretch. "I let my cock lead me rather than good sense, and I got caught with my trousers down. By my brother, of all people. You'd think he would keep his mouth shut, but Rich always has to do the honorable thing."

If looks could kill, Drew would be dead ten times over. Lana might refuse to speak to him for years to come.

Some of the fight drained from Reggie. "What are ya saying? Yer bein' forced to marry?"

Drew offered a sardonic grin. "I wouldn't say *forced*. I have a choice. I can live in poverty—no thank you—or I can do the honorable thing and marry the chit." He doubted the man knew anything of his financial state, so it seemed the safest of any lie he had told thus far.

Reggie narrowed his beady eyes. "Then why come lookin' for 'er?"

Drew's next revelation was risky, and he hesitated, weighing the possible consequences. "She is with child and my father knows it. Do you think the self-righteous Duke of Foxhaven would forgive me if I didn't search for her? I had no idea she would actually be here." Drew nearly winced when he realized his blunder.

Reggie moved farther away from Lana. "'Ow did ya know to look 'ere?"

Drew's left eye twitched. He couldn't reveal that Reggie's sister was dead. There was no way to predict his reaction, but it seemed unlikely he would shake Drew's hand and offer his appreciation.

Drew affected a sneer. "Siblings are all alike, gent. They can only be trusted to a certain point. Betsy pointed the finger at you when she was caught. I beat the authorities, but they'll be here soon. And you'll be swinging from the gallows."

"That double-crossing bitch. I'll kill 'er."

Reggie threw his head back and howled like the wild animal he was before grabbing the oil lamp and hurling it against the wall. Shards of glass flew through the air, a piece nicking Drew's cheek. Flames trailed like crooked fingers along the floor and engulfed the wall.

"They'll be nothin' left of ya when they come," Reggie screamed, spewing hatred everywhere before storming from the cottage.

Drew hadn't factored this pickle into the odds, but then again, he rarely gambled with madmen.

Forty-three

LANA'S JAW DROPPED, ALL HER BREATH RUSHING FROM her as the roaring flames mesmerized her like a snake charmer's flute.

"Lana." Drew's shout broke the spell. "Your hands are free. Save yourself."

Leaping to action, she bolted upright on the bed and slipped one knot enough to free her foot. A simple slide and she released the other. She scrambled to the edge of the bed and hopped to the floor to hurry to Drew.

"Get out of here."

She ignored his shouted command and dropped to her knees to work the knots free. "You can't be so desperate to escape marriage you would perish in a fire."

The heat singed her back, urging her to move faster, as flames climbed to the roof. The cottage was going up like tinder, and at the rate the fire grew, it would collapse on them in a matter of minutes.

"Lana, this is no time prove your stubbornness. Save our child."

She ignored his pleas and wedged her finger into the knot. Her nail ripped as she tugged at the fastenings Drew's thrashings had tightened.

"I can do this," she said aloud as much to convince herself as Drew. "Now, do be quiet so I may work." She tunneled her finger farther into the knot and tugged. "I've got it. One minute more."

He looked up at the blazing ceiling. "We don't have another minute. I demand you leave."

"Perhaps we should clear up a certain matter, my lord." Another pull released part of the knot. "I don't follow commands, yours or anyone else's."

With one loop untied, Lana maneuvered the other twists as she'd learned years ago, and the rope fell to the floor. Drew shot to his feet, grasped her upper arm, and hauled her to his side.

"Wait." She tried to break free from his hold, intent on recovering the pistol under the bed, but Drew dragged her from the fiery shelter.

Heat from the inferno rolled into the chilled night air as they raced out the door. Lana stumbled, and Drew swept her into his arms without breaking stride. He didn't stop running until they were a safe distance from the cottage. She clung to him.

Heavens. It felt good to be in his arms again.

The roof collapsed, the beams snapping and the walls folding in on themselves with a loud crash that rumbled through the night. The roaring flames lit what was once the yard. Reggie appeared to be gone, thank goodness, along with Drew's horse.

Drew lowered her to her feet. "Lana, what the hell were you thinking? You could have been killed."

"A simple thank you will suffice."

He shoved his hands through his hair and issued a frustrated growl. Grabbing her shoulders, he jerked her close and kissed her soundly. When he set her away, he didn't release his hold. "You cannot risk yourself. If you lost the baby…"

Lana's heart skipped. She hadn't realized how important issue would be to him that he would sacrifice himself. Drew had never wished to marry until he thought her with child. What would he think once he learned the truth? Tears flooded her eyes.

Drew wrapped his arms around her and pulled her into his chest. "Please don't cry, peach. I'm sorry."

His crooning and gentle touch encouraged her release, but Lana held tight to her emotions. The last thing they needed was a blubbering ninny slowing them down.

"Do you think you can walk? Lady Dohve's manor is close, but it will mean walking a fair distance."

She nodded, wanting to escape this terrible place. Her heart leapt into her throat. "Reggie has a firearm."

Drew checked his holster. "Damnation. Did he take my pistol?"

She glanced back at the roaring heap. "It's in there. I was trying to recover it."

"He likely thinks we're dead and is hiding to save his own skin." Drew shrugged off his jacket and placed it around her shoulders. "Let's try to be quick."

"I don't need your jacket," she protested.

"Let us get *this* straight, my sweet. I am the gentleman. By rights, I decide who will and won't wear my jacket."

Away from the heat of the fire, the frigid wind swept over her. She shivered and pulled the garment tightly around her body. "Who am I to argue with authority?"

"Indeed." Drew snuggled her against his side, and they began the trek to Lady Dohve's house.

A full moon created an eerie sort of daylight, illuminating their breath as it formed a fog around them. Lana glanced sideways at his profile. Had he truly offered for her out of obligation? She hadn't believed it to be so, but his words to Reggie rang with truth. The duke had been unhappy when he learned of their union, and Drew's brother had demanded he offer for her hand.

She couldn't contemplate it now. Not when every effort went toward forcing her legs to move.

"This is the family cemetery," Drew said. "It won't be much farther."

Lana nodded, but her dry throat prevented her from speaking. They walked for what seemed like another half hour before the bulky outline of the house loomed in the distance.

Thank God. She took three more steps before her knees buckled, sending her crashing to the earth.

Drew kneeled beside her. "We're almost there, peach."

She struggled to stand, but her legs refused to cooperate and she sank back down. "Go on without me," she said, too weary to go another step. "I will catch up later."

Drew cocked his head and chuckled. "How considerate, Miss Hillary. But I see little point in going any farther without you, and I don't relish sitting in the cold." He scooped her in his arms and stood.

"You can't carry me."

His chest vibrated with a low chuckle. "Do you disparage my manhood, peach? We really must have a serious discussion about who is in charge once we return to London."

She laid her head against his shoulder and closed her eyes. "I believe I could eat an entire horse once we reach home."

He kissed her forehead. "Perhaps Lady Dohve has

something more appetizing. I'm afraid we must stay the night at Choate Manor. I will arrange transportation on the morrow."

"Drew," she said, "thank you for coming for me."

"I truly had no other choice. There is an empty spot in my bed belonging to you."

⤜⊷

Drew climbed the front steps with Lana in his arms and burst through Lady Dohve's door in complete disregard for propriety. "Lady Dohve. It is Andrew Forest. I need assistance."

A glow from the drawing room where he'd met with the baroness earlier drew him.

Lady Dohve was in mid-lift from her chair when he crossed the threshold with Lana in his arms.

"Oh, dear." She hurried to his side. "Maynard. Elsie. Come quickly."

Lady Dohve touched Drew's elbow and guided him to the settee.

"Dear heavens, my lord, where ever did you find a young lady?"

Elsie, the maid, hustled into the drawing room, awaiting instructions.

"Retrieve a blanket, posthaste," the baroness said.

Lana reached her hand toward Lady Dohve. "My name is Lana Hillary, a daughter to James Hillary of Sussex."

"Poor dear, your lips are turning blue."

Drew placed Lana on the settee and examined her face. Indeed, her lips had a bluish tint, and though she pulled off the look with ease, he didn't care for the indication. He stalked to the fireplace and tossed two more logs on the glowing embers.

The maid returned with a blanket at the same time the manservant appeared.

"If only Reggie were here to help." Lady Dohve twisted her hands. "Elsie, find some nourishment for this young lady and Lord Andrew. And Maynard, please prepare the west wing suite."

The elderly man hobbled toward the staircase. Drew cringed with the thought of him navigating the steps. "Lady Dohve, I realize this is highly irregular, but would you allow me to prepare the room? I don't mind since your usual help is otherwise engaged."

The lady glanced toward her unsteady manservant. "Oh, dear."

"I would appreciate your permission. I'd feel responsible if Maynard fell on the stairs."

She gave a sharp nod while the servant scowled.

Pride be damned. Sometimes a man had to admit when he couldn't do things any longer.

"I don't require anything special," Lana argued. "Just a place to lay my head."

"I'll at least start a fire in the grate," Drew said. "Where might I find more firewood?"

Maynard directed him to the dwindling supply, and Drew gathered six logs in his arms to carry with him.

Upstairs, he started a respectable fire and shook out the linens before remaking the bed. He made a few more trips to gather enough logs to keep the room toasty throughout the night. He'd stay here with Lana to keep her safe and warm, and perhaps steal a kiss or two.

When he returned to the drawing room, Lana held a glass of wine, and she snuggled into the blanket, pulling it to her chin as he approached. Her lips had regained their rosy pinkness, and Drew sighed with relief.

Lady Dohve offered a solicitous smile as if she had expected their visit. "Lord Andrew, would you care for a drink?"

"Thank you, my lady. Perhaps you will allow me to pour it myself?"

"Certainly."

He sloshed the dark liquid into a tumbler then assumed the place next to Lana on the sofa.

The baroness's brows pinched together. "Lord Andrew, I am puzzled by how you came to encounter Miss Hillary?"

Drew gulped his drink this time, not wishing to bring more unpleasantness into the lady's life. "I know of no easy way to introduce the topic. Therefore, I will be forthright. Miss Hillary, my betrothed, was abducted from her home yesterday."

"Oh, heavens." Lady Dohve retrieved her dutiful fan. "How horrible, my dear."

Lana shivered beside him, and he longed to wrap himself around her to warm her. "I managed to escape unscathed, thanks to Lord Andrew."

"Yes, thank the Lord above for this divine intervention." Lady Dohve raised her eyes to the heavens, making Drew look up, too. There was a nice mural on the ceiling. A bit risqué, but he had seen less appropriate works of art.

"I must admit," Lady Dohve said, "I'm uncertain how your unfortunate circumstances led to Lord Andrew's discovery, or how it is you arrived at Choate Manor?"

"That is the part I believe will be most difficult to hear," Drew answered. "As you may or may not be aware, Betsy March was employed as Miss Hillary's lady's maid."

"Yes?" Lady Dohve leaned forward. "But you aren't

suggesting Betsy had anything to do with Miss Hillary's kidnapping, are you? She would never do anything untoward. She was always a dutiful child."

He smiled in sympathy. "I'm sorry to say Miss March played a role in Miss Hillary's kidnapping."

Lady Dohve's hand flew to her chest. "I can't believe that's possible, Lord Andrew. Betsy radiated kindness. She would do nothing to harm anyone."

Lana covered Drew's hand to silence him. "I can see you have sincere affection for Betsy, as did I, so this must be shocking. Unfortunately, Lord Andrew speaks the truth."

Lady Dohve's chest heaved with a ragged sigh.

Lana tossed the blanket aside and went to kneel at the baroness's feet. Reaching out, she squeezed the older woman's hand. "I'm unconvinced Betsy behaved without undue influence, my lady. I suspect her brother may have masterminded the ploy."

Drew bit his tongue. The man couldn't mastermind his way out of a burlap sack.

Lady Dohve shook her head. "No, I cannot believe Reggie would do anything as reprehensible either. I'm afraid you are mistaken, Miss Hillary."

Maynard had returned and hovered on the edge of the room but hobbled toward his mistress. "If I may be so bold as to interrupt, Lady Dohve, my grandson has not been the pillar of society I may have led you to believe."

"Indeed, Maynard? How can you say as much? Isn't Reggie here daily to assist with the upkeep of the manor?"

From the disrepair of the home, it appeared Reggie did little in the way of assisting.

"Yes, my lady," Maynard said, wringing his hands together, "but we both know items have gone missing."

"I have always wanted to believe the items had been put away without any memory of where I placed them."

The servant came even closer. "Which is the reason I've remained silent." He turned to Lana. "May I ask what happened to you, miss?"

"I'm certain Betsy laced my tea with a sleeping draught. She left me in her brother's care while she delivered the ransom note, but she never came back. It must be true she was apprehended."

Lady Dohve peered over Lana's shoulder to meet Drew's eyes. "I thought she had met with an accident."

Lana glanced over her shoulder, and he nodded. "Oh," she answered in a small voice, appearing to digest this news. "When Betsy didn't return, I didn't have long to wonder what had happened. Lord Andrew found me in the cottage on your property."

"I see." The corners of the baroness's mouth drooped. "We must call for the magistrate in the morning, but you both require sustenance and rest. Maynard, please secure all the doors and windows."

"Yes, my lady."

Once they'd eaten, Drew assisted Lana up the staircase and ushered her into the toasty room.

She collapsed on the bed. "I feel filthy."

"Shall I bring water for the basin?"

Lana nodded. "Please."

He sought out warm water then carried it upstairs for her use. She slumped forward like a wilted flower. Placing the basin on the washstand, he soaked the cloth then lathered it with a sliver of lavender soap the housemaid provided. He wrung out the excess water and carried the cloth to Lana.

She sat with her eyes closed, too tired to even stay

upright. He pulled back the counterpane, removed her slippers, and encouraged her to recline on the pillow. Then taking the cloth, he wiped the dirt from her face.

"Lavender," she said on a breath. "Much better than onions and sheep."

Drew arched a brow in question, but she had closed her eyes again.

"You don't have to do this," she said, but didn't try to stop him.

From her face, he slid the cloth along her neck and across her chest to the neckline. He was careful not to touch her breasts for fear he would be unable to stop himself. They would become the cleanest part on her person.

He quickly moved to her arms before he changed his mind. Pushing up her sleeves, he smoothed the cloth over each arm before cleaning the red marks on her wrists.

Her stockings were tattered beyond reason, so he removed them and tried to inch her skirts higher to clean her legs.

She grasped her skirts and held them in place. "No. Please don't."

He drew back slowly. "As you wish."

The ordeal had shaken her more than she had allowed him to see. Once he covered her with the counterpane, he placed tiny kisses on both wrists and pulled down her sleeves. Lana's breath grew deep and steady as she surrendered to slumber. When he judged her soundly asleep, he moved from the bedside intending to turn the lock in the door.

Her eyes flew open and she reached toward him. "Drew, please don't leave me alone."

He kissed her hand and then settled into a chair close to her bed, facing the door to stand guard.

"Shh, I'm not going anywhere." In fact, it might be a long time before he left her side again.

Forty-four

HORSES APPROACHED CHOATE MANOR. LANA PUSHED back from the breakfast table to hurry into the foyer, her gaze flicking to the spiral stairs. Should she wake Drew?

Lady Dohve followed behind Lana at a slower pace. "Who would be calling this early?"

When there was a rap on the door, Lana's steps faltered. *What if it's him?* She chided herself for being silly. Her abductor wouldn't show his face at Choate Manor, surely. And he wouldn't travel in a pack.

Pushing her irrational thoughts aside, she turned the locks and opened the door a crack. "Papa!" She threw open the heavy oak door and launched into her father's arms.

He gathered her in a firm hug. "Lana, precious girl. You are safe. Thank God."

As soon as her father released her, Jake pulled her into his squeezing embrace. "Thank God is right. Forest found you. Where is he?"

"Is he all right?" a less familiar voice asked.

She peeked around her brother to discover Lord Richard hanging back, fumbling his hat.

Lana stepped from Jake's arms. "He's sleeping, my

lord. He suffered a blow to the head, but he doesn't seem to have any lasting injuries."

"Maybe the blow has knocked some sense into him." Despite Lord Richard's bluster, worry showed in the lines on his forehead. "Perhaps I should see to my brother."

Lady Dohve stepped aside and swept a hand toward the stairs. "Of course, you should, my lord. Maynard will show you to the chamber."

"No need," Drew's voice drifted down the stairwell making Lana's heart trip. "I heard a commotion and thought I should investigate." He ambled down the stairs to greet her family and his brother. "The cavalry arrives at last. And late. I could've used your help earlier."

Drew's brother gathered him in a rough hug, pounding his back as if he burped an infant. Well, an especially hearty one. "You should've asked me to accompany you," Lord Richard said. "What were you thinking?"

Drew offered a sheepish grin. "In retrospect, I agree."

Lana gestured toward their hostess. "Lord Richard, Papa, Jake. You remember Lady Dohve, do you not? The baroness provided us with safe haven last night."

Her father bowed to the baroness. "You have my undying gratitude, my lady. We've been sick with worry these last two days."

"As would be any parent with a missing child, even if she's a grown woman. Please, join us for breakfast."

With hats in hand, they trailed into the breakfast room where there was no servant to attend to their needs. Once the men prepared their plates with the meager offering, Lady Dohve sighed.

"We've had more than our share of heartache at Choate Manor these past months, so I'm relieved to see your situation has a happy ending."

Everyone offered sympathetic mutterings, seeming unsure in what to say. The baroness didn't require any encouragement to continue.

"I learned only yesterday Betsy March was killed in an accident." Lady Dohve sipped her tea. "Betsy was like a daughter, you know."

Lana studied her family. Her father's lips twisted into a poor imitation of sympathy. "I did not know. My sympathies, my lady."

Jake fiddled with his napkin, his face turning red as he held his tongue.

"That is kind of you, sir." Lady Dohve pulled a handkerchief from her sleeve and blotted the tears welling in her eyes. "Four months ago we lost my great-nephew to a fever. Philip had only arrived from Bavaria when he grew ill."

Jake's eyes rounded. "Philip Bollrud?"

"Did you know him, Mr. Hillary?"

He shook his head. "Not personally, my lady."

Lana's father turned to Drew, effectively ending discussion of Bollrud. "We didn't know what to think when you didn't return last night, so we left at dawn to call on Lady Dohve. I'm elated to find you and Lana safe. What happened?"

Drew met Lana's gaze before throwing a glance toward the baroness. "Perhaps after breakfast we may speak in private."

Lana understood he wanted to spare Lady Dohve. "Do you have a library, my lady? I would love a book to occupy my mind."

The baroness puffed her chest and smiled. "Yes, it is lovely. My husband collected many books on a multitude of subjects. I've been fortunate to retain it these last few years."

❦

Drew sent a smile of gratitude to Lana when she escorted Lady Dohve from the breakfast room.

Jake tapped his knuckles against the table. "So that blackguard *isn't* Bollrud? I knew he was queer as Dick's headband."

Drew recalled thinking the same thing when Bollrud first appeared at Irvine Castle. "His real name is Reggie March, Betsy's brother. It was a ruse to access Lana's dowry."

He filled them in on the events at the cottage, ending with their escape.

"Where is the bugger now?" Rich asked, fury making his face hard.

Unlike Drew, March didn't have the loyalty of his kin to protect or hide him.

"He has no other ties," Drew said, "and we know he has no money, or very little."

Mr. Hillary rose from his seat at the end of the table. "Jake will collect the local magistrate. Drew and Lord Richard, you search the outer property. Return to the cottage and see if you can track him. I will walk the grounds closest to the house." The man handed out orders like a decorated general.

Drew didn't feel at ease leaving Lana, even if her father kept watch over her. Yet, he was the only one who knew the location of the cottage.

He heaved a sigh and rolled his shoulders. "I'll need a horse."

"You may use mine," Mr. Hillary said.

Before Drew left, he sought out Lana in the drawing room. She excused herself from Lady Dohve's company and followed him to the foyer.

"Lana, I must leave for a short while, but your father will keep watch over you."

She gripped his arm. "Where are you going?"

"Rich and I are hunting Reggie March."

"Can't we go home and be done with the matter?"

"I'm afraid if we don't find him, he will turn up again." And March still had Drew's horse, or more aptly his father's. There would never be an end to his father's bellyaching if Drew lost Demetrius.

Lana's blue-green eyes locked with his, and in them, he read a mixture of apprehension and knowing. "Please, proceed with caution."

"Nothing will happen to me, peach. I have responsibilities." Drew wrapped her in his arms and placed a quick kiss on her lips before anyone interrupted. "My carefree days are over."

Lana drew back with a frown.

"I meant care*less*." He winked, hoping his teasing would ease her worries. "My careless days have come to an end, though my carefree ones seem numbered as well if that dark scowl is any indication."

He placed a kiss on the tip of her nose, relieved to hear her soft chuckle.

❧

Lana's mind wandered as Lady Dohve chattered about the weather, her favorite holiday, and her past associations in London.

She wanted to be home where she could take a real bath and sleep in her bed, but it appeared she might be stuck at Choate Manor another night.

"Miss Hillary, I would like you to be frank with me."

Lana looked up to find the baroness studying her with

a firm gaze. "Did my Betsy ever give reason to believe she was a bad person? Aside from her involvement with your abduction, of course."

Yes, there was that small matter. Difficult to overlook, really. Lana thought back to her earlier experiences with Betsy. Her maid had been a sweet young woman. Lana was as shocked by Betsy's betrayal as Lady Dohve. "I had no reason to suspect her."

The lady offered a sad smile and gazed at her hands resting on her lap. "I am sorry for what happened to you, and I apologize for my questions of a personal nature. It's quite heartbreaking to learn the unadulterated truth about a loved one."

Lana nodded. "I can only imagine the depth of your hurt."

"Miss Hillary, the gentlemen referenced my nephew in their discussion. How do they know of him? Philip had been abroad most of his life."

She glanced at the baroness. Should she reveal Reggie's deception? The lady seemed fragile, and Lana didn't know if she could cope with much more.

Lady Dohve twisted at the waist to open a drawer on the side table beside her chair. Retrieving a miniature, she handed it to Lana. "This was my nephew, Philip."

Lana accepted the painting. The young man's dark hair waved back from his handsome, youthful face and a secretive smile played about his lips. The name Bollrud would always conjure Reggie's snarling face in her mind, and this thought made her sad. He had tainted the reputation of a gentleman deeply loved by his family, likely a kind man if he was anything like his aunt. Lady Dohve deserved to know what additional damage Reggie had caused.

"Mr. March portrayed himself as your nephew. He traveled to Irvine Castle and told everyone he was Lord Bollrud. He claimed he sought a wife but he had already chosen me as his target."

She searched Lady Dohve's face for any expression of emotion, but it remained impressively blank. Lana was unsure if the baroness had even heard her given her lack of any reaction.

Finally, she wrinkled her forehead and bit her lower lip. "Miss Hillary, please forgive my questions, but I must know, what happened at the cottage?"

Lana wished to put the entire affair behind her, so she provided an abbreviated summary of events at the cottage.

"Reggie threatened you with a pistol, you say?" Lady Dohve's manner remained on par with one inquiring into one's holiday in Bath.

"Yes, my lady."

"Oh, dear." The baroness struggled to push herself from her chair with a grunt. "Will you excuse me, Miss Hillary?" Without waiting for a reply, she swept from the room.

What had gotten into Lady Dohve to necessitate her sudden disappearance? Lana blushed as it dawned on her the lady likely rushed for the water closet. She returned her attention to her book, but after half an hour, Lana began to worry the gravity of the situation had gotten to the baroness.

For the next few moments, Lana glanced over her shoulder, hoping to catch a glimpse of Lady Dohve beyond the drawing room doors. Finally, she set her book aside and shifted her weight to rise from the sofa, but a rustling of skirts stopped her. Lady Dohve returned with her sewing basket and resumed her spot by the fire.

"You don't mind if I attend to my embroidery, do you?" Lady Dohve's voice was full of cheer.

The lady was taking everything surprisingly well. Lana's fears of the baroness swooning or dissolving in a fit of tears remained unfounded. In fact, her jolly demeanor struck Lana as bizarre given everything that had transpired.

Lady Dohve looked up from her sewing. "Would you care for any refreshment, dear? Betsy always favored chocolate biscuits. Would you like me to ring for tea?"

"N-no thank you."

The baroness sat back with a smile. "How silly of me. We just enjoyed breakfast, did we not?"

There was something off about the lady. Lana scooted to the edge of her seat, preparing to stand. "My lady, are you well? Should I call for assistance?"

Lady Dohve chuckled. "I'm right as rain, my dear. Thank you for your concern. Please, rest."

Easing back against the sofa cushion, Lana lifted the book from her lap, but her attention stayed on her hostess.

The baroness's needle stilled and she cocked her head, staring into space. She froze, her posture rigid, for several moments before clucking her tongue and shaking her head.

Lana's concern for the lady increased. Was the baroness suffering an apoplectic fit? Her behavior was decidedly strange.

Lady Dohve plopped back against the chair. "My dear girl, I believe I left my spectacles in the library. Would you please retrieve them?" When Lana didn't move at once, the baroness waved her hand impatiently. "Go on, do as I say. *Now.*"

Good heavens above. The woman was too overbearing by half, which may account in part for her lack of servants under her employ.

"As you wish." Lana rose from the sofa and took refuge in the library. Closing the door, she sank against it. She didn't mind escaping the other woman's company for a bit. The way Lady Dohve spoke incessantly about Betsy troubled her.

She wandered the room lined with shelves reaching all the way to the soaring ceiling, inactively seeking the spectacles. The inner room had no windows, probably to protect the books from damage, but this meant she had no view outside. And no quick means of escape should the baroness choose to follow and impose her peculiar company on Lana.

Perhaps she could convince her father to take her home. She opened the library door and slipped into the foyer, hoping the lady wouldn't hear her escape.

"I'll ask ya once more, where is she?" Reggie's gruff voice stopped Lana, and she pressed back against the wall. Blast! How did he gain access inside the manor house?

"Don't affect that tone with me, young man." Lady Dohve's voice rang out strong, a testament to her aristocratic lineage. "I haven't any idea who you mean."

"That trollop, Lana Hillary. I saw 'er pa walkin' the grounds. Tell me where she is."

Lana held her breath. If Lady Dohve kept her secret, she promised to be much more tolerant of the baroness's oddities.

Forty-five

"REGGIE, REGGIE, REGGIE." LADY DOHVE CHUCKLED. "I told myself there was only so much you could take from me and once you had depleted everything, you would have no choice but to abandon your thievery. I had nothing of great value any longer, so I looked the other way."

"W-wot makes ya think *I* took yer jewels?"

"I never mentioned jewels, you simpleton." The baroness's voice was hardened and sharp. "But I was wrong, wasn't I? Once you depleted my valuables, you didn't leave me alone."

"I don't know wot yer sayin'."

"You've besmirched my nephew's name, Reggie. Or should I refer to you as Lord Bollrud?"

"That was Betsy's idea. Everything," he said, his voice rising in pitch. "She planned the whole thing."

Lana pursed her lips. How like a brother to blame his younger sister.

"Ah, yes. Thank you for the reminder of another loss at your hands, my darling Betsy." Lady Dohve's calm tone sent a shiver down Lana's back. "You corrupted my little girl, Reggie."

"She was yer *maid*, you batty old woman. Not your daughter."

"Perhaps not by blood, but Betsy was only an infant when she came to Choate Manor. I'll never forget the feel of her in my arms. Betsy fulfilled my deepest wishes."

"Yer mad," Reggie snarled. "You should be locked away."

"You stole her from me, Reginald. *You* killed her."

"I did not. Betsy got 'erself caught and betrayed me."

Lady Dohve's laugh was nothing more than a hollow imitation. "A carriage ran her down in the street, my dear boy. I imagine she didn't see its approach, because she was trying to evade capture."

"That's a lie."

"How I wish that were true. But stealing from me, ruining my great-nephew's reputation, and even taking Betsy from me wasn't your worst mistake, Reggie, my boy."

He scoffed. "Indeed? An' wot might that be?"

Tension saturated the air as Lady Dohve remained silent, leaving Lana with the eerie feeling that once she responded, Reggie wasn't going to care for the lady's answer.

Lady Dohve cleared her throat. "I know you took Lord Dohve's dueling pistol."

"Is that so?" Reggie said with a derisive snort. "And 'ow is *that* a mistake?"

"You should have taken both of them."

"Wot the—?"

A bone-rattling bang shattered the air, and Lana cried out. An immediate thud shook the floor and then there was silence. Had the baroness just shot Reggie? She must be beside herself. Lana dashed to the drawing room to check on the poor lady.

Lady Dohve looked up when Lana appeared in the doorway. The pistol rested on the side table and she had returned to her needlepoint. "There you are, my dear. Did you locate my spectacles?"

Lana shook her head, speechless.

The baroness flicked a dismissive hand. "That is quite all right, dear. I keep an extra pair of spectacles in my sewing box."

❧

Drew's blood froze in his veins while the rest of him broke into a sweat when he heard the gunshot. He pushed the stallion into a gallop, reaching the manor house in a matter of a few seconds. Pulling back on the reins, he leapt from the horse and dashed inside. Rich wasn't far behind.

Lana stood in the foyer, wrapped in her father's embrace. "What happened, peach?"

She glanced up at him with wide, green eyes. "Lady Dohve shot Reggie."

"The hell you say," he said under his breath and continued to the drawing room to see for himself.

The baroness sat in the drawing room working on her needlepoint, smiling when he and Rich entered. "Lord Richard and Lord Andrew, how nice to see you again. I do hope you enjoyed your ride. Choate Manor boasts the most beautiful vistas." She nodded toward the body. "Do watch your step, gentlemen."

Drew and Rich exchanged glances before proceeding to Reggie's crumpled body to check for signs of life. His brother knelt, placing his hand in front of the man's nose.

"No breath," Rich mumbled. "He's dead."

"Yes, quite dead I imagine," Lady Dohve answered.

"I shot him through the heart. Dohve made an excellent teacher, and he boasted that I was his most adept student. Do you think you might assist me with removing his body? Such a bloody nuisance."

Drew balked. "My lady, what happened?"

"I heard the vermin sneaking through the back door, the one he always uses, so I sent Miss Hillary to the library." She looked up as if just remembering Lana. "She is a delightful young woman. I would love to have her extend her stay. Do you think she might?"

The lady had lost her mind. A pistol lay beside Reggie on the Aubusson, out of place in the once pristine drawing room.

"It appears to have been self-defense," Rich commented.

"Oh, no," Lady Dohve interjected as if discussing the weather. "It was justice. He deserved what he got as payment for all he took from me."

Maynard hovered in the doorway. "Don't listen to her, my lords. She has grown a bit addled in her elder years."

Lady Dohve skewered her servant with a furious glare, but then returned her attention to her thread and needle, humming a happy tune as she worked.

"I heard the entire exchange, and it was self-defense, my lords."

"What did I miss?" Jake asked from the foyer. He had brought the magistrate with him.

Mr. Hillary repeated what they knew with certainty. Lady Dohve was an excellent markswoman.

The magistrate, a brawny fellow with windblown black hair, ambled into the drawing room, his dispassionate eyes taking in the scene. "I take it this is the kidnapper."

He walked to the body and pushed the man's arm with the toe of his boot as if to reassure himself he was dead.

With a swipe of his hand across his forehead, he stared down at the gruesome sight. "What happened here?"

Maynard stepped forward. "Her ladyship defended herself and her guest against my grandson. He waved a firearm at the baroness and threatened her. He would have shot my mistress if she hadn't fired first."

Lady Dohve rolled her eyes and continued her needlepoint.

"We believe she's in shock," Rich explained. "Perhaps a doctor could be summoned for her ladyship."

"Along with the undertaker," the magistrate agreed, "for the body, that is."

Unable to stomach any more, Drew left the drawing room. He wanted to hold Lana and be reassured she remained unharmed. But when he arrived outside, she sat in front of Jake on his horse.

"I'm taking her home, Forest. Lana has been through enough. She will feel better once she's back in familiar surroundings."

Drew should be the one carrying her home. "At least cover her better." He shrugged off his coat and tossed it to Jake. Lana's brother accepted his offering and wrapped it around her shoulders.

"I'll come to Hillary House as soon as I can leave here," Drew said.

Lana met his eyes and gave a small nod.

"Take good care of her, Jake."

"I always do. Just hurry with clearing up matters here so I may turn the responsibility over to you. I don't know if my nerves can take another day."

"I'm sitting right here," Lana grumbled. "You do realize I can hear you."

Drew chuckled. He hoped being back in London

among the comforts of home would erase some of the trauma she had experienced over the last two days, but from what he could gather so far, Lana would be fine.

Mr. Hillary rounded the side of the house. "Your black stallion is in the mews. I'm leaving with Lana and Jake, but come by as soon as you return." Lana's father grabbed him in a rough hug. "You have my undying gratitude, Drew. I don't know what I would have done if anything had happened to her."

"Me either, sir." Thank goodness none of them would ever have to find out.

❦

Back home, Lana sank into the hot tub, welcoming how the water enveloped her aching limbs. With no lady's attendant any longer, she'd accepted her mother's offer of help. Her mother's silence and gentle touch surprised her. She never asked Lana about her experience. Her mother had changed within the last two days, opening Lana's eyes to how much she must love her and how terrifying everything must have been for her, too.

She captured her mother's hand and pressed a kiss to it. "Thank you, Mama."

"It's nothing, my darling daughter." Her mother choked out the words.

But it wasn't nothing. Lana's mother had kept her promise. She hadn't retreated into her sadness, and she was here for her when Lana most needed her.

"I love you, Mama."

Tears flowed down her mother's cheeks. "I love you too, Lana. More than you will ever know."

Once Lana had finished her bath and dressed in a clean

gown with her mother's help, she went to her father's study. Over the last couple of hours, she had considered her relationship with Drew. She loved him completely, which meant she couldn't see him miserable.

She stood at the doorway. Her father sat behind his desk, holding his head in his hands. "Papa?"

He startled, but his face broke into a radiant grin. "Lana. Please, come in."

She entered his study. Even with the warm bath, a chill resided in her bones, so she chose a chair close to the crackling fire. Her father stood and came around his desk to lean against it.

"I suppose I shouldn't grow too comfortable with your presence at Hillary House. Soon Drew will take you to his home."

How could she broach the subject with her father without feeling like a failure? She cleared her throat. "Papa, I believe Lord Andrew may wish to bow out of our betrothal."

Her father's eyebrows shot up, but he held his tongue.

"If this is his wish, I would like him to be released from our agreement without penalty."

"Why, Lana? I thought you fancied him."

"I do. I love him, Papa, which is why I must let him go. I suspect he offered for me out of a sense of obligation." She shuddered when she glanced up to discover her father's eyes burning with great intensity.

"What type of obligation? What are you suggesting, Lana?"

"It's hard to explain. I... We..." Tears burned her eyes and a knot formed in her throat, making it impossible to confess her transgression.

Her father sighed. "I see."

Lana's head fell. She was a horrible daughter, a huge disappointment. "I'm so ashamed, Papa."

Her father's hand on hers brought more tears. "My darling, you are not the first, nor will you be the last, to surrender to passion. Do you carry his child?"

She shook her head. "B–but he believes I do. And I cannot allow him to marry me for this reason. I'd rather die than have Drew resent me for forcing him into marriage. Just look how horrid it has been for you and Mama."

Her father grasped her chin gently. "Your mother and I were not forced to marry."

"But, I thought—"

"Your mother told you she had no choice." When Lana nodded, he released her chin and turned away with a huff. "Marrying was mutually beneficial for both of us. I assure you we were not forced."

He spun to face her again with hardened features, but his anger dissolved quickly. "When a man... um... exhibits a—Well, when he shows certain tendencies or... um, *interests*, this indicates..."

Her face heated and she squirmed, reaching a new level of embarrassment.

"Damnation, Lana. This is difficult for me. Could you please accept my word that the young man loves you?"

Lana couldn't discuss Drew's *interests* with her father without dying of mortification, but his interests extended beyond her. She was simply the only one foolish enough to risk pregnancy. Plus, there was the matter of discovery that had prompted his courtship.

"I must know he wants me for me, and not to fulfill a sense of duty. Please, Papa, if he wants out of the agreement, will you release him?"

Her father stared until Lana began to fidget again. He issued a tired sigh. "I wouldn't have you marry someone who doesn't love you, my girl."

The squeezing in her chest moved upward until her throat was almost too constricted to swallow. She experienced no relief at learning of her father's agreement.

"Would you like me to be present when you speak with Lord Andrew?"

Her eyes flew to his stern face. "Heavens, no."

"Will you speak with him today when he calls?"

Lana twisted her fingers in her lap. She couldn't face Drew yet. "Just one more day? Tell him I'm resting, please." She needed one more day to gather her courage.

Her father frowned. "You shouldn't keep him waiting long. The poor gent has been tortured enough the last several days."

Lana nodded. Drew had been through a lot with almost dying.

"Very well," her father conceded. "When he calls today, I'll request he return early tomorrow morning."

"Thank you, Papa."

Forty-six

LANA ROSE WITH THE SUN, HER NERVES A TANGLED MESS. Her father had informed her before she retired to bed Drew would call at nine o'clock. In three hours, she would offer to release him from his commitment.

She shuffled through Hillary House as if in a thick fog, barely touching her breakfast, unable to concentrate on any task. At nine o'clock, she waited in her father's study, sitting primly on an overstuffed leather chair. She sat on her hands, fighting the urge to run, when there was a light tap on the door.

"Enter," her father called.

Hogan opened the massive oak door and crossed the room to offer a card to Lana's father. "His lordship requests an audience."

Her father's questioning gaze shot to Lana. "Are you certain you want to do this?"

Her mind screamed no, but she took a deep breath and nodded.

His thinning lips and tight expression served as evidence of her father's disapproval of her decision. "Show Lord Andrew in right away."

"Yes, sir." Hogan's steps seemed reluctant. How much did the butler know about this meeting?

Her stomach churned with the violence of a tempest, and she readjusted her position.

When Drew stepped into her father's study, her hand fluttered to her chest. He looked splendid, the most dashing fellow in all of England. His gray breeches molded to his muscled thighs, his pristine white shirt and expertly tied cravat stood stark against his tailored-to-perfection navy jacket. His polished hessians gleamed. Even his toffee waves were as tamed as she'd ever seen them. Most appealing of all, he wore his dimpled smile. His only flaw was the nick on his cheek, but it had begun to heal and would likely disappear within the week. Lana suppressed the urge to fling herself into his arms.

It would be easy to marry Drew, continuing the pretense, but she couldn't ask him to commit to her without knowing she didn't carry his child.

"Welcome, Lord Andrew," her father greeted. "Please, come in."

She didn't miss the coolness in her father's tone, but she couldn't fault him given her confession.

Drew sauntered into the room and remained standing, his eyes never leaving her. She returned his gaze, her cheeks heating under his scrutiny.

"I'll leave you alone," her father announced before looking at Lana, "but I'll be close if I'm needed."

Lana's heart hammered as her father crossed the room and pulled the door closed.

"Your father said you wished to speak with me, peach."

❦

Drew admired the sight before him. Lana was as beautiful as he always found her. He would never lose his desire for her; the hunger simply bound him tighter to her.

After receiving a blistering set down from Mr. Hillary for compromising his daughter, the man had taken pity on him and suggested he come prepared to convince Lana to continue their engagement. In reality, Mr. Hillary would not allow his daughter out of the marriage, but he'd impressed upon Drew the importance of leaving no doubts as to his constancy.

"Why have you summoned me, Lana?"

She wiggled on the chair, and Drew held back his grin. Damn, how he'd love to have her wiggling on his lap instead.

Lana took a shaky breath and let it out slowly. "My father has agreed to release you from the engagement if you so choose."

He ambled toward her, rubbing his chin with his thumb and index finger. "Hmm, I imagine it would be quite a scandal if we chose to remain unmarried."

Her eyelashes fluttered and an attractive blush colored her cheeks.

"Yes," he continued, moving closer, "it would shock the *ton*, especially when I intend to keep you in my bed for days on end."

Her gaze shot to his, and he offered a seductive smile. Her nervous movements increased as she adjusted her position on the chair again.

"Please don't toy with me, Drew. I know you offered to marry me out of obligation."

He moved closer until his knees brushed against hers. "Are you clairvoyant, love? You never revealed this little talent. Do tell me. What am I thinking at this moment?"

Lana's green eyes stole a look, and her breath caught in an audible hitch. Good, she still desired him. He counted on that to help him show her the error of her thinking.

Drew hauled her to stand in front of him, making sure her body touched his. Capturing her face, he caressed his thumb along the ridge of her ear. She leaned into his touch, her eyelids growing heavy.

"I-I don't know wh-what you're thinking."

He brushed his lips against hers and she quivered. It took all of his willpower not to devour her right there. "Not even a guess?" he whispered against her lips. He didn't kiss her again, but placed his hand on her waist in preparation.

He saw no fear, only a flicker of passion waiting to ignite.

"No," she replied softly.

He breathed in Lana's scent, airy and fresh, one he would forever associate with love. As he slid his hand to cup her bottom, her body arched into his. "You have no guesses at all, peach?" His voice sounded strained, as it should. Lana Hillary pushed his self-control to the breaking point.

She chuckled softly and relaxed a little in his arms. "I-I have *some* idea."

"So that there's no misunderstanding, I'll tell you anyway." He nibbled her earlobe. She shivered in response. "I'm fantasizing about making the only woman I've ever loved my wife." This time he pecked her lips. "And *then*, I'm going to strip every article of her irksome clothing so I can lavish her with endless adoration."

"Oh," Lana said on an exhale. "Does... does she know about me?"

Drew dropped his forehead against hers and chuckled under his breath. "That's one of the things I love about you, peach. Not a sentimental bone in your gorgeous body."

She laughed too, and he gathered her against him. Lana buried her face in his neck and wrapped her arms around his waist. They stayed that way a long time. She tried to break contact when she eased from his embrace, but he kept hold of her hands.

"Drew, I know you desire me, as I do you, but that doesn't make for a solid marriage." She pulled her hands again and he released her, for the moment. She wandered to the fireplace and stared into the flames. "I've spoken with my father. He has agreed to allow you out of the marital contract."

He blew out a deep breath, exasperated by her inability to hear him. "Lana, I've proclaimed my intentions repeatedly. Why do you push me away?"

She glanced over her shoulder, her bottom lip trembling and tears welling in her eyes. "But in the cottage…"

Drew rushed forward, sweeping her against him. "Lana, don't you realize I lied? I would have said anything to keep that bastard from hurting you. It was torture watching him maul you, but I couldn't allow *him* to know." He rubbed his cheek against her silky hair, loving the feel of it against his skin.

A gasping sob broke free from her, and he pulled her snug against him, running his hands along her back and kissing her temple. "My poor darling, I thought you understood. It was all a lie. I love you."

They held each other, swaying back and forth in a comforting dance until Lana's tears subsided. He loosened the embrace and pulled a handkerchief from his pocket.

She examined the darkened spot on his jacket, her cheeks turning pink. "I'm sorry for dampening your jacket."

"That's quite all right. I hope to shed it soon."

She dabbed her eyes and took a shuddering breath. "Drew, there's something I must know. Did you propose marriage to save me from ruin?"

Drew pinched the bridge of his nose. For heaven's sake, of course he had in the beginning, but he'd fallen in love. He refused to answer a pointless question. "I love you, Lana. I want to marry you and raise our child together. That's the only thing relevant."

Tears pooled in her eyes again. "I'm not with child. I... discovered this at the cottage."

"Oh." He raked his fingers through his hair, trying to sort his feelings. She had seemed certain only a week ago. "I'm sorry, love. I can see how this upsets you."

Her emerald gaze locked on him. "But what about you? How does this knowledge affect you?"

He debated being honest with her, fearing she might not appreciate his feelings, but he wouldn't begin their marriage on a lie. Lana sat on the settee as she awaited his answer.

"Naturally, I'm disappointed, but if I may be honest, I'm relieved also."

Lana's back stiffened. "Which is the reason I must release you from our agreement. There is no child. You're under no obligation to marry me."

She turned her head away when he kneeled before her.

"Lana, don't be silly—"

"My chances of securing another match are nonexistent, but I can't bring myself to marry anyone else. I'll retire to the country and live the life of a spinster." Lana attempted to pull away, but he wouldn't allow it. Not anymore.

"If you would allow me to explain, love. You could

at least extend me that courtesy as your betrothed, couldn't you?"

Her troubled gaze landed on him, and eventually, she inclined her head.

"I realize I am being selfish," he said, "but I'm relieved, because I don't wish to share you yet. When the time is right, we'll have our children. I wish to cherish this time with you. I want you as my wife. The only thing dictating my decision is my heart. But what about you, Lana? Do you love me, or did you agree to wed because you thought you were with child?"

Her eyes rounded, and she sucked in a sharp breath. "How could you even ask such a pudding-headed question?"

Leave it to his peach to find *his* question ridiculous while hers were perfectly logical. "Then it's settled. We will marry," he said.

"Agreed. We shall marry."

Drew lifted her in a hug. "Thank God. I thought I would be an old man before you finally married me."

Lana tossed her head back with a giggle. "Drew."

"It's true, peach. You've changed your mind with greater frequency than a lady changes her gowns."

She broke into a heart-stopping smile. "Yes, yes. Enough of your whining. How long must I wait for your endless adoration to begin?"

"Not long." He covered her lips with his.

⁓

When Lana allowed Drew to guide her out of her father's study, her mother's presence caught her off guard. Her body heated at the thought of her mother overhearing such an intimate moment.

Drew handed Lana over to her mother. "Mrs. Hillary, if

you would be so kind as to escort my bride to her chambers to ready herself for our nuptials, I'd be forever grateful."

Lana gasped. "We're getting married today?"

"Within the hour. The vicar has other engagements today, after all." Drew turned toward her mother. "Promise you won't allow her out of your sight."

"Not on my life, Lord Andrew." Her mother linked arms with her before pulling her up the staircase.

Lana had never suffered from a lack of beautiful dresses, especially since she visited the most exclusive modiste in Town. She selected a Pomona green gown, one of her favorites. Ivory ribbon trimmed the capped sleeves and crisscrossed the bodice, making her appear more endowed than she actually was. Her mother's maid placed tiny sprigs of baby's breath from the hothouse in her hair, and a string of pearls adorned her neck.

"I'm ready, Mama." She wheeled around to discover her mother with tears shining in her eyes.

"You look lovely. Shall we find your groom?"

Lana couldn't hold back a smile as she reached out to grasp her mother's hand.

As Lana entered the drawing room, Phoebe rushed to hug her. "Thank heavens you're back safe and sound."

All of Drew's family had come to witness the exchanging of their vows, including his eldest brother.

The vicar inspected the mantle clock while blotting beads of sweat on his upper lip with a handkerchief. "Shall we begin?"

Drew offered his hand and she placed her smaller one in his. Standing side-by-side in front of the clergyman, they pledged their commitment. When she recited her promise to love, honor, and obey, Drew winked, bringing heat to her cheeks and solidifying his place in her heart. Despite her initial embarrassment over their secret vow, she welcomed the chance to fulfill her promise every day for the rest of their lives and grinned like a fool.

After the ceremony, everyone gathered in the dining room for breakfast. The simplicity of the celebration pleased Lana, and for once, she ate everything on her plate: eggs, ham, sliced peaches, and a roll. She knew from experience she would need sustenance for the coming night, if she and Drew made it that long.

Lana's mother approached her toward the end of the meal. "I had my lady's maid pack a few things for you. You may take her with you, if you like. We've known Jane for ages and know she may be trusted."

Lana's hand fluttered to her chest. Her mother's gesture was overwhelming. "Thank you, Mama, but what will you do? Won't you miss Jane?"

"You mustn't worry about me. I don't mind losing her to you."

She hugged her mother and kissed her cheek. "You are a lovely person, Mama."

Once in the carriage, Drew pulled Lana onto his lap and whispered in her ear, "I've rented a room for us until the house is finished."

She slipped her arms around his neck and kissed his cheek. "I want to see the house."

Drew sported an uncharacteristic scowl. "Now?"

"Oh, please, Drew. I can't wait any longer."

"Very well," he grumbled before delivering his orders to the waiting servant. "But I can't wait much longer either."

The carriage lurched as he took possession of her mouth, his hot lips igniting her passion. She indulged herself, drinking in his kisses, allowing his tongue to probe the recesses of his mouth. She loved his smell, rich and decadent like the finest dark chocolate.

His hand cupped her breast as his thumb swept across her nipple. Lana murmured her approval as he drew circles around the hardened tip, making her squirm with pleasure, wanting more.

Drew broke the kiss, closed his eyes, and took a deep breath. "I don't want to take you in the carriage." A miserable groan accompanied his words.

"Why not?" She worked the buttons of his waistcoat before stealing her hand into the opening of his shirt. "I have such fond memories." Under her fingertips, his chest was like rock covered by the finest silk. She nibbled his neck while her fingers found his nipple.

He grasped her hand to still her movements. "Stop that, Lana Forest."

She gave him the most devilish smile possible before kissing him, but he jerked his head away at the last moment. Huffing, she snatched her hand back. "You started it."

He clasped her hand in her lap and kissed her cheek. "And I intend to finish it too, but not until I can see every part of you. Do indulge your husband and be good, or I shall have to be stern."

The twinkle in his eye belied his words. Drew would never be anything other than a gentle, loving man, just as he had proven over the last several weeks.

For good measure, she glared anyway. "Be good, he says."

"It's only temporary," he teased. "Then you may be as naughty as you wish once we are alone."

Forty-seven

"THE DOWNSTAIRS NEEDS MORE WORK," DREW SAID AS they reached the entrance of their new home. "The workmen promised it would be completed by next week, but I have my doubts."

Lana reached for the door handle, eager to see inside, but her husband stepped in front of her, blocking her access. "Where do you think you're going?"

She wrinkled her nose before attempting to push him aside. "Drew, I wish to see *inside*, too."

"I believe it is customary for the groom to carry his bride over the threshold." He scooped her in his arms with such speed, she squealed.

"I had no idea you were so superstitious," she teased, placing a chaste kiss on his cheek.

"If you're even half as clumsy as your brother, I don't want to take any chances. Nothing but good luck from here on out."

With Drew holding her, she twisted the knob and opened the door with a tiny shove. "You need better help around here, Drew."

"We'll start interviews soon, but you're the most attractive butler I have ever seen. I'm loath to replace you."

Quiet greeted them as they entered the house. "It appears no one is here."

Drew frowned. "I'm not surprised, lazy buggers. If we move in before Michaelmas, it will be a miracle."

Lana only saw the promise of what their home would become. "It's wonderful."

Drew set her on her feet and grasped her hand to lead her farther into the house. "I hope you like it."

The worry line between his brows tugged at her heart. She'd never seen Drew unsure of anything. His obvious desire to please her was sweet.

She squeezed his hand to reassure him. "I already love it."

He escorted her to the doorway of a half-painted room. The cheerful buttery yellow captured the light and reflected her high spirits.

"This will be the drawing room," he said and then gestured to another door off the entry. "And through there, you'll find the dining room."

Lana meandered around the future drawing room, admiring the towering windows and gleaming wood-work. "Oh, my."

Drew lagged behind as she explored the ground floor. Her breath caught when she spied the dusty chandelier in the dining room. It would be exquisite once polished. More windows overlooking the garden welcomed the bright sunlight while a set of French doors invited her to wander outside to the terrace.

Lana shivered as the cool air engulfed her. "We'll host beautiful soirees here."

"Come back inside before you catch a chill."

She did as he bid and continued her exploration inside. The next room was empty save for rolls of masculine wall coverings. "I assume this is to be your study. Everything is lovely."

"It's nothing like Hillary House," Drew said.

She glanced over her shoulder and caught him watching her, the adorably anxious crease still marring his brow. "No, it's much warmer, even without fires in the grates."

"Obviously, this floor needs more work," he added, "but the second and third floors are refinished, and furnished as well."

Her eyes flicked to the ceiling and then back at Drew. She smiled mischievously. "Are you saying...?"

Drew's eyes darkened. A simple jerk of his thumb toward the doorway was all the encouragement she required. Lana dashed from the room, Drew following close behind, lightly pinching her bottom as she ran up the stairs.

"Stop that," she admonished with a laugh. At the top of the stairs, she came to a sudden halt. "Which room?"

"It doesn't matter," he growled. Tossing her over his shoulder, he carried her into the first room they reached. He kicked the door closed and strode to the bed, where he laid her on her back before joining her.

Stretching his lean form over her, he settled between her thighs, resting his weight on his elbows. His forget-me-not eyes brightened with tenderness as his thumb caressed her jaw, stroking back and forth. "You're so beautiful. I could look at you forever."

Her heart leapt. "I hope you do more than look," she murmured as she cradled the back of his neck and pulled him down for a kiss. His gentle lips pressed against hers, his breath flowing into her, filling her with a craving for more of him.

Her desire flamed and she deepened the kiss. Opening

her mouth, she tentatively traced his lips with her tongue. They parted to allow her leisurely expedition. Emboldened, Lana's hands slipped inside his jacket, pushing it down his shoulders.

Drew shifted and climbed from the bed to shed his clothes.

"No," she protested as his hands went to his cravat. Her cheeks warmed as she contemplated making her request, but she gathered her nerve, inhaling deeply before voicing her desire. "May *I* undress you?"

Without hesitation, his hands dropped to his sides as a seductive smile graced his lips. "Nothing would bring me more pleasure, love."

She moved to the edge of the bed and held out her hand. "Come closer," she coaxed. Drew placed himself between her knees, pressing his body against hers. With his jacket already cast off, her fingers grazed his chest as she unfastened the buttons of his waistcoat.

Grasping his cravat, she tugged him lower. He parted his lips and allowed her to test the waters again. She loved his taste: pure man with a touch of honey from the morning rolls they'd consumed earlier. He moaned against her lips, encouraging her to work faster.

With his torso finally bared, she traced his well-defined muscles. A light sprinkling of caramel curls fanned across his chest, narrowing to a thin line that ran down his abdomen and disappeared into his trousers. She nuzzled her cheek against the soft hair, eliciting a sharp gasp from her husband.

Kissing his belly, she undid his trousers before dragging them down his lean thighs. His shaft sprang free and strained toward her. She tentatively brushed over the top before running the backs of her fingers down his length.

Drew shuddered and placed his hand over hers, showing her how to grasp him and encouraging a firmer touch. She caressed him with slow strokes.

"Lana, I'm more than ready, love." His husky voice washed over her, and she glanced up to discover his eyes had grown nearly black with desire.

"Oh," she said on an exhale. "I-I wasn't quite done yet."

Drew adored his new bride, and her willingness to explore his body was more than gratifying. It was also the most delicious torment. He didn't know how much more he could endure. Yet, gazing into her magnificent, wonder-filled eyes, he resolved to try his best. Her delicate fingers encircled him, her touch almost reverent as she waited for his permission to continue.

"Why don't you undress for me, peach?"

Her answering smile was a relief. The last thing he wanted was to stifle her sensuality.

Drew assisted with the fastenings of her gown before reclining on the bed to savor the moment. She slid the dress down her arms, allowing it to fall around her waist, revealing a white corset trimmed in delicate lace. Though Lana didn't need the undergarment, Drew couldn't deny he liked the way it plumped her breasts. With a wiggle of her hips, the garment slithered down her shapely legs to pool at her feet.

Once she had removed the last article of clothing, she stood nude before him, unashamed. Her ivory skin glistened like the most luxurious satin in the warm sunlight pouring through the windows. He longed to feel her against him, to kiss every silken inch of her.

"Come here, Lana." He reached out and she placed her hand in his. Rolling to his back, he urged her to climb atop him.

When she straddled his hips, he sucked in a hissing breath, catching his lower lip between his teeth and biting back a tortured groan. She was more than ready for him, but the wicked glint in her eyes said she wasn't finished with him yet.

Lana captured both of his wrists and clasped them above his head while sliding her body along his. Her heat glided along his length, setting a sinuous rhythm, the tips of her breasts brushing against his chest with each pass. Drew's hips lifted to grind against her dewy skin.

When she released his wrists, he caught her hips, positioning her over his shaft. He had to bury himself inside her or go insane. Lana accepted him, surrounding him like molten lava.

Fully seated inside her, they both sighed with satisfaction. The scent of her arousal taunted him, making him ache to drive into her, but he held back. He would allow her to relish her position of control, unwilling to take that pleasure from her.

He fondled her breasts as she moved against him, her beautiful auburn locks tumbling around her shoulders. Her eyes fluttered, her delicate lashes lying against her cheeks, as she arched into his touch.

God, how he loved her passionate nature. His wife was bold, adventurous, and lusty; his equal in every way. Her pace sped, her breathing heavy and fast. When she opened her eyes and locked them on him, desire blazed in their emerald depths. Drew groaned. He was so close to the edge he didn't know if he could hold back.

Lana threw her head back and cried out. Her body gripped him in waves as bliss filtered across her beautiful face. He grabbed her hips, thrusting deep inside his wife, spilling his seed as pleasure ripped through him. Lana collapsed against his chest, her lips seeking his. "I love you," she whispered.

He settled her into the crook of his arm, her cheek resting against his chest. Never would he have guessed the most pleasurable experience known to man would be found within the union of marriage.

"You have a fantastic way of showing your love, peach. Absolutely sensational." He rubbed his chin against her hair. "Next time it's my turn. And I get to choose the room."

She lifted to her elbow, a frown on her pretty face. "*You* chose this time."

"It was simply the closest."

"But you did choose," she argued. "Just because it was the first one means nothing."

"Perhaps we should develop a fair system."

Lana grinned. "Very well. Whoever exerts the most effort and ends on top chooses the location of our next tumble."

He rolled her to her back and kissed her long and slow before gazing into her eyes. "Lana, I truly love you, but you will lose repeatedly."

"Well, with you dictating our pleasure, how could I possibly complain?"

"I would be a disgrace of a man if you did." He kissed her again, successfully ending their playful banter. He would make certain his lovely wife was well pleased.

JAKE HILLARY WAS A KEEPER—KEEPER OF HIS FAMILY'S
secret, keeper of his wayward brother, and most tragically,
keeper of a hopeless love for his best friend's wife. But at
least for now, he wouldn't think on the torturous evening
to come of admiring Amelia from afar. His brother was
due for a thrashing, and Jake planned to deliver it.

Yanking on his watch fob, he extracted the gold
timepiece from his pocket. He could barely make out the
hands in the dim light.

"Blast and damn."

He slipped the watch back into his pocket. There
wasn't enough time to pound Daniel before the party.
Instead, Jake hammered his fist against the solid door of
his brother's rented room, rattling it in the frame.

"Aye!" Daniel bellowed.

Apparently, his brother had discarded common courtesy *and* manners while he was at sea, although Daniel
had never been one to adhere to etiquette. Based upon
his ill-mannered response, it seemed unlikely he intended
to cross the room to admit Jake. Irritated, he threw the
door open and barged inside.

"Dan—"

"Right there, luv." Daniel threw his head back against the chair as a blonde burrowed her face into his crotch. "Oh, yes!"

"Damnation." Jake covered his eyes and spun on his heel, cracking his elbow against the door frame. "Ouch!" He muttered another curse under his breath.

"What the hell, Jake? Haven't you heard of knocking, you reprobate?"

"I did knock. Next time I shall make more noise," he drawled. Surely all that pounding could have been heard on the other side of Mayfair. "Inform me once you have set yourself to rights."

Jake shook his head as he strolled into the corridor to wait. What a sight to stumble upon, his brother getting his butter churned. And all before dinner. It was enough to spoil his appetite.

When the foul smell from the stairwell hit him again, his lip curled. Daniel might indulge in whores and spirits, but he wasn't throwing away his fortune on rented rooms. Paper peeled from the walls in great sheets, and stains of an unknown origin splattered the scarred floor. *Smells like the bloody mews in here.* Fitting, given his brother was behaving like a jackass.

After a series of bumps and muffled curses, the door flew open. His brother filled the doorway, every bare inch of him.

Jake smirked. "I asked you to summon me *after* you had dressed."

"Get in here."

Pushing away from the wall, Jake reentered the apartments. "Is your guest decent now?"

A crooked leer replaced Daniel's scowl. "Why? You want a turn?"

"Show some respect. The woman deserves at least as much for tolerating your vulgarity."

A feminine giggle drifted from the back room. "Thank you, Mr. Hillary, but I find the captain's vulgarity tolerable indeed." The young woman appeared in the threshold, her nudity now concealed with a faded, ruby dress. Her lackluster hair was pinned up in a haphazard coiffure.

"Oh, my!" Her brown eyes rounded as she looked Jake up and down before turning back to Daniel. "Your brother is delicious, Captain Hillary."

Delicious? Like a meat pie? Jake coughed into his fist, uncomfortable with the nature of her compliment given there were no rules to dictate his response. Yet, he considered it bad-mannered to discount her outright. "Yes, well. Thank you."

Daniel winked at her. "You fancy the rotter, do you?"

She wandered over to Jake's brother with a smile pulling at her plump lips. "I would wager he is the most handsome of the Hillary clan."

"Aside from me."

"Aye. That goes without saying." The woman accepted the purse Daniel offered and pressed a kiss to his cheek. "Same time tomorrow, sir?"

Daniel swatted her behind. "I'll send word."

Jake moved aside to allow his brother's, um… *friend* passage into the corridor.

As she moved past him, she grazed her fingers over the lapel of his jacket. "You're definitely the pinkest of the pinks. I would be happy to pay *you* a call sometime."

Jake's smile was forced. "That's a generous offer, miss."

"Not at all, sir." She tipped her head to the side and batted her lashes, looking up at him in expectation.

When Jake offered no encouragement, she heaved a sigh and sauntered to the stairway.

Daniel chuckled. "What are you about, choirboy?"

Jake closed the door and walked further into the apartments. "I cannot decide which smell is more offensive, the corridor or you. Get cleaned up. You haven't much time."

"Time for what?" Daniel flopped onto the tattered chair in a perfect display of insolence, among other things.

Jake looked up at the ceiling to avoid catching another glimpse of his brother. "I have it on good authority you received the invitation to the dinner party Mother has planned in your honor, although you did not bother responding. *Again*. Now, get dressed. The guests will be arriving in…" He checked his watch again. "Forty-five minutes."

"Is that tonight?"

"Yes, and you can either make yourself presentable, or I will drag your smelly arse across Town as is. Either way, you are attending."

Daniel smirked. "I'd like to see you attempt it. Come on. Make me attend Mother's boring dinner party."

Jake cracked his knuckles and rolled his neck. "Must we go through this *every* time? You learned nothing from the last time I thrashed you. Why do I bother?"

Daniel threw his head back and laughed. "I only vaguely recall the incident now, but you had the advantage since I was foxed."

"You're not far from that now," Jake said dryly. "Put some clothes on. Mother has expended a lot of effort on your behalf. Try to show a little gratitude."

"Mummy, Mummy, Mummy," Daniel mocked, a spark of enjoyment brightening his eyes. "One would think you're still in leading strings."

"You must discover novel ways to abuse me. I grow weary of the same insults." Jake refused to be bothered by his older sibling. He had too many serious concerns on his mind at the moment, such as not making a cake of himself in front of Amelia this evening.

"Would you hurry?" he snapped when Daniel made no move to ready himself.

"Oh, very well." His brother dragged his carcass from the chair and lumbered toward the back room. "Who will be in attendance? Anyone interesting?"

Jake folded his arms and rocked heel-to-toe, toe-to-heel, impatient with Daniel's tardiness. "No one important. Unless you count your *family*."

Daniel stuck his head through the doorway, a jaunty grin in place. "I said anyone interesting. Do you ever listen?"

"If you would only pay a visit to our parents when you return to London, Mother wouldn't orchestrate these affairs."

"Mother would be as happy to forget me as she is her past. She has ulterior motives for this evening's event."

Jake didn't bother arguing this time. It was true their mother was too sensitive to her bourgeois origins, but she desired the best for her children. Sometimes Jake wondered if Daniel's decision to captain his own ship had been designed simply to upset her. If so, his efforts were jolly successful.

Daniel walked from the back room dressed in his best and looking like a proper gentleman. Of course, he still smelled like a barrel of rum, but Jake couldn't do anything to correct that unfortunate problem. The acrid scent emanated from Daniel's skin.

"Pay Mother one call when you arrive, and you needn't trouble yourself with her motives," Jake said.

"I would like to see how quickly you would run home to Mum after being at sea. The first thing I need is the touch of a woman, and *not* the one who gave birth to me. Unlike you, I'm not content to dote on Mother."

"Sod off."

Jake craved a woman's touch, too, but not just any female. Daniel knew well where his allegiances lay. Unfortunately, the woman he desired didn't want him. And thanks to his maniacal rant in her foyer months earlier, she no longer spoke to him either.

Daniel donned his coat and adjusted his cravat. "How is Lady Audley these days? Enticed her to your bed yet?"

Searing heat crept up Jake's neck to the tips of his ears. "My personal matters are none of your concern." The last thing he wished to disclose was how he had ruined any chance for an attachment to Amelia while his brother had been abroad.

Daniel's eyebrows arched in question. "I will take your grumbling as a no. Pity. What has it been? A year?" He strolled to the outer door and tugged it open. "Perhaps *I* will try my hand with the lady tonight."

"The hell you will."

The thought of Daniel touching Amelia under *any* circumstances set Jake's blood on fire, but after what he'd walked in on a moment ago… "Just stay clear of the lady. She deserves better than the likes of you."

"Like you, Mummy's Boy?" Daniel chuckled as he disappeared into the darkened corridor. "I tire of waiting for you to woo the lady. I say tonight, may the better man win the lovely widow."

Jake stalked after his brother. "I am the better man."

❧

Amelia, Lady Audley, leaned against the carriage seat, dreading the coming evening. She would rather be any place than a guest in Jake Hillary's home, but she couldn't snub the Hillarys, not after their generous donation to the children this afternoon. Besides, Mrs. Hillary had always been exceptionally kind to her. Amelia could face Jake this evening for his mother's sake, even if the task required herculean strength.

Amelia's dearest friend and silent partner in the foundling house renovation project, Bianca Kennell, leaned forward with a frown. "Amelia, you look as if we are attending a funeral instead of a dinner party. At least *try* to appear enthused for my sake. You know how I love parties."

"I am not attending this affair for my own pleasure. Mrs. Hillary has spoken with Lady Eldridge and the Duchess of Foxhaven about the renovation. She assures me both ladies are amenable to publicly lending their support, but they wish to inquire into my specific intentions."

Bibi yawned loudly, covering her mouth in a grand gesture. "Oh, pardon me. All this talk of orphans and charity is putting me into a sleeping trance."

Amelia shook her head, smiling reluctantly. She really should be more severe with Bibi, but her dramatics amused more than vexed her. "How thoughtless of me, dearest. I shall endeavor to be more stimulating in my conversation."

"Thank you." Bibi pinched both cheeks, patted her ebony curls, and then readjusted her breasts so they swelled over the neckline of her emerald gown like rising dough. "How do I look?"

"You look lovely, as always."

Bibi flashed a brilliant smile, a wicked twinkle in her eye. "Good enough to eat?"

Amelia grinned cheekily. "Mrs. Hillary serves three

course meals. You needn't worry about anyone stuffing an apple in your mouth and serving you on a platter."

Bibi huffed and lifted her nose in the air. "You have a sharp wit tonight, Lady Audley. Try not to slice anyone to ribbons with it."

"I shall wield my weapon with care," she answered with mock graveness.

"See that you do." Bibi crossed her arms and slumped in her seat, her bottom lip protruding as she practiced her pout. "You comprehended my meaning."

Amelia lifted one shoulder, the heat of a blush flooding her cheeks. Unfortunately, she did know her friend's meaning. "Must everyone be privy to your private affairs?"

"Just because you have chosen to remain celibate, does not mean I must."

Amelia hadn't chosen celibacy. Her life was simply too complicated to entertain thoughts of a liaison at the moment, and she had sworn off complications the day Jake had condemned her in her own house. She certainly didn't have time for the caliber of gentlemen Bibi took to her bed. One scoundrel had proven one too many for Amelia.

Bibi tossed her head. "What other benefit is there to being widowed if I can't enjoy a tumble or two here and there?"

As the carriage rolled to a stop, Amelia recited a silent prayer of thanks. She didn't wish to continue this discussion.

"Do whatever you like, Bibi, but please practice discretion. I need the support of the ladies attending tonight."

"Prudes."

Amelia's brows lifted. "Must we hurl names at them?"

Bibi didn't answer. The footman opened the carriage

door and offered her his hand. As she climbed down the steps, she tossed a look back at Amelia. "You were more fun before Jake Hillary attached that millstone of guilt around your neck."

Amelia's heart leapt into her throat as she noted other guests alighting from their carriages or wandering into the house. "Hush, silly girl."

She joined Bibi on the drive and they linked arms, both staring up at the massive Italianate home. Despite visiting Hillary House many times, Amelia never ceased to be amazed by the grandeur. Why, the Hillarys could house hundreds of children without ever crossing paths with a single one!

The foundlings would not have as grand a home as the wealthy landowner, but their living conditions would improve by no small amount once she had the support of a few more philanthropic souls. Of course, she couldn't approach the true holders of the purse strings, which meant she must convince their wives to do so on her behalf.

Amelia's stomach churned. Perhaps it had been a mistake to arrive with her friend. Lady Kennell had been deemed bad *ton* by several of the ladies who had developed a disliking for her. She hazarded a sideways glance. Bibi flashed an enthusiastic smile, causing Amelia's heart to soften. When she looked at Bibi, all she saw was the loyal friend who had been with her since childhood. *To the devil with those ladies.*

She hugged Bibi closer to her side and whispered in her ear. "Thank you for accompanying me tonight."

"Where else would I be?"

Indeed. Bibi remained Amelia's constant ally in whatever ventures she undertook.

As they approached the front doors propped open to admit the elegantly attired guests, Amelia patted her dearest friend's hand. "Are you ready to face the *ton*?"

"Face them? I am prepared to conquer, my dear."

Amelia laughed softly. "Well, go easy on them for my sake."

If she had any hope of helping the orphans, she needed the ladies to view them as benefactresses of a worthy cause, not the wanton widows of Mayfair.

The Virtuoso

by Grace Burrowes

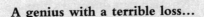

A genius with a terrible loss…

Gifted pianist Valentine Windham, youngest son of the Duke of Moreland, has little interest in his father's obsession to see his sons married, and instead pours passion into his music. But when Val loses his music, he flees to the country, alone and tormented by what has been robbed from him.

A widow with a heartbreaking secret…

Grieving Ellen Markham has hidden herself away, looking for safety in solitude. Her curious new neighbor offers a kindred lonely soul whose desperation is matched only by his desire, but Ellen's devastating secret could be the one thing that destroys them both.

Together they'll find there's no rescue from the past, but sometimes losing everything can help you find what you need most.

For more Grace Burrowes, visit:

www.sourcebooks.com

Lord and Lady Spy

by Shana Galen

No man can outsmart him...

Lord Adrian Smythe may appear a perfectly boring gentleman, but he leads a thrilling life as one of England's most preeminent spies, an identity so clandestine even his wife is unaware of it. But he isn't the only one with secrets...

She's been outsmarting him for years...

Now that the Napoleonic wars have come to an end, daring secret agent Lady Sophia Smythe can hardly bear the thought of returning home to her tedious husband. Until she discovers in the dark of night that he's not who she thinks he is after all...

"An excellent book, full of great witty conversation, hot passionate scenes, and tons of action."—BookLoons

"The author's writing style, how this story is built and all of the delicious scenes, and the characters themselves are just so rich, so enjoyable I found myself smiling and absolutely enjoying every single page."—Smexy Books

For more Shana Galen, visit:

www.sourcebooks.com

The Rogue Pirate's Bride

by Shana Galen

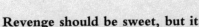

Revenge should be sweet, but it may cost him everything...

Out to avenge the death of his mentor, Bastien discovers himself astonishingly out of his depth when confronted with a beautiful, daring young woman who is out for his blood...

Forgiveness is unthinkable, but it may be her only hope...

British Admiral's daughter Raeven Russell believes Bastien responsible for her fiancé's death. But once the fiery beauty crosses swords with Bastien, she's not so sure she really wants him to change his wicked ways...

Praise for Shana Galen:

"Lively dialogue, breakneck pace, and great sense of fun."—Publishers Weekly

"Galen strikes the perfect balance between dangerous intrigue and sexy romance."—Booklist

For more Shana Galen, visit:

www.sourcebooks.com

A Gentleman Never Tells

by Amelia Grey

—— ❦ ——

A stolen kiss from a stranger...

As if from a dream, Lady Gabrielle walked from the mist and into Viscount Brentwood's arms. Within moments, he's embroiled in more scandal than he ever thought possible...

Can sink even a perfect gentleman...

Beautiful, clever, and courageous, Lady Gabrielle needs Brent's help to get out of a seriously bad situation. But the more she gets to know him, the worse she feels about ruining his life...

Enter the unforgettable world of Amelia Grey's sparkling Regency London, where a single encounter may have devastating consequences for a gentleman and a lady...

—— ❦ ——

"A stubborn heroine clashes with an equally determined hero in the latest well-crafted, canine-enhanced addition to Grey's Regency-set Rogues' Dynasty series."—Booklist

"The book is delightful... charming and unforgettable."—Long and Short Review

For more Amelia Grey, visit:

www.sourcebooks.com

Fortune's Son

by Emery Lee

She is the ultimate gamble…

Beautiful young widow Susannah, Lady Messingham, refuses to belong to any man again. Until she inadvertently draws handsome Lord Philip Drake into an exhilarating game of terrifying stakes and unimaginable rewards…

And he'll risk everything on a toss of the dice…

Philip is a seasoned gambler who knows all the tricks and isn't afraid to use them. He'd do anything for Susannah, including sacrificing his honor and his freedom…

"Lee brings the atmosphere of the Georgian era to life with lush descriptions that beg the reader to see, hear, feel and touch it all."—RT Book Reviews

"This proves to be a very enjoyable read with a multi-dimensional (and, surprisingly, male) protagonist."—Historical Novel Review

For more Emery Lee, visit:

www.sourcebooks.com

About the Author

This is Samantha Grace's debut as a Regency romance author. It is her belief that everyone has a story worth remembering, and she cherishes her work with aging adults, immersing herself in their tales of eras gone by. She is happily writing her next book and loves blogging with fellow authors at Lady Scribes. Samantha is married to her best friend, strives to stay one step ahead of their two precocious offspring, and lives in Onalaska, Wisconsin.